"A genre of one."

—*Bookreporter.com*

"Compulsively readable."

—*The New Orleans Times-Picayune*

"Truly masterful."

—*The Herald* (Ireland)

"Dark . . . and haunting."

—*Fantasy Book Critic*

"Strongly recommended for plot, characterization, authenticity . . . horror . . . and humanity."

–*Library Journal* (starred review)

"Powerful . . . Both harrowing and memorable."

—*Kirkus Reviews* (starred review)

"One of the best thriller writers we have."

—#1 *New York Times* bestselling author Harlan Coben

"A unique voice."

—*New York Times* bestselling author Michael Connelly

"The intensity of a madman and the subtlety of a poet."

—#1 *New York Times* bestselling author Vince Flynn

"Think Thomas Harris by way of Stephen King."

—*Publishers Weekly*

"Leaves unshakable images lurking on the edge of the reader's consciousness."

—*Booklist*

"He writes like a poet about terrible horrors . . . His words sing."

—*Houston Chronicle*

"For Connolly, the 'unknown' remains unknown, lending an air of mystery and tension that's as unrelenting as it is unsettling. Connolly truly understands both horror and crime fiction, and his deft blend of the two makes for a powerful and heady brew, resulting in one of the most potent and emotionally wrenching P.I. series in recent memory. And his characterizations are so sharp they could draw blood."

—*The Thrilling Detective*

THE WRATH OF ANGELS

"Connolly writes seamlessly about an array of forces both criminal and supernatural, killings, and torture alongside the plethora of more prosaic human failings that he delineates so compassionately."

—*Library Journal* (starred review)

"Few thriller writers can create a sense of menace and evil as deftly as Connolly does. Compelling."

—*The Irish Independent*

"An exciting fusion of the occult and the hard-boiled . . . a gruesomely entertaining ride."

—*Publishers Weekly*

"The best kind of book for long winter nights."

—*New York Newsday*

"It's Evil versus Good versus an entity indifferent to both."

—*Booklist*

THE WOLF IN WINTER

"Connolly is at his very best here. . . . A brilliant performance from one of our finest writers."

—*The Irish Times*

A SONG OF SHADOWS

"Strongly recommended for plot, characterization, authenticity . . . horror . . . and humanity."

—*Library Journal* (starred review)

"Gripping . . . fast-paced action builds to a shocking ending."

—*Publishers Weekly*

"Connolly's work just gets better and better."

—*Florida Times-Union*

"Parker fans will . . . hang on every word."

—*Suspense Magazine*

A TIME OF TORMENT

"Connolly again displays his mastery at combining the hard-boiled with the supernatural."

—*Publishers Weekly* (starred review)

For Swati Gamble

ATRIA PAPERBACK

An Imprint of Simon & Schuster, Inc
1230 Avenue of the Americas
New York, NY 10020

Gerald Hausman kindly gave permission to quote from his book *Meditations with the Navajo* (Bear & Company/InnerTraditions, 2001).

"The Divine Wolf" by Adonis, translated by Khaled Mattawa, is cited with the kind permission of the author and the Yale University Press, publisher of *Adonis: Selected Poems* (2010), in which this poem appears.

First Emily Bestler Books/Atria paperback edition October 2016

EMILY BESTLER BOOKS / ATRIA PAPERBACK and colophons are trademarks of Simon & Schuster, Inc.

For information about special discounts for bulk purchases, please contact Simon & Schuster Special Sales at 1-866-506-1949 or business@simonandschuster.com.

The Simon & Schuster Speakers Bureau can bring authors to your live event. For more information or to book an event, contact the Simon & Schuster Speakers Bureau at 1-866-248-3049 or visit our website at www.simonspeakers.com.

Manufactured in the United States of America

10 9 8 6 5 4 3 2 1

Library of Congress Cataloging-in-Publication Data

Connolly, John.
  The wolf in winter : a Charlie Parker thriller / by John Connolly.—First Emily Bestler Books/Atria Books Hardcover edition.
    pages cm
  I. Title.
  PR6053.O48645W65 2014
  823'.914—dc23
                          2014004196

ISBN 978-1-4767-0318-3
ISBN 978-1-5011-2270-5 (pbk)
ISBN 978-1-4767-0320-6 (ebook)

THE WOLF IN WINTER

A CHARLIE PARKER THRILLER

JOHN CONNOLLY

EMILY BESTLER BOOKS

—

ATRIA PAPERBACK

NEW YORK   LONDON   TORONTO   SYDNEY   NEW DELHI

AUTHOR INTRODUCTION

As a series progresses, writers—or those writers with some kind of conscience—begin to worry about tiredness setting in. It's difficult to sustain a series without encountering the occasional trough, although the trick is to ensure that readers can't reach any unanimity on where the trough in question may lie.

Looking back over the Parker books, I tend to consider the first four novels as forming a kind of self-contained quartet published between 1999 and 2002. When the series resumed in 2005, after a two-year break for the writing and publication of *Bad Men* and *Nocturnes*, I'd made some decisions about how I might try to create a sequence of books that did its utmost to avoid shortchanging its readers while also enabling me, the writer, to continue to produce a body of work revolving around a single character without sacrificing enthusiasm or experimentation. In large part, that meant creating a saga to which each individual book would contribute to varying degrees, enabling a momentum to build through the careful revelation of crucial information as the sequence continued.

Of course, that inevitably led to the question I have been asked most frequently by readers in recent years, namely if I have an ending in mind for the series. It's interesting that readers use that word "ending," which has a certain finality to it. Even my own editors have a tendency to employ it, as though Parker's fate were somehow written in stone, and that stone might take the form of a gravestone.

In a way, *The Wolf in Winter* plays upon those expectations—or fears, if you prefer, because I recognize that my readers have an affection for Parker, Angel, Louis, and the rest—and the nature of the books means their concerns for these characters grow with each installment. Also, Parker is no superman. He suffers. He is vulnerable. There is even a little part of him that might embrace an end to his pain, if it were offered. He doesn't want to die, but he is not afraid of death. When it comes, he suspects that he will greet it with a kind of warmth.

When I commenced work on *The Wolf in Winter*, I knew that it would be a significant marker in the series, in much the same way that *The Black Angel* had been almost a decade earlier. I wanted some of those questions raised over the course of the series to be confronted. I wanted Parker to be given the choice of whether to live or die. He would drift no longer.

I understood, too, that I wished to shift the nature of the narrative in the books. The Parker novels have always employed a number of voices. Parker's first person narration is to the fore, but the action of the novels is not seen exclusively through his eyes. It's something that has occasionally been commented upon by readers and reviewers, as though this somehow breaks an unwritten pact. (My view remains that the novels are constructed from a series of perspectives, organized by an overall consciousness that may or may not be the author's.) Nevertheless, a major transition in narration occurs about halfway through *The Wolf in Winter*, with the result that the novels to follow could not be the same. They would be tonally different, just as Parker himself would be altered.

I think that I also did not want to accept a certain article of faith about ongoing mystery series. Some years ago, I was having drinks with the very fine mystery writer Dennis Lehane, who remarked that nobody ever picks the tenth, or the twelfth, novel in a series as a favorite. It's always an earlier book, perhaps because familiarity sets in on the part of the reader, or the novelist finds him- or herself locked into a framework that, although not rigid, is less flexible than might be wished. In Lehane's words, I heard the sound of a gauntlet being thrown down. *The Wolf in Winter*, and the books that came after it, would be my attempt at a riposte.

But this book is also among the most European of my novels, even though it barely ranges beyond the state of Maine. It is infused with what might be termed "folk horror," a particular branch of supernatural fiction in which the threat emerges from a rural setting, and is deeply embedded in notions of land and place. I had always been fascinated by the Green Man mythos, the placement of pagan images on early Christian churches, a nod to older gods and atavistic belief systems, and I saw an opportunity to fuse the American mystery novel with something uniquely European.

Part of my fascination with Maine lies, I think, in those deep woods that cover so much of the state. Residents view them with a certain practicality—as places in which to hunt, hike, snowmobile, and the like—although they're well aware of the danger inherent in becoming lost in such a wilderness. But for me, forests tap into a mythic, folkloric tradition. They are the setting for dark fairy tales. They hide monsters. I would locate just such a monster in *The Wolf in Winter*, and bury it beneath a church.

Oddly enough, my first exposure to the Green Man came not through pictures, or books, or even an exploration of the churches themselves. Instead, I have long been a fan of the fine English band XTC, and one of their final albums, 1999's *Apple Venus Volume 1*, contains a song entitled "Green Man." That was the beginning of my fascination with these odd figures, and I was fortunate that the band subsequently agreed to let me use the song on the soundtrack CD that originally accompanied early hardback copies of this book.

I was aided in the construction of the book's mythology by the discovery of the existence of the Familists, a deeply peculiar sixteenth-century religious sect that believed in a time before Adam and Eve, and in a god that was part of nature. They were religious chameleons, shielding themselves from the potentially fatal consequences of refusing to align themselves with the Church of England by hiding in its congregations, and paying lip service to its beliefs while secretly worshipping a stranger god entirely. Mind you, unearthing them required digging through many volumes of religious and architectural history, but the search was worth it in the end. As so frequently happens when I'm researching, reality proved at least a match for my strangest imaginings.

You know, I find that somewhat worrying.

John Connolly
Dublin 2015

1

HUNTING

He fled in fear and reached the silent fields
And howled his heart out, trying in vain to speak.

Ovid, *Metamorphoses*

I

The house was studiedly anonymous: not too large or too small, and neither particularly well kept nor in any sense dilapidated. Situated on a small patch of land not far from the outskirts of the city of Newark, Delaware, in the densely populated county of New Castle, the town had taken a hit when Chrysler's Newark assembly plant closed in 2008, along with the nearby Mopar distribution center. However, it was still the home of the University of Delaware, and twenty thousand students can spend a lot of money if they put their minds to it.

Newark was an unsurprising choice of location for the man we were hunting. It was close to the borders of three states—Pennsylvania, New Jersey, and Maryland—and only two hours from New York City by car. Then again, it was just one of any number of rat's nests that he had established for himself, acquired over the years by the lawyer who protected him. The only distinguishing feature of this property lay in the degree of power consumption: the utility bills were steeper than for the others we had discovered. This one looked as if it was used regularly. It was more than a storehouse for elements of his collection. It was a base of sorts.

He called himself Kushiel, but we knew him as the Collector. He had killed a friend of ours named Jackie Garner at the end of the previous year. The Collector would have called it an eye for an eye in his version of justice, and it was true that Jackie had made an appalling error—one that resulted in the death of a woman who was close to the Collector. In revenge, the Collector had shot Jackie down without mercy while he was unarmed and on his knees, but he had also made it clear that we were all under his gun now. We might have been hunting the Collector for what he had done to one of ours, but we also knew that it was only a matter of time before he decided we might be less of a threat to him with six feet of earth above our heads. We intended to corner and kill him long before it came to that.

A light burned in one room of the house. The others were all dark. A car stood in the driveway, and its arrival had alerted us to the possibility of the Collector's presence. We had placed a dual wireless break-beam alert system in the undergrowth halfway up the drive. The system was timer-based, so an alert would be sent to our phones only if the two beams weren't broken twice within a ten-minute period. In other words, it allowed for deliveries, but a vehicle that entered the property and remained on it for any length of time would trigger the alarm.

Of course, this assumed that the Collector would not arrive on foot, or by cab, but we figured that he had too many enemies to leave his escape routes to chance, and he would keep at least one well-maintained vehicle. A windowless garage stood to the right of the house, but we had not risked breaking into it when we first discovered the existence of the property. Even planting the little wireless infrared transmitters was a calculated gamble, and had been undertaken only after a sweep of the yard revealed no similar alarm system beyond whatever was used to secure the house itself.

"What do you think?" said Louis.

His dark skin caught something of the moonlight, making him seem even more a creature of the night than usual. He wore dark cotton trousers cinched at the ankles, and a black waxed-cotton Belstaff jacket from which all the buckles and buttons had been removed and replaced with non-reflective equivalents. He looked cool, but then he always looked cool.

"My legs are cramping up, is what I think," said Angel. "If we don't make a move soon, you'll have to carry me in there on a sedan chair."

Angel didn't care about cool. His clothing was functional and un-labeled. He just preferred things that way. His gray hair was hidden beneath a black beanie. Without the cap, he looked his years. He was older than Louis and me, and had grown quieter and more cautious in recent times. Mortality shadowed him like a falcon mantling its wings over dying prey.

We squatted in the grass by the side of the road, Angel to my left and Louis to my right, each of us armed with a suppressed Glock 9mm loaded with subsonic ammunition. We'd lose something in ve-locity, but if we found the Collector we'd be working at close range. There were properties to the east and west of the house, and the area was quiet. We didn't want to bring local law enforcement down on our heads by replicating the sound of the Gunfight at the O.K. Corral. All three of us also carried Russian-made anti-fog gas masks. They cost less than Louis's boots, but they hadn't let us down yet.

"You two take the back," I said. "I'll cover the front."

Louis reached into the pocket of his jacket and produced a tear-gas grenade. Angel had a second, and I had two more.

"Try not to get shot before you've thrown them," Angel told me.

"I'll try not to get shot after I've thrown them as well," I said.

It wasn't an ideal situation. We'd need to break glass to get the gre-nades into the house, and hope that we didn't take fire in the process. If the Collector was cornered and chose to take his chances inside, then Angel and Louis would have to go in and get him, or flush him out to where I would be waiting. Grenade launchers might have been more effective, but your average grenade launcher tended to attract a certain amount of attention in the suburbs, and was hard to hide under a jacket, even one as expensive as Louis's. The other option might have been to try and break down the doors and come in shooting like gangbusters, but we risked looking kind of stupid—and kind of dead—if the doors were reinforced or booby-trapped in any way. The Collector was very protective of his health.

This was the third of the Collector's nests that we had targeted, and we were becoming almost accomplished by this point. We went in fast, and hit both sides of the house simultaneously, the panes of three windows shattering as one. The grenades delivered a combination of military-grade pepper spray and tear gas, and could cover a range of more than 20,000 cubic feet in less than a minute. Anyone who was in those rooms when they exploded wouldn't be staying there for long.

I was edgy before the first grenade went in, but I was doubly so as I prepared to toss the second. If shots were going to come, they would come now, but there was no reaction from inside the house. After a minute, I heard more glass shattering. Angel and Louis were going in through a window, not through the door. It was a calculated risk: expose yourself while climbing in through the busted frame, or try the door and hope that it wasn't wired. They'd opted for the former. I pulled back from the front of the house and took cover behind the car in the drive. It was a midsize Chevy sedan, the kind that an accountant might drive. The interior was pristine, and the seats were bare.

Nothing happened. There were no shouts, and no gunshots. I could hear doors banging open in the house, but no more than that. After three minutes, my cell phone rang. It was Louis. He was breathing heavily. Behind him I could hear Angel coughing.

"He's gone," said Louis.

———

WE ALLOWED THE GAS to disperse before heading back inside. This house was better furnished than the others we had seen. There were books on the shelves—political biographies and modern histories, for the most part—and an effort had been made to decorate the rooms. The wood floors were partly covered with cheap but tasteful rugs, and abstract prints hung on some of the walls. The kitchen closets contained canned goods, rice, pasta, a couple of jars of instant coffee, and a bottle of Martell XO cognac. A small portable refrigerator hummed on the floor. Inside were candy bars, fresh milk, and a six-pack of diet soda. A TV in the living room was hooked up to a DVD player, but there was no cable connection. A copy of that day's *Washington Post* lay on the floor by the single armchair. Beside it was a mug of coffee, still warm. We must have missed him by minutes, seconds.

My eye caught an object hanging from the reading lamp by the chair. It was a bear-claw necklace. The Collector had taken it from Jackie's truck either before or after he killed him. It had once hung from Jackie's rearview mirror. It was his good-luck token, but his luck had still run out. In the end, everyone's luck does.

The Collector always kept souvenirs of his kills. He had not abandoned this one lightly. It was a message for us: a taunt, or perhaps a gesture of recompense, depending upon how one chose to take it.

I stepped carefully to the window and risked a glance at the small back yard. Two houses backed onto this one, and in the distance I saw the lights of Newark. I could feel him out there. He was watching us. He knew that we wouldn't come after him on foot over unfamiliar ground, and at night. He was waiting to see what we would do next.

"We got more trinkets," I heard Angel say.

He joined me at the window, his back to the wall. Even in the darkness, he didn't want to make a target of himself. In his gloved hand he held a gold charm bracelet, a photograph of a young woman in an ornate silver frame, and a baby shoe that had been cast in bronze, each a token of a life taken.

"How did he get out?" I asked.

"Through the back door?"

"It's still locked from the inside," I said. "The front door was the same way. And you had to break a window to get in. They only open at the top, and a child could barely fit through the gap."

"In here," said Louis from the main bedroom.

We joined him there. Like all the other rooms in the house, it had a low ceiling. A hole for an AC unit had been cut in the wall by the main window, but there was no unit in place, and the hole appeared to have been boarded up. A chair was nearby. Louis stood on it and tested the board. It was hinged at the top, and moved like a pet door with the pressure of his hand. The hole looked small, but then Louis flipped up the frame surrounding it, and suddenly the space was big enough to allow an average-sized man to squeeze through.

"Bet the board on the other side is hinged too," said Louis. "He crawled out of here like the bug that he is."

He stepped down from the chair. The night was clear. No clouds obscured the moon.

"He's out there, isn't he?" he said.

"Probably."

"Can't go on like this. Eventually he's going to get tired of running."

"Maybe. Who knows how many of these bolt holes he has. But somewhere there's one that matters more than the others, even more than this one. That's where he's keeping the lawyer."

The lawyer Eldritch steered the Collector in the direction of those who had, in his eyes, forfeited the right to life—perhaps even the right to their immortal souls. He presented the case for the prosecution, and the Collector took care of the punishment. But Eldritch was injured in the same incident that had killed the woman and brought the Collector down on Jackie, and the Collector had spirited the old lawyer away. Who knew, Eldritch might even be dead. If that was the case, the Collector would be off the leash entirely. If nothing else, Eldritch held his hunting dog in some form of check.

"We going to keep looking for this refuge?" asked Louis.

"He killed Jackie."

"Maybe Jackie brought it on himself."

"If you believe that, then we all bring it on ourselves."

"That might just be true."

Angel joined us.

"Why hasn't he hit back? Why hasn't he tried to take us out?"

I thought that I had the answer.

"Because he believes that he violated his own code when he killed Jackie. Jackie's life wasn't his to take, whatever mistakes he might have made. Somewhere in what passes for his conscience, the Collector suspects that we may have earned the right to come after him. It's like Louis said: maybe we all bring it on ourselves.

"And then, like us, the Collector is just a pawn in a greater game. He might know more about the rules of the game than we do, but he has no idea of the state of play, or how close anyone is to winning or losing. He's afraid to kill us in case it tips the balance against him, although I don't know how long that situation will continue."

"What about us?" said Angel. "If we kill him, will there be blowback?"

"The difference is that we don't care," I said.

"Oh," said Angel. "I must have missed that memo."

"Basically, it said 'Fuck 'em if they ain't on our side,'" Louis explained.

"Yeah, I would have remembered seeing that one," said Angel. "So we keep hunting him until we corner him, or until he just rolls over and dies?"

"We hunt him until he tires, or we tire," I said. "Then we'll see how it plays out. You got anything better to do?"

"Not lately. Not ever, to be honest. So what now?"

I looked again into the darkness beyond the house.

"If he's out there, let's give him something to watch."

———

WHILE ANGEL WENT TO retrieve our car, Louis and I broke into the Chevy and pushed it against the door of the house. I could already smell the gas from the stove in the kitchen as Louis doused the interior of the Chevy with the Collector's cognac, saving about a third of the liquid. He stuck a kitchen rag into the neck of the bottle and shook it to soak the material. When Angel was sure that the road was clear, he signaled Louis with his headlights, and Louis lit the rag, tossed the bottle into the car, and ran.

The Chevy was already burning as we drove away, but the two explosions—the first from the car, the second from the house itself—came sooner than anticipated and occurred almost simultaneously, catching us by surprise. We didn't stop to watch the fireball rise above the trees. We just kept driving, taking Telegraph Road into Maryland as far as the intersection with Route 213, then headed north into Pennsylvania. We handed the car over to a woman in Landenberg, took possession of our own vehicles, and separated without another word, Louis and Angel heading for Philly while I drove north to the Turnpike.

———

ON THE OUTSKIRTS OF Newark, a man in a dark coat watched fire trucks pass. The sleeve of his coat was torn, and he limped slightly as he walked, favoring his right leg. The lights of the trucks briefly illuminated his thin face, his dark, slicked-back hair, and the thin trickle of blood that ran from his scalp. They had come close to catching him this time, so very close. . . .

The Collector lit a cigarette and inhaled deeply as his house burned.

II

The wolf was a young male, alone and in pain. His ribs stood out beneath his rust-brown fur, and he limped as he drew closer to the town. The wolf's pack had been annihilated by the shores of the St. Lawrence River, but by then the urge to roam had already taken him, and he had just begun moving south when the hunters came. His had not been a large pack: a dozen animals in all, led by the alpha female that was his mother. They were all gone now. He had escaped the slaughter by crossing the river on winter ice, flinching at the sound of gunfire. He came across a second, smaller group of men as he neared the Maine border, and sustained an injury to his left foreleg from a hunter's bullet. He had kept the wound clean, and no infection had set in, but there was damage to some of the nerves, and he would never be as strong or as fast as he once had been. The injury would bring death upon him, sooner or later. It was already slowing him down, and slow animals always became prey in the end. It was a wonder that he had come so far, but something—a kind of madness— had driven him ever onward, south, south.

Now spring was approaching, and soon the slow melting of snow would commence. If he could just survive the remainder of the winter, food would become more plentiful. For the time being, he was re-duced to the status of a scavenger. He was weak from starvation, but that afternoon he had picked up the scent of a young deer, and its spoor had led him to the outskirts of the town. He smelled the deer's fear and confusion. It was vulnerable. If he could get close enough to it, he might have enough strength and speed left to take it down.

The wolf sniffed the air, and picked up movement among the trees to his right. The deer stood motionless in a thicket, its tail raised in warning and distress, but the wolf sensed that he was not the cause of it. He tested the air again. His tail moved between his legs, and he drew back, his ears pinned against his head. His pupils dilated, and he exposed his teeth.

The two animals, predator and prey, stood united in fear for a moment, and then retreated, the wolf heading east, the deer west. All thoughts of hunger and feeding had left the wolf. There was only the urge to run.

But he was wounded, and tired, and winter was still upon him.

———

A SINGLE LIGHT BURNED in Pearson's General Store & Gunsmithery. It illuminated a table around which sat four old men, each of them concentrating on his cards.

"Jesus," said Ben Pearson, "this is the worst hand I've ever seen. I swear, if I hadn't watched it dealt myself I'd never have believed it. I didn't even know cards went this low."

Everybody ignored him. Ben Pearson could have been holding four aces dealt by Christ himself and still he'd have bitched. It was his version of a poker face. He'd developed it as a way of distracting attention from his regular features, which were so expressive as to give away his every passing thought. Depending upon the story that one was telling, Ben could be the best or the worst audience a man might wish for. He was almost childlike in his transparency, or so it seemed. Although he was now in his seventies, he had a full head of white hair, and his face was comparatively unlined. It added to his air of youthfulness.

Pearson's General Store & Gunsmithery had been in Ben's family for four generations in one form or another, and yet it wasn't even the oldest business in the town of Prosperous, Maine. An alehouse had stood on the site of what was now the Prosperous Tap since the eighteenth century, and Jenna Marley's Lady & Lace had been a clothing store since 1790. The names of the town's first settlers still resounded around Prosperous in a way that few other such settlements could boast. Most had roots back in Durham and Northumberland, in the northeast of England, for that was where Prosperous's first settlers had originally come from. There were Scotts and Nelsons and Liddells, Harpers and Emersons and Golightlys, along with other more singular names: Brantingham, Claxton, Stobbert, Pryerman, Joblin, Hudspeth. . . .

A genealogist might have spent many a profitable day scouring the town's register of births and deaths, and some had indeed journeyed this far north to investigate the history of the settlement. They were received courteously, and some cooperation was offered, but they invariably left feeling slightly dissatisfied. Gaps in the town's annals prevented full and thorough research, and making connections between the settlers of Prosperous and their ancestors back in England proved more difficult than might first have been expected, for it seemed that those families which departed for the shores of the New World had done so in their entirety, leaving few, if any, stray branches behind.

Of course, such obstacles were hardly unfamiliar to historians, whether amateur or professional, but they were frustrating nonetheless, and eventually the town of Prosperous came to be regarded as a dead end, genealogically speaking, which perfectly suited the inhabitants. They were not unusual in that part of the world in preferring to be left untroubled by strangers. It was one of the reasons their forefathers had ventured so far into the interior to begin with, negotiating treaties with the natives that held more often than not, giving Prosperous a reputation as a town blessed by the Lord, even if its inhabitants declined to allow others to share in their perceived good fortune, divinely ordained or otherwise. Prosperous did not invite, or welcome, new settlers without specific connections to the northeast of England, and marriages outside the original primary bloodlines were frowned upon until the late nineteenth century. Something of that original pioneering, self-sufficient spirit had transmitted itself down the generations to the present population of the town.

Now, in Pearson's General Store, cards were exchanged, and bets were placed. This was nickel-and-dime poker in the most literal sense, and it was a rare evening when any man went home with his pockets more than a dollar or two lighter or heavier. Still, bragging rights for the rest of the week could be gained from a good run of cards, and there had been times when Ben Pearson's fellow players had chosen to avoid his store for a couple of days in order to let Ben's triumphalism cool a little.

"I'll raise you a dime," said Calder Ayton.

Calder had worked alongside Ben Pearson for the better part of half a century, and envied him his hair. He owned a small share in the store, a consequence of a brief period of financial strife back in the middle of the last century, when some of the townsfolk had allowed their attention to wander, what with the war and all, and ancient, careful habits had been set aside for a time in the hope that they might eventually be abandoned altogether. But folk had learned the foolishness of that way of thinking, and the older inhabitants had not forgotten the lesson.

Thomas Souleby pursed his lips and gave Calder the cold eye. Calder rarely went above a nickel unless he had a straight at least, and he'd flipped his dime so fast that Thomas was certain he was holding a flush or better. They always played with one-eyed royals as wild cards, and Thomas had caught a glimpse of Calamity Jane squinting at him from Calder's hand—Thomas not viewing it as cheating if someone was careless enough to display his hand to all and sundry. It was what had made him a good businessman in his day, back when he worked in corporate acquisitions. You took whatever advantage came your way, and you milked it for all it was worth.

"I'm out," said Luke Joblin.

At sixty he was the youngest of the quartet, but also the most influential. His family had been in real estate ever since one caveman looked at another and said to himself, "You know, his cave is much bigger than mine. I wonder if he'd see his way to moving out. And if he doesn't see his way to moving out I'll just kill him and take his cave anyway." At which point some prescient seed of the Joblin clan had spotted an opportunity to make a percentage on the deal, and perhaps prevent some bloodshed along the way.

Now Luke Joblin made sure that real estate in Prosperous stayed in the right hands, just as his father and his grandfather and his great-grandfather had done before him. Luke Joblin knew the state's zoning and land-use regulations backward and forward—not surprising, given that he'd helped write most of them—and his eldest son was Prosperous's code-enforcement officer. More than any other family, the Joblins had ensured that Prosperous retained its unique character and identity.

"The hell do you mean, you're out?" said Ben Pearson. "You barely looked at those cards before you dropped them like they was poisoned."

"I got nothing but a hand of cultch," said Luke.

"You got nearly a dollar of mine from the last eight hands," said Thomas. "Least you can do is give a man a chance to win his money back."

"What do you want me to do, just hand your money over to you? I got no cards. This is a game of strategy; you gamble when you're strong, you fold when you're weak."

"You could try bluffing," said Thomas. "You could at least make some kind of effort."

It was always like this between them. They liked each other well enough, but the pleasure each derived from the other's company was directly proportionate to the degree of pickle he could give over the course of an evening.

"I brought the whisky," Luke pointed out. "It wasn't for me, you'd be drinking Old Crow."

There were murmurs of agreement.

"Ayuh, this one's a sippa," said Calder, laying on the accent with a trowel. "Wicked good."

Each man took it in turn to provide a bottle for the weekly poker night, although it usually sufficed for two evenings, and it was a point of pride to bring along something that satisfied all tastes to a degree. Luke Joblin knew Scotch better than any of them, and that night they were drinking an eighteen-year-old from Talisker, the only distillery on the Isle of Skye. It was a little spicy for Thomas's palate, but he had to admit that it was far superior to The Glenlivet, which had been his selection some weeks earlier. Then again, Thomas had never been one for hard liquor, preferring wine. He gave the whisky a second swirl from habit, and took a small mouthful. He was starting to like it more and more. It certainly grew on a fella.

"Maybe I'll let you off this once," said Thomas.

"That's generous of you," said Luke.

In the end, Calder took the pot with a flush, just as Thomas had anticipated. Thomas was enduring a mauling that night. If things kept going the way they were, he'd have to break another dollar.

By unspoken consent, they rested for a while. Talk turned to local matters: business dealings, rumors of romances, and problems in the town that needed to be addressed. Tree roots were just about coming through the sidewalk on Main Street, and the Town Office needed a new boiler. A dispute had also arisen over the old Palmer house, with three families seeking to acquire it for their children. The Palmers, a private couple even by the town's standards, had died without issue, and represented the end of their line in Prosperous. The proceeds of their estate were to be dispersed among various charities, with a portion going also to the town's central fund. But living space was at a premium in Prosperous, and the Palmer house, though small and in need of repair, was much coveted. In any ordinary community, market forces would have been allowed to prevail, and the house would have gone to the highest bidder. Prosperous, though, didn't operate that way. The decision on the sale of the house would be made according to who was owed it, who had the best claim on it. Discussions would be held, and a consensus reached. The family that eventually acquired the house would make some reparation to the others. Luke Joblin would get his commission, of course, but he would earn it.

In effect, the poker night functioned as an unofficial meeting of most of the board of selectmen. Only Calder Ayton didn't contribute to the discourse. Meetings bored him, and whatever Ben Pearson decided was always fine with him. Old Kinley Nowell, meanwhile, was absent on this occasion, laid up in the hospital with pneumonia. There was a general feeling that Kinley didn't have long on this earth. Possible replacements had to be considered, and Ben now raised the matter with his fellow selectmen. After a little back-and-forth, they decided that some younger blood wouldn't hurt them. They'd approach the elder Walker girl, Stacey, once the chief selectman had given her consent. Hayley Conyer—she didn't care to be called a selectwoman, didn't approve of that kind of nonsense—was not one for poker games or whisky evenings. Ben Pearson said that he would talk to Hayley in the morning and sound her out, but he told the others that he didn't anticipate any refusal, or any problems with the nomination. Stacey Walker was a clever girl and a good lawyer, and it never hurt to have lawyers on call.

Thomas Souleby wasn't so sure. He felt certain that Hayley Conyer would object, and she retained a rarely used power of veto when it came to nominations to the board. Conyer was a strong woman who

preferred the company of men, and had no particular sense of obligation to others of her sex who might be a threat to her position. She
wouldn't welcome the arrival of someone as young and vibrant as
Stacey Walker, and Thomas believed that, in the case of the Walker
girl, Conyer might well have a point. He had ambitions of his own to
lead the board once Conyer was gone, whenever that might be, and
had worked long and hard to ensure that he had as little competition
as possible. Stacey Walker was just a mite too clever, and too ambitious, for Thomas's liking. While he frequently clashed with Conyer,
he would not object to her using her veto to shoot down the Walker
nomination. Someone more suitable could be found; someone more
substantial, more experienced.

Someone more malleable.

Thomas stretched and took in the old store, with its curious mix of
expensive artisan products alongside the regular items that you could
buy for half the price in a Hannaford or a Shaw's. Ben certainly wasn't
shy with his pricing, Thomas would give him that, but there was also
the matter of convenience, and exchanging gossip, and supporting
local businesses to consider. It was important that money stayed
within the town's precincts wherever possible. Once cash started leak-
ing out, Prosperous would be financially sound in name only. For the
early settlers, the name had been part prayer, part aspiration. Now it
was a reflection of the reality of the town's situation: it had the highest
per capita income in Maine, a fact that might not have been immediately apparent were a visitor to judge it on appearances alone. Prosperous maintained a low profile, and did not call attention to itself.

The four men were seated at the western side of the store, where
Calder had set up some tables beside a picture window that looked out
on his yard and on the woods beyond. In summer there were picnic
benches at which to sit, but now icy snow still lay on the grass, and the
air was pierced by a damp chill that made an old man's bones hurt. To
Thomas's left, a locked door led into the gun shop, and behind that

was the gunsmithery itself. A tattered and yellowed sign on the door advised that a deposit of thirty dollars was required for each weapon accepted for service, with a further twenty-five levied if the weapon was presented without the required magazine. Thomas didn't even know why the sign was still in place. The only people who presented Ben Pearson with weapons to be serviced were locals, and they were hardly likely to forget that they'd left them with Ben. Similarly, if they neglected to bring along the magazine, they could just drop by with it later in the day.

Thomas's wife, Constance, used Ben's services occasionally—she had been a competitive rifle shooter for most of her life, and hadn't been far shy of Olympic standard as a young woman, although, at that level, the gap between what she could do and what was required might as well have been as deep and wide as an abyss—but she was one of the exceptions in Prosperous. Even allowing for those who hunted, the town had one of the lowest rates of gun ownership in the state. The gunsmith element of Ben Pearson's business was little more than a hobby for him. He kept only a small range of rifles and pistols for sale, mostly high-end stuff, but he seemed to enjoy the metalwork aspect of the job, the threading and fluting and jeweling. He was also reputed to make very fine custom-built stocks, if that was what floated your boat.

Thomas yawned and checked his watch. The whisky had gone to his head, and he was wishing for his bed. He glanced to his right. The light from their table illuminated only a few feet of snow on the yard outside. Beyond was darkness.

Something pale flickered in the shadows. It looked like a moth. As Thomas watched, it grew larger and larger. It took on the form of a young woman wearing a stained white dress, the color of it nearly lost against the snow, so that he thought he might almost have been dreaming her. Her feet were bare as she ran, and there were leaves caught in her dark hair. Closer and closer she came. Thomas opened his mouth to speak, but no words emerged. He rose from his chair just as the girl impacted against the glass, shaking it in its frame. Her fingernails were torn. They left trails of blood on the window.

"Help me," she cried. "Please help me."

Her words turned to clouds on the air, and the wind snatched them away and bore them into the listening woods.

CHAPTER

III

Miles to the south, in the city of Portland, a homeless man was dying.

His name was Jude—no last name, just Jude—and he was well known both to his fellow street people and to those in law enforcement. He was not a criminal, although there were some in Portland who seemed to regard being homeless as a criminal act, punishable by the withdrawal of services and support until death took care of the problem. No, Jude had always been law-abiding, but he had been on the streets so long that he knew every nook and cranny of the city, every crack in the sidewalk, every raised brick. He listened carefully to the reports from others of his kind—the appearance of strangers among them, men of vicious demeanor, or the news of abandoned properties that had previously provided some shelter and were now being used by dealers of narcotics—and traded that information with the police. He did not do so for his own benefit, although there were times when the nights were cold and he was offered the comfort of a cell in which to rest, or even a ride to South Portland or farther afield if a cop was feeling particularly generous or bored.

Jude functioned as a kind of father figure to the homeless of Portland, and his relationship with the police allowed him to intervene on behalf of men and women who sometimes found themselves in trouble with the law for minor infractions. He also acted as a go-between for the operators of the city's homeless services, keeping an eye on individuals who were most at risk, and therefore least likely to maintain a consistent relationship with anyone who might be in a position to help them. Jude knew where everyone slept, and at any time he could name the number of homeless in the city to within a handful of people. Even the worst of them, the most violent and troubled, respected Jude. He was a man who would rather go a little hungrier himself, and share what he had with a brother or sister, than see another starve.

What Jude declined to share with others was much of his own history, and he rarely sought anything beyond the most basic assistance for his own needs. He was clearly an educated man, and the backpack he wore on his shoulders always contained a book or two. He was well versed in the great works of fiction, but preferred history, biography, and works of social commentary. He spoke French and Spanish, some Italian, and a little German. His handwriting was small and elegant, not unlike its practitioner. Jude kept himself clean, and as neatly turned out as his situation allowed. The Goodwill stores on Forest Avenue and out by the Maine Mall, and the Salvation Army on Warren Avenue, all knew his sizes by heart, and would often put aside items that they thought he might appreciate. By the standards of the streets, one might even have said that Jude was something of a dandy. He rarely spoke of any family, but it was known that he had a daughter. Of late, she had become a topic of conversation among Jude's few intimates. It was whispered that Jude's daughter, a troubled young woman, had fallen off the radar again, but Jude spoke little of her, and refused to bother the police further with his private concerns.

Because of his efforts, and his decency, the city's advocates for the homeless had tried to find Jude permanent housing, but they soon learned that something in his character rendered him ill suited to settling down. He would stay in his new home for a week, or a month, and then a social worker would respond to a complaint and find that Jude had given up his apartment to four or five others, and had himself returned to the streets. In winter, he would seek a bed at the Oxford Street Shelter or, if no such bed was available, as was often the case when the weather turned harsh, he would lie down on a thin mat on the floor of the nearby Preble Street community center, or take a chair in the lobby of Portland's general-assistance office. On such nights, with the temperature at seventeen degrees and the wind so cold that it penetrated his layers of wool and cotton, of newspaper and flesh, right down to his bones, he would wonder at those who claimed that Portland was too attractive to the homeless, because it found a place for anyone who sought shelter. But he would consider, too, the flaws in his own personality that rendered him unable to accept the comforts that he sought for others. He knew that this meant he would die on the streets. He was not surprised, therefore, by the fact that death had now come for him at last, but merely by the form it had taken.

He had been living in the basement of a run-down and gutted condo near Deering Oaks for a week or more. He was eating little, apart from what he could scavenge and what the shelters provided, trying to balance the need to save money with the basic requirements of staying alive.

He would be of no use to her if he died.

Was it genetic? Had he passed on his own flaw, his destructive love affair with the streets, to his only daughter? In his colder, more logical moments, he thought not. He had never had difficulties with drugs or alcohol. Substance addiction was not in his nature. His daughter, by contrast, started using shortly after Jude left home, or so her mother had told him before all communication between them ceased. His wife had died hating him, and he could hardly blame her. She would tell him that she did not know what she had done wrong, what grave offense she had given that caused her husband to leave her and their child, for she could not accept that she had done nothing. Something had broken inside him, that was all. He had walked away from every-thing—his job, his family, even his dog—because, had he not done so, he would have taken his own life. His was a psychological and emo-tional disturbance of untold, awful depth, mundane and yet tragic in its very ordinariness.

He had tried talking to his daughter, of course, but she would not listen. Why would she? Why should she take lessons in life from a man who had been unable to come to terms with happiness, with being loved? She threw his failings back in his face, as he knew she would. If he had stayed, if he had been a true father, then perhaps she too might have remained where she was, and this beast would not have taken her in its clutches and slowly drained the life from her. You did this to me, she said. You.

But he had done what he could for her, in his way. Just as he kept careful watch on those in his charge on Portland's streets, so others did the same for his daughter, or attempted to. They could not save her from herself, for she had a self-destructive urge that was kin to her father's fractured nature. Whatever had come from her mother's estate went into her arm or the arms of others, or briefly lined the pockets of boyfriends who were one step above pimps and rapists.

Now she had traveled north. He had heard reports of her in Lew-iston, and Augusta, then Bangor. The news from an old homeless woman, traveling south, was that his daughter was clean and seeking somewhere to live, as a place of her own would be the first step toward finding a job.

"How did she look?" Jude asked.

"She looked well. She's pretty, you know that? Hard, but pretty."

Yes, he thought. I know that. Pretty, and more than pretty.

She is beautiful.

So he took the bus north, but by then all trace of her was gone. There was talk, though. She had been offered a job. He learned that a

THE WOLF IN WINTER

young woman living and working at the Tender House, a shelter for homeless mothers and their children in Bangor, had spoken with her. His daughter had seemed excited, or so Jude was told. She had money in her hand. She was going to take a shower, buy some new clothes, maybe get a haircut. There was work for her. A couple, a nice older couple, needed someone to help maintain their house and their big yard, perhaps cook a meal or two as well, or drive them places when the need arose. For the sake of their own security, and to calm any concerns that the girl might have, they told her that they'd drop by the local police department on the way to the house, just so that she could confirm that they were on the level and meant her no harm.

"They showed me a picture of their house," Jude's daughter told the young woman from the Tender House. "It's beautiful."

What was the name of this town? Jude asked his informant.

Prosperous.

Its name was Prosperous.

But when Jude traveled to Prosperous, and went to the police department, he was told that no such girl had ever passed through its doors, and when he asked on the streets of the town about his daughter he was met with professions of ignorance. Eventually, the police came for him. They drove him to the town limits, and told him not to return, but he did. The second time he got a night in a cell for his troubles, and it was different from the cells in Portland or Scarborough, because he was not there of his own volition, and the old fears came upon him. He did not like being shut in. He did not like locked doors. That was why he roamed the streets.

They drove him to Medway the next morning, and escorted him onto the bus. He was given a final warning: stay out of Prosperous. We haven't seen your daughter. She was never here. Quit bothering people, or next time you'll be up before a judge.

But he was determined not to stay away. There was something wrong in Prosperous. He felt it on that first day in the town. Living on the streets had made him sensitive to those who carried a bad seed inside them. In Prosperous, one of those seeds had germinated.

He shared none of this with others, and certainly not with the police. He found excuses to remain silent, although one in particular came more naturally than others: his daughter was a drifter, an addict. Such people routinely disappeared for a while before turning up again. Wait. Wait and see. She'll come back. But he knew that she would not return, not unless someone went looking for her. She was in trouble. He sensed it, but he could not bring himself to speak of it. His vocal cords froze on her name. He had been on the streets for too long. The illness that caused him to leave his family had left him unable to open himself up, to express weakness or fear. He was a locked box inside which tempests roiled. He was a man enshadowed by himself.

But there was one whom he trusted, one to whom he might turn: an investigator, a hunter. He worked for money, this man, and with that realization came a kind of release for Jude. This would not be charity. Jude would pay him for his time, and that payment would buy Jude the freedom he needed to tell his daughter's story.

This night, his final night, he had counted his money: the handful of notes that he had hidden in a box in the damp earth of the base-ment; the small savings he had entrusted to one of the social workers, reclaimed that day; and a bag of filthy bills and coins, just a small frac-tion of the loans that he had given out to others and now repaid at a quarter on the dollar by those who could afford to do so.

He had just over a hundred and twenty dollars, enough to get him beaten up by some, or killed by others.

Enough, he hoped, to hire the detective for a couple of hours.

———

BUT NOW HE WAS DYING. The rope, suspended from a ceiling beam, was tightening around his neck. He tried to kick, but his legs were being held. His arms, previously restrained by his sides, were released, and he instinctively raised his hands to the noose. His fingernails were ripped from his flesh, but he barely felt the pain. His head was exploding. He felt his bladder release, and knew that the end was coming. He wanted to cry out to her, but no words came. He wanted to tell her that he was sorry, so sorry.

The final sound that he made was an effort to speak her name.

IV

I t was left to Thomas Souleby to calm the girl down. He had four daughters of his own, and they, in turn, had so far gifted him only with female grandchildren, so he had more experience in placating women than anyone else in the room. This particular woman needed more placation than most: her first act, after they had let her in through the back door of the store, was to grab the nearest knife and keep them at bay. None of Thomas's offspring had ever pulled a knife on him, although he wouldn't have put it past one or two of them during their teenage years.

"Easy, honey," he said. He stayed out of range of the knife, and spoke as softly as he could. "Easy, now. What's your name?"

"Annie," she replied. "Call the police. Please, just call the police."

"We will," he said. "But we just—"

"*Now!*" she screamed, and the sound just about busted Calder Ayton's hearing aid.

"Okay, we're calling them," said Thomas. He motioned to Ben, who already had his cell phone in hand. "But what are we supposed to tell them?"

"You tell them that some bitch and her fucker husband locked me in a basement and fattened me up like a pig for slaughter," she said. "That's what you tell them."

Thomas looked at Ben and shrugged.

"You maybe don't have to use those exact words," Thomas told him. Ben nodded, and started dialing.

"Put it on speaker, Ben," said Thomas. "Just so Annie here knows we're on the up and up."

Ben tapped the screen on his phone and turned the volume to maximum. They all listened to it ring. On the third tone, a voice broke in.

"Chief Morland," it said.

The girl seemed to relax at the sound of the voice, but Thomas could still see her casting glances over his shoulder, staring out the picture window in the direction from which she had come. She couldn't know how long it would be before her captors noticed that she was gone and came looking for her. She didn't trust four old coots to keep her safe.

"Lucas, this is Ben Pearson over at the store. We got a girl here in some distress. She says her name is Annie, and that someone has been holding her in a basement. I'd appreciate it a whole lot if you could get here real soon."

"On my way," said the chief. "Tell her to sit tight."

The connection was cut.

"How far away is the police station?" asked Annie.

"Less than a mile, but I called the chief on his cell phone," said Ben. "He could be closer than that, or a little farther away, but this isn't a big town. It won't be long before he's here."

"Can we get you something, honey?" said Thomas. "You want water, or coffee? We got whisky, if that helps. You must be freezing. Ben, find the girl a coat."

Ben Pearson moved to the rack to get one of the men's coats. His motion brought him almost within reach of the knife, and the girl slashed at the air in warning.

"Jesus!" said Ben.

"You stay back!" she warned. "All of you, just keep back. I don't want anyone to come near me—not until the police get here, you understand?"

Thomas raised his hands in surrender.

"Anything you say, but I can see that you're shivering. Look, Ben will go to the rack and slide a coat across the floor to you. None of us will come near you, okay? Seriously, nobody here is in a hurry to get cut."

The girl considered the offer, then nodded. Ben took his big old L.L.Bean goose-down parka from the rack and slid it across the floor. The girl squatted and, never taking her eyes from the four men, slipped her left arm into the sleeve. She rose, and in one quick movement changed the knife from her right hand to her left so that she could put the parka on fully. The men remained completely still while she did so. The girl then moved sideways across the room to the poker table, poured herself a glass of the whisky, and tossed it back in one gulp. Luke Joblin looked slightly pained.

"These people who held you captive," said Thomas. "Did you get a look at them?"

"Yes."

"Do you know their names?"

"No." The girl relented, and soon the words were tumbling from her lips. "They weren't the ones who brought me here first, though. They were an older couple, David and Harriett Carpenter, if those were even their real names. They showed me some ID when we first met, but what do I know about IDs? As soon as we got to the outskirts of this shithole, they handed me over to another couple, younger than them. They were the ones who kept me in their damn basement. I know their faces. They didn't even bother to keep them hidden from me. That's how I knew they were going to kill me in the end. Others came too. I caught them looking at me through the slit in the door. I pretended to be asleep, but I saw some of their faces as well."

Thomas shook his head in disbelief, and sat down heavily. Ben

Pearson looked toward the woods, just as the girl had done, waiting for figures to appear out of the gloom, hell-bent on dragging her back to captivity. Luke Joblin watched the young woman, his expression unreadable. Calder Ayton's attention was drawn to the wrinkles on his hands. He traced them with the tips of his index fingers—first the left, then the right—as though surprised to find this evidence of his aging. No further words were spoken, no more reassurances given. This was Morland's business now.

Annie walked over to the register, where she could keep an eye on the parking lot outside the store. Blue lights shone in the distance. The police were on their way. She watched the four men, but they seemed stunned into inaction. She was in no danger from them.

An unmarked Crown Vic pulled into the lot, a flashing blue light on its dashboard. Although Ben had killed the outside spots when he closed the store, there were motion-activated lights above the porch. Those lights now illuminated the lot, bathing Chief Morland in their glow as he stepped from the car.

"I feel sick," said Annie. "I need to go to the bathroom."

"The chief has just arrived, honey," said Thomas.

"It's the whisky," said the girl. "It's done something to my stomach." She bent over, as if in pain.

"I need to puke or shit—I don't know which."

Ben didn't want her to do either in his place of business, so he directed her to a door at the rear of the store. It led into his private quarters, where he sometimes stayed the night, particularly if he was working late in the gunsmithery. His house was less than a mile away, but since the death of his wife it had felt too big and empty for him. He preferred the store. That was his place now.

"It's the second door on the left," he said. "You take your time. You're safe now."

She headed toward the back of the store, her hand over her mouth, seconds before the chief entered. He was a big man, six feet three and topping out at about two hundred pounds. He was clean-shaven, and his eyes were gray, like the cold ashes of old fires. He had been Prosperous's chief of police for nearly a decade, and had taken over the job from his father. Before that, he served his apprenticeship in the Maine State Police. That was how he always described it: "my apprenticeship." Everyone knew that Prosperous was the only place that mattered. He walked with the slightest of limps, a consequence of a car accident near Augusta back in the day. No one had ever suggested that his injured limb might affect his ability to carry out his job, and the chief had never given anyone cause to do so.

"Where is she?" he asked.

"In the bathroom," said Ben. "She wasn't feeling good."

Morland had been in Pearson's store often enough to know it nearly as well as he did his own house. He went straight through to the bathroom and knocked on the door.

"Miss?" he called. "My name is Lucas Morland, and I'm the chief of police here in Prosperous. Are you okay in there?"

There was no reply. A cold breeze flipped the ends of Morland's trousers against his shoes and legs. It was coming from under the bathroom door.

"Shit!" he said.

He stepped back, raised his right foot, and kicked hard against the lock. The lock held, but the jamb broke on the second attempt. The door opened to reveal an empty bathroom. The small window above the toilet gaped open. Morland didn't even waste time trying to look out. The girl would already be seeking the cover of darkness.

Thomas Souleby had followed behind the chief, and was almost bowled over by him as he moved back into the store.

"What is it?" he asked, but Morland didn't answer. He was trying to hide the pain in his left leg. This damn weather always played hell with it, and he'd be glad when summer came. He stomped into the parking lot and turned left at the corner of the store. Pearson's was close to the intersection of two roads; the front faced north on the main road into Prosperous, while to the west was the highway. Morland's eyesight was good, even in the dark, and he could see a figure moving fast between two copses of trees, making for the highway. The road crested a hill at Prosperous's western boundary. As he watched the girl, the lights of a truck appeared on the hill.

If she reached it, he was lost.

———

ANNIE RAN.

She'd been so close to safety, or so she'd thought, and then the cop had appeared. She'd recognized him at once: the shape and size of him, but most of all the way that he limped. She'd seen him twice before. The first time was just after the handover, when she was brought to the basement. She'd fought against them as they carried her from the truck, and the cloth across her eyes had slipped a little. The cop had been there, supervising the operation, following behind as they took her to her cell. The second was on one of the occasions when they permitted her to shower, although they always kept her hands and feet manacled. She had glanced to her right as she left her basement cell, and caught a brief glimpse of the man with the gray eyes at the top of the stairs before the door closed. On neither occasion had he been in uniform, otherwise she would have known better than to let the old geezers call the cops.

The couple had kept her well fed. That, at least, was something. She had strength, perhaps more than she'd had in many years. There was no alcohol in her system, and she was clean of drugs. Her own speed surprised her.

Annie saw the truck at the same time that Morland did. If she could get to the highway in time, she could stop it and beg for a ride to another town. There was a chance that the cop might come after them, but any truck driver in his right mind would be able to see her bare, bloodied feet and her tattered nightgown, and know that something terrible had befallen her. If that wasn't enough to convince him, she was sure that her story would do the rest. He—or she, if she was lucky enough to be picked up by a woman—could take her to the cops in Bangor, or to the nearest state police troop house. The truck driver could haul her to the FBI in Washington, DC, for all Annie cared. She just wanted to get away from this godforsaken town.

The ground began to slope upward as she neared the road. She stumbled slightly as her feet hit a rock, and there was a terrible, sharp pain. She'd broken the big toe of her right foot. She was sure of it. It slowed her down, but it didn't stop her. The truck was still some distance away, but she would reach the highway long before it passed her spot. She was prepared to stand in the middle of the road and risk being hit if that was what it took. She'd rather die quickly under its wheels than be taken back to that basement.

Something pushed her from behind, and she fell to the ground. An instant later, she heard the shot, and there was a pressure in her chest, followed by a burning that set her lungs on fire. She lay on her side and tried to speak, but only blood flowed from between her lips. The truck passed barely an arm's length from where she lay, the driver oblivious of her dying. She stretched her fingers toward it, and felt the breeze of its passing. The burning inside her was no longer fiery but cold. Her hands and feet were growing numb, the ice spreading inward to the core of her being, freezing her limbs and turning her blood to crystals.

Footsteps approached, and then two men were looking down at her. One was the limping cop, the other the old man who had given her his coat. He was holding a hunting rifle in his arms. She could see the rest of his friends following behind. She smiled.

I got away. I escaped. This wasn't the ending that you wanted.

I beat you, you fuckers.

I . . .

———

BEN PEARSON WATCHED THE life depart the girl, her body deflating as its final breath left it. He shook his head in sorrow.

"And she was a good one too," he said. "She was scrawny, but they were fattening her up. If we were lucky, we could have got ten years or more out of her."

Chief Morland walked to the road. There were no more vehicles coming their way. There was no chance that they would be seen. But what a mess, what a godawful mess. Somebody would answer for it.

He rejoined the others. Thomas Souleby was closest to him in height. These things mattered when you were dealing with a body.

"Thomas," he said, "you take her arms. I'll take her legs. Let's get this all cleaned up."

And together the two men carried the remains of Annie Broyer, lost daughter of the man named Jude, back to the store.

V

They saw the cars pull into their drive and knew that they were in trouble.

Chief Morland was leading, driving his unmarked Crown Vic. The dash light wasn't flashing, though. The chief wasn't advertising his presence.

The chief's car was followed by Thomas Souleby's Prius. A lot of folk in Prosperous drove a Prius or some other similarly eco-conscious car. Big SUVs were frowned upon. It had to do with the ethos of the town, and the importance of maintaining a sustainable environment in which to raise generations of children. Everybody knew the rules, unofficial or otherwise, and they were rarely broken.

As the cars pulled up outside the house, Erin gripped her husband's hand. Harry Dixon was not a tall man, or a particularly handsome one. He was overweight, his hair was receding, and he snored like a drill when he slept on his back, but he was her man, and a good one too. Sometimes she wished that they had been blessed with children, but it was not to be. They had waited too late after marriage, she often thought, and by the time it became clear that the actions of nature alone would not enable her to conceive they had settled into a routine in which each was enough for the other. Oh, they might always have wished for more, but there was a lot to be said for "enough."

But these were troubled times, and the idyllic middle age they had imagined for themselves was under threat. Until the start of the decade, Harry's construction company had weathered the worst of the recession by cutting back on its full-time employees and paring quotes to the bone, but 2011 had seen the company's virtual collapse. It was said that the state had lost forty-eight hundred jobs in March of that year alone, which contributed to making Maine the nation's leader in lost jobs. They'd both read about the arguments between the Maine Department of Labor and the Maine Center for Economic Policy, the latter basing its figures on higher Bureau of Labor Statistics job loss figures that the former refuted. As far as the Dixons were concerned, that was just the state's Department of Labor trying to sweep the mess under the carpet. It was like telling a man that his feet are dry when he can feel the water lapping at his chin.

Now Harry's company was little more than a one-man operation, with Harry quoting for small jobs that he could complete with cheap labor, and bringing in skilled contractors by the hour as he needed them. They could still pay their mortgage, just about, but they'd cut back on a lot of luxuries, and they did more and more of their buying outside Prosperous.

Erin's half sister, Dianne, and her surgeon husband had helped them out with a small lump sum. They were both hospital consultants, and were doing okay. They could afford to lend a hand, but it had hurt the couple's pride to approach them for a loan—a loan, what's more, that was unlikely to be repaid anytime soon.

They had also tapped the town's discretionary fund, which was used to support townsfolk who found themselves in temporary financial trouble. Ben Pearson, who was regarded as one of the board's more approachable members, had taken care of the details, and the money—just over two thousand dollars—had helped the Dixons out a little, but Ben had made it clear that it would have to be paid back, in cash or in kind. If it wasn't, the board would start delving more deeply into their situation, and if the board started snooping it might well find out about Dianne. That was why the Dixons had agreed, however reluctantly, to keep the girl. It would serve as repayment of the loan, and keep their relationship with Dianne a secret.

Erin had only discovered her half sister's existence some three years earlier. Erin's father had left Prosperous when she was little more than an infant, and her mother had subsequently remarried—to a cousin of Thomas Souleby's, as it happened. Her father hadn't been heard from again, and then, at the end of 2009, Dianne had somehow tracked Erin down, and a tentative if genuine affection had sprung up between them. It seemed that their father had created a whole new identity for himself after he left Prosperous, and he never mentioned the town to his new wife or to their child. It was only following his death, and the death of her mother, that Dianne had come across documents among her father's possessions that explained the truth about his background. By then she was on her second marriage—to a man who, coincidentally or through the actions of fate, lived in the same state that had spawned her father, and not too far from the town and the life that he had fled.

Erin had professed complete ignorance of the reasons that their father might have gone to such lengths to hide his identity, but when Dianne persisted she hinted at some affair with a woman from Lewiston, and her father's fear of retribution from his wife's family. None of it was true, of course—well, none of the stuff about the affair. Her father's fear of retribution was another matter. Nevertheless, she made it clear to Dianne that it would be for the best if she kept her distance from Prosperous and didn't go delving into the past of their shared father.

"Old towns have long memories," Erin told Dianne. "They don't forget slights."

And Dianne, though bemused, had consented to leaving Prosperous to its own business, aided in part by her half sister's willingness to share with her what she knew of their father's past, even if, unbeknownst to Dianne, Erin had carefully purged all the information she offered of any but the most innocuous details.

So Erin and Harry were the poor relatives, bound to Dianne and her husband by the shade of a father. They were content to play that role, though, and to keep the existence of Dianne and her husband hidden from the citizens of Prosperous. Unspoken between them was the fact that they might have need of Dianne at some point in the future, and not only for money, for the Dixons wanted nothing more than to leave Prosperous, and that would be no easy task. The board would want to know why. The board would investigate. The board would almost certainly find out about Dianne, and the board would wonder what secrets Erin Dixon might have shared with her half sister, the daughter of a man who had turned his back on the town, who had stolen its money and, perhaps, whispered of the deal it had made to secure itself.

Keeping all their fears from Dianne and her husband wasn't easy. To further complicate matters, Harry and Erin had asked that the money be paid in cash. She could still remember the look on Dianne's face: puzzlement, followed by the dawning realization that something was very wrong here.

"What kind of trouble are you two in?" Dianne asked them, as her husband poured the last of the wine and gave them the kind of disapproving look he probably reserved for patients who neglected to follow his postoperative advice and then seemed surprised when they started coughing blood. His name was Magnus Madsen, and he was of Danish extraction. He insisted on the pronunciation of his first name as "Mau-nus," without sounding the "g," and had resigned himself to correcting Harry's literal pronunciation whenever they met. Harry just couldn't seem to manage "Mau-nus," though. That damned "g" kept intruding. Anyway, it wasn't as if Magnus Madsen was fresh off a Viking longship. There were rocks that hadn't been in Maine as long as the Madsens. His family had been given plenty of time to learn to speak English properly, and drop whatever airs they'd brought with them from the Old Country.

"We'd just prefer it if people in Prosperous didn't know that we were having serious difficulties," said Harry. "It's a small town, and if word got out it might affect my chances of bidding successfully for work. If you pay us in cash, then we can make pretty regular lodgments into our account until we find our feet again, and nobody will be any the wiser."

"But surely any dealings you have with your bank are entirely confidential," said Magnus. "Couldn't you ask your bank manager for an extended line of credit? I mean, you're still working, and you must have paid off the bulk of your mortgage by now. That's a nice house you have, and it's worth a fair sum, even in these difficult times. It's hardly like asking for an unsecured loan."

There was so much that Harry wanted to say at that point, but it could have been summarized as "You and I do not live in similar worlds." Those words "unsecured loan" bit at him as well, because that was precisely what they were asking of Magnus and Dianne, but mostly he knew that Magnus had no conception of the way the town of Prosperous worked. If he did, it would turn his hair white.

And, shortly after that, he'd be dead.

Magnus and Dianne gave them the money in the end, and Harry used it to pump up the deposits being made at the bank, but the borrowed cash was almost gone now, and he didn't think that his in-laws could be tapped again. In any normal situation, Harry and Erin would have sold up and moved on. Sure, they'd take a bit of a hit on the house, but with a little luck they might come out of it with a high five- or low six-figure sum once the mortgage was paid off. They could start again, maybe rent for a while until the economy recovered.

But this wasn't a normal situation. They knew that they probably weren't the only ones in the town who were suffering; there were rumors, and more than rumors. Even Prosperous wasn't entirely immune from the vagaries of the economy, just as, throughout its history, it had never been completely protected from conflict, or financial turmoil, or the wrath of nature. Yet it had always been better protected than most. The town took steps to ensure that this was the case.

"What do you think happened?" Erin now whispered to her husband, as they watched the men approach. "Did she get away?"

"No," said Harry. "I don't believe she did."

If she had escaped, these others wouldn't be here on their doorstep. There were only two possibilities. The first was that the girl had been captured before she could leave Prosperous, in which case the chief was going to be mad as hell with them for failing to keep her locked up, and they could only hope that the girl had sense enough to keep any suspicions about the ease of her escape to herself. The second possibility was that she was dead, and Harry found himself wishing that the latter was true. It would be easier for all of them.

They didn't give the chief time to knock on the door. Harry opened it to find Morland with his fist raised, and he flinched instinctively in anticipation of the blow. There was a doorbell, but it wouldn't have been like Lucas Morland to use it under the circumstances. Psychologically, a sharp knock was far more effective.

Harry stepped aside to admit them, the chief with his face set hard and Thomas Souleby looking more disappointed than angry, as though Harry and Erin were errant teenagers who had failed some crucial parental test.

"We know why you're here," said Harry.

"If you know why we're here," said the chief, "then why didn't you call to tell us about the girl?"

"We only just found out she was gone," said Erin. "We were about to call, but—"

She looked to her husband for help.

"But we were frightened," he finished for her.

"Frightened of what?"

"That we'd let you down—that we'd let the whole town down. We knew you'd be angry."

"Did you try looking for her?"

"Sure," said Harry. "I mean, no, not yet, but we were about to. See, I'd put my boots on." He pointed at his feet, which were, indeed, booted. He never wore footwear in the house—Erin bitched about the carpets—but he'd put his boots on that night, just in case it all went to hell. "I was ready to head out when you arrived."

"Did you find her?" asked Erin. "Please tell me that you found her."

She was good, Harry gave her that. It was just what she should have said, just what the chief would have expected to hear.

Morland didn't reply. He was leaving them to stew for a while, waiting to see what they might reveal to him. They'd have to step carefully now. What would the girl have said when she was caught? What would she have told them?

Nothing, Harry figured. She'd have kept quiet. That was why he and Erin had simply left the doors mostly unsecured and gone about their business. If the girl was caught, they'd have deniability.

Morland leaned against the kitchen table and folded his arms.

"How did it happen?" he asked.

"It was my fault," said Erin. "I left the door unlocked. I didn't mean to. Sometimes, if I knew she was asleep, I'd just shoot the bolt and let the shackle hang loose on the mechanism. I was tired, though, and I may have forgotten to put the padlock on. She must have worked the bolt free from the inside. I found a piece of cloth on the floor that she could have used. Maybe she tore it from her nightgown."

"How did she know that you hadn't locked the door?" asked Souleby.

Damn you, thought Harry. I always felt you were too smart for anyone's good. Souleby, the miserable bastard, reminded Harry of an old
stork: all beak and limbs.

"I don't know," said Erin. "My guess is that she never gave up trying
to escape. She probably tested the door every time I left the room, and
this time she just got lucky."

"Got lucky, huh?" said Morland.

He permitted himself a little smile.

"Show me the door," he said. "Explain it all to me again."

They went down to the basement, and Erin showed him the cell,
and the bolt, and the padlock. Just as she had told him, there was a
piece of white material on the floor, stained with grease from the bolt.
The chief examined it, and toyed with the bolt and the padlock for a
while.

"Get inside," he said to Erin.

"What?"

"Go on. Get inside that cell." He handed her the strip of cloth. "And
take this with you."

She did as she was told. The chief closed the door on her and slid
the bolt, but did not secure it with the padlock.

"Now," he said, "open it."

The saliva dried up in Harry's mouth. He would have prayed, but
he had long since stopped believing in God. The continued existence
of Prosperous was one of the strongest arguments he could come
up with against the possibility of a benevolent deity watching over
humankind.

After a couple of attempts, Erin managed to get the cloth through
the gap between the door and the frame, and over the bolt. There
was, though, no way that she could pull the other end back in. Harry
closed his eyes. This was it.

A thin shaft of broken wood poked through the gap, caught the strip of cloth, and pulled it back through to the other side of the cell door. Slowly, Erin began to twist it back and forth. The bolt moved: not by much, but it moved. With some perseverance, it would be only a matter of time before Erin managed to unlock the door from the inside, as she claimed the girl had done.

Morland stared at Harry. Despite what he had witnessed, Harry knew that the chief still didn't quite believe what he'd been told. If he was expecting Harry to crack, though, he would be disappointed, unless he resorted to torture, and even Morland was probably above that.

"Let her out," he told Souleby, and Souleby pulled the bolt.

Erin stepped out of the cell, flushed but triumphant.

"Where did you get the wood?" said the chief.

"It was on the floor by the girl's bed," she said. "I saw it when I was trying to figure out how she did it."

She handed him the fragment of pine. The chief tested it with his finger, then went to the bed and found the spot from which it had been taken.

"Looks new," he said.

"She hasn't been gone but an hour," said Erin.

"Uh-huh." Chief Morland took the stick in both hands and snapped it. It was the first outward demonstration that he had given of the rage he was feeling.

"You still haven't told us if you found her," said Harry.

"Oh, we found her all right," said the chief.

"Where is she?"

"In the trunk of my car."

"Is she—?"

"Is she what?"

"Is she . . . dead?"

The chief didn't answer immediately. He closed his eyes and wiped his face with his right hand. His shoulders sank. That was when Harry knew that they were okay, for now.

"Yes, she's dead," said Morland finally. "Just not the right kind of dead. You got a shovel?"

"Sure," said Harry. "In my toolshed."

"Good," said the chief. "Because you're going to help me bury her."

CHAPTER

VI

I had a ticket for the 8:55 P.M. flight with US Airways out of Philadelphia, if I chose to use it, but I realized that I would either kill
myself trying to make it or end up with a ticket for speeding. Neither possibility particularly appealed to me, so I changed my flight to
9:30 A.M. the following morning and checked into a motel off Bartram
Avenue. I had dinner in a bar that was one step up from eating food
off the street, but I didn't care. Once the adrenaline had stopped flow-
ing after the events in Newark, I experienced a comedown that left me
shaking and nauseated. It didn't matter what I ate: it would have tasted
foul anyway, but I thought I needed something in my stomach. In the
end, I left most of the food on the plate, and what I ate didn't stay in
my system for long once I was back in my room.

In truth, such reactions were becoming increasingly common as the
years went on. I suppose I had always been frightened as I faced situations like that night's—anyone who has found himself looking down
the barrel of a gun, or confronting the possibility of injury or death,
and claims to have done so without fear is either a liar or insane—but
the more often you do it and survive, the more aware you become that
the odds are inevitably swinging against you. If cats could count, they'd
start getting nervous around the time they put paid to their fifth life.

I also wanted to watch Sam, my daughter, grow up. She was long past those early years when children, though cute, don't do a whole lot except babble and fall over, much like a certain type of really old person. I found her endlessly fascinating, and regretted the fact that I was no longer with Rachel, her mother, although I didn't think Rachel was about to move back in just so that I could spend more time with Sam. Then again, I didn't want Rachel to move back in, so the feeling was mutual. Still, with Rachel and Sam in Vermont, and me in Portland, arranging to spend time with my daughter took some planning. I supposed that I could always move to Vermont, but then I'd have to start voting socialist, and finding excuses to secede from the Union. Anyway, I liked Portland, and being close to the sea. Staring out over Vermont's Lake Bomoseen wasn't quite the same thing.

I checked my cell phone messages as I lay on the bed. There was only one, from a man in Portland named Jude. He was one of a handful of the local street folk who'd proved helpful to me in the past, by providing either information or the occasional discreet surveillance service, as people tended not to notice the homeless, or pretended not to. Naturally there was no callback number for Jude. Instead, he had suggested leaving a message with the folk at the Portland Help Center or on the bulletin board at the Amistad Community on State Street to let him know when I might be available to meet.

I hadn't seen Jude around in a while, but then I hadn't really been looking out for him. Like most of Portland's homeless, he did his best to stay off the streets in winter. To do otherwise was to risk being found frozen in a doorway.

Me, I wasn't doing so badly. Work had picked up over the winter because I'd developed a nice sideline in process serving. It wasn't glamorous work, but it paid reasonably well, and occasionally required the exercise of more than a handful of brain cells. The day before I headed down to Newark to join Angel and Louis, I'd cashed a check for two thousand dollars, including a goodwill bonus payment, for just one job. The subject of the subpoena was an investment analyst named Hyram P. Taylor, who was involved in the initial stages of serious and hostile divorce proceedings with his wife, who was represented by my lawyer—and, for the most part, my friend—Aimee Price. Hyram was such a compulsive fornicator that even his own lawyer had privately acknowledged the possibility of his client's possessing a penis shaped like a corkscrew, and eventually his wife had just become tired of the humiliation. As soon as she filed for divorce, Hyram set about hiding all records relating to his wealth, and moving said wealth as far as possible from his wife's reach. He even abandoned his office in South Portland and tried to go to ground, but I tracked him down to the apartment of one of his girlfriends, a woman called Brandi, who, despite having a stripper's name, worked as an accountant in New Hampshire.

The problem was that Hyram wouldn't so much as pick up a piece of paper from the street for fear that it might be attached to an unseen piece of string ending in the hand of a process server. He didn't go anywhere without Brandi in tow, and she was the one who paid cash for newspapers, groceries, and drinks in bars. Hyram didn't put his hand on anything if he could help it. He probably had Brandi check him before he peed in the morning, just in case someone had attached a subpoena to his manhood while he slept.

His weakness—and they all have a weakness—was his car. That was how I found him. He drove a six-liter black Bentley Flying Spur Speed: ten miles to the gallon in the city, 0–60 in 4.8 seconds, and $200,000 worth of vehicle, at the very least. It was his pride and joy, which was probably why he stood up so suddenly that he spilled coffee over himself when I walked into the Starbucks on Andrews Road and asked if anyone owned a hell of a nice Bentley, because I'd just knocked off the wing mirror on the driver's side.

Hyram wasn't a slim man, but he could move fast when the need arose, even with hot coffee scalding his thighs. He went past me at full sail and arrived at his car to find that, sure enough, the mirror was hanging on to the body of the car only by wires. It had been harder to knock off than I'd anticipated, requiring two blows from a hammer. The Bentley may have been expensive, but it was clearly built well.

"I'm real sorry," I told him when I found him stroking the car as though it were a wounded animal that he was trying to console. "I just wasn't looking. If it's any help, I got a brother who runs an auto shop. He'd probably give you a good deal."

Hyram seemed to be having trouble speaking. His mouth just kept opening and closing without a sound. I could see Brandi hurrying across the parking lot, still trying to struggle into her coat while juggling her coffee and Hyram's jacket. Hyram had left her in his wake, but she'd be with us within seconds. I needed to hook Hyram before she got here, and while he was still in shock.

"Look," I said, "here are my insurance details, but if you could see your way clear to just letting me pay cash to cover the damages I'd surely be grateful."

Hyram reached out for the paper in my hand without thinking. I heard Brandi cry out a warning to him, but by then it was too late. His fingers had closed on the subpoena.

"Mr. Taylor," I said, "it's my pleasure to inform you that you've just been served."

It said a lot about Hyram P. Taylor's relationship with his car that he still seemed more upset by the damage to it than he was by being in receipt of the subpoena, but that situation didn't last long. He was swearing at me by the time I got to my own car, and the last I saw of him was Brandi flinging her coffee at his chest and walking away in tears. I even felt a little sorry for Hyram. He was a jerk, but he wasn't a bad guy, whatever his wife might have thought of him. He was just weak and selfish. Badness was something else. I knew that better than most. After all, I'd just burned a man's house down.

I made a note to get in touch with Jude, then turned out the light. The post-adrenaline dip had passed. I was now just exhausted. I slept soundly as, back in Portland, Jude twisted on his basement rope.

VII

Harry Dixon and Chief Lucas Morland drove to the burial site in Morland's car. There wasn't a whole lot of conversation between them. The last body Harry had seen was that of his own mother, and she was eighty-five when she passed on. She died in a hospice in the middle of an October night. The call had come to Harry at 3 A.M., informing him that his mother's last hours on earth were approaching and perhaps he might like to be with her when she went, but by the time he got to her she was already dead. She was still warm, though. That was what Harry remembered the most, the nurse telling him that he ought to touch her, to feel his mother's warmth, as though warmth equated to life and there might still be something of her inside that shell. So he placed his hand on her shoulder, for that appeared to be what was expected of him, and felt the heat gradually leave her, the spirit slowly departing until at last there was nothing left but cold.

He had never, he realized, seen anyone who wasn't supposed to be dead. No, that wasn't right, but he couldn't put it any better to himself. It had been his mother's time to go. She was sick, and old. Her final years had mostly been spent sleeping, misremembering, or forgetting entirely. Only once in her last months of life could he recall her speaking with any lucidity, and then he had just been thankful that they were alone together in the room. He wondered if, in her dementia, she had spoken of such matters to the nurses. If she did, they must have dismissed them as the ravings of an old woman on her way to the grave, for nobody had ever mentioned them to him. Those words came back to him now.

"I saw them do it once," she had said, as he sat beside her in an uncomfortable hospice chair. "I wanted to look. I wanted to know."

"Really?" he replied, only half listening, practiced in the art of nodding and ignoring. He was thinking of his business, and money, and how it had all gone so wrong for Erin and him when it continued to go well for so many others, both within and beyond the boundaries of Prosperous. After all, he and Erin played their part in the business of the town. They did as they were asked, and did not complain. How come they were suffering? Weren't the benefits of living in Prosperous supposed to be distributed equally among all? If not, what was the point of being part of the community in the first place?

And now his mother was rambling again, dredging up some inconsequential detail from the mud of her memories.

"I saw them take a girl. I saw them tie her up and leave her, and then—"

By now he was listening to her. Oh, he was listening for sure, even as he cast a glance over his shoulder to make sure that the door was closed.

"What?" he said. "Then what?" He knew of that which she spoke. He had never seen it himself, and didn't want to see it. You weren't supposed to ask; that was one of the rules. If you wanted to be certain, you could become a selectman, but selectmen in Prosperous were chosen carefully. You didn't put yourself forward. You waited to be approached. But Harry didn't want to be approached. In a way, the less he knew, the better. But that didn't stop him wondering.

"Then—"

His mother closed her eyes. For a moment he thought that she might have fallen asleep, but as he watched a tear crept from her right eye and her body began to shake. She was crying, and he had never seen his mother cry, not even when his father died. She was a hard woman. She was old Prosperous stock, and they didn't show frailty. If they had been frail, the town would not have survived.

Survived, and bloomed.

"Mom," he said. "Mom."

He took her right hand in his, but she shook it away, and only then did he realize that she wasn't crying but laughing, giggling at the memory of what she had witnessed. He hated her for it. Even in her slow dying, she had the capacity to horrify him. She stared at him, and she could see by his face how appalled he was.

"You were always weak," she said. "Had your brother lived, he would have been stronger. He would have become a selectman. The best of your father's seed went into him. Whatever was left dribbled into you."

His brother had died in the womb three years before Harry was born. There had been a spate of miscarriages, stillbirths, and crib deaths during the same period, a terrible blight upon the town. But the board of selectmen had taken action, and Prosperous had been blessed with only healthy, live children for many years thereafter. Harry's mother had never ceased to speak of his dead brother, though. Earl: that was the name she had given him, a melancholy echo of the status he might have attained had he lived. He was the Lost Earl. His royal line had died with him.

There were times in her dotage when Harry's mother called him Earl, imagining, in her madness, a life for a son who had never existed, a litany of achievements, a great song of his triumphs. Harry suffered them in silence, just as he had endured them throughout his life. That was why, when his mother's end approached at last, he had left Erin in bed, put on his clothes, and driven for two hours to get to the hospice on a miserable fall night to be with her. He simply wanted to be certain that she was dead, and few things in their relationship had given him greater pleasure than feeling the warmth leave her body until just the withered husk of her remained. Only consigning her to the flames of the crematorium had been more rewarding.

"You still awake there?" said Morland.

"Yes," said Harry. "I'm awake."

He didn't look at the chief as he spoke. He saw only his own reflection in the glass. I resemble my mother, he thought. In Prosperous, we all look like our parents, and sometimes we look like the children of other folks' parents too. It's the gene pool. It's too small. By rights it shouldn't be deep enough to drown a kitten, and every family should have a drooling relative locked away in an attic. I guess we're just blessed, and he smiled so hard, and so bleakly, at his choice of the word "blessed" that he felt his bottom lip crack.

"You're very quiet," said the chief.

"I never had to bury anyone before."

"Me neither."

Now Harry did look at him.

"You serious?" he said.

"I'm a cop, not an undertaker."

"You mean nothing like this has ever happened before?"

"Not to my knowledge. Seems this may be the first time."

It didn't make Harry feel any better. There would be repercussions. This trip with the chief was only the beginning.

"You didn't tell me what happened to the girl," said Harry.

"No, I didn't." The chief didn't speak again for a time, stringing Harry along. Then: "Ben Pearson had to shoot her."

"Had to?"

"There was a truck coming. If she'd stopped it—well, we would have had an even more difficult situation than the one we're currently in."

"What would you have done?" asked Harry.

The chief considered the question.

"I'd have tried to stop the truck, and I'd have been forced to kill the driver."

He turned his gray eyes on Harry for a moment.

"And then I'd have killed you, and your wife too."

Harry wanted to vomit, but he fought the urge. He could taste it at the back of his throat, though. For the first time since he had gotten into the car with Morland, he felt frightened. They were in the darkness out by Tabart's Pond, just one of many locations around Prosperous that was named after the original English settlers. There were no Tabarts left now in Prosperous. No Tabarts, no Mabsons, no Quartons, no Poyds. They'd all died early in the history of the settlement, and the rest had seemed set to follow them before the accommodation was reached. Now Harry was about to dig a grave in a place named after the departed, the lost, and a grave could accommodate two as easily as one.

"Why?" said Harry. "Why would you have killed us?"

"For forcing me to do something that I didn't want to do. For making life harder than it already is. For screwing up. As an example to others. You take your pick."

The chief made a right turn onto a dirt road.

"Maybe I'll have another look at that lock on your basement when we're done," he said. "Something about all this doesn't sit quite right with me. Kinda like the lock itself, it seems."

He grinned emptily at Harry. The beams of the headlights caught bare trees, and icy snow, and—

"What was that?" said Harry. He was looking back over his right shoulder.

"Huh? I didn't see nothing."

"There was something there. It was big, like an animal of some kind. I saw its eyes shining."

But the chief was paying him no attention. As far as Morland was concerned, Harry's "something" was just a ruse, a clumsy attempt to distract him from the business of the basement door. But Morland wasn't a man to be turned so easily. He planned to walk both Harry and his wife through their versions of the escape. He'd do it over and over until he was either satisfied with their innocence or convinced of their guilt. He'd been against entrusting the girl to them from the start, but he was overruled. He wasn't a selectman, even though he could sit in on the board's meetings. No chief of police had ever been a selectman. It was always felt that it was better to have the law as an instrument of the board's will.

The board had wanted to test Harry and Erin Dixon. Concerns had been raised about them—justifiable concerns, it now appeared. But it was a big step from doubting the commitment of citizens of Prosperous to taking direct action against them. In all the town's history, only a handful of occasions had arisen when it became necessary to kill one of their own. Such acts were dangerous, and risked sowing discontent and fear among those who had doubts, or were vulnerable to outside influence.

Morland now regretted telling Harry Dixon that he might have killed his wife and him. He didn't like Dixon, and didn't trust him. He'd wanted to goad him, but it was a foolish move. He'd have to reassure him. He might even have to apologize and put his words down to his justifiable anger and frustration.

But the test wasn't over. The test had only just begun. Harry Dixon would have to make amends for his failings, and Morland was pretty sure that Harry Dixon wouldn't like what that would entail, not one little bit.

"So what was it that you thought you saw?" said Morland.

"I believe I saw a wolf."

VIII

The ground was hard. Not that Harry should have been surprised; he'd lived in Penobscot County long enough to have no illusions about winter. On the other hand, he'd never had to dig a grave in any season, and this was like breaking rocks.

Morland left him to his own devices at the start. The chief sat in his car, the driver's door open but the heat on full blast, and smoked a series of cigarettes, carefully stubbing each one out in the ashtray. After a while, though, it became clear that Harry would be hacking at the ground until summer if he was forced to dig the grave alone, and so Morland opened the trunk of his car and removed a pickax from it. From where he stood, Harry caught a glimpse of something wrapped in transparent plastic sheeting, but he didn't look for long. He figured he'd have seen more than enough of it by the time the night was over.

Morland broke the ground with the pickax, and Harry cleared the earth away with the shovel. They worked without speaking. They didn't have any energy to spare. Despite the cold, Harry felt sweat soaking into his shirt. He removed his coat and was about to hang it on the low branch of a tree when Morland told him to put it in the car instead. Harry assumed it was because the car would keep his coat warm, until Morland made it clear that Harry's health and well-being were the last things on his mind.

"With luck, she'll stay down here and never be found," said Morland. "But you never know. Prepare for the worst and you won't be disappointed. I've seen crime scene investigators put a man behind bars for the rest of his life on the basis of a thread left on a branch. We take no chances."

Morland wasn't concerned about leaving tracks on the ground. It was too hard for that. Neither was he worried about being seen. Nobody lived nearby, and anyone who might be passing would, in all likelihood, be a citizen of Prosperous, and would know better than to go sticking a nose into Chief Morland's affairs even if he or she was foolish enough to come and investigate in the first place. Anyway, by now news of what had happened to the girl would have been communicated to those who needed to know. The roads around Prosperous would be quiet tonight.

They continued to dig. When they got to three feet, they were both too exhausted to go farther. The chief was a big, strong man, but Harry Dixon was no wilting flower either; if anything, he'd grown fitter over the previous year, now that he was required to be more active on his construction sites than he had been in decades. That was one of the few good things to come out of the financial mess in which he found himself. He had spent so long supervising, and ordering, and taking care of paperwork, that he had almost forgotten the pleasure of actual building, and the satisfaction that came with it—that, and the blisters.

Morland went to the car and took a thermos of coffee from the backseat. He poured a cup for Harry, and drank his own directly from the neck. Together they watched the moon.

"Back there, you were kidding about the wolf, right?" said Morland.

Harry was wondering if he might have been mistaken. At one time, there had been wolves all over Maine—grays and easterns and reds—and the state had enacted wolf bounties until 1903. As far as he could recall, the last known wolf killing in the state was back in 1996. He remembered reading about it in the newspapers. The guy had killed it thinking it was a large coyote, but the animal weighed more than eighty pounds, twice the size of the average coyote, and had the markings of a wolf, or a wolf hybrid. There had been nothing since then, to his knowledge: sightings and rumors, maybe, but no proof.

"It was a big animal, and it had a doglike head. That's all I can say for sure."

Morland went to light another cigarette, but found that the pack was empty. He crushed it and put it carefully into his pocket.

"I'll ask around," he said. "Wouldn't be a wolf, but if there's a coyote in the woods we'd best let folk know, tell them to keep a watch on their dogs. You done?"

Harry finished the last of the coffee and handed the cup back to the chief. Morland screwed it back on and tossed the thermos to the floor of the car.

"Come on, then," said Morland. "Time to put her in the ground."

———

THE TRUNK LIGHT SHONE on the plastic, and the girl inside it. She was lying on her back, and her eyes were closed. That was a mercy, at least. The exit wound in her chest was massive, but there was less blood than Harry might have expected. The chief seemed to follow the direction of his thoughts.

"She bled out on the snow of Ben's yard," he said. "We had to shovel it up and spread some more around to hide what we'd done. Take her legs. I'll lift from the head."

It was difficult to get her out of the trunk. She hadn't been a big girl, which was why they'd decided to fatten her up first, but for the first time Harry understood what was meant by "dead weight." The heavy-duty plastic was slippery, and Morland struggled to get a grip. Once she was out of the car, he had to drop her on the ground, put his foot under her to raise her upper body, and then wrap his arms around her chest to carry her, holding her to him like a sleeping lover. They stood to the right of the grave, and on the count of three tossed her in. She landed awkwardly, in a semi-seated position.

"You'd best get down there and straighten her," Morland told Harry. "If the hole was deeper I'd be inclined to let it go, but it's shallow as it is. We don't want the ground to sink and have her head peeping up like a gopher's."

Harry didn't want to get into the grave, but it didn't seem as though he had much choice. He eased himself down, then squatted to grip the ends of the plastic. As he did so, he looked at the girl. Her head was slightly lower than his, so that she seemed to be staring up at him. Her eyes were open. He must have been mistaken when he first saw her lying in the trunk. Perhaps it had been the reflection of the internal light, or his own tiredness, but he could have sworn . . .

"What's the problem?" said Morland.

"Her eyes," said Harry. "Do you recall if her eyes were open or closed?"

"What does it matter? She's dead. Whether we cover her up with her eyes wide open or squeezed shut is going to make no difference to her or to us."

He was right, thought Harry. He shouldn't even have been able to see her eyes so clearly through the plastic, but it was as though there was a light shining inside her head, illuminating the blue of her irises. She looked more alive now than she had in the basement.

He shook the thought from his head and pulled sharply on the plastic, dragging the girl's body flat. He didn't want to see her face again, so he turned away from it. He'd tried. She'd been given a better chance than any of the others, of that he was certain. It wasn't his fault that Ben Pearson had put an end to her hopes.

Suddenly, all the strength was gone from his body. He couldn't haul himself from the grave. He could barely raise his arms. He looked up at Morland. The chief had the pickax in his hands.

"Help me up," said Harry. But the chief didn't move.

"Please," said Harry. His voice cracked a little, and he despised himself for his weakness. His mother was right: he was half a man. If he'd been gifted with real courage, he'd have put the girl in his car, driven her to the state police in Bangor, and confessed everything to them, or at least dropped her off in the center of the city, where she'd be safe. Standing in the grave, he imagined a scenario in which the girl agreed to keep quiet about what had occurred, but it fell apart as soon as he saw himself returning to Prosperous to explain her absence. No, he'd done the best that he could for her. Anything more would have damned the town. Then again, it was already as close to damnation as made no difference.

He closed his eyes and waited for the impact of the pickax on his head, but it never came. Instead, Morland grabbed Harry's right hand, leaned back, and their combined strength got him out of the grave.

Harry sat on the ground and put his head in his hands.

"For a second, I thought you were going to leave me down there," he said.

"That would be too easy," said Morland. "Besides, we're not done yet."

And Harry knew that he wasn't referring to the filling in of the grave alone.

———

THE GIRL WAS GONE, covered by the earth. The ground had clearly been dug up, but Morland knew that whatever remained of the winter snows to come would take care of that. When the thaw came in earnest, the ground would turn to mire. As it dried, all traces of their activity would be erased. He just hoped that they'd buried the girl deep enough.

"Shit!" he said.

"What is it?" said Harry.

"We probably should have taken her out of the plastic. Might have helped her to rot quicker."

"You want to dig her up again?"

"No, I do not. Come on, time to go."

He wrapped the blade of the shovel and the head of the pickax in plastic bags, to keep the dirt off the trunk of his car. Tomorrow he'd clean it inside and out, just to be sure.

Harry had not moved from his place beside the grave.

"I have a question," he said.

Morland waited for him to continue.

"Isn't there a chance that she might be enough?" said Harry.

Morland might have called the look on Harry's face hopeful, if the use of the word "hope" weren't an obscenity under such circumstances.

"No," said Morland.

"She's dead. We killed her. We've given her to the earth. Why not? Why can't she be enough?"

Chief Morland closed the trunk before he replied.

"Because," he said, "she was dead when she went into the ground."

CHAPTER

IX

It was just after five on the evening after my return to Portland when I arrived at the Great Lost Bear on Forest Avenue. The bar was buzzing, as it always was on Thursdays. Thursday was showcase night, when the Bear invited a craft brewery to let folks taste its wares, always at a discount and always with a raffle at the end. It really didn't take much to keep customers loyal, but it always amazed me that so many businesses couldn't work up the energy to make the minimal extra effort required.

I found Dave Evans, the Bear's owner, marshaling the troops for the assault to come. I hadn't worked there in a while. Like I said, business had been good for me in recent months, maybe because, like the Bear, I tended to go the extra mile for my clients. In addition, some ongoing litigation relating to the purchase of my grandfather's old house on Gorham Road had been settled in my favor, and a lump sum had found its way into my accounts. I was solvent, and likely to remain so in the foreseeable future. Still, I liked to keep my hand in at the Bear, even if it was only once or twice a month. You hear a lot from people in bars. Admittedly, most of it is useless, but the occasional nugget of information creeps through. Anyway, my presence would allow Dave to take the rest of the night off, although he was strangely reluctant to leave.

"Your buddies are here," he said.

"I have buddies?"

"You used to. I'm not sure if the word still applies where those two are concerned."

He indicated a corner of the bar that was now looking significantly smaller than it usually did, thanks to the addition of two massive men in polyester jogging suits: the Fulci brothers. I hadn't seen them since Jackie Garner's funeral. His death had hit them hard. They had been devoted to him, and he had looked out for them as best he could. It was hard for men so large to keep such a low profile, but somehow they'd managed it during the months since Jackie's death. The city might even have breathed a bit easier for a while. The Fulcis had a way of sucking the oxygen from a room. They had a way of knocking it from people too. Their fists were like cinder blocks.

Dave's concern was therefore understandable. But despite their appearance, and an undeniable propensity for violence that seemed resistant to all forms of pharmaceutical intervention, the Fulcis were essentially brooders by nature. They might not brood for very long, but they did tend to take some time to consider which bones they might enjoy breaking first. The fact that they'd stayed away from me for so long meant that they'd probably been considering the fate of their friend with a certain degree of seriousness. That boded either well or very badly for me.

"You want me to call someone?" said Dave.

"Like who?"

"A surgeon? A priest? A mortician?"

"If they've come here to cause trouble over Jackie, you may need a builder to reconstruct your bar."

"Damn, and just as the place was coming together."

I worked my way through the crowd to reach their table. They were both sipping sodas. The Fulcis weren't big drinkers.

"It's been a long time," I said. "I was starting to worry."

To be honest, I was still worrying, and maybe more than before, now that they'd shown up at last.

"You want to take a seat," said Paulie.

It wasn't a question. It was an order.

Paulie was the older, and marginally better adjusted, of the two brothers. Tony should have had a lit fuse sticking out of the top of his head.

I took the seat. Actually, I wasn't too worried that the Fulcis might take a swing at me. If they did, I wouldn't know a lot about it until I woke up, assuming that I ever did, but I'd always gotten along well with them, and, like Jackie, I'd tried my best to help them whenever I could, even if it meant just putting in a word with local law enforcement when they stepped over the line. They'd done some work for me over the years, and they'd put themselves in harm's way on my behalf. I liked to think that we had an understanding, but Timothy Treadwell, that guy in the Herzog documentary who was eaten by the grizzlies he'd tried to befriend, probably felt the same way until a bear's jaws closed on his throat.

Paulie looked at Tony. Tony nodded. If things were going to turn bad, they would do so now.

"What happened to Jackie, we don't blame you for it," said Paulie.

He spoke with great solemnity, like a senior judge communicating a long-considered verdict.

"Thank you," I said, and I meant it, not only because my continued good health appeared assured but because I knew how important Jackie was to them. I wouldn't have been surprised if they'd held some residual grudge against me, but it appeared there would be none. With the Fulcis, it was all or nothing. We had a clean slate.

"Jackie done something very bad," said Tony, "but that didn't mean he should have been shot down from behind because of it."

"No," I said.

"Jackie was a good guy," Tony continued. "He took care of his mom. He looked out for us. He—"

Tony choked. His eyes were tearing up. His brother patted him on a muscled shoulder.

"Whatever we can do," said Paulie, "whatever help you need to find the man who did this, you let us know. And, anytime you want us to step up for you, you just call. Because Jackie would have stepped up, and just because he ain't around no more don't mean we ought to let these things slide, you understand? Jackie wouldn't have wanted that."

"I hear you," I said.

I reached out and shook their hands. I didn't even wince, but I was relieved to get the hand back.

"How's his mom doing?" I asked.

Jackie's mother had been given a diagnosis of Creutzfeldt-Jakob disease the previous year. Her illness was the only reason Jackie had committed the acts that led to his death. He just needed the money.

"Not so good," said Paulie. "Even with Jackie she would have struggled. Without him . . ."

He shook his head.

Jackie's insurance company had invoked a clause in his life-insurance policy relating to criminal activity, arguing that his death had resulted from participation in a criminal enterprise. Aimee Price was fighting the case on a pro bono basis, but she didn't believe the insurance company was going to modify its position, and it was hard to argue that it didn't have a point. Jackie was killed because he screwed up: he was careless, somebody died, and vengeance fell. I made a mental note to send a check to Jackie's mother. Even if it helped only a little, it would be something.

The Fulcis finished their drinks, nodded their goodbyes, and left.

"You're still alive," said Dave, who'd been keeping one eye on proceedings and another on his bar, in case he didn't get to see it again in its present form.

"You seem pleased."

"Means I get my night off," he said, as he pulled on his overcoat. "Would have been hard to leave otherwise."

———

I ENJOYED THAT EVENING in the Bear. Perhaps it was partly relief at not having incurred the wrath of the Fulcis, but in moving between the bar and the floor I was also able to empty my head of everything but beer taps, line cooks, and making sure that, when Dave returned the next morning, the Bear would still be standing in more or less the same condition it was in when he left it. I drank a coffee and read the *Portland Phoenix* at the bar while the night's cleanup went on around me.

"Don't tax yourself," said Cupcake Cathy, as she nudged me with a tray of dirty glasses. "If you strained something by helping, I don't know how I could go on living."

Cathy was one of the waitstaff. If she was ever less than cheerful, I had yet to see it. Even as she let off some steam, she was still smiling.

"Don't make me fire you."

"You can't fire me. Anyway, that would require an effort on your part."

"I'll tell Dave to fire you."

"Dave just *thinks* we work for him. Don't disillusion him by making him put it to the test."

She had a point. I still wasn't sure how the Bear operated, exactly; it just did. In the end, no matter who was nominally in charge, everyone just worked for the Bear itself. I finished my coffee, waited for the last of the staff to leave, and locked up. My car was the only one left in the lot. The night was clear, and the moon bright, but already there was a layer of frost on the roof. Winter was refusing to relinquish its hold on the Northeast. I drove home beneath a sky exploding with stars.

————

OVER BY DEERING OAKS, the door to Jude's basement opened.

"Jude, you in here?"

A lighter flared. Had there been anyone to see, it would have revealed a man layered in old coats, with newspaper poking out of his laceless boots. The lower half of his face was entirely obscured by his beard, and dirt was embedded in the wrinkles on his skin. He looked sixty but was closer to forty. He was known on the streets as Brightboy. He once had another name, but even he had almost forgotten it by now.

"Jude?" he called again.

The heat from the lighter was burning his fingers. Brightboy swore hard and let the flame go out. His eyes were getting used to the dark, but the basement was shaped like an inverted "L," which meant that the moonlight penetrated only so far. The dogleg to the right remained in darkness.

He hit the lighter again. It was a cheap plastic thing. He'd found a bunch of them, all still full of fluid, in a garbage can outside an apartment building that was being vacated. In this kind of weather, anything that could generate heat and flame was worth holding on to. He still had half a dozen left.

Brightboy turned the corner, and the light caught Jude's brown boots dangling three feet above the floor. Brightboy raised the flame slowly, taking in the reddish-brown overcoat, the green serge pants, the tan jacket and waistcoat, the cream shirt, and the carefully knotted red tie. Jude had even managed to die dressed like a dandy, although his face was swollen and nearly unrecognizable above the knot in his tie, and the noose that suspended him above the floor was lost in his flesh. A backless chair was on its side beneath his feet. To its right was a wooden box that he had been using as a nightstand. His sleeping bag lay open and ready next to it.

On the box was a plastic bag filled with bills and coins.

The lighter was again growing hot in Brightboy's hand. He lifted his thumb, and the flame disappeared, but the memory of its light danced before his eyes. His left hand found the bag of money. He put it carefully into his pocket, then dragged Jude's pack into the moonlight and rifled it for whatever was worth taking. He found a flashlight, a deck of cards, a couple of pairs of clean socks, two shirts fresh from Goodwill, and a handful of candy bars just one month past expiration.

All these things Brightboy transferred to his own pack. He also took Jude's sleeping bag, rolling it up and tying it to the base of his pack with string. It was better than his own, newer and warmer. He didn't even think about Jude again until he was about to leave. They had always got along okay, Brightboy and Jude. Most of the other homeless people avoided Brightboy. He was untrustworthy and dishonest. Jude was one of the few who tried not to judge him. True, Brightboy had sometimes found Jude's obsession with his appearance to be an affectation, and he suspected that it helped to make Jude feel superior to his brothers and sisters on the streets, but Jude had been as generous with Brightboy as he had been with everyone else, and rarely had a harsh word passed between them.

Brightboy thumbed the lighter and held it aloft. Jude seemed frozen in place. His skin and his clothing were spangled with frost.

"Why'd you do it?" said Brightboy. His left hand dipped into his pocket, as though to reassure himself that the money was still there. He'd heard that Jude had been calling in loans. Brightboy himself had owed Jude two dollars. That was one of the reasons he'd come looking for him; that and a little company, and maybe a swig of something if Jude had it to spare. Someone had said that Jude wanted the money urgently, and it was time to pay up. Jude rarely asked for anything from the rest of his kind, so few resented him calling in his debts, and those that had it paid willingly enough.

So why would a man who had succeeded in putting together what Brightboy guessed to be at least a hundred dollars suddenly give up and take his own life? It made no sense, but then a lot of things made no sense to Brightboy. He liked his street name, but he had no conception of the irony that lay behind it. Brightboy wasn't smart. Cunning, maybe, but his intelligence was of the lowest and most animal kind.

Whatever had led Jude to finish his days at the end of a rope, he had no need for money where he now was, while Brightboy was still among the living. He walked to St. John Street, ordered two cheeseburgers, fries, and a soda for five dollars at the drive-through window of McDonald's, and ate them in the parking lot of a Chinese restaurant. He then bought himself a six-pack of Miller High Life at a gas station, but it was so cold outside that he had nowhere to drink the beers. With no other option available, he headed back to Jude's basement and consumed them while the dead man hung suspended before him. He unrolled Jude's sleeping bag, climbed into it, and fell asleep until shortly before dawn. He woke while it was still dark, gathered up the bottles for their deposit, and slipped from the basement to seek out breakfast. He stopped only to make a 911 call from a public phone on Congress.

It was the least that he could do for Jude.

CHAPTER

X

Jude died without enough money to pay for his own funeral, so he was buried by the city at taxpayers' expense. It cost fifteen hundred dollars, give or take, but there were those who resented spending even that much to give a decent burial to a man who seemed to them to have been nothing but a burden on the city for most of his life. The only consolation they could derive was that Jude was unlikely to trouble them for a handout again.

He was interred in an unmarked grave at Forest City Cemetery, in South Portland, when the medical examiner had finished with his body. A funeral director recited a psalm as the coffin was lowered into the ground, but, unlike most city cases, Jude did not go to his rest unmourned. Alongside the cemetery workers stood a dozen of Portland's homeless, men and women both, as well as representatives of the local shelters and help centers who had known Jude. I was there too. The least that I could do was acknowledge his passing. A single bouquet of flowers was laid on the ground above him once the grave had been filled in. Nobody lingered. Nobody spoke.

The medical examiner's opinion was that Jude's injuries were consistent with asphyxiation, with no indication of a suspicious death. The investigation was ongoing, though, and the police and the attorney general were under no obligation to accept the ME's opinion as gospel. Still, in this case it was unlikely that the Portland PD would reject it. When a homeless man died at the hands of another, it was usually in a brutal manner, and there was little mystery to it. Jude, despite the care that he took with his appearance, was a troubled man. He suffered from depression. He lived from meal to meal, and hand-out to handout. There were more likely candidates for suicide, but not many.

If there was anything unusual about this case, it was that the medical examiner had found no trace of drugs or alcohol in Jude's system. He was clean and sober when he died. It was a minor detail, but one worthy of notice. Those who choose to take their own lives often need help with the final step. Either they set out with the intention of killing themselves, and find something to relax them in those last hours and minutes, or the mood induced by alcohol or narcotics is the trigger for the act. Suicide isn't easy. Neither, whatever the song might say, is it painless. Jude would have learned that as he kicked at the air from the end of a rope. I don't know how much help booze might have been under the circumstances, but it couldn't have made his situation any worse.

To be honest, I let Jude slip from my mind after the funeral. I'd like to say that I was better than everybody else, but I wasn't. He didn't matter. He was gone.

———

LUCAS MORLAND PULLED UP in front of Hayley Conyer's home on Griffin Road. It wasn't the biggest house in Prosperous, not by a long shot, but it was one of the oldest, and, being partly built of stone, conveyed a certain authority. Most of it dated from the end of the eighteenth century, and by rights it should probably have been listed on the National Register of Historic Places, but neither generations of Conyers nor the citizens of Prosperous had seen fit to nominate the house. The town didn't need that kind of attention. The old church presented them with enough problems as it was. Anyway, the Conyer house wasn't particularly noteworthy in terms of its situation or its design, and had no interesting historical associations. It was just old, or at least old by the standards of the state. The leading citizens of Prosperous, cognizant of their heritage, of their links to a far more ancient history back in England, took a more nuanced view of such matters.

Hayley Conyer's Country Squire station wagon stood in the drive. There seemed to be even more bumper stickers on it than Morland remembered: "Obama/Biden"; a "No Tar Sands in Maine" protest badge; "Maine Supports Gay Rights" over a rainbow flag; and a reminder that sixty-one percent of the electorate had not voted for the current governor of the state. (Blame the state's Democrats for that, thought Morland; trust them to split their own vote and then act surprised when it came back to bite them on the ass. Jesus, monkeys could have handled the nomination process better.) The station wagon was so ancient that it was probably held together by those stickers. He'd heard Hayley arguing with Thomas Souleby about the car, Souleby opining that the old gas-guzzler was causing more environmental pollution than a nuclear meltdown, and Hayley responding that it was still more environmentally friendly than investing in a new car and scrapping the old one.

Morland's own Crown Vic had been acquired from the Prosperous Police Department back in 2010, while it was still in perfect running order. By then, Ford had announced that it would cease production of the Police Interceptors in 2011, and Morland decided to secure one of the department's Crown Vics for himself before his officers drove the fleet into the ground. The Crown Vic had two tons of rear-wheel drive, and a V8 engine under the hood. If you crashed in a Crown Vic, you had a better chance of walking away alive than you did in a lighter patrol car, like the increasingly popular Chevy Caprice. The car was also spacious, and that meant a lot to a big man like Morland. The sacrifice was getting only thirteen miles to the gallon, but Morland reckoned the town could afford that small gesture on his behalf.

Hayley appeared on her porch as Morland sat musing on his car. She was still a striking woman, even as she left seventy behind. The chief could remember her in her prime, when men had circled like insects, flitting around her as she went about her business and did her best to ignore them or, if they grew too persistent, swatted them away with a flick of her hand. He had no idea why she had never married. That rainbow bumper sticker on her car might have caused some folk to suggest an explanation, but Hayley Conyer was no lesbian. She was, if anything, entirely asexual. She had committed herself to the town: it was hers to have and to hold, to love and to cherish. She had inherited her duty to it, for more members of the Conyer family than any other in Prosperous had served on the board. Hayley herself had been the first selectman for more than four decades now. There were those who whispered that she was irreplaceable, but Morland knew better. Nobody was irreplaceable. If that were true, Prosperous would never have thrived for so long.

But in the dark corners of his mind Morland was starting to feel that it might be for the best if Hayley Conyer made way for another. It would take her death to do it, for she would never relinquish control while there was breath in her body, but it was time that the Conyer reign came to a close. There was a lot to be said for the discipline of married life. It forced one to learn the art of compromise, and to remedy the flaws in one's nature. Morland himself was still a work-in-progress after two decades of marriage, but he liked to think that his wife might be as well. Hayley Conyer, on the other hand, simply grew more resolute in her self-belief, more intransigent in her views, and more ready to embrace the use of diktats to get her way. She was helped by the rules of the board, which gave the first selectman the equivalent of two votes. It meant that, even if the board was evenly divided on an issue, Hayley's side would triumph, and she could force a stalemate with only one other selectman on her side. It was also a simple fact that the rest of the board combined had less testosterone than she did. It was increasingly left to Morland to try to deal with Hayley, and to encourage her to moderate her behavior, but he had been having less and less success in recent months. A body left hanging in a Portland basement was testament to that.

"I was just admiring your car," said Morland.

"You going to tell me that I need to replace it too?" she said.

"Not unless pieces of it start coming off on the highway and injuring folk, although that's starting to seem increasingly likely."

She folded her arms over her chest, the way she did at meetings when she wanted to let people know that she had done listening to their arguments and her decision was made. She wasn't wearing a brassiere, and her breasts hung low beneath her shirt. With her flowered skirt and her sandaled feet, and her long gray hair held back by a scarf, she came across as the typical earth mother, all bean sprouts and wheatgrass and organic milk. It wasn't entirely inapt, even if it didn't hint at the hardness beneath.

"It's mine," she said, "and I like it."

"You're only holding on to it because the Thomas Soulebys of this world keep telling you to get rid of it," he said. "If they started stroking it and admiring it, you'd sell it for scrap in a heartbeat."

Her scowl softened. Morland had a way of disarming her that few others could lay claim to. His father had enjoyed the same gift. Daniel Morland's relationship with Hayley Conyer had been almost flirtatious, at least when his wife wasn't around. Whether Hayley chose to embrace sexual activity or not, she was an attractive woman, and Alina Morland wasn't about to stand by and let her husband play patty-cake with her just to ensure the smooth running of the town. Neither had Alina been concerned by the power that Hayley wielded as chief selectman, because that was all politics and this was about a wife and her husband. The town could have decided to make Hayley Conyer its official queen, and Alina would have knocked her crown off for stirring even the slightest of sexual feelings in her husband.

This demonstrated one of the curious truths about Prosperous: in most things it ran pretty much like any other town of similar size. It had its rivalries, its intrigues. Men cheated on their wives, and wives cheated on their husbands. Hugo Reed didn't talk to Elder Collingwood, and never would, all because of an incident with a tractor and a garden gate some forty years earlier. Ramett Huntley and Milicent Rawlin, although superficially polite to each other, were obsessed with their bloodlines, and both had made regular pilgrimages back to the northeast of England over the years in an effort to trace their lineages to royalty. So far neither had been successful, but the search went on. In Prosperous, business as usual was the order of the day. The town differed in only one crucial way from the rest, and even that had become a version of normal over the centuries. It was surprising what folk could accustom themselves to, as long as they were rewarded for it in the end.

"You want some tea, Lucas?" said Hayley.

"Tea would be good."

In Prosperous, you were more likely to be offered tea than coffee. It was a hangover from the Old Country. Ben Pearson was probably the only store owner for fifty miles who regularly ran out of loose-leaf Earl Grey and English Breakfast, and Yorkshire Tea teabags. And, damn, was there trouble when he did.

Inside, Hayley's home resembled a Victorian house museum: dark-wood antique furniture, Persian rugs, lace tablecloths, overstuffed chairs, and wall upon wall of books. The chandeliers were late nineteenth-century reproductions by Osler & Faraday of Birmingham, based on classic eighteenth-century Georgian design. Morland thought them excessively ornate, and ill suited to the house, but he kept that opinion to himself. Still, sitting at Hayley's dining table always made him feel as if he were preparing for a séance.

Hayley boiled some water and set the tea to brew. The teapot was sterling silver, but the tea would be served in mismatched mugs. China would have been too much of an affectation. She poured milk into each of the mugs, not bothering to ask Morland how much he wanted, or whether he might prefer to do it himself. By now she knew his habits and preferences almost as well as his wife did. She added the tea, then found some shortbread biscuits and emptied four onto a plate. Biscuits, not cookies; it said so on the packaging, which was also decorated with Highland cattle, tartans, and ancient ruins.

They sipped their tea, nibbled the shortbread, and spoke of the weather and the repairs that would have to be made to the town office once winter was gone, before moving on to the real business of the afternoon.

"I hear they buried that hobo," said Hayley.

Morland wasn't sure that the man named Jude had been a hobo, strictly speaking. As far as he knew, hobos were migratory workers. Technically, Jude had been a bum.

"Apparently so," said Morland.

"Has there been any fuss?"

"Not that I've heard."

"I told you there wouldn't be. I had to listen to all that bitching and moaning for nothing."

Morland didn't dispute the point. He had done all his arguing when the board's decision was communicated to him, but by then it was too late. He'd tried to talk Hayley around, but on that occasion she had proved immune to his charms.

"It would have been preferable if he'd just disappeared," said Morland.

"That would have cost more—a lot more. Books have to be balanced."

"It might have been worth it. I don't think anyone would have come looking for a missing homeless man, and it's hard to prove the commission of a crime without a body."

"Nobody's trying to prove that a crime was committed. A hobo hanged himself, and that's the end of it."

Not quite, thought Morland. Hayley was thinking like a selectman, Morland like a lawman.

"The problem, as I see it, is that we now have two dead bodies to no good end," said Morland.

"Ben told me that he had no choice but to shoot the girl. You agreed."

Yet I didn't agree to the killing of her father, Morland was about to say, but he stilled the words before they reached his tongue.

"This town has survived, and flourished, by being careful," he said.

"You don't have to tell me that!" said Hayley. A little blood found its way into her pale cheeks. "What do you think I've been doing all these years? Every decision I've made has been with the best interests of the town at heart."

I've made, he noticed, not *we've* made. He wondered if this was how all despots began. At some point, someone had to speak truth to power. Then again, those who did frequently ended up with their heads on stakes.

"I'm not questioning your commitment to the town, Hayley. Nobody is. But two dead from the same family could attract attention."

"One dead," she corrected him. "There's one body, not two. Has the girl even been reported missing yet?"

"No," he conceded.

"And she won't be either, because the only one who might have been concerned about her is now in the ground. By acting as we did, we solved the problem—or we would have if that damn fool Dixon hadn't let the girl go."

"That's an interesting choice of words," said Morland.

He hadn't raised his suspicions with Hayley before. He wanted to let them percolate some before he started pouring them out. Hayley nibbled on her shortbread, her tiny white teeth chipping away at it with the actions of a hungry rodent.

"You think he's telling lies about what happened?" she said.

"I went to their house and tried using a scrap of material to open the bolt from the inside, like he and Erin claimed the girl did."

"And?"

"It worked."

"So?"

"It took a while, and I had to use a piece of wood to pull the cloth in and form a loop, just as Erin Dixon did when I put her in the basement and asked her to demonstrate how the girl might have escaped. She told me she'd found the wood on the floor, and that the girl must have broken it off the bed. She showed me the bed, and there was a long splinter of wood missing that matched the piece in Erin's hand."

"I'm waiting for a 'but.'"

"But there was blood on the floor by the bed when I let Erin out, and it was fresh."

"Could it have been the girl's? She couldn't have been gone for but an hour by then."

"If it was, the blood would have congealed."

"If it was Erin's blood, maybe she cut herself when she was examining the wood."

"Maybe."

Hayley set her shortbread down by her mug. She seemed to have lost her taste for sweetness.

"Why would they let her go?"

"I don't know. There are rumors about Harry's business."

"I've heard. I've been concerned since they took that loan."

"The paintwork on his house needs a new coat, and that old truck of his might just be the only vehicle in Prosperous that's in worse shape than yours. I didn't have time to take a good look around his kitchen when I visited, but I saw that some groceries had been unpacked and hadn't yet been put away. They're buying cheap bread, generic pasta, a couple of packs of chicken joints that were about to expire but would be okay if you froze them, that kind of thing."

"They could have been for the girl. They weren't going to be feeding her filet mignon."

"It just doesn't sit right with me." He regarded her closely. "It sounds to me like you're trying to defend them."

"I'm not defending anyone," said Hayley. "I'm trying to understand. If what you're suggesting is true, we have a major problem on our hands. We'll have to act, and that could cause unrest in the town. We don't turn on our own."

"Not unless our own start turning on us."

"I still can't figure out why they'd want to release her."

"Pity? Guilt?"

"It's not like we were asking them to kill her," said Hayley. "They just had to take care of her until we were ready. She was too thin. All this might have been avoided if Walter and Beatrix hadn't brought us a junkie."

"It's been a long time since we've had to find someone," said Morland. "It's harder now. The safest way is to take the vulnerable, the lost, the ones that nobody will miss. If that means junkies and whores, then so be it."

"Junkies and whores may not be good enough."

"It's been many years, Hayley. Some people are wondering if it might not be necessary at all."

She flared up.

"Who? Tell me!" Her eyes grew sly. "The same ones who are whispering about my 'commitment' to the town?"

He should have stepped more carefully. She heard everything, turning the details over in her mind and examining them the way a jeweler might consider gemstones before deciding which to keep and which to discard.

"I know there are some who are starting to doubt me," she said.

Hayley stared at Morland, as though willing him to confess that he himself had been guilty of such thoughts, but he did not. She leaned over the table and grasped his hand. Her skin was cold, and its look and feel reminded him of the cheap cuts of chicken at the Dixon house.

"That's why this is so important," she said. "If I'm to go, I want to leave knowing the town is secure. I want to be sure that I've done all that I can for it."

She released her grip on him. She had left marks on the back of his hand, as if to remind him that she was still strong and should not be underestimated.

"What do you suggest?" he said.

"We talk to the Dixons. We tell them to find us another girl, fast. And no junkie either; we want someone clean and healthy. If they come through for us, we'll see what more the town can do to help them out if they're in trouble."

Morland had more to say about the Dixons, but he kept it to himself, for now.

"And if they don't?"

Hayley stood and started clearing the table. She was tired of talking with him. The discussion was over.

"Then they're a threat to the security of the town. There's still money in the discretionary fund, thanks to the decision not to disappear the hobo instead of just leaving him to be found.

"And," she added, "our friends will be grateful for the work."

XI

I was sitting at a table in Crema Coffee Company, on Commercial, when the man who called himself Shaky found me. It was just after nine in the morning, and while a steady stream of people kept the baristas busy, most of the tables remained empty. It was that time of day when folk wanted to order and go, which suited me just fine. I had a nice sun-dappled spot by the window, and copies of the *New York Times* and the *Portland Press Herald*. Crema had one of the best spaces in town, all bare boards and exposed brickwork. There were worse places to kill an hour. I had a meeting later in the morning with a prospective client: trouble with an ex-husband who hadn't grasped the difference between keeping a protective eye on his former wife and stalking her. It was, depending on whom you asked, a thin line. Neither did he appear to understand that if he really cared about his wife he should pay her the child support that he owed. On such misunderstandings were hourly rates earned.

Shaky was wearing black sneakers, only slightly frayed jeans, and an overcoat so big that it was just one step away from being a tent. He looked self-conscious as he entered Crema, and I could see one or two of the staff watching him, but Shaky wasn't about to be dissuaded from whatever purpose he had in mind. He made a beeline for my table.

It wasn't just Shaky who called himself by that name. Apparently, everyone on the street did. He had a palsied left hand that he kept close to his chest. I wondered how he slept with it. Maybe, like most things, you learned to get used to it if you had to endure it long enough.

He hovered before me, the sunlight catching his face. He was clean-shaven, and smelled strongly of soap. I may have been mistaken, but it struck me that he'd tidied himself up and dressed in his best clothing to come here. I remembered him from the funeral. He was the only one present to shed a tear for Jude as he was lowered into his grave.

"You mind if I sit down?" he asked.

"Not at all," I said. "Would you like a coffee?"

He licked his lips, and nodded. "Sure."

"Any preference?"

"Whatever's the biggest, and the warmest. Maybe sweet too."

Since I was mainly a straight-filter kind of guy, I had to rely on the girl behind the counter to guide me on warm and sweet. I came back with a maple latte and a couple of muffins. I wasn't too hungry, but Shaky probably was. I picked at mine to be polite while Shaky went back to the counter and loaded up his latte with sugar. He tore into the muffin as soon as he resumed his seat, then seemed to realize that he was in company, and nobody was likely to try and steal the snack from him, so he slowed down.

"It's good," he said. "The coffee as well."

"You sure there's enough sugar in there for you?" The stirrer was pretty much standing up by itself in the coffee.

He grinned. His teeth weren't great, but the smile somehow was.

"I always did have a sweet tooth. I guess it's still in there somewhere. I done lost most of the rest."

He chewed some more muffin, holding it in his mouth for as long as he could to savor the taste.

"Saw you at the cemetery," he said, "when they put Jude in the ground. You're the detective, right?"

"That's correct."

"You knew Jude?"

"A little."

"What I heard. Jude told me that he did some detecting for you, couple of times."

I smiled. Jude always did get a kick out of being asked to help. I could hear some skepticism in Shaky's voice, just a hint of doubt, but I think he wanted it to be true. He kept his head down as he stared up at me, one eyebrow raised in anticipation.

"Yes, he did," I said. "Jude had a good eye, and he knew how to listen."

Shaky almost sagged with relief. Jude hadn't lied to him. This wasn't a wasted errand.

"Yeah, Jude was smart," he said. "Wasn't nothing happened on the streets that Jude didn't know about. He was kind too. Kind to everyone. Kind to me."

He stopped eating, and for an instant he looked terribly lonely. His mouth moved soundlessly as he tried to express emotions that he had never shared aloud before: his feelings for Jude, and about himself now that Jude was gone. He was trying to put loss into words, but loss is absence, and will always defy expression. In the end, Shaky just gave up and slurped noisily at his latte to cover his pain.

"You were friends?"

He nodded over the cup.

"Did he have many friends?"

Shaky stopped drinking and wiped his mouth with the back of his hand.

"No. He kept most people at a distance."

"But not you."

"No."

I didn't pursue it. It was none of my business.

"When did you last see him alive?"

"Couple of days before he was found in that basement. I was helping him to collect."

"Collect?"

"Money. He was calling in the debts he was owed, and he asked me to help. Everyone knew that me and him was close, and if I said I was working on his behalf then it was no word of a lie. He put it all down on paper for me. As I'd find someone I'd cross the name off the list and record how much they'd given me."

He reached into one of his pockets and produced a sheet of paper, which he carefully unfolded and placed before me. On it was a list of names written neatly in pencil. Beside most of them, in a considerably messier hand, figures were scrawled: a dollar or so, usually, and no sum more than two bucks.

"Sometimes I'd get to a person after he did, and maybe they'd already have paid up, and maybe they wouldn't have. Jude was soft, though. He believed every hard-luck story, because it was his way. Me, I knew some of them was lying. As long as they was breathing, they was lying. I made sure that, if they could, they paid."

I took the piece of paper and did a little rough addition on the numbers. The total didn't come to much: a hundred dollars and change. Then I realized that, while it wasn't much to me, that kind of sum could get a man beaten to a pulp if he fell in with the wrong company. It might even be enough to bring death upon him.

"What did he want the money for?" I said.

"He was looking for his daughter. Told me she used to be a junkie but she was straightening out. Last he heard she was up in Bangor looking for work, and seems like she found some. I think—"

He paused.

"Go on."

"I think she'd come up here because she wanted to be near him, but not so near that it would be easy for him," said Shaky. "She wanted him to come find her. Jude had abandoned her momma and her way back, and he knew that the girl blamed him for everything that had gone wrong in her life since then. She was angry at him. She might even have hated him, but when there's blood involved love and hate aren't so different, or they get all mixed up so's you can't tell one from the other. I guess he was considering moving up to Bangor and having done with it. But Jude didn't like Bangor. It's not like here. They tore the heart out of that city when they built the mall, and it never recovered, not the way Portland did. It's a bad place to be homeless too—worse than here. But Jude wanted to make up to the girl for what he'd done, and he couldn't do it from Portland."

"How long did it take you and Jude to get the money together?"

"A week. Would have taken him a month if he'd been working alone. I ought to get me a job as a debt collector."

He used the forefinger of his right hand to pull the scrap of paper back to him.

"So my question is—" he began, but I finished it for him.

"Why would a man who had just spent a hard week calling in his debts, and who was fixated on mending his relationship with his daughter, hang himself in a basement just when he's managed to get some cash together?"

"That's right."

"So, what: he was going to give his daughter the money, or use it to move to Bangor?"

"Neither," said Shaky. "If I understood him right, I think he was hoping to hire you to find her."

He seemed to remember that he still had his coffee. He drank half of what remained in one go, and turned an eye to the muffin on my plate. I pushed it toward him.

"Go ahead," I said. "I'm not as hungry as I thought."

———

WE SPOKE FOR AN hour, sometimes about Jude, sometimes about Shaky himself. He'd served in the military, and that was how he had come by his bad arm; it was nerve damage of some kind, caused by a jeep tire exploding.

"Not even a proper wound," as Shaky told me. "I used to lie about it to make myself sound brave, but it just don't seem worth the effort no more."

At the end of our conversation, two things were clear to me: Shaky knew Jude better than almost anyone else in Portland, and he still didn't really know him at all. Jude had shared only the barest of information about his daughter with him. To Shaky, it seemed as though the more troubles his friend encountered the more reluctant he was to seek help with them, and that was how men ended up dying alone.

I bought Shaky another maple latte before I left, and he gave me instructions for how best to reach him. As with Jude, he used the Amistad Community and the good folk at the Portland Help Center for such communications. I then drove to South Portland to meet my prospective client at her home, and she gave me details of where her husband was working, where he was living, just how much of an asshole he now was, and just how much of an asshole he didn't used to be. For her children's sake, she didn't want to involve the police, and she hated her lawyer. I was the least bad of the remaining options, although she did ask if I knew someone who would break her husband's legs once I had made it clear that this wasn't something I was prepared to take on—or not without a better reason.

Since I had nothing else to do, I went to visit the errant husband at his office in Back Cove, where he was a partner in some hole-in-the-wall financial advice and investment business. His name was Lane Stacey, and he didn't look pleased when he discovered that I wasn't there to give him money to invest. He did some hollering and grandstanding before it became clear to him that I wasn't about to be intimidated back onto the street. A calm demeanor always helped in these situations—calmness, and having a good forty pounds on the man on the other side of the argument.

Like the Bentley-owning Hyram P. Taylor, Stacey wasn't a bad guy. He wasn't even as priapic as Hyram. He was lonely, he missed his wife and kids, and he didn't think anybody else would be willing to have him. His wife had just fallen out of love with him, and he, to a lesser degree, with her, although he had been more willing to keep things going as they were in order to secure a roof over his head and have someone around to nurse him when he caught cold, and maybe sleep with him occasionally. Eventually I ended up having lunch with him at the Bayou Kitchen, where I explained to him the importance of not stalking his wife, and of paying to support his children. He, in turn, confessed that he'd been hoping to force her to take him back by starving her—and his kids—into submission, which went some ways toward explaining why his fears that he might not find anyone else to put up with him had some basis in truth. By the time lunch was over I'd secured some guarantees about his future behavior, and he'd tried to sell me on a short-term bond so risky that it was little more than a personal recession waiting to happen. He took my rejection on the chin. He was, he said, "optimistic" about the country's financial future, and saw only great times ahead for his business.

"Why is that?" I asked.

"Everybody loves the promise of a quick buck," he said. "And the sucker store never runs out of stock."

He had a point.

After all, I'd just paid for lunch.

CHAPTER

XII

A couple of calls gave me the name of the detective whose name graced the file on Jude's case. It came as both good and bad news. The good news was that I knew the detective personally. The bad news was that I had once kind of dated her. Her name was Sharon Macy, and "dated" might have been too strong a word for the history between us. She'd come into the Bear a couple of times when I was bartending, and we had dinner once at Boda, on Congress, which wasn't far from her apartment on Spruce Street. It had ended with a short kiss, and an agreement that it might be nice to do it again sometime soon. I wanted to, and I think she did too, but somehow life got in the way, and then Jackie Garner died.

Sharon Macy was an interesting character, assuming you were content to accept the Chinese definition of "interesting" as resembling a kind of curse. Some years earlier, she was temporarily stationed on an island called Sanctuary, out in Casco Bay, when a group of hired guns with a grudge came calling, and a lot of shooting had resulted. Macy came through unscathed, but she bloodied herself along the way, and had acquired no small degree of respect as a cop with clean kills. As a result, she hadn't been destined to stay in uniform for long, and no one was surprised by her move to detective. She worked in the Portland PD's Criminal Investigation Division, and was also heavily involved in the Southern Maine Violent Crimes Task Force, which investigated serious incidents in the region.

Macy's cell phone was off when I called her number, and I didn't bother to leave a message. She wasn't at her apartment when I went by, but a neighbor said that she had gone to drop off her laundry at the eco place on Danforth. The guy at the Laundromat confirmed that she'd been in, and said that he thought she might be waiting in Ruski's while he did a fast wash-and-fold for her.

Ruski's was a Portland institution, opening early and serving food until late. It had long been a destination for those whose working hours meant that breakfast was eaten whenever they happened to want it, which was why Ruski's served it all day. On Sundays it was a magnet for regulars, including cops and firefighters from anywhere within an easy drive of Portland who wanted somewhere dark and friendly in which to kill an afternoon. It boasted darts, a pretty good jukebox, and a shortage of places to sit, and it never changed. It was what it was: a neighborhood bar where the prices were better than the food, and the food was good.

Macy was sitting by the window when I walked up, drinking and chatting with a patrol cop named Terrill Nix. I knew Nix a little because one of his brothers was a cop out in Scarborough. Nix was in his late forties, I guessed, and probably already thinking about cashing out. His hair was thinning, and his face had assumed a default expression of pained disappointment. The remains of a hangover special—hash, toast, eggs, home fries—lay on the plate beside him, but he didn't look as if he was trying to beat down a hard night. His eyes were bright and clear. He could probably see all the way to retirement.

Macy looked like Macy: small, dark, with quick eyes and an easy smile. Damn. I tried to remember why I hadn't called her again. Oh, yeah. Life, whatever that was. And some dying.

Nix spotted me before Macy did, as she had her back to the door. He nudged Macy's left leg with his right foot to alert her. It didn't look as though there was anything between them, just two cops who happened to cross paths in Ruski's, where cops crossed paths with one another all the time. Anyway, Nix's wife would have emasculated him and left him to bleed out before decorating the hood of her car with the pieces if she even caught a whiff of another woman off him, not to mention the fact that Nix's brother had married Nix's wife's sister. The whole family would have helped weigh down his corpse in the Scarborough marshes.

"Charlie," said Nix. "Detective Macy, do you know Charlie Parker, our local celebrity PI?"

Macy's initial surprise at seeing me gave way to a lopsided grin.

"Yes, I do. We had dinner once."

"No shit?" said Nix.

"Mr. Parker never called for a second date."

"No shit?" Nix said again. He clucked at me like a disappointed schoolmarm. "Hurtful," he opined.

"Uncouth," said Macy.

"Maybe he's here to make amends."

"I don't see any flowers."

"There's always the tab."

"There is that," said Macy. She hadn't taken her eyes off me since I'd come in. She wasn't flirting, but she was enjoying herself.

"So if he's not here to apologize for blowing you off, why is he here?" said Nix.

"Yes, why are you here?" said Macy.

"He's going to put trouble on someone's plate," said Nix.

"Are you going to put trouble on someone's plate?" said Macy.

"Not if I can help it," I said, just happy to be getting a word in at last now that Nichols and May had paused for breath. "I had a couple of questions about the Jude case. Your name came up in connection with it."

Nix and Macy exchanged a look, but Nix left it up to Macy to comment if she chose. She was, after all, the detective.

"Small world," said Macy.

"Really?" I said.

"Nix was first responder," said Macy. "And there is no 'Jude case'—unless," she added, "you know different."

"It was a nice, clean hanging," said Nix, and I knew what he meant. You took those when they came along. They were paperwork, and not much else.

I pointed at their bottles, which were mostly suds. "You want another?"

Nix was drinking a Miller High Life. There was something about Ruski's that made people want to do strange stuff like drink High Life. Macy was on Rolling Rock. Both of them agreed to let me spend my money on them, and Nix wondered aloud if buying a drink constituted a second date in my world. I ignored the peanut gallery and ordered the drinks, along with a Rolling Rock for myself as well. I tried to remember the last time I ordered a Rolling Rock, but couldn't. I suspected a fake ID might have been involved.

Nix, I noticed, had the sports section of the *Press Herald* beside him, open to the basketball page.

"You a fan?" I asked.

"My kid's a Yachtsman," he said.

The Yachtsmen were Falmouth High's basketball team. The previous season they'd taken the kind of beating from their local rivals, Yarmouth, that usually requires years of therapy to overcome: 20–1 in the regional final. They had looked dead and buried, but so far this season they'd been beaten only once, by York, and had won their first sixteen games by an average margin of more than twenty points. Now they had the state final in their sights, and Coach Halligan, who had also taken Falmouth to nine state soccer titles in his twenty-six-year career, was considered a candidate for sainthood.

"Better season than last," I said.

"They got stronger kids this year," said Nix. "My boy plays soccer too, and he skis. Kid is built like a racehorse, and he's got another year left. He's ready for the move to Class A."

He took a long tug on his beer. Once again, he was leaving it to Macy to do the heavy lifting.

"So, what do you want to know about Jude?" said Macy.

"How was he found?"

"Nine-one-one call from a public phone on Congress. No name given. We figure it was one of his homeless buddies."

"Anything odd about it?"

She looked to Nix, who thought about the question. "It was an unfinished dirt basement, L-shaped, so kind of split in two by the angle of the walls. It looked like someone else had slept in there that night. There was a depression in the earth, and we found a couple of beer caps. Whoever it was had also taken a dump, and used a copy of that day's newspaper to clean himself off. But the ME's report said that Jude had been dead for at least thirty-six hours when we found him. You do the math."

"Somebody spent a night with the corpse."

"They maybe slept with their back to it, but yeah. You know, it was wicked cold, and if you don't have anywhere else to go . . ."

"What about his possessions?"

"Sleeping bag was gone," said Macy. "And it looked like his pack had been rifled for valuables."

"Any money found?"

"Money? Like what kind of money?"

"More than a hundred dollars. Not much in the normal scheme of things, but a lot to a guy like that."

"People have died for less."

"Amen."

"No, there was no money. What, you think he might have been killed for it?"

"Like you said, people have died for less."

"Sure," said Macy, "but it's hard to hang a man who's struggling against it, and harder still to make it look like a suicide. The ligature marks were consistent with the downward momentum of the body, and the ME found no excessive injury to the neck. The victim did scratch at the rope, but that's not unusual."

"Any idea where the rope might have come from?"

"Nope. It wasn't new, though. Like Jude, it had been around the block a couple of times. It had been cut to size to make the noose."

"At the funeral, I heard that he had no alcohol or narcotics in his system."

"That's right."

"Which *is* unusual."

"Depends on how you read it," said Nix. "If you're talking Dutch courage, then, yes, you might have expected him to take something to ease the pain. On the other hand, if you're looking for evidence of a homicide made to look like a hanging suicide, then some drugs or alcohol might be useful if you wanted to subdue the victim first."

I let it go.

"The money is the other thing," I said.

"How come?" said Macy. She was interested now. I could see it in her eyes. A lot of detectives wouldn't have cared much to have a snoop question a neat, closed case, but Macy wasn't one of them. I doubted that she had ever been that kind of cop, and whatever happened out on Sanctuary had done nothing to change her. If anything, it had simply strengthened that aspect of her character. She hadn't told me much about what occurred on the island beyond what was in the official record, and I hadn't pressed her on it, but I'd heard stories. Sanctuary was a strange place, even by the standards of this part of the world, and some of the bodies from that night had never been found.

"Jude went to a lot of trouble to collect it," I said. "It seems that he was worried about his daughter. Her name was Annie—ex-junkie, trying to go straight, living in a shelter up in Bangor. He was trying to reestablish a relationship with her when she disappeared. He was worried about her. The money was to help him search for her. In fact, I think he might even have hoped to hire me with the cash."

"What would it have bought him?" said Nix. "A couple of hours?"

"I'd have given him a discount."

"Even so."

"Yeah."

Nix took another hit on his beer. "Well, chances are that whoever slept in the basement and cherry-picked Jude's possessions also took the money. I don't think they'd have gone to the trouble of trying to stage it as a suicide, though. A homeless person would have been more likely to use fists, or a blade. It wouldn't have taken much to put Jude down. He wasn't a strong guy."

"It still doesn't explain," I said, "why a man who has gone to the trouble of calling in his debts, and who's concerned about his daughter, should end it all in a basement and leave her to whatever trouble she was in. And, as you said, Jude wasn't a strong man. A breeze could have lifted him off the street. A big man, or two big men, could have held him long enough to hoist him up on a chair, put a rope around his neck, and kick the chair out from under him. They'd have left marks on his body, I guess. Couldn't not have."

I was thinking aloud now. Macy set aside her beer unfinished.

"You got a couple of minutes?" she said to me.

"Sure."

"You want to head down to Rosie's, I'll join you there for one more. I got some laundry to pick up along the way."

Nix decided to stay at Ruski's for another beer. He knew better than to tag along, regardless of any history between Macy and me. If she chose to share more about Jude's death with a PI, then that was her business. He didn't want, or need, to know.

I did cover his tab, though, including his drink for the road. He sighed theatrically as I left.

"And I bet you won't even call," he said. "I just feel so . . . *used*."

CHAPTER

XIII

Harry and Erin Dixon were deep in discussion when they heard the car approach.

"We have to leave," said Erin.

"And go where?" said Harry.

"I don't know. Anywhere. We could promise not to tell if they just let us go and didn't follow."

Harry tried not to laugh, but he couldn't stop himself. The idea that Prosperous had survived for so long just by allowing those who were uncomfortable with its edicts to leave was so preposterous as to be beyond belief. Erin, of all people, should have known that. They had hunted her father, Charlie Hutton, for years, and they had never given up. He had been clever, and lucky. He was also a teller at the bank, and he didn't leave with his pockets empty: he raided the town's discretionary fund before he ran. The money bought him time, and some room to maneuver. It allowed him to set himself up with a new identity and a new life, but Harry was sure that he spent his days fearing every knock on the door and searching the faces on the street for the gaze that lingered too long.

Charlie hadn't been afraid that they'd set the police on him. That wasn't the way Prosperous worked. Anyway, the money that he stole didn't officially exist, and the fund was used for purposes about which it was better that the law knew nothing. What had always stayed with Harry was that Erin's father had never told. He could have gone to the police and tried to explain the nature of Prosperous, but it was so fantastic that he would have risked being dismissed as a madman. Even if they had chosen to believe him, there were no bodies to which he could point, no shallow graves to be dug up and bones to be exhumed. Harry wondered how deep you'd have to go to find the victims of Prosperous, if anything of them truly remained at all. Any searchers would have given up long before they first struck rock, and some of the bodies probably lay even deeper than that. And then there was the fact that rarely did it happen more than once every twenty or thirty years, and those responsible kept the secret of it to themselves. To descry any kind of pattern would be almost impossible, and the names of those who had been taken were forgotten as soon as they were belowground. In many cases, they had never been known at all.

But there was another probable reason that Erin's father had remained silent, a deeper reason: he was bound to Prosperous, and one didn't slough off one's loyalties to a place so old, and so strange, with any ease. He stayed loyal to the town even as he sought to put as much distance between him and it as possible, for he couldn't deny the truth, even if he wanted no further part in it.

But the town learned from what had happened with Charlie, and steps were taken to ensure that it wouldn't occur so easily again. It kept a close watch on its inhabitants in the guise of caring for their well-being, and it bound them together with bonds of matrimony, familial and business loyalties, and fear.

"You want to be like your father?" said Harry, once his laughter had ceased. He hadn't cared much for the sound of it. It held a distressingly lunatic tone. "You want to be hunted all your life?"

"No," she said softly. "But I don't want to stay here either."

But Harry wasn't listening to her. He was on a roll now.

"And he had money. We have nothing. You don't think they're

watching our spending habits, our patterns of deposits and withdraw-
als? They *know*, or at least they suspect. We're vulnerable, and that
means they're concerned about how we might act. No, we have no
choice. We have to wait this out. We have to hope that our situation
improves. When it does, we can start putting money away. We can
plan, just like Charlie must have done. You don't leave Prosperous on
a whim. You don't—"

And then there came the sound of the car. Lights washed over the
house, and the words died in Harry Dixon's mouth.

XIV

Rosie's wasn't too dissimilar from Ruski's, but your chances of getting a seat at Rosie's were greater than at Ruski's simply because Rosie's had more chairs. I didn't want another beer, so I ordered coffee instead, and watched the cars go by on Fore Street. Music was playing, a song that I thought I recognized, something about seas of charity and unchosen exiles. I called Rachel while I waited, and she put Sam on. We chatted for a while about events in elementary school, which seemed to involve a lot of painting, and a certain amount of argument with a boy named Harry.

"His mom and dad named him after Harry Potter," Sam explained. She didn't sound as though she approved. A whole generation of adults who had dressed up as wizards when they should have known better now seemed destined to inflict whimsy on their offspring. I wasn't a big fan of whimsy. Whimsical people were the type who got run over by cars without anybody really noticing or caring that much beyond the damage to the vehicle, which was usually minimal anyway, whimsical folk being kind of lighter than most.

"He draws lightning on his forehead," said Sam.

"Does he?" I said.

"Yeah. He says it's real, but it comes off when you rub hard."

I decided not to ask how she knew this, although I was pretty certain that, however she'd discovered it, the boy named Harry had been an unwilling participant in the experiment. Talk moved on to the trip to Florida that she was taking the following weekend, where she and Rachel would join Rachel's parents in their new winter vacation home. Rachel's current boyfriend, Jeff, wouldn't be going along with them, Sam informed me.

"Oh," I said, keeping my voice as neutral as possible. I didn't like Jeff, but it didn't matter. Jeff liked himself enough for both of us.

"Daddy!" said Sam. "You don't have to pretend you're sad."

Jesus.

"Are you sure you're just in elementary school?" I said. "You're not studying psychology on the side?"

"Mom knows psycottagy," said Sam.

"Yes, she does." Not enough of it to avoid dating a jackass like Jeff, but solving other people's problems was often easier than taking care of your own. I considered sharing that insight with Rachel but decided against it. Maybe I was learning at last that discretion was the better part of valor. "Just put your mom back on. I'll see you when you get back."

"Bye. Love you," said Sam, and my heart broke a little.

"Bye, hon. Love you too."

I chatted with Rachel for a minute or two more. She seemed happy. That was good. I wanted her to be happy. If she was happy, Sam would be happy. I just wished Rachel could be happy with someone other than Jeff. It reflected badly on her good taste, but then there were those who might have said the same about her time with me.

"What are you working on?" asked Rachel.

"Nothing much. Process serving. Errant husbands."

"Is that all? It won't keep you out of mischief for long."

"Well, there's this thing with a homeless guy too. He hanged himself, and I can't figure out why."

"I'll bet he didn't pay you in advance."

"You know, it's funny you should say it, but someone in this city might have the money that he would have used to hire me."

"Do I need to tell you to be careful?"

"No, but it always helps."

"I doubt that, but for the sake of your daughter . . ."

"I'll be careful."

"You in a bar?"

"Rosie's."

"Ah. A date?"

Macy arrived. She had some photocopied pages in one hand and a mug in the other. Like me, she had sought coffee.

"No, I wouldn't say that."

Rachel laughed. "No, you wouldn't, would you? Go on, get lost."

I hung up. Macy had been hanging back in an effort to give me privacy. Now she stepped forward and laid the papers on the table as she sat.

"You can read," she said, "but I'm not leaving them with you, okay?"

"Understood."

It was the ME's report on Jude's body. I could probably have bargained a look at it out from the ME's office, but this saved me the trouble of a trip to Augusta. The rope used in the hanging was cotton, with a running knot placed above the occipital region. Some rope fibers and remnants had been found on a table nearby, along with marks in the wood that were consistent with the cutting action of a sharp knife.

"Did you find a knife at the scene?" I asked Macy.

"No, but it could have been with the other possessions that were taken."

"I guess."

Rigor mortis and postmortem staining on both legs, distal portion of upper limbs, and area of waist above the belt line. Both eyes partially open; conjunctiva congested and cornea hazy. Mouth partially open, tongue protruding.

I moved on to the ligature mark. The ME found that it encircled the whole neck, apart from a small gap beneath the knot, consistent with the drag weight of the body. The ligature ran backward, upward, and toward the occipital region. The ligature marks were slightly wider on the left of the neck than on the right, but only by about a fifth of an inch. Dissection of the neck revealed no evidence of fracture of the thyroid cartilage or hyoid bone, as is often the case in forced strangulation, which seemed to rule out the possibility that Jude had been attacked. Likewise, there was no extravasation—forced flow—of blood in the neck tissues. The ME had concluded that the cause of death was asphyxia due to suicidal hanging by ligature.

The only other noteworthy inclusion in the report was a list of bruises, scars, and abrasions to Jude's body. They were considerable enough to make me wince. As if to compound the issue, Macy slid another sheet of paper across the table. It was a color copy, and the quality wasn't great. This was a small mercy, given what the two photographs on it revealed about the battering that Jude had taken over the years. Falls, fights, beatings: all were recorded on a map of skin and flesh, and all were concealed beneath the trappings of a thrift-shop dandy. Anyone who was dumb enough to imagine that life on the streets of Portland was some kind of state-funded outdoor vacation needed just one look at the picture of Jude's torso and limbs to be set straight.

"The ME says some are recent, but most are pretty old," said Macy. "One or two might have been received in the hours prior to his death. These here are interesting."

She pointed to marks on Jude's upper right and left arms.

"What are they?"

Macy handed over a final sheet. She had a flair for the dramatic. The pictures showed enlargements of the marks.

"They look like grips," I said, "as though someone held him hard from behind."

"That's what I thought," said Macy. "But it doesn't mean they're connected to his death. This was a man who took knocks on a regular basis."

"You going to ask around?"

"I wasn't until you showed up. Look, I still think he took his own life, but I'll admit that you've raised enough questions to make me wonder again about why he did it. Might be useful if we could find the contents of his pack, though—or, better still, talk to whoever made that call. You never know what we might learn."

"You try asking around?"

"Nix did, as best he could. If anybody knew anything, they were keeping quiet. But if I came across a dead man, and then rifled his belongings and stole what little money he had, I'd probably keep quiet about it too."

Macy gathered up the photocopies and finished her coffee.

"So, you doing much pro bono work these days?"

"No, but I hear it's good for the soul."

"Which is why you'll keep on this—for the good of your soul, and the fact that you think you might owe Jude some hours?"

"Whatever I owe him, it's not hours," I said.

"You still have my number?"

"Yes."

"Good. I thought you might have lost it, seeing as how you never called and all."

"I'm sorry about that."

"Don't be. It was a good dinner, and you did pay for it."

"It was, but I still should have called. I don't know why I didn't."

"I do," she said. "The same things that stopped me from calling you. Life. Death."

She stood.

"You know how to find me," she said. "I'd appreciate a heads-up if you learn anything."

"Done," I said.

She turned back briefly as she walked away.

"It was good seeing you again."

"And you," I said.

I watched her go. A couple of other guys did too.

Damn.

CHAPTER
XV

Morland sat on one side of the kitchen table, Hayley Conyer to his right. Harry and Erin sat on the other side, facing them. The Dixons had never entertained Hayley in their home before. They had never entertained her anywhere. Neither had they ever set foot in her house. They had heard that it was beautiful and ornate, if gloomy. Erin was secretly pleased that, while their own home might not have been anything special, it wasn't lacking in cheer. The kitchen was bright, and the living room that connected to it was even brighter. There was a shadow over all of it now, though. Hayley Conyer seemed to have brought something of the night in with her.

"You have a lovely home," she said, in the manner of one who was surprised at how far the little people could stretch a nickel but still wouldn't want to live like them.

"Thank you," said Erin.

She had made coffee. She had a vague recollection that Hayley Conyer preferred tea, but she deliberately hadn't offered her any. She wasn't even sure that there was tea in the house. If there was, it had been there for so long that nobody would want to drink it.

"I noticed that the paintwork on your windows is flaking," said Morland. "You ought to do something with it before it gets much worse."

· Harry's smile didn't waver. It was a test. Everything was a test now, and the only thing that mattered in a test was not failing.

"I was waiting for winter to pass," he said. "It's hard to paint a window frame when your hands are shaking with cold. You're liable to end up with windows that you can't see much out of."

Morland wasn't about to let it go.

"You could have taken care of it last summer."

Harry was finding it hard to keep his smile in place.

"I was busy last summer."

"Yeah?"

"Yeah."

"Doing what?"

"Making a living. Is this an interrogation, Chief?"

Hayley Conyer intervened.

"We're just worried about you, Harry. With this downturn in the economy, and the way it's hit construction—well, you're more . . . *vulnerable* than most. Businesses like yours must be suffering."

"We're getting by," said Erin. She wasn't going to let her husband be cornered alone by these two. "Harry works hard."

"I'm sure he does," said Conyer.

She pursed her lips, and then pulled from memory the semblance of a concerned expression.

"You see, it's the job of the board to protect the town, and the best way we can do that is by protecting the *people* of the town."

She didn't look at Harry. She had her eyes on Erin. She spoke to Erin as though to a slow child. She was goading her, just as Morland had goaded Harry. They wanted a reaction. They wanted anger.

They wanted an excuse.

"I understand that, Hayley," said Erin. She didn't allow even a drop of sarcasm to pollute her apparent sincerity.

"I'm glad. That's why I asked Chief Morland here to look into your affairs some, just to be sure that all was well with you."

This time, Erin couldn't conceal her anger.

"You *what*?"

Harry placed a hand on her arm, leaning into it so that she felt his weight.

Calm, calm.

"Would you mind explaining to me what that means?" said Harry.

"It means," said Morland, "that I talked to some of your suppliers, and your subcontractors. It means that, when the mood has struck me, I've followed you around these last few weeks. It means that I've had a meeting with Allan Dantree at the bank, and we had a discreet conversation about your accounts."

Harry couldn't help but close his eyes for a moment. He'd tried so hard, but he'd underestimated Morland, and Hayley Conyer, and the board. He wasn't the first to have tried to hide his difficulties, and he wouldn't be the last. He should have known that, over the centuries, the town had learned to spot weakness, but he had exposed himself by applying to the town's fund for that loan. Perhaps they'd all just been more alert than usual to strange patterns, blips in behavior, because of the economy. So many folk were struggling in the current climate. That was why the board had acted. That was why they had taken the girl.

"Those are our private affairs," said Erin, but her voice sounded hollow even to her. In Prosperous nothing was private, not really.

"But what happens when private difficulties affect all?" said Hayley, still speaking in that maddeningly reasonable, insidiously patronizing tone. God, Erin hated her. It was as though cataracts had been removed from her eyes, the old clouded lenses replaced with ones that were new and clear. She saw the town as it really was, saw it in all its viciousness, its self-regard, its madness. They had been brainwashed, conditioned by centuries of behavior, but it was only when it arrived at their own door, in the form of the girl, that Harry and Erin realized that they could no longer be a part of it. Releasing the girl was an imperfect solution, the action of those who were still not brave enough to take the final step themselves and hoped that another might do it for them. The girl would go to the police, she would tell her story, and they would come.

And what then? The girl would have been able to give the police a description of Walter and Beatrix, and of Harry and Erin. All four would have been questioned, but Walter and Beatrix wouldn't have buckled under interrogation. They had been responsible for finding and taking the last two girls, but they were now nearing death. They were as loyal to the town as Hayley Conyer was, and they weren't likely to roll over on it in the final years of their life. At best, it would have been their word against that of Harry and Erin.

They threatened us. They told us to get them a girl or they'd burn our house down. We're old. We were frightened. We didn't know what they wanted with the girl. We didn't ask. . . .

And Hayley Conyer, and the selectmen, and Chief Morland? Why, there'd be nothing to connect them to the girl, nothing beyond the word of Harry and Erin Dixon, who'd kept her trapped in their basement before leaving a door unlocked, and it could be that they did so only because they'd lost the courage to follow through on whatever it was they had planned for her. They would have been liable to felony charges of kidnapping and criminal restraint—a Class A crime, or a Class B if the prosecution accepted that they'd voluntarily released the victim alive and in a safe place, and not suffering from serious bodily injury. It was the difference between ten years behind bars and thirty years, but it would still have been more time than either of them wanted to spend in a cell.

And maybe, just maybe, someone might have believed their story.

But no, that was the greatest fantasy of all.

"Harry? Erin? You still with us?"

It was Morland speaking.

Erin looked at her husband. She knew that their thoughts had been running along similar lines.

What if, what if . . .

"Yes," said Harry. "We're listening."

"You're in financial difficulties—far more serious difficulties than you chose to share with Ben when you asked for a loan—and you tried to keep them from us."

There was no point in denying it.

"Yes, that's true."

"Why?"

"Because we were ashamed."

"Is that all?"

"No. We were frightened as well."

"Frightened? Frightened of what?"

There was no going back now.

"Frightened that the town might turn against us."

Now Hayley Conyer spoke again.

"The town does not turn against its own, Harry. It protects them. That's the reason for its existence. How could you doubt that?"

Harry squeezed the bridge of his nose with the index finger and thumb of his right hand. He could feel a migraine coming on.

"I don't know," he said. "With all that was going on, with all our problems . . ."

"You lost faith," said Conyer.

"Yes, Hayley, I suppose we did."

Conyer leaned across the table. Her breath smelled of mints and dying.

"Did you let the girl go?" she asked.

"No," said Harry.

"Look me in the eye and tell me true."

Harry took his hand away from his nose and stared Conyer down.

"No, we did not let the girl go."

She didn't want to believe him. He could see that. Like Morland, she had her suspicions, but she couldn't prove them, and the town wouldn't allow her to move against them without proof.

"All right, then," she said. "The question is, where do we go from here? You'll have to make amends, both of you."

The pain was pulsing in Harry's head now, and with it came the nausea. He knew what was coming. He'd known from the moment Morland arrived at their house with the body of the girl in the trunk of his car. He wanted to tell them of the dreams he'd been having, but he bit back the words. He hadn't even told his wife about them. In his dreams, the girl wasn't dead. They'd put her in the grave alive, because dead girls didn't open their eyes. She was alive and scratching at the plastic, and somehow she had managed to tear through it and dig her way out of the ground, except that when she emerged she really was dead. She was a being transformed, a revenant, and when she opened her mouth she spewed darkness, and the night deepened around her.

"What do you want us to do?" said Harry, but he asked only because it was what was expected of him. He might as well have been reading from a script.

Hayley Conyer patted his hand. It was all he could do not to yank it away at her touch.

"Find us another girl," said Conyer. "And quickly."

XVI

I got to the Preble Street Soup Kitchen just as the dinner service was coming to an end. A woman named Evadne Bryant-Perkins, who worked at the Portland Help Center, a mental health and community support facility off Congress, had directed me to the kitchen. Shaky had given me her name as a contact person, but she told me that she hadn't seen him in a day or two, and suggested that he might drop by Preble Street for a bite to eat.

Preble Street served three meals per day not only to the city's homeless but to seniors and families who were struggling to get by on welfare. That added up to almost five hundred thousand meals per year, but the meals were just a starting point. By getting people in the door, the staff was in a position to help them with housing advice, employment, and health care. At the very least, they could give them some clean, warm socks, and that meant a lot during winter in Maine.

One of the volunteers, a young woman named Karyn, told me that Shaky had been through earlier in the evening, but had finished his meal and headed back out almost immediately after. This was unlike him, she said. He was more sociable than some, and he usually appreciated the company and warmth of the shelter.

"He hasn't been the same since his friend Jude died," she said. "They had a bond between them, and they looked out for each other. Shaky's talked to us a little about it, but most of it he's kept inside."

"Do you have any idea where he might have gone?"

Karyn called over another volunteer, a kid of about college age.

"This is Stephen," she said. "He was one of the coordinators of this year's homeless survey. He might be able to help you."

She went back to cleaning tables, leaving me with Stephen. He was a tall young man. I pretty much had to lean back just to look him in the eye. He wasn't as open as Karyn had been. He had his arms crossed as he spoke to me.

"Can I ask why a private detective is looking for Shaky?" he said.

"He came to talk to me about Jude's death. I think he set tumblers falling in my mind. If I'm to take it any further, there are some questions that he might be able to help me answer. He's in no trouble. I give you my word on that."

I watched him consider what I'd told him before he decided that I wasn't about to make Shaky's existence any more difficult, and he loosened up enough to offer me coffee. Between the beer I'd had at Ruski's and the coffee at Rosie's, I was carrying more liquid than a camel, but one of the first things I learned when I started out as a cop was always to accept if someone you were trying to talk with offered you a coffee or a soda. It made them relax, and if they were relaxed they'd be more willing to help you.

"Karyn mentioned something about a survey," I said, as we sipped coffee from plastic cups.

"We're required by the Department of Housing and Urban Development to do a census of the homeless each year," said Stephen. "If we don't know how many folk need help, we can't work out budgets, staffing, even how much food we're likely to require over the months to come. But it's also a chance to make contact with the ones who've avoided us so far, and try to bring them into the fold."

I must have looked puzzled.

"You're wondering why anyone who's hungry would pass up the chance of a hot meal, right?" said Stephen.

"I guess it doesn't make much sense to me."

"Some people who take to the streets don't want to be found," he said. "A lot of them have mental health issues, and if you're a paranoid schizophrenic who believes that the government is trying to kill you the last thing you're going to want to do is turn up at a shelter where someone might start prying into your business. Then there are others who are just plain scared. Maybe they've gotten into a fight with someone in the past, and they know that there's a knife out there looking to sink itself into them, or they've had a bad experience with the authorities and prefer to keep their heads down. So, for one night of the year we go out in force, looking under bleachers and behind Dumpsters, and we try to reach them all. I mean, we're out there at other times of the year, too, but the sustained focus of survey night, and the sheer weight of volunteers on the streets, means that we get a hell of a lot done in a few hours."

"So where does Shaky hang out?"

"Shaky likes to come into the shelter, if there's a mat available to sleep on. He hasn't been in so much since Jude died, which means that he's either set up camp somewhere off the interstate, probably around Back Cove Park, or he's sleeping at the rear of one of the businesses on Danforth or Pleasant, where the cops can't see him. That's where I'd look."

He toyed with his coffee cup. He wanted to say more. I didn't hurry him.

"Did you know Mr. Jude?" he eventually asked.

I'd never heard anyone call Jude "Mister" before. He was always just Jude. It made me warm more to the kid.

"A little," I said. "I'd sometimes put money his way if I needed someone to watch a car or an address for a while. He never let me down."

"He was a smart man, and a good one too," said Stephen. "I could never quite figure out how he ended up in the situation he was in. Some of the men and women here, I can see it. There's a trajectory you can reconstruct. But not in Mr. Jude's case. The best I can tell, there was a weak bolt in the machinery, and when it broke the whole mechanism ground to a halt."

"You're not an engineering student by any chance, are you?"

He grinned for the first time. "Know a man by his metaphors."

"You sound as though you liked Jude," I said.

"Uh-huh, I did. Even in the midst of his own troubles, he still had time for others. I tried to follow his lead by helping him in turn."

"You're talking about his daughter?"

"Yeah, Annie. I was kind of keeping an eye on her for him."

"Really?"

"Because of my work with the shelter here, I was in a position to talk to others in the same business. I made an occasional call to the Tender House in Bangor, where Annie was staying, just so I could re-assure Mr. Jude that she was doing okay. When she disappeared, I—"

He stopped.

"You felt responsible?"

He nodded, but didn't speak.

"Did Jude say anything to make you believe he felt the same way?"

"No, never. It wasn't in his nature. It didn't help, though. It didn't make me feel any less guilty."

Stephen was clearly a good kid, but he had the egotism of youth. The world revolved around him, and consequently he believed that he had the power to change how it worked. And, in the way of the young, he had made another's pain about himself, even if he did so for what seemed the best of reasons. Time and age would change him; if they didn't, he wouldn't be working in soup kitchens and shelters much longer. His frustrations would get the better of him and force him out. He'd blame others for it, but it would be his own fault.

I thanked him and left my cell phone number, just in case I couldn't find Shaky, or he chose to come into the shelter for the night after all. Stephen promised to leave a note for the breakfast and lunch volunteers as well, so that if Shaky arrived to eat the next day they could let me know. I used the men's room before I left, just to ensure that my bladder didn't burst somewhere between the shelter and Back Cove. An old man was standing at one of the sinks, stripped to the waist. His white hair hung past his shoulders, and his body reminded me of the images I'd seen of Jude's poor, scarred torso, like some medieval depiction of Christ after he'd been taken down from the cross.

"How you doing?" I said.

"Livin' the dream," the old man replied.

He was shaving with a disposable razor. He removed the last of the foam from his cheek, splashed water on his face, and rubbed his skin to check that it was smooth.

"You got any aftershave?" he asked.

"Not with me," I said. "Why, you got a date?"

"I haven't been on a date since Nixon was president."

"Another thing to blame him for—ruining your love life."

"He was a son of a bitch, but I didn't need no help on that front."

I washed my hands and dried them with a paper towel. I had money in my pocket, but I didn't want to offend the old man. Then I thought that it was better to risk hurting his feelings. I left a ten on the sink beside him. He looked at it as though Alexander Hamilton might bite him if he tried to pick it up; that, or I might ask him to bite me as part of some bizarre sexual fetish.

"What's that for?" he said.

"Aftershave."

He reached out and took the ten.

"I always liked Old Spice," he said.

"My father wore Old Spice."

"Something stays around that long, it has to be good."

"Amen," I said. "Look after yourself."

"I will," he said. "And, hey?"

I looked back.

"Thanks."

XVII

It's a full-time job being homeless. It's a full-time job being poor. That's what those who bitch about the underprivileged not going out there and finding work fail to understand. They have a job already, and that job is surviving. You have to get in line early for food, and earlier still for a place to sleep. You carry your possessions on your back, and when they wear out you spend time scavenging for replacements. You have only so much energy to expend, because you have only so much food to fuel your body. Most of the time you're tired, and sore, and your clothes are damp. If the cops find you sleeping on the street, they move you on. If you're lucky, they'll give you a ride to a shelter, but if there are no beds free, or no mats available on the floor, you'll have to sleep sitting upright in a plastic chair in an outer office, and the lights will be on full, because that's what the fire code regulations require, so you go back out on the streets again, because at least there you can lie down in the dark, and with luck you'll sleep. Each day is the same, and each day you get a little older, and a little more tired.

And sometimes you remember who you once were. You were a kid who played with other kids. You had a mother and a father. You wanted to be a fireman, or an astronaut, or a railroad engineer. You had a husband. You had a wife. You were loved. You could never have imagined that you would end up this way.

You curl up in the darkness, and you wait for death to kiss you a final, blissful good night.

———

SHAKY WAS BACK ON the streets. He'd been tempted to stay at one of the shelters and find a mat on which to sleep. His arm ached. It always pained him in winter, leaving him with months of discomfort, but it had been hurting more since Jude died. It was probably—what was the word? He thought and thought—*psychosomatic*, that was it. It had taken him a good minute to recall it, but Jude would have known the word instantly. Jude knew about history, and science, and geography. He could tell you the plot of every great novel he'd ever read, and recite whole passages from memory. Shaky had once tested him on a couple, and had jokingly remarked that, for all he knew, Jude could have been making up all those quotations off the top of his head. Jude had responded by claiming that Shaky had impugned his honor—that was the word he'd used, *impugned*—and there had been nothing for it but for the two of them to head down to the Portland Public Library on Congress, where Shaky had pulled *The Great Gatsby* from the shelves, along with *The Adventures of Huckleberry Finn*, *Lolita*, *The Grapes of Wrath*, *As I Lay Dying*, *Ulysses*, and the poems of Longfellow and Cummings and Yeats. Jude had been able to quote chunks of them without getting a word wrong, without a single stumble, and even some of the librarians had come over to listen. By the time he got on to Shakespeare, it was like being in the presence of one of those old stage actors, the kind who used to wash up in small towns when there were still theaters in which to perform, their costumes and props in one truck, the cast in another, and put on revues, and comedies, and social dramas, or maybe a condensed Shakespeare with all the dull parts removed, leaving only the great moments of drama: ghosts, and bloodied daggers, and dying kings.

And there was Jude in his old checked suit and two-tone shoes, the heels worn smooth and cardboard masking the holes in the soles, surrounded by curious readers and amused librarians. He was lost in words, lost in roles, someone other than himself for just a little while, and Shaky had loved him then, loved him as he basked in the glow of pleasure that emanated from Jude's face, loved him as his eyes closed in reverie, and he said a prayer of gratitude for the presence of Jude in his life even as he wondered how one so clever and so gifted could have ended up scavenging in Dumpsters and sleeping on the streets of a city forever shadowed by winter, and what weakness in Jude's being had caused him to turn away from his family and his home and throw himself to the winds like a leaf at the coming of fall.

Shaky's pack weighed heavily on him. He thought again about the shelter. He could have left his belongings there—even if there was no bed for him, someone might have been willing to look after them—and returned to pick them up later, but increasingly he found the presence of others distressing. He would look at the familiar faces, but the one he sought was no longer there, and the presence of the rest only reminded him of Jude's absence. How long had they been friends? Shaky couldn't remember. He had lost track of the years a long time ago. Dates were of no consequence. He was not marking wedding anniversaries, or the birthdays of children. He left the years behind him, discarded without a thought, like old shoes that could no longer fulfill even his modest needs.

He was near Deering Oaks. He kept returning there, back to the place in which Jude had breathed his last. He was a mourner, and a pilgrim. He stopped outside the house, its windows boarded. Someone had placed a new lock and bolt on the basement door since Jude's death: the police, maybe, or the owner, assuming it was still owned by a person and not a bank. Crime scene tape had been placed across the door, but it was torn now. It drifted in the night's breeze.

Shaky felt no sense of Jude at the house. That was how he knew that Jude had not taken his own life. Shaky didn't believe in ghosts.

He didn't even believe in God, and if he turned out to be wrong, well, he and God would have some words about the dog-shit hand that Shaky had been dealt. But Shaky did have a certain sense about people and places. Jude had it too. You needed it if you wanted to survive on the streets. Shaky knew instinctively whom to trust, and whom to avoid. He knew the places in which it was safe to sleep and the places, though empty and apparently innocuous, in which it was best not to rest. Men and women left their marks as they moved through life, and you could read them if you had a mind to. Jude had left his mark in that basement, his final mark, but it didn't read to Shaky like the mark of a man who had given in to despair. It read to Shaky like the mark of one who would have fought if he'd had the strength, and if the odds had not been against him.

He walked down to the basement door and took the Swiss Army knife from his pocket. It was one of his most valuable possessions, and he maintained it well. There was one blade that he kept particularly sharp, and he used it now to make two signs on the stonework beside the door. The first was a rectangle with a dot in the center, the old hobo-alphabet symbol for "danger." The second was a diagonal line joined halfway by a smaller, almost perpendicular line. It was the warning to keep away.

He spent the rest of the night asking questions. He did it carefully, and discreetly, and he approached only those whom he trusted, those he knew would not lie to him or betray him. It had taken him a while to figure out what he should do. Talking to the detective had crystallized things for him. Someone had taken Jude's money, and the contents of his pack. It might have been those responsible for his death, but it didn't seem likely that they'd then call in his hanging corpse to the cops. Neither would they have taken the money if they wanted his death to appear as a suicide. Anyway, from what Shaky had learned, Jude had been dead for a day or more before his body was found.

All this suggested to Shaky that the person who had called in the killing, and the person who had taken the money and rifled Jude's belongings, were one and the same, and it seemed to Shaky that it might well be one of their own, a street person. One of the city's homeless had either stumbled across Jude's sleeping place by accident or, more likely, had gone looking for Jude to begin with. The word was out: Jude was calling in his loans. He needed money. The unknown person could have been seeking Jude out in order to pay his debts, but, equally, there were those on the street who would not be above hunting Jude down in order to steal whatever cash he had managed to accumulate. It didn't matter; either way someone had found Jude hanging in that basement and looted his belongings in the shadow of his corpse.

Shaky well knew that a hundred and twenty dollars was a lot of money for someone who struggled by on a couple of bucks a day. The instinct would be to celebrate: booze, or perhaps something stronger; and fast food—bought, not scavenged. Alcohol and narcotics made people careless. Rumors would start to circulate that one of their own had enjoyed a windfall.

By the time he returned to his tent at Back Cove Park, Shaky had a name.

Brightboy.

XVIII

The next morning, Shaky didn't join the line for breakfast at the shelter. He kept his distance, and fingered the note in his pocket. It had been pinned to the bulletin board at Preble Street. The detective wanted to talk. Shaky had memorized the number, but he kept the note, just in case. He knew that the years on the streets had addled his brain. He would sometimes look at a clock face, and see the hands pointing at the numbers, and be unable to tell the time. He could be in a store, the price of a six-pack or a bottle of liquor clear to read on the sign, his change laid out in his hand ready to pay, and fail to make the connection between the cost of the booze and the money in his possession.

Now, as he stood in the shelter of a doorway on Cumberland Avenue, he repeated the cell phone number over and over to himself. He had considered calling the detective and telling him what he knew, but he wanted to be sure. He wanted to present the detective with hard evidence. He wanted to prove himself, both for his own sake and for Jude's, so he stood in the shadows and watched his fellow homeless gather for breakfast.

———

IT DIDN'T TAKE HIM long to spot Brightboy. He arrived shortly before eight, his pack on his back. Shaky's keen eyes were drawn to Brightboy's boots. They were tan Timberlands, better than what Brightboy usually wore. It was possible that he'd found them, but, equally, they were the kind of Goodwill purchase that even a moron like Brightboy might have the sense to make while he had money in his pocket. A good pair of boots would keep your feet warm and dry, and make days spent walking the streets a little easier. He watched Brightboy exchange greetings with those whom he knew, but for the most part he kept to himself. Brightboy had always been a loner, partly out of choice, but also because he couldn't be trusted. There were those with whom one could leave a pack and know that it would be safely looked after, that its contents would not be searched and its valuables—socks, underwear, a candy bar, a can opener, a permanent water bottle—looted. Brightboy was not such a man, and he had taken beatings in the past for his thievery.

Shaky had learned that Brightboy had been on a drunken tear these past few days, and a serious one too: Mohawk Grain Alcohol 190 and Old Crow bourbon, bottle after bottle of it. As was his way, Brightboy had declined to share the contents of his portable liquor cabinet. Had he done so, there might not have been quite so many whispers of discontent.

Shaky didn't follow Brightboy into the shelter, but instead waited on the street and nibbled on a bagel from the previous day. Shaky was known in most of the city's bakeries and coffee shops, and rarely left them without having something to eat pressed upon him. He was careful to spread his lack of custom evenly, and by now he had his weekly routine down: this place on Monday morning, this one Tuesday, this one Wednesday . . . They had grown to expect him, and if he missed a visit questions would be asked of him when he returned. What happened? Were you ill? You doing okay? Shaky always answered honestly. He never played sick when he wasn't, and he never lied. He didn't have very much, which made retaining some semblance of dignity and honor all the more important.

Brightboy emerged an hour later. Shaky knew that he'd have eaten, and used the bathroom. He would probably have half a bagel, or a piece of toast, wrapped in a napkin in his pocket for later. Shaky let Brightboy get some distance ahead of him, then followed. When Brightboy stopped to talk to a woman known as Frannie at Congress Square Park, Shaky slipped into the Starbucks across the street and took a seat at the window. With his damaged arm, and the slight stoop that came with it, he felt like the unlikeliest spy in the world. Undercover Elephant would have been less conspicuous. Fortunately, it was Brightboy he was following. Brightboy was dumb, and self-absorbed. He was nearly as bad as the regular folk in his failure to notice what was going on around him.

Portland was changing. The old Eastland Hotel was being renovated by a big chain—Shaky had lost count of the number of new hotels and restaurants the city had added in recent years—and it looked as if part of Congress Park, the old plaza at Congress and High, would be sold to the hotel's new owners. A Dunkin' Donuts had once stood at the corner of Congress Park, and it became a gathering spot for the city's homeless, but it was long gone now. The businesses that had occupied the space over the years sometimes seemed to Shaky as transient as some of those who frequented its environs. It had been a laundry, a Walgreens, the Congress Square Hotel, and, way back, a wooden row house. Now it was a brick-and-concrete space with a sunken center and a few planting beds, where people like Brightboy and Frannie could conduct their business.

Brightboy's encounter with Frannie ended with the woman screaming abuse at him, and Brightboy threatening to punch her lights out. Shaky wished him luck. Frannie had been on the streets for a decade or more, and Shaky didn't even want to think about the kind of treatment she'd endured and survived in that time. The story was that she'd once bitten off the nose of a man who tried to rape her. This was subsequently described as an exaggeration: she hadn't bitten off all of his nose, said those who knew of such matters, just the cartilage below the nasal bone. Shaky figured that it must have taken Frannie a while, because she didn't have more than half a dozen teeth in her head worth talking about. He had a vision of her holding on to the guy by his ears, gnawing away at him with her jagged shards. It gave him the shivers.

He kept after Brightboy for two hours, watching him search for coins in pay phones and around parking meters, and halfheartedly rummaging through garbage cans. At the intersection of Congress and Deering Avenue, Brightboy took a detour on Deering past Skip Murphy's sober house. He lingered outside for a time, although Shaky didn't know why. Skip's accepted only those who were in full-time employment, or students with some form of income. More to the point, it took in only those who actually wanted to improve themselves, and Brightboy's best chance of improving himself lay in dying. Maybe he knew someone in there, in which case the poor bastard in question would be well advised to give Brightboy a wide berth, because Shaky wouldn't have put it past Brightboy to try and drag someone who had embarked on a twelve-step back down to his own level. It was the only reason Brightboy might offer for sharing a drink. Misery loved company, but damnation needed it.

Brightboy moved on, Shaky trailing him, and at last they came to Brightboy's stash, where he kept the stuff that he couldn't, or didn't want to, carry. There were some who used a shopping cart to haul their possessions, but they were mostly the ones who tried to make a bit extra by scavenging. Brightboy didn't have that kind of resolve. He had hidden whatever was worth keeping behind a warehouse on St. John Street, stashing it in the bushes beside a Dumpster that looked as if it hadn't been emptied since plastic was invented. He was crouched over the bushes when Shaky turned the corner, so intent on whatever he was doing that he didn't hear Shaky approach.

"Hey," said Shaky.

Brightboy was squatting with his back to Shaky. He looked over his shoulder, but didn't try to get up. Shaky could see his right hand moving in the bushes.

"Hey," said Brightboy in reply. His hand kept searching. Shaky knew that it had found what it was seeking when he saw Brightboy smile. Glass flashed in the sunlight as Brightboy withdrew his hand. He started to rise, but Shaky was too quick for him. Some might have called him a cripple behind his back, but he was far from it. His left foot was forward, his right moving in a strong arc to join and then pass it. The toe of his boot caught Brightboy in the side of the head. Brightboy gave a single yelp and fell sideways. The empty bottle of Old Crow fell from his hand and rolled across the ground. Shaky aimed a second kick at Brightboy, just to be sure, and because he wanted to. He had never liked Brightboy. Jude hadn't cared much for him either, even if his personal code of ethics forbade him to turn his back on him. Jude's attitude toward Brightboy was proof positive to Shaky that his late friend had not been without flaw.

This time, Shaky landed a glancing blow to Brightboy's chin. Brightboy started to crawl away, and Shaky finished him off with a toe to the groin from behind. Brightboy stopped moving and lay on the ground, cupping himself with his hands as he moaned softly.

The previous night's breeze was no more, and the day was still. Shaky began to search Brightboy's possessions. It took him only a minute to find Jude's old canvas bag. Jude had used it to transport what he called his "essentials": wipes, toothbrush, comb, and whatever book he happened to be reading at the time. It was small enough to carry easily, and big enough to take any treasures he might scavenge along the way, while he left his main pack in a locker at Amistad. Brightboy must have swept Jude's valuables into it before he left the basement.

Shaky sank down against the Dumpster. The sight of the bag, the feel of it in his hands, brought home to him with renewed clarity that Jude was gone. Shaky started to cry. Brightboy looked up at him from the ground. His eyes were glazed, and he was bleeding from the mouth.

"You took this from him," said Shaky. "You took it from him while his body was still warm."

"His body weren't warm," said Brightboy. "It was cold as shit."

He tried to sit up, but his balls still hurt. He lay down again, rocking with pain, but managed to keep talking.

"Anyway, Jude would have wanted me to have it. He couldn't take it with him. If he could've talked, he'd have told me so."

God, Shaky hated Brightboy. He wished that he'd kicked him hard enough to drive his balls up into his throat and choke him.

"Even if he'd given this to you, you wouldn't have deserved to have it," Shaky told him.

Inside the bag he found the last of Jude's money—forty-three dollars, still wrapped in the same rubber band—and Jude's toothpaste and comb. The wipes were gone. Strangely, the book Jude had been reading at the time of his death, an architectural history of early churches in England, was also among the books stolen by Brightboy. Jude had ordered it specially, Shaky remembered. The people at Longfellow Books had found a paperback copy for him, and refused to accept payment for it. Jude had picked it up days before he died, just after returning from his most recent trip north. Shaky had put the selection down to another manifestation of Jude's magpie intellect, but his friend had been different about this book. He hadn't wanted to discuss it with Shaky, just as he hadn't wanted to tell him exactly where he had gone when he left Portland those final two times.

"Bangor?" Shaky had pressed him.

"It doesn't matter."

"Your daughter still up there, you think?"

"No, I believe she went . . . someplace else."

"You find her?"

"Not yet."

Jude had begun to mark the pages as he read. Shaky flipped through them, and some bus tickets fell out. He tried to grab them, but at that moment the wind came up again from out of nowhere and snatched the tickets away. It blew them into some briars, and Shaky tore the skin on his right hand trying to retrieve them. He almost gave up, but he hadn't come this far to let anything slide that might help the detective. He knelt down and reached into the bush, ignoring the pain and the damage to his coat.

"Damn you," he whispered. "Damn bushes."

"No," said a voice behind him. "Damn you, you fuck!"

The sunlight caught the bottle of Old Crow again. This time it didn't roll away, but shattered against Shaky's skull.

———

SHAKY CAME BACK TO consciousness as the paramedic tended his wounds. Later he would learn that a driver had come into the lot to turn, and spotted him lying on the ground. The driver thought he was dead.

"We'll need to get you stitched up," said the paramedic.

He and his colleague wore blue plastic gloves that were stained with Shaky's blood. Shaky tried to rise, but they held him down.

"You stay there. We got you."

Shaky felt something in his right hand. He looked and saw the bus tickets crumpled in his fist. Carefully he put them into the pocket of his coat, and felt his fingers brush against the piece of paper with the detective's number on it.

"You got someone we can call?" said the paramedic, and Shaky realized that they didn't know he was homeless. He had laundered his clothes only a day earlier, and showered and shaved at Amistad while they were drying.

"Yes," said Shaky, and despite the blow to the head he recited the detective's cell phone number from memory before promptly losing consciousness again.

XIX

By the time I got to Maine Medical, a doctor had picked the shards of glass out of Shaky's scalp and stitched him up. He was woozy from the mild sedative they'd given him, but he wasn't going to be kept overnight. X-rays had revealed no sign of skull fracture. He'd just have a hell of a headache, and his scalp looked as if it had been sewn together by Victor Frankenstein.

He silently pointed me to his possessions, which were contained in a plastic bag. The nurse told me that, before his lights went out behind the warehouse, he insisted that the medics retrieve his book. That was in the bag as well.

"A history of early English churches?" I said, waving it at Shaky as he lay on the gurney, his eyes heavy. "I have to say that I'm surprised."

Shaky swallowed hard and gestured toward the water pitcher nearby. I poured him a glass and held it to his mouth. He only dribbled a little.

"It was a friend's," he said.

"Jude's?"

He nodded, but it clearly made his head hurt, because he winced and didn't try to do it again.

"Coat," he said.

I went through the pockets of his coat until I found the bus tickets, along with the scrap of paper containing my cell phone number. The tickets were for two Portland–Bangor round-trips with Concord, and then two further onward round-trips on the Cyr Bus Line that connected Bangor to Aroostook and points between, this time from Bangor to Medway, in Penobscot County.

"Where did he get the money for these tickets?" I asked Shaky. "From earlier loans he called in?"

"Guess so," said Shaky. "And bottles and cans."

Portland's homeless, like most people in their position, made a little money by scouring the trash for drink containers. Tuesday evenings were particularly profitable, since Wednesday was pickup day for recycling.

"Did he say why he wanted to go to Medway?"

"No."

"But it must have been something to do with his daughter?"

"Yeah. Everything had to do with his daughter these last few weeks."

I looked again at the tickets. The main reasons to go to Medway were hunting, fishing, snowmobiling, and skiing, and I couldn't see Jude doing any of those, whether they were in season or not. Perhaps his daughter had ended up there, but at this time of year there wasn't a whole lot happening. Eventually the snow would melt, but a lull would follow before the summer tourists began arriving.

I flicked through the book. There was something there, something that I couldn't quite grasp. It danced at the edge of my awareness. Maine and English churches.

Then it came to me: a town with an ancient church, an English church.

"Prosperous," I said aloud, and a nurse gave me a curious glance. "But what the hell would Jude be doing in Prosperous?"

———

IT DIDN'T TAKE LONG for the police to find Brightboy. He'd bought himself a half gallon of Caldwell Gin and found a quiet spot in Baxter Woods in which to drink it. He hadn't even bothered to ditch the items that he'd taken from Jude's basement. After they cuffed him and put him in the back of the car, Brightboy told them, without prompting, that he wasn't sorry for hitting Shaky with the empty Old Crow bottle.

"I'd have hit him with a full one," he said, "if'n I could have afforded to."

When he was questioned at Portland PD headquarters, once he'd sobered up some, Brightboy could add little to the sum of knowledge about Jude's death, and Shaky didn't want to press charges over the assault, arguing that "Jude wouldn't have wanted me to." Then again, Jude was dead, and he wasn't the one who'd been smacked over the head with the Old Crow.

A bed was reserved for Shaky at one of the shelters, and the staff had agreed to keep an eye on him for any signs of concussion. He looked comfortable when I spoke to him about Brightboy, but an emergency shelter didn't seem the best place in which to try to recover from a head injury. As good fortune had it, Terrill Nix was one of the respondents to the initial assault, and between us we agreed to see if something could be done to move Shaky up the housing-placement list in return for his efforts in tracking down Brightboy.

The police continued to question Brightboy about Jude, and what he might or might not have seen in the basement. Brightboy didn't prove too helpful on that count—not out of unwillingness but because he had seen nothing beyond Jude's corpse and the consequent open season on his possessions. The cops could have charged Brightboy with both petty theft, for the total value of the cash and other items taken from the basement was less than five hundred dollars, and with interfering with a possible crime scene, but in the end they decided just to put him back on the streets. The court and the prison systems were overburdened as it was, and a spell behind bars was unlikely to have much of an impact on Brightboy one way or another.

Macy joined Nix while I was at the hospital, and I mentioned the bus tickets to her, and the book on church architecture.

"What the hell would someone like Jude be doing in Prosperous?" she said.

"You know," I replied, "those were almost exactly my own words."

"I've talked to my lieutenant," said Macy, "and his view is that all this is just complicating what should be kept simple. We have enough to keep us busy for the next twelve months without adding Jude to the list. He thinks we should let it slide for now. I'll keep an open mind on it, though. If you find out anything solid, you let me know. Terrill?"

She looked to Nix for his view. I had to admire the way she worked. There were detectives who wouldn't have bothered to cut a patrolman in on a discussion like this, let alone seek his opinion. The potential downside was that it could make the detective look indecisive, or lead to a situation where patrol cops might feel they had the right to drop in their two cents' worth without an invitation, but I got the impression Macy wouldn't have those problems. She didn't give too much. She gave just enough.

Nix took the path of least resistance.

"The more I sleep on it, the more it looks like Jude took the drop of his own free will. I spoke to one of the psychiatrists at the Portland Help Center. He said that Jude suffered from depression most of his life. It was one of the reasons he couldn't hold down the permanent housing they tried to find for him. He'd just get depressed and head back to the streets."

I understood their position. Jude wasn't a pretty USM sophomore, or a nurse, or a promising high school student, and the narrative of his death, however incomplete, had already been written and accepted. I'd been there myself, once upon a time.

"Did someone ask Brightboy about a knife?" I said. I was still wondering how Jude had cut the rope, assuming that he had even done so himself.

"Shit!" said Macy.

She slipped away and made a call. When she returned, she looked troubled.

"Brightboy had a penknife in his possession when we picked him up, but he says it's his own. He didn't recall seeing a knife at the scene. He could be lying, though, and he admits that he was out of his skull most of the time he was in that basement. I don't think Brightboy remembers much of anything, even at the best of times."

But she seemed to be talking more to convince herself than to convince me. I let it go. The seed had been planted. If it took root, all the better.

Macy left with Nix. I watched her go. A passing doctor watched her too.

"Damn," he said.

"Yeah," I replied. "My sentiments exactly."

The next time I saw Macy, I was dying.

XX

A pall hung over the house of Harry and Erin Dixon after the departure of Chief Morland and Hayley Conyer. A visit from either of them would have been enough to unnerve the Dixons at the best of times, for they were the two most powerful citizens in Prosperous, even allowing for the fact that Morland didn't sit on the board. But a visit from both of them, especially under the circumstances, was sufficient to push Harry and Erin to breaking point.

They had let the girl go because they wanted to be free of this madness—and perhaps because she reminded them of the daughter they had never had, but for whom they had always wished—and now they were being drawn deeper into the town's insanity just because they had tried to do the right thing. In a way, Erin thought, it might be the shock to the system that they needed. Something of their torpor, their acquiescence to the town's edicts, had already been challenged, or they could not have acted as they had in freeing the girl. Now, faced with the prospect of kidnapping a replacement, any remaining illusions they had were being profoundly dissipated.

As their vision grew clearer, so too did their desperation to get away from Prosperous increase, but neither had yet spoken about what was being asked of them. To a greater (in the case of Harry) or lesser extent (in the case of his wife), they were like children, hoping that by ignoring the problem it might go away, or that some other solution might present itself. Harry, in particular, had sunk into denial. He found himself almost wishing that some stray girl—a waif, a runaway—might pass through Prosperous, or be picked up at the side of the road by one of the selectmen: a safe, older man like Thomas Souleby or Calder Ayton, who would offer her a ride into town and buy her soup and a sandwich at Gertrude's. He would excuse himself to go to the men's room, and a conversation would ensue behind closed doors. A woman would approach the girl, a mother figure. Concern would be expressed for her. A place to stay would be offered, if only for a night or two until she had a chance to clean herself up. There might even be work for her at Gertrude's, if she wanted it. Gertrude's was always shorthanded. Yes, that would work; that would do it. That would take the pressure off Harry and Erin, and they could continue to plan for their eventual escape. Yes, yes . . .

A day went by. Harry avoided speaking with his wife, finding excuses to be away from her. That was not how their marriage had survived for so long. True, Harry might sometimes be a reluctant participant in conversations about feelings, hurt or otherwise, but he had come to accept their value. While Erin could not know the direction of his thoughts, she understood him well enough to guess them.

Father, if thou be willing, remove this cup from me . . .

He sometimes quoted that particular piece of Scripture—Luke 22:42, if she remembered correctly—in times of mild difficulty, like when she asked him to take out the trash if it was raining or, occasionally (and annoyingly) when they were about to make love. Her husband had his weaknesses. She had no illusions about them, just as, she assumed, he was aware of hers in turn, although she liked to think that hers were venal, and of less consequence. Harry disliked confrontation, and was poor at making serious decisions. He preferred to have responsibility for the latter taken from him by circumstance, for then he would not be blamed if the consequences were negative. Erin had never said so aloud, but, had her husband demonstrated a little more backbone, a pinch more ruthlessness, some of their financial problems might have been avoided.

But would she have loved him as much if he had? Ah, there was the rub.

Like her husband, she attended church every Sunday. Most of the people of Prosperous did. They were Baptists, and Methodists, and Catholics. Some had even embraced roadside churches whose denominations were unclear even to their adherents. They believed, and yet did not believe. They understood the difference between the distant and the immanent, between the creator and what was created. But Erin derived more consolation from the rituals than her husband did. She could feel him zoning out during services, for he had little or no interest in organized religion. Sunday worship was a form of escape for him, though only in the sense that it gave him some peace and quiet in which to think, daydream or, occasionally, nap. But Erin listened. She didn't agree with all that she heard, but so much of it was unarguable. Live decently, or what was the point in living at all?

And the people of Prosperous did live decently, and in most matters they behaved well. They gave to charity. They cherished the environment. They tolerated—no, embraced—gays and lesbians. Entrenched conservatives and radical liberals all found their place in Prosperous. In return, the town was blessed with good fortune.

It was just that, sometimes, the town needed to give fortune a push.

But had her husband listened a little more attentively to what was being said at services, and perhaps read the Bible instead of just picking up random quotations from it, he might have recalled the second part of that verse he so loved to throw her way as she began to nuzzle his neck late at night.

. . . *nevertheless not my will, but thine, be done.*

It was the town's will that had to be done.

"We need to talk about it," said Erin as they sat at the table to eat an early dinner. She had made a pot roast, but so far neither of them had done more than pick at it.

"There's nothing to talk about," said Harry.

"What?" She stared at her husband with absolute incredulity. "Are you out of your mind? They want us to abduct a girl. If we don't, they'll kill us."

"Something will turn up," said Harry. He forced himself to eat some of the pot roast. It was strange—or maybe it wasn't strange at all—but ever since he and Chief Morland had buried the girl, Harry had experienced something of a turn against meat. He'd started consuming a lot of cheese, and bread smeared with peanut butter. The pot roast tasted so strong that he had to force himself not to spit it back onto the plate. Somehow he managed to chew it long enough to enable him to swallow. He separated the meat from the vegetables and the potatoes, and proceeded to eat them instead.

"They won't kill us," he said. "They can't. The town has survived by not hurting its own. The board knows that. If they kill us, others will start to fear that it might be their turn next. The board will lose control."

Or they'll tighten it, thought Erin. Sometimes it was necessary to make an example, just to keep the rest in line, and most of those in town—the ones who knew, the ones who participated—would have little time for anyone who placed the present and the future of Prosperous at risk. Any townsfolk who might have some sympathy for the Dixons' predicament were those most like themselves, the ones who were secretly struggling. But there was no chance of them turning against Prosperous once the Dixons were gone, not as long as Chief Morland and Hayley Conyer didn't show up at *their* door and demand that they go hunting for a young woman. Young men didn't work as well. Prosperous had learned that a long time ago.

"You're wrong," said Erin. "You know you are."

He wouldn't look up at her. He speared half a potato with his fork and stuffed it into his mouth.

"What would you have me do?" he asked.

"We have to tell someone."

"No."

"Listen to—"

"*No!*"

She shrank back from him. Harry rarely raised his voice—not in joy, and certainly not in anger. That was one of the reasons she had been so attracted to him. Harry was like a strong tree; he could be buffeted by storms, but he always remained rooted. The downside of his disposition was that tendency not to act but to react, and then only when no other option presented itself. Now he found himself in a situation that he had always hoped to avoid, and since he did not know how to extricate himself from it he had responded with inertia, coupled with a peculiar misplaced faith in a combination of good luck and the possibility of a change of mind on the part of the board.

"I'm dealing with it," he said.

His voice had returned to its usual volume. That brief flash of anger, of energy, was gone, and Erin regretted its passing. Anything was better than this lassitude.

Before she could continue, their doorbell rang. They had heard no car approaching, and had seen no lights.

Harry got up and went to the door. He tried not to think of who might be out there: Morland, asking to look at their basement again, querying further the manner of the girl's escape; or Hayley Conyer, come to check on their progress, to see if they'd started trawling the streets yet.

But it was neither of them. On the step stood Luke Joblin's son, Bryan. He had a bag at his feet. Bryan was twenty-six or twenty-seven, if Harry remembered correctly. He did some lifting work for his father, and was good with his hands. Harry had seen some furniture that Bryan had made, and was impressed by it. The boy had no real discipline, though. He didn't work at developing his gifts. He didn't want to be a joiner or a carpenter or a furniture maker. Mostly, he just liked hunting, in season and out; anything from a crow to a moose, Bryan Joblin was happy to try and kill it.

"Bryan?" said Harry. "What are you doing out here?"

"My dad heard that you might need some help," said Bryan, and Harry didn't like the gleam in his eye. He didn't like it one little bit. "He suggested I ought to stay with you for a week or two. You know, just until you get back on top of things again."

It was only then that Harry spotted the rifle case. A Remington 700 in .30-06. He'd seen Bryan with it often enough.

Harry didn't move. He felt Erin's presence behind him, and it was only when she put her hand on his shoulder that he realized he was trembling.

"There's no problem, is there, Mr. Dixon?" said Bryan, and his tone made it clear that there was only one right answer to the question.

"No, there's no problem at all," said Harry.

He stepped back to admit Bryan. The boy picked up his bag and gun and stepped inside. He greeted Erin with a nod—"Mrs. Dixon"—and the food on the table caught his attention.

"Pot roast," he said. "Smells good."

Erin had not taken her eyes off Harry. Now they looked at each other across the Joblin boy, and they knew.

"I'll show you to your room, Bryan," said Erin, "and then you can join us for a bite to eat. There's plenty to go round."

Harry watched her lead the boy down the hall to the spare room. When they were both out of sight, Harry put his face in his hands and leaned against the wall. He was still standing in that position when Erin returned. She kissed his neck and buried herself in the scent of him.

"You were right," he whispered. "They're turning on us."

"What will we do?"

He answered without hesitation.

"We'll run."

The wolf was in agony. His injury was worsening. In his earlier pain and fear, he had traveled far from the place of his pack's destruction, but now he was having trouble walking even a short distance. Somewhere in the depths of his consciousness the wolf recognized the fact of his own dying. It manifested as a gradual encroachment of darkness upon light, a persistent dimming at the edges of his vision.

The wolf feared men, dreading the sound and scent of them, remembering still the carnage they had wrought by the banks of the river. But where men gathered, so too was there food. The wolf had been reduced to scavenging among trash cans and garbage bags, but in doing so he was eating better than he had in weeks. He had even managed to take a small mongrel dog that had ventured too far into the woods. The wolf could hear the noise of men calling and whistling as he tore the dog's throat apart, but the prey's body was light enough to clamp in his jaws and carry away. He took it far from the sounds of pursuit, and consumed it until just fur and small bones remained.

But the wolf remained hungry.

Now it was night, and his nose was twitching. He smelled decaying meat. He came to the place where the scent was strongest, and found that the ground was soft and broken.

Ignoring the ache in his wounded leg, he started to dig.

2

TRAPPING

"We! Lord," quoth the gentyle knyght,
"Whether this be the Grene Chapelle?
Here myght aboute mydnyght
The Dele his matynnes telle!"

Sir Gawain and the Green Knight

XXII

Prosperous looked like a lot of Maine towns, except that those towns lay mostly Down East and were kept wealthy by tourists who didn't balk at spending fifty dollars on decorative lobster buoys. But Prosperous was well off the tourist trail, and its stores and businesses relied on local trade to remain solvent. Driving down Main Street, I took in the antique streetlamps, and the carefully maintained storefronts, and the absence of anything resembling a chain outlet. Both coffee shops were small and independent, and the pharmacy looked old enough to be able to fill prescriptions for leeches. The Prosperous Tap reminded me of Jacob Wirth, in Boston, even down to the old clock hanging above the sign, and the general store at the edge of town could have been dropped into the nineteenth century without attracting a single sidelong glance.

That morning I had done a little reading up on Prosperous in the library of the Maine Historical Society, in Portland, before making the journey northwest. Prosperous's home-ownership rate was as close to a hundred percent as made no difference, and the median value of property inside the town limits was at least fifty percent higher than the state average. So too was median household income, and the number of residents who held a bachelor's degree or higher. Meanwhile, if Prosperous had any black residents they were keeping themselves well hidden, and it was the same for Asians, Latinos, and Native Americans. In fact, if the census figures were correct, Prosperous had no foreign-born residents at all. Curiously, the number of residents per household was much higher than the state average as well: nearly four, while the average was 2.34. It seemed that kids in Prosperous liked to stay home with mom and dad.

There was one other strange fact that I discovered about Prosperous. Although its percentage of military veterans was roughly proportional to its size, none of the townsfolk had ever been fatally wounded while serving their country. Not one. All had returned home safely. This extraordinary feat had been the subject of an article in the *Maine Sunday Telegram* following the return of Prosperous's last serving soldier from Vietnam in 1975. The town's good fortune had been ascribed to the "power of prayer" by its pastor, a Reverend Watkyn Warraner. His son, Michael Warraner, was the current pastor. While there were various Catholic, Baptist, Methodist, and Presbyterian houses of worship in the surrounding area, the only church within the town limits was the tiny, and peculiarly named, Congregation of Adam Before Eve & Eve Before Adam, and it was of this flock that Michael Warraner was apparently shepherd.

Which was where things got really interesting: Prosperous's church, which was stone-built and barely large enough to hold more than twenty people, had been transported to Maine in its entirety from the county of Northumberland, in England, at the beginning of the eighteenth century. Each stone of the church had been carefully marked and its position in the structure recorded, then all were carried as ballast on the ships that brought the original congregation to Bridgeport, Connecticut, in 1703. From there, these pilgrims journeyed north to Maine and, over a period of decades, eventually founded the town of Prosperous and rebuilt their church, which had been placed in storage for the duration.

The reason they left England, and took their church building with them, came down to religious persecution. The Congregation, as it became known, was an offshoot of the Family of Love, or the Familists, a religious sect that emerged in sixteenth-century Europe. The Family of Love was secretive, and reputedly hostile to outsiders to the point of homicide, although that may just have been anti-Familist propaganda. Marriage and remarriage were kept within the sect, as was the precise nature of its followers' beliefs. As far as I could make out, the Familists believed that hell and heaven existed on earth, and that there was a time preceding Adam and Eve. In the seventeenth century, the majority of Familists became part of the Quaker movement, with the exception of a small group of Northumbrian members who rejected a formal rapport with the Quakers or anyone else, and continued to worship in their own way, despite efforts by King Charles II to crack down on nonconformist churches in England. All officials in towns were required to be members of the Church of England, all clergy had to use the Book of Common Prayer, and unauthorized religious gatherings of more than five people were forbidden unless all were members of the same family. The Familists were among those persecuted in this way.

But the sect proved hard to suppress. The Familists learned to hide themselves by joining established churches while continuing to conduct their own services in secret, and they maintained that charade during the worst years of the crackdown on nonconformism. Also, as intermarriage between families was common, they could easily circumvent the rule about religious gatherings.

In 1689, Parliament passed the Toleration Act, which gave nonconformists the right to their own teachers, preachers, and places of worship, but it seemed that some Familists had already made the decision to abandon the shores of England entirely. They may simply have grown weary of hiding, and had lost faith in their government. The only hint of a deeper discontent lay in the footnotes of an essay that I found titled "The Flight West: Nonconformist Churches and the

Goodness of God in Early New England Settlements," in which the
author suggested that the Familists who formed the Congregation had
been forced out of England because they were so nonconformist as to
be almost pagan.

This corresponded to a couple of paragraphs in Jude's book on
church architecture, which stated that the Congregation's church was
notable for its carved figurines, including numerous "foliate heads,"
part of a tradition of carving ancient fertility symbols and nature spirits on Christian buildings. Such decorations were routinely tolerated,
even encouraged, on older houses of worship. They were a kind of tacit
recognition by the early church fathers of the link between the people
and the land in agrarian communities. In the case of the building that
eventually found its way to Maine, though, the general consensus
among the sect's opponents was that the heads were more than merely
decorative: they were the object of Familist worship, and it was the
Christian symbols that were incidental. As I parked just off Main Street,
it struck me as odd that a congregation with a history of concealment
should have placed enough value on an old church building to transport it across the Atlantic Ocean. This might be a church worth seeing.

The interior of the Town Office, housed in a nineteenth-century
brownstone with a modern extension to the rear, was bright and clean.
When I asked to see the chief of police, I was directed to a comfortable
chair and offered coffee while a call was put through to his office. The
coffee came with a cookie on a napkin. If I stayed long enough, someone would probably have offered me a pillow and a blanket. Instead,
I passed the minutes looking at the images of Prosperous through the
years that decorated the walls. It hadn't changed much over the centuries. The names on the storefronts remained mostly the same, and
only the cars on the streets, and the fashions of the men and women
in the photographs, gave any clues to the passage of time.

A door opened to my right, and a man in uniform appeared. He
was taller than me and broader in the back and shoulders, and his

neatly pressed dark-blue shirt was open at the neck to reveal a startlingly white T-shirt beneath. His hair was dark brown. He wore rim-
less bifocal spectacles, and a SIG as a sidearm. All things considered,
he looked like an accountant who worked out most evenings. Only his
eyes spoiled the effect. They were a pale gray, the color of a winter sky
presaging snow.

"Lucas Morland," he said, as he shook my hand. "I'm chief of police
here."

"Charlie Parker."

"I'm very pleased to meet you, Mr. Parker," he said, and he appeared
to mean it. "I've read a lot about you. I see you've already been given
coffee. You need a top-off?"

I told him I was fine with what I had, and he invited me to step into
his office. It was hard to tell what color the walls might be, as they
were covered with enough certificates and awards to render paint
pretty much superfluous. On his desk were various photographs of a
dark-haired woman and two dark-haired boys. Chief Morland wasn't
in any of them. I wondered if he was separated. Then again, he may
just have been the one taking the photographs. I was in danger of
becoming a "glass half empty" kind of guy. Or a "glass emptier" guy.

Or maybe a "What glass?" guy.

"You have a nice town," I said.

"It's not mine. I just look out for it. We all do, in our way. You considering moving here?"

"I don't think I could afford the taxes."

"Try doing it on a cop's salary."

"That's probably how Communism started. You'd better keep your
voice down, or they'll start looking for another chief."

He leaned back in his chair and folded his hands across his stomach. I noticed that he had a small belly. That was the problem with
quiet towns: there wasn't much that one could do in them to burn
calories.

"Oh, we have all kinds here," said Morland. "Did you notice the motto on the sign as you came into town?"

"I can't say that I did."

"It's easy to miss, I guess. It's just one word: 'tolerance.'"

"Pithy."

He looked out the window and watched a stream of elementary school kids waddle by, each with one hand clinging tightly to a pink rope. It was a clear day, but cold, and they were wrapped in so many layers that it was impossible to see their faces. Once the kids had disappeared from view, and he was content that nothing had befallen them, or was likely to, he returned his attention to me.

"So how can I help you, Mr. Parker?"

I handed him a copy of a photograph of Jude that I'd found at the Portland Help Center. It had been taken at a Christmas lunch the previous year, and Jude, wearing a tan suit and a white shirt accessorized with a piece of tinsel in place of a tie, was smiling. A pedant would have pointed out that the suit was too close to cream for the time of year, but Jude wouldn't have cared.

"I was wondering if you'd seen this man around Prosperous recently, or if he'd had any contact with your department," I said.

Morland wrinkled his nose and peered at the photograph through the lower part of his bifocals.

"Yes, I recall him. He came in here asking about his daughter. His name was . . ."

Morland tapped his fingers on his desk as he sought the name.

"Jude," he said finally. "That was it: Jude. When I asked him if that was his first or last name, he told me it was both. Is he in trouble, or did he hire you? To be honest, he didn't seem like the kind of fella who had money to be hiring private detectives."

"No, he didn't hire me, and his troubles, whatever they were, are over now."

"He's dead?"

"He was found hanged in a basement in Portland about a week ago."

Morland nodded.

"I think I recall reading something about that now."

The discovery of Jude had merited a paragraph in the *Press Herald*, followed by a slightly longer feature in the *Maine Sunday Telegram* about the pressures faced by the city's homeless.

"You say that he was asking about his daughter?"

"That's right," said Morland. "Annie Broyer. He claimed that someone at a women's shelter in Bangor told him that she was headed up this way. Apparently she'd been offered a job here by an older couple, or that was the story he'd heard. He wanted to know if we'd seen her. He had a photograph of her, but it was old. He described her well, though, or well enough for me to be able to tell him that no young woman of that description had found her way into this town—or none that I knew of, and I know them all."

"And was he happy with that?"

Morland's face bore an expression I'd seen a thousand times. I'd probably worn it myself, on occasion. It was the face of a public servant who just wasn't paid enough to deal with the unhappiness of those for whom the reality of a situation wasn't satisfactory.

"No, Mr. Parker, he was not. He wanted me to take him to every house in Prosperous that might be occupied by an older couple and have me show them the photograph of his daughter. In fact, he went so far as to suggest that we ought to *search* the houses of everyone over sixty, just in case they had her locked up in their home."

"I take it that wasn't an option."

Morland spread his hands helplessly.

"He hadn't reported his daughter missing. He didn't even know if she *was* missing. He just had a feeling in his bones that something was wrong. But the more we got into it the more apparent it became that he didn't really know his daughter at all. That was when I discovered that she'd been living in a women's shelter, and he was homeless, and they were estranged. It all got messy from there."

"What did you do in the end?"

"I made a copy of the photograph, put together a description of his daughter to go with it, and told him I'd ask around. But I also tried to explain to him that this wasn't the kind of town where people took in street women they didn't know and offered them beds in their homes. To be honest, I don't know a whole lot of towns where anyone would behave in that way. The story just didn't ring true. He gave me a couple of numbers for shelters and soup kitchens where a message could be left for him, and then I gave him a ride to Medway so he could catch the bus back to Bangor."

"Let me guess," I said. "The offer of a ride to Medway wasn't one that he could refuse."

Morland gave me the long-suffering public servant expression again.

"Look, it was a last resort. He said he was going to get a cup of coffee, and next thing I knew he was stopping folks on the streets to show them the picture of his daughter, and taping crappy photocopies to streetlights. I'd told him that I'd do what I could to help him, and I meant it, but I wasn't going to have a bum—even a well-dressed bum—harassing citizens and defacing public property. I like my job, Mr. Parker, and I want to keep it. Most of the time it's easy, and even when it's hard it's still kind of easy. I like this town too. I grew up here. My father was chief of police before me, and his father before him. It's our family business, and we do it well."

It was quite a speech. I'd have voted for him if he ran for office.

"So you drove Jude to Medway"—I resisted suggesting that Jude had literally been given the bum's rush—"but I'll venture that he didn't take the hint."

Morland puffed his cheeks.

"He started calling my office two or three times a day, asking if there had been any progress, but there was none. Nobody here had seen his daughter. He'd been given bad information. But he wouldn't accept that, so he came back. This time, he didn't pay me the courtesy of a visit, just went from house to house, knocking on doors and peering in windows. Naturally, I started getting telephone calls from panicked residents, because it was getting dark. He was lucky he didn't get himself shot. I picked him up and kept him in a cell overnight. I told him I could have him charged with criminal trespass. Hell, he even ended up in the cemetery more than half an hour after sunset, like that fella in Dickens."

"Magwitch," I said.

"That's the one."

"What was he doing in the cemetery?"

"Trying to get into the church. Don't ask me why; we keep it locked, and visits are only by appointment. We've had incidents of vandalism in the past. Do you know about our church?"

I told him that I did, and that I'd be curious to see it before I left, if that was possible. Morland perked up slightly at the prospect of my leaving town. He was tiring of talking about the problems of dead bums and their daughters.

"In conclusion, the next morning I drove him back to Medway—*again*—and told him that if he showed his face in Prosperous one more time he would be arrested and charged, and he'd be no help to his daughter from a jail cell. That seemed to get through to him, and, apart from a phone call or ten, that was pretty much the last I saw or heard of him, until now."

"And nobody in town knew anything about his daughter?"

"No, sir."

"But why would his daughter have said that she was going to Prosperous if someone hadn't given her reason to do so? It sounds like an odd story to make up."

"She might have been trying to impress the other street people.

Worst case, she spoke to someone in Bangor who told her they were from Prosperous when they weren't. It may be that this Jude was right, and something did happen to her, but if so, it didn't happen to her here."

Morland returned the photo of Jude and got to his feet. We were done.

"So you want to see the church before you go?"

"If it's not too much trouble," I said. "At least you won't have to drive me to Medway after."

Morland managed a thin smile, but said nothing. As I stood, I let my arm brush one of the photographs on the desk. I caught it before it hit the floor, and returned it to its place.

"Your family?" I said.

"Yes."

"Good-looking boys. No girls?"

Morland gave me a peculiar look, as though I had intimated something unpleasant about him and the nature of his familial relations.

"No, no girls," he said. "I'm happy about that, I got to say. My friends with daughters tell me they're more trouble than boys. Girls will break your heart."

"Yes," I said. "Jude's daughter certainly broke his."

Morland took the photograph from me and restored it to its place on his desk.

"You had a daughter, didn't you?"

"Yes," I said. "She died," I added, preempting whatever might have followed. I was used to it by now.

"I know," said Morland. "I'm sorry. You have another little girl now, don't you?"

I looked at him curiously, but he appeared nothing but sincere.

"Did you read that somewhere too?" I asked.

"You think there's anyone in Maine law enforcement who doesn't know your history? This is a small-town state. Word gets around."

That was true, but Morland still had a remarkable memory for the family histories of men he had never met before.

"That's right, I have another little girl," I conceded.

Morland seemed on the verge of saying something, then reconsidered, contenting himself with, "Maybe if this man Jude hadn't walked out on his family his daughter might not have ended up the way she did."

Morland had a point—Jude, had he still been alive, might even have agreed with him—but I wasn't about to point the finger at Jude's failings as a husband and a father. I had my own guilt to bear in that regard.

"He tried to make up for it at the end," I said. "He was just doing what any father would have done when he came looking for her in Prosperous."

"Is that a criticism of how he was treated by my department?"

Morland didn't bristle, but he wasn't far off it. "My department," I noted, not "me."

"No," I said. "You just did what any chief of police would have done."

That wasn't quite the truth, but it was true enough. Maybe if Morland had a daughter of his own he would have behaved more compassionately; and if Jude hadn't been a bum, and his daughter a homeless ex-junkie, Morland would have tried a little harder—just a little, but sometimes that's all it takes. I didn't say any of this aloud, though. It wouldn't have helped, and I couldn't guarantee that, in his position, and with his background, I would have behaved any differently.

We walked from his office. Morland told the receptionist that he was heading out to the chapel. She looked surprised, but said nothing.

"This woman, Annie Broyer, you think she's dead?" asked Morland as we stepped outside.

"I don't know," I said. "I hope not."

"So you're going to keep looking for her?"

"Probably."

"And you've been hired to do this by whom?"

"I haven't been hired by anyone."

"So why are you looking for her?"

"Because nobody else will," I said.

Morland took this in, then told me to follow his car.

He was still shaking his head as he pulled away.

XXIII

The Chapel of the Congregation of Adam Before Eve & Eve Before Adam, to give it its full title, was situated in the middle of a forest about half a mile northwest of Prosperous. A road marked PRIVATE, and secured with a lock and chain for which Chief Morland had a key, wound through the woods until it came to iron railings painted black, within which lay the town's original cemetery and the church. Morland parked his car on a narrow strip of grass beside the railings, and I parked on the road. There was a gate in the railings, also kept closed with a lock and chain, but it was already open when we arrived.

"I gave Pastor Warraner a call along the way and asked him to join us," said Morland. "It's just good manners. The church is in his care. I have a key, but it's only in case of an emergency. Otherwise, I leave all such matters to him."

I looked around, but I could see no sign of the pastor. The church was even smaller and more primitive than I had expected, with walls of rough-hewn gray stone, and a western orientation instead of the more usual eastern. I did one full circuit of the building, and it didn't take long. A heavy oak door seemed to be the only point of entry or exit, and there were two narrow windows on its northern and southern walls, sealed with glass from within and bars without. The wall behind what I presumed to be the altar was blank and windowless. The roof was relatively new, and appeared incongruous above the ancient stones.

The main decorative features, the faces for which the church was famous, were in the upper corners of each wall, creating a kind of Janus effect where they met, an impression compounded by the fact that the lengths of carved ivy and branches of which the decorations were composed flowed between the faces and continued along the upper lengths of the walls, so that the visages all appeared to spring from the same source. They had weathered over the centuries, but not as much as might have been expected. Intricate constructions of stone leaves formed a protective screen around them, from which the faces peered out. They reminded me of childhood, and fairy tales, and of the way in which the markings on the trunks of very old trees sometimes took on the appearance of contorted, suffering people, depending on the light and the angle at which they were examined.

But what struck me most was the sheer malevolence of the expressions on the carvings. These were not manifestations of gentle emotions, or signifiers of hope. Instead, they boded only ill for all who looked on them. To my mind, they had no more place on a church building than a pornographic image.

"What do you think?" said Morland, as he joined me.

"I've never seen anything like them before," I said, which was the most neutral reply I could offer.

"There are more inside," he said. "Those are just the opening acts."

As if on cue, the door to the chapel opened and a man stepped out.

"Pastor Warraner," said Morland, "this is Mr. Parker, the detective I told you about."

Warraner wasn't what I had expected of a cleric who had charge of a building that was almost a millennium old. He wore jeans and battered work boots, and a brown suede jacket that had the look of a garment long reached for instinctively when warmth and comfort were required. He was in his late forties, with heavily receding hair, and as we shook hands I saw and felt the calluses on his skin, and caught a faint smell of timber and wood shavings on him.

"Call me Michael," he said. "I'm glad I was around to say hello."

"Do you live nearby?" I asked. I hadn't seen any other vehicle when we arrived.

"Just the other side of the woods," he said, gesturing over his right shoulder with his thumb. "Five minutes on foot. Same time it takes me in my truck by the less scenic route, so it makes more sense to walk. May I ask what brings a private detective to our town?"

I stared at the church carvings, and they stared back. One had its mouth wide open, and a tongue poked obscenely from between its carved lips. It seemed to mock any hope I might have of finding Annie Broyer alive.

"A homeless man named Jude came to Prosperous recently," I said. "Chief Morland tells me that he may have trespassed on the church grounds in the course of one of those visits."

"I remember," said Warraner. "I was the one who found him here. He was very agitated, so I had no choice but to call Chief Morland for assistance."

"Why was he agitated?"

"He was concerned about his daughter. She was missing, and he was under the impression that she might have found her way to Prosperous. He felt that he wasn't getting the help he needed from the police. No offense meant, Chief."

"None taken," said Morland, although it was hard to tell if he was sincere, as he had kept his sunglasses on against the glare of winter sun on snow. I barely knew Morland, but I had already figured him for a man who guarded any slights jealously, nurturing them and watching them grow.

"Anyhow, I tried to calm him down, but I didn't have much success," said Warraner. "I told him to leave the grounds, and he did, but I was worried that he might attempt to break into the church, so I called the chief."

"Why would you think he'd want to break into the church?" I asked.

Warraner pointed at the faces looming above his head.

"Disturbed people fixate," he said, "and this wonderful old building provides more opportunities for fixation than most. Over the years, we've had attempts to steal the carvings from the walls, and to deface them. We've found people—and not just young ones either but folk old enough to know better—having sex on the ground here because they were under the impression it would help them to conceive a child, and, of course, we've been visited by representatives of religious groups who object to the presence of pagan symbols on a Christian church."

"As I understand it, this town was founded by the Familists, and it was originally their church," I said. "Their belief system strikes me as more than a complicated variation on Christianity."

Warraner looked pleasantly surprised at the question, like a Mormon who had suddenly found himself invited into a house for coffee, cake, and a discussion of the wit and wisdom of Joseph Smith.

"Why don't you step into my office, Mr. Parker?" he said, welcoming me into the chapel.

"As long as I'm not keeping you from anything important," I said.

"Just kitchen closets," he said. "I run a joinery service."

He fished a card from his pocket and handed it to me.

"So you're not a full-time pastor?"

Warraner laughed. "I'd be a pauper if I was. No, I'm really just a caretaker and part-time historian. We no longer have services here; the Familists are no more. The closest we have are some Quaker families. The rest are mainly Baptists and Unitarians, even some Catholics."

"And what about you?" I said. "You still keep the title of 'pastor.'"

"Well, I majored in religion at Bowdoin, and studied as a Master of Divinity at Bangor Theological Seminary, but I always did prefer woodworking. Still, I guess you could say that the theological gene runs in the family. I hold a weekly prayer group, although often I'm the only one praying, and there are people in town who come to me for advice and guidance. They tend to be folk who aren't regular churchgoers but still believe. I don't probe too deeply into what it is that they *do* believe. It's enough that they believe in some power greater than themselves."

We were in the church now. If it was cold outside, it was colder still inside. Five rows of hard wooden benches faced a bare altar. There were no crosses, and no religious symbols of any kind. Instead, the wall behind the altar was dominated by a foliate face larger than any that decorated the exterior. Two slightly smaller faces of a similar kind were visible between the windows.

"Do you mind if I take a closer look?" I said.

"By all means," said Warraner. "Just watch your step. Some of the stones are uneven."

I approached the altar along the right aisle of the church. As I passed, I glanced at the first of the faces. It was more detailed than the ones outside, and had a grinning, mischievous expression. As I looked at it more closely, I saw that all its features were made from stone re-creations of produce: squash, pea pods, berries, apples, and ears of wheat. I had seen something like it before, but I couldn't recall where.

"Wasn't there an artist who painted images like this?" I asked Warraner.

"Giuseppe Arcimboldo," he replied. "I've always meant to study up on him, but there never seems to be enough time. I imagine that he and the creators of these carvings would probably have had a lot to discuss, particularly the intimate connection between man and the natural world, had they not been separated by the ages."

I moved to the altar and stood before the carving on the wall. If the face on the right was almost cheerful—albeit in the manner of someone who has just watched a puppy drown and found it amusing—and evoked images of the earth's bounty, this one was very different. It was a thing of roots, thorns, and nettles, of briars, bare winter bushes, and twisting ivy. Branches bristling with spines poured from its open mouth and seemed both to form its features and to suffocate them, as though the image were tormenting itself. It was profoundly ugly, and startlingly, vibrantly present, an ancient being brought to life from dead things.

"It's the same visage, or the same god, depending upon one's inclination," said Warraner from behind me.

"What?"

He pointed to his right, at the face made from produce, to his left at another constructed from blossoming flowers, and finally at a fourth face that I had not noticed before, as it was above the door: a face composed of straw, and leaves that had just begun to wither and die.

"All versions of a similar deity," said Warraner. "In the last century, the name 'Green Man' was coined for him—a pagan god absorbed into the Christian tradition, a symbol of death and rebirth long before the idea of the resurrection of Christ came into being. You can see why a building decorated in such a manner would have appealed to the Familists, a sect that believed in the rule of nature, not God."

"And are you a Familist, Pastor Warraner?" I asked.

"I told you," he answered. "The Familists no longer exist. Frankly, it's a shame. They were outwardly tolerant of the views of others while repudiating all other religions entirely. They refused to carry arms, and they kept their opinions and beliefs to themselves. They attracted the elite, and had no time for the ignorant. If they were still around today, they'd regard most of what passes for organized religion in this country as an abomination."

"I read that they were accused of killing to defend themselves," I said.

"Propaganda," said Warraner. "Most of those allegations came from John Rogers, a sixteenth-century cleric who hated Christopher

Vitel, the leader of the Familists in England. He called the Family of Love a 'horrible secte,' and based his attacks on depositions given by dissenting ex-Familists. There's no evidence that the Familists ever killed those who disagreed with them. Why should they? The sect's members were quietists; they didn't even identify themselves publicly, but hid among other congregations to avoid being identified and put at risk."

"Like religious chameleons," I said, "blending into the background."

"Exactly," said Warraner. "Eventually, they simply became what they pretended to be."

"Except the ones who traveled here to found Prosperous."

"And in the end even they vanished," said Warraner.

"Why did the Familists leave England?" I asked. "It wasn't clear from the little that I could find out about them. As far as I can tell, religious persecution was already dying when they departed. Why flee when you're no longer threatened?"

Warraner leaned against a pew and folded his arms. It was a curiously defensive gesture.

"The Familists entered a state of schism," he said. "Disagreements arose between those who advocated following the Quaker way and those who wished to adhere to the sect's original belief system. The traditionalists feared being named as something more dangerous than dissenters, particularly when it was suggested that the building we're in should be razed. They viewed this church as the wellspring of their faith, which was probably why those who had chosen to follow an alternative path so desired its destruction. A wealthy cadre of the faithful came together to save the church, and their sect, from annihilation. The result was an exodus to New England, and the founding of Prosperous."

He glanced at his watch.

"Now, I'm sorry," he said, "but I really do need to get back to my kitchen closets."

I took one more look at the largest of the faces on the wall, the image of a winter god, then thanked him and joined Morland, who had waited throughout by the door. We watched Warraner lock the chapel with a key from a heavy ring and check that it was securely closed.

"One last thing," I said.

"Yes?"

He sounded impatient. He wanted to be gone.

"Wasn't Christopher Vitel a joiner too?"

Warraner thrust his hands into his pockets and squinted at me. The sun was setting, and the air was growing colder, as though the chill inside the chapel had permeated the outside world while the door was open.

"You really have done your homework, Mr. Parker," he said.

"I like to keep myself informed."

"Yes, Vitel was a joiner. It was used against him by his enemies to suggest that he was nothing but a vagabond."

"But he was much more than that, wasn't he? I understand that he was also a textile merchant in the Low Countries, and it was there that he encountered the founder of the Familists, Hendrik Niclaes, except at that time he was Christopher Vitell. He dropped the second 'l' when he returned to England to spread the doctrine of the Familists, effectively giving himself a new identity."

"That may be true," said Warraner. "Such changes of spelling were not uncommon at the time, and may not even have been deliberate."

"And then," I continued, "around 1580, when the government of Queen Elizabeth was hunting the Familists, Vitel simply disappeared."

"He is not present in the historical record from that time on," said Warraner. "It's not clear why. He may have died."

"Or assumed another identity. A man who changed his name once could easily do so again."

"What are you suggesting, Mr. Parker?"

"Maybe preaching isn't the only talent you inherited from your genes."

"You should have been a historian, Mr. Parker. A speculative one, perhaps, but a historian nonetheless. But then isn't historical research a form of detection too?"

"I suppose it is. I hadn't really considered it."

"In answer to your suggestion, I have no idea if my line stretches back to Vitel, but I would consider myself blessed indeed if that were the case."

He tested the door one last time, and began walking toward the gate.

"It's been interesting talking to you, Mr. Parker," he called back just before he reached it. "I hope you get to visit us again sometime."

"I think I'll be back," I said, but only Morland heard me.

"It's a dead end," he said. "Whatever you're looking for isn't here."

"You may be right," I said, "but I'm not sure what it is that I'm looking for, so who's to know?"

"I thought you were looking for a missing girl."

"Yes," I said, as Warraner vanished into the woods without a backward glance. "So did I."

Morland escorted me from the churchyard and locked the gate behind us. I thanked him for his time, got into my car, and drove away. I thought he might have followed me to the town limits to make sure that I was leaving, but he didn't. When I turned right, he went left to go back to Prosperous. I kept the radio off and played no music as I drove. I thought about Jude, and Morland, and my time with Pastor Warraner. One small detail nagged at me. It might have been nothing, but, like a fragment of thorn buried in my flesh, it itched as I headed south, and by the time I reached Bangor it was impossible to ignore.

Warraner had not asked me anything more about Jude, or my reasons for visiting Prosperous, once we left the subject of Jude's intrusion on the cemetery. It might simply have been the case that Warraner wasn't curious about Jude or his missing daughter. He may have become distracted as we talked about his beloved chapel. Or there was a third possibility: Warraner didn't ask about Jude because he knew that Jude was dead, but if that was so, why not mention it? Why not ask who had hired me, or why I had come so far north to ask about a homeless man? Yes, Morland could have told Warraner the reason for my visit while I was following him to the churchyard, but if so, why would Warraner have bothered to ask me the same question a second time?

My headlights caught bare branches and twisted trees, and every shadow concealed the face of the Green Man.

XXIV

Morland drove to the outskirts of Prosperous and sat in his car, drinking coffee from his thermos and watching the cars enter and leave the town. His Crown Vic rested on a small hill partially concealed by trees, a site that he often used as the location for a speed trap when the mood took him. His father had shown him this location, pointing out to him the sweet spot, the perfect position from which to watch without being seen while also giving an unrestricted view of the road. On this occasion, Morland left the radar gun in its case. He didn't want to be disturbed. He wanted to think.

Hayley Conyer would have to be informed of the detective's visit, and it was better that Morland be the one to do it rather than Pastor Warraner. Who knew what poisons Warraner would pour into Hayley's ear? It was the pastor who had shouted loudest for the killing of the one named Jude, even as Morland tried to divert the board from a course of action that had now brought a dangerous man down upon them.

For the detective was dangerous, of that Morland had no doubt. The chief had not been busy when the detective arrived at the Town Office, and could have seen him immediately, but he had taken time to compose himself, to run through the possible reasons for the man's visit. Morland had been surprised when the detective mentioned

Jude's name, but had hidden it well. He had struggled harder to retain his composure when the detective wanted to visit the chapel, but he shouldn't have: it was a perfectly understandable request to make, given the unusual nature of the building, although Morland had offered the detective an opening by mentioning that Jude had been arrested on church grounds. As for Warraner, he regularly received letters and emails from interested parties asking for permission to view the building, even if he was careful to limit such visits to those whose reasons were entirely without ulterior motive.

But Morland believed that the detective did *nothing* without an ulterior motive. He wasn't the kind of man to go sightseeing at an old church simply because he had time on his hands. He was looking for connections. Morland could only hope that he had left Prosperous without making any. The chief ran over the details of their conversation again and again, adding what he'd heard of the detective's discussion with Warraner. Morland tried to see the situation through the detective's eyes, and by the time the thermos was empty he had decided that there was nothing about the day's business that could have added to any half-formed suspicions the detective might have brought with him. It had been a fishing expedition, nothing more, and the hook had come back bare. Still, Morland hadn't liked the way the detective watched Warraner as the pastor departed, or his suggestion that the girl's disappearance might not be the sole purpose of his visit. The detective's first hook might not have caught on anything, but he had left others trailing.

Morland climbed from the car and went into the bushes to take a leak. It was dark now, but the moon shone silver on the small body of water known as Lady's Pond. This was where the women of Prosperous would go to congregate and bathe, undisturbed by their menfolk, in the early decades of the township. Morland wondered how many of them knew of the town's true nature, even then. Probably only a handful, he thought. More of the townsfolk understood Prosperous now, but far from all. Some chose to be blind to it, and others were deliberately kept in the dark. It was strange, thought Morland, how generations of Prosperous families had never been entrusted with the truth, yet still had reaped its benefits. It was stranger still that the town's secret had remained undiscovered by outsiders over the centuries, even allowing for the killings that had occurred in order to silence those who were ready to betray it. Perhaps it was a circular argument: the town was always at risk because it required murder to survive, but by spilling blood it accrued the blessings that enabled it to keep that risk to a minimum, and assure the town's continued prosperity. Put that way, it sounded simple, logical.

Morland wondered if, like his father and his grandfather before him, he had become such a monster that he almost failed to notice his own moral and spiritual deformity anymore.

The issue of betrayal brought him back to the Dixons. It had been Morland's decision to place Luke Joblin's son with them. He hoped that Bryan Joblin's presence would keep the Dixons in line and force them to act according to the board's wishes, but he had his doubts. If the Dixons actually managed to produce a girl to replace Annie Broyer, Morland would give up coffee for a year.

But there was a part of the chief that hoped Harry Dixon was right—that the fact of the girl's killing and the soaking of her blood into the soil of Prosperous might be enough. The town was hurting, but not as much as the rest of the state. People were getting by. Morland imagined a situation where Pastor Warraner informed the board that all was now well and the chapel remained quiet, so no further action was required. But Warraner was both fanatical and weak, and Morland had not yet decided whether the latter quality was useful or dangerous. It depended upon the circumstances, he supposed, but it meant that Warraner had a habit of attacking from behind when it came to disputes. He was no honest broker. Morland wished that Warraner's father were still alive and in charge of the chapel. Old Watkyn

Warraner had been a cautious man by all accounts, but he steered the congregation for more than half a century without blood being spilt more than once. It was the longest such period of contentment the town had known.

Well, we're paying for it now, thought Morland. Two bodies—one here and one in Portland—and it appeared that they were not enough. Now a detective was asking questions, a strange man with a reputation for excavating long-buried secrets and annihilating his enemies. Under the circumstances, Warraner could argue that the spilling of blood was more necessary than ever, for only by blood would the town be saved, and the selectmen might well be inclined to agree. They were all old, and fearful—even Hayley Conyer, but she just hid her fear better than most. Younger people were needed on the board, but most of the town's youths weren't ready to take on the burden of protecting Prosperous. It took decades for the town to seep into one's soul, for the recognition of one's obligations to it to form. It was a kind of corruption, a pollution passed down through the generations, and only the oldest were corrupt and polluted enough to be able to make the tough decisions required to keep the town alive.

Morland used a bottle of water to wash his hands before drying them on the legs of his trousers. It was time to talk with Hayley Conyer. He called his wife and told her that he would be home late. No, he wasn't sure when. He knew only that a long evening stretched ahead.

Morland drove to the Conyer house and parked outside. The drapes were drawn on all the windows, but a sliver of light was visible from Hayley's mausoleum of a living room. He wasn't surprised to find her home. Unless she was out on board business, Hayley was always home. Morland couldn't remember the last time she'd left town for more than a couple of hours. She was afraid the place would collapse into the ground without her. That was part of the problem, of course.

"Bitch," he said softly, as he stepped from the car. The wind

whipped the word away, and he found his right hand twitching invol-
untarily, as if it were hoping to catch the insult before it reached the
ear of Hayley Conyer.

He rang the doorbell, and Hayley answered.

"I'm sorry to disturb you—" Morland began to say, but Hayley held
up a hand to interrupt him.

"It's quite all right," she said. "I've been expecting you."

She invited him to step inside, then led him to the living room,
where Pastor Warraner had already made himself at home in an
armchair.

Shit, thought Morland.

XXV

The woman on desk duty at the Tender House in Bangor was named Molly Bow, and she looked as if she should have been fixed to the prow of a ship. She was big and weathered, but attractive in a matronly way, and at one point I had to take a couple of steps back to avoid being crushed by her breasts as she passed me to get to a filing cabinet in her office.

"Comin' through," she said as I flattened my back against a wall. She gestured toward her bosom. "I was born large. Backache apart, it's been useful in life. People make an effort to get out of my way."

Once again, I had an image of a schooner or, better still, a man-of-war cleaving a path through the waves, but I kept my eyes fixed on a neutral spot on the opposite wall, well above chest height.

The Tender House had no signs outside to mark its presence. It was housed in a pair of adjoining clapboard buildings surrounded by a white picket fence that was only slightly higher than those of its neighbors. Two cars were parked in the drive, which was secured by an automatically operated steel gate, also painted white. Inside the front door of the main building was a waiting room containing toys, a library of self-help books, boxes of tissues, large containers of secondhand clothes organized according to type and size, from infant to adult, and, in a discreet corner, toothbrushes, toothpaste, and toiletries. Behind the reception desk was a small playroom.

The Tender House wasn't a homeless shelter but, rather, a "crisis center" for women, where homelessness was only one of the problems it tackled. It catered to victims of domestic and sexual abuse, runaways, and women who simply needed a place to stay while they tried to improve their situation. Its staff liaised with the police and the courts, advising on everything from restraining orders to educational and job opportunities, but it generally steered the long-term homeless toward other agencies and centers.

"Got it," said Bow, waving a file. She licked an index finger and flipped through some pages. "We had her for about eleven days, apart from the fifth night, when someone broke out a couple of half gallons of Ten High over by Cascade Park. We had some sore heads the next day, Annie's among them."

"Was she an alcoholic?"

"No, I don't think so. She'd been a user, but she claimed to be clean by the time she arrived at our door. We made it clear to her that we had a zero-tolerance policy when it came to drugs. If she got high, she'd be back on the streets."

"And alcohol?"

"Officially, we're down on that too. Unofficially, we give some leeway. Nothing on the premises, and no intoxication. Actually, I was disappointed when Annie came back to us all raw from the Ten High. I had her pegged as a young woman who was genuinely trying to change her life. We sat her down and had a talk with her. Turned out her estranged father had come looking for her, and his presence in town had thrown her. She was offered a sip or two to steady herself, and it all got sort of blurry for her after that."

"Did she say anything about her relationship with her father?"

Bow was clearly reluctant to share confidences. I could understand her reservations.

"Annie is missing, and her father is dead," I said.

"I know that. He hanged himself in a basement down in Portland."

I gave it a couple of seconds.

"He was found hanging in a basement in Portland," I corrected her. It was minor, but it was important.

Molly sat behind her desk. She'd been standing until then. We both had. As she sat, so did I.

"Is that why you're here—because you don't think it was suicide?"

"So far I don't have any proof that it wasn't," I said. "A couple of small details are just snagging like briars."

"Such as?"

"Such as the fact that he loved his daughter, and clearly wanted to reestablish contact with her. He had spoken of heading up here permanently to be closer to her. He'd also gone to a lot of trouble to pull together some money in the days before he died. He succeeded too. Those aren't the actions of a suicidal man."

"What was the money for?"

It struck me that I was on the wrong side of an interrogation: I should have been asking the questions, not her, but sometimes you had to retreat an inch to gain a foot.

"To support him as he tried to find his daughter. I think he was also hoping to hire me to help look for her."

"So how much money did he manage to collect?"

"More than a hundred dollars."

"Do you work that cheap?"

"Funny, you're the second person who's asked me that. I could have given him a couple of hours, or more if I took the time from some of my wealthier clients."

"Isn't that unethical?"

"Only if I don't tell them I'm doing it. They pay by the hour, even if the job only takes five minutes. I don't do fractions. Look, do you think *I* might get to ask a question at any point?"

Bow smiled. "You just did."

Hell.

She leaned back in her chair, like a reigning champ who had dispensed with another challenger to her crown, then threw me a bone of consolation.

"I'm joshing with you," she said. "You'd be surprised how many people I get in here asking questions about the women in our care. I have to be careful, for their sakes."

"What kind of people?"

"Sometimes we have women who turn tricks when times are desperate, and a john will come looking for one of them just because he's a creep, or he's got a beef about the service he received, or he liked it so much he wants a second bite. We get husbands and boyfriends trying to take back their possessions, because the kind who come storming in here mostly regard women as chattel. Oh, they'll do their best to dress it up as nicely as they can—they want to talk things over, to give the relationship another try, and they're sorry for whatever it is that they've done, which usually involves a fist or a boot, often with a little domestic rape thrown in along the way—but I've developed a nose for the worst of them. It's not hard. As soon as you put an obstacle in their way the threats start to emerge, but those ones are usually pretty dumb along with it. They mooch around in the hope that they'll be able to snatch their woman off the street, but we have a good relationship with the Bangor PD, and they'll get here before I've hung up the phone.

"But we've had men try to break in, or beat up volunteers. Last year, one even tried to burn us down by starting a fire at the back door. At the same time, we try to keep channels of communication open between women and their families. This is a place to which women—and their children—come when they're desperate. It isn't a long-term solution. We make that clear to them from the start, but I've been seeing some of the women who pass through these doors on and off for the past ten years. They just get older and more bruised. There are times when I wonder how far we've come as a society where women are concerned. Whenever I turn on the TV to hear some jackass in a blazer bleating about feminists I want to set him on fire, and don't get me started on those dumb bitches who find themselves on the top of the pile only to reject the whole concept of feminism, as though their success wasn't built on the struggles of generations of women. I defy them to spend one day here with a forty-year-old woman whose husband has been stubbing out cigarettes on her for so long that he has to search for a spot where it still hurts, or a nineteen-year-old girl who has to wear diapers because of what her stepfather did to her, and tell me that they're not feminists."

What was strange about Molly Bow's speech was that, by the end of it, she was still leaning back in her chair and her voice hadn't grown even slightly louder. It was as though she had seen too much to want to expend valuable energy on useless rage. Better to direct it into more productive channels.

"And where did Annie fit into all this?"

Molly's fingers stroked the file, as if Annie Broyer were seated on the floor beside her and she was still capable of consoling her, of offering her some assurance that the world might be gentler with her in time.

"She was deserted by her father, and her mother died when she was a teenager. That doesn't mean she had to become an addict, and find herself on the streets, but she did. She wasn't weak, though. She had real strength to her. I don't like to use the word 'rescue,' or make out like I'm on some kind of mission to turn round the life of every woman who passes through our doors. It's just not possible, and we do what we can here, but there was something about Annie, something bright and untouched. It was why I let the drinking go, and the fact that she couldn't keep curfew to save her life—"

She suddenly stopped talking as she became aware of the dual meaning of what she had just said. A spasm of pain convulsed her, and she looked away.

"But that's not what happened, is it?" I said. "She didn't vanish from the streets in the night."

"No," she said, once she was certain that her voice wouldn't break, although she still didn't look at me. "She came in the sunlight, and she packed her bags and left. I wasn't even here. She asked one of the other volunteers to thank me for what I'd done, but I hadn't done anything, not really."

She touched the file again.

"Do you think she's dead?" she asked.

"Do you?"

"Yes. I hate to say it, but yes; I have a feeling of absence. I have no sense of her in the world. Do you think—?"

"What?"

"Is it possible that her father might have hurt her—killed her—and then taken his own life out of remorse?"

I thought about what I knew of Jude.

"No, I don't believe so."

"Call me a cynic," she said, "but I had to ask. He wouldn't have been the first."

The office was very quiet for a time. The silence was disturbed by a young woman who appeared at the reception desk from somewhere upstairs. She wore a yellow T-shirt that extended to her thighs, and she was almost unbearably beautiful. She had hair so blond that it shone white, and her skin was without blemish. She held in her arms a girl of two or three who might have been her daughter or, given the youth of the woman who carried her, perhaps even her younger sister. The child had clearly been crying, but the sight of two adults silenced her. She laid her face against the young woman's neck and watched me carefully.

"I'm sorry," said the older girl. "She wants hot milk, but we finished our milk earlier. I was hoping—"

She proffered a plastic cup, the kind with a lid and a perforated mouthpiece.

"Sure, honey," said Molly, accepting the cup. "Just take a seat. I won't be but a minute."

Molly went to the refrigerator, removed a half-gallon container of milk, and disappeared into the little kitchen that adjoined the reception area. I could see the young woman from where I sat, and she could see me. I smiled at the child in her arms. She didn't smile back, but peered out from under the safety of the older girl's chin before burying her face in her chest. I decided not to bother either of them and went back to finding interesting spots on the wall at which to stare. Eventually Molly returned with the hot milk, and the two children—because that's what they were—vanished back upstairs.

"Do I even want to know?" I asked when Molly returned.

"It's bad," she said. "But we've had worse. There's always worse. That's the hell of it. And we don't usually allow men on the premises after five, so your presence here probably threw her some. Don't take it personally. Sorry, where were we?"

"Annie, and the day she left the shelter."

"Right."

"I'd like to talk to the woman who saw her last. Is she still here?"

Molly nodded.

"Candice, but she likes being called Candy."

"Will she speak with me?"

"Probably, but you'll have to be patient. She's special . . ."

———

CANDY WAS IN HER late thirties. She wore pink bunny slippers, over-sized jeans, and a T-shirt that announced she would work for cookies. Her hair was red and unruly, and her chin was speckled with acne. Her eyes were slightly too small for her face, but she had a radiant smile. Had Molly not told me about her while we waited for her to come down, I might not have guessed that she had mild Down syndrome. Molly told me that women like Candy were often referred to as "high-functioning," but this was a phrase that was generally disliked in the Down community, as it implied a hierarchy among those with the condition. Candy was the daughter of the shelter's original founders. Both were now deceased, but Candy remained. She cleaned the rooms, helped around the kitchen, and provided company and consolation to those who needed it. As Molly put it, "Candy gives good hugs."

Candy took a seat on the couch in the office while Molly made her a mug of hot chocolate.

"Not too much marshmallow," warned Candy. "I'm watching my weight."

She patted her belly, but still looked disappointed when the hot chocolate arrived with a Weight Watcher's sprinkling of tiny marshmallows.

"Oh," she said. She poked disconsolately at the melting islands of pink and white. "Not many marshmallows."

Molly raised her eyes to heaven.

"You told me you were watching your weight," she said.

"I am watching my weight," said Candy. "But I'm not fat. It's all right. Don't worry."

She stuck out her lower lip and gave a long-suffering sigh. Molly went to the kitchen and returned with enough marshmallows to cover the entire surface of the hot chocolate and then some.

"Thank you," said Candy. "Very kind."

She slurped noisily at her drink, and surfaced with a chocolate mustache.

"Aaah. That's good."

Molly placed a hand on Candy's arm.

"Charlie here would like to ask you about Annie," she said.

"Annie?"

"Yes. You remember Annie."

Candy nodded.

"Annie was my friend."

Molly had said that Candy had been unusually fond of Annie, and that Annie, in turn, had been particularly good with Candy. Some of the women in the shelter found it harder to deal with Candy than others. They treated her like a defective, or a child. Annie did neither. She simply treated Candy as Candy.

"Do you remember when you saw her last?" I said.

"January twenty-second," said Candy. "A Tuesday."

"Can you tell me what you talked about?"

Candy's eyes welled up.

"She told me she was going away. Got a job. I was sad. Annie was my friend."

Molly patted her on the arm again.

"Did she say where the job was?" I asked.

"Prosperous." Candy struggled with the word slightly, so that it came out as "Prospuss."

"You're sure?"

"Yes. She said. She told me she was going to Prospuss. She had a job. Was going to clean, like Candy."

"And did she mention who had given her the job?"

Candy thought.

"No. They had a blue car."

"How do you know? Did you see them?"

"No. Annie told me."

"Candy is very interested in cars," Molly explained.

"I like to know colors," said Candy. "What color is your car?"

"I have two cars," I said.

"Two cars!" Candy said, clearly shocked. "What color?"

"One red, and one blue. I used to have a green car too, but—"

"Yes? But?"

"I didn't really like the color."

Candy considered this. She shook her head.

"I don't like green. Like red."

"Me too."

Candy grinned. We'd bonded. Clearly, anyone who preferred red cars to green could not be all bad.

"Annie didn't tell you the make of car, did she?" I said.

"No, just blue."

"And the people who owned it, did she tell you anything about them?"

"They were old."

She took another sip of her hot chocolate.

"How old?" I asked. "Older than I am?"

Candy giggled. "You're not old."

"So older?"

"I think so." She yawned. "Tired. Time for bed."

We were done. Candy stood to leave, carefully holding her mug of hot chocolate so that it didn't spill.

"Candy, is there anything else you can tell me about Annie?" I said. The blue car was something, but it wasn't much.

"Annie told me she'd write to me," said Candy. "She promised. But she didn't write."

She turned her attention back to Molly.

"Must go to Prospuss," said Candy. "Find Annie. Annie's my friend."

"Charlie is going to look for Annie," said Molly. "Aren't you, Charlie?"

"Yes," I said. "I'll look for Annie."

"Tell her Candy said she must write," said Candy. "Mustn't forget her friend Candy."

With that, she trotted off to her room. Molly and I said nothing else until we were sure she was gone.

"She would have written," said Molly. "She wouldn't have wanted to disappoint Candy."

She swallowed hard.

"If I'd been here when she left, I'd have made sure that she gave us details of where she was going. I'd have asked to meet these people who were offering her work. But all the full-time staff were at a meeting that day with the Department of Health and Human Services over on Griffin Street, and we just had volunteers manning the shelter. Volunteers, and Candy."

Anything I might have said would have sounded trite, so I said nothing. Instead, I took one of my business cards from my wallet and handed it to her.

"If you or Candy can think of anything else that might help me, or if anyone else comes around asking about Annie, I'd appreciate it if you'd give me a call. Also . . ."

"Yes?"

"I don't think Candy should talk too much about that blue car. I think it might be better if she kept it to herself."

"I understand. We didn't lie to Candy, did we? You are going to keep looking for Annie? I mean, I'd hire you myself if I could afford to."

"You forget: I work cheap."

This time she didn't smile.

"Somehow, I don't believe that's true. What you charge and how you work are two different things."

I shook her hand. "I'll be in touch."

Molly showed me to the door. As she opened it, there was movement behind us. Candy was sitting on the stairs, just out of sight of the office.

She was crying, crying beyond consolation.

———

I FOUND SHAKY IN his bed at the Oxford Street Shelter. They'd done their best to keep him comfortable while the injury to his head was healing. He still had a headache, and his scalp had begun to itch, but otherwise he was doing as well as could be expected for someone who had been hit over the skull with a liquor bottle. I put him in my car and took him to the Bear for a burger and a beer. When he was settled in his seat, with a rodeo burger on order and a Shipyard Old Thumper in a glass before him, and Cupcake Cathy had fussed over him some, I told him a little of the day I'd had. After all, I was working for him. I'd made him pay me a dollar while he was lying on the hospital gurney. One of the nurses had taken it amiss, and my reputation at Maine Medical was now probably lower than that of most ambulance chasers.

"So he definitely went to Prosperous?" said Shaky.

"He didn't just go there; he got run out of town. Twice. The first time politely, the second time less so."

"He could be a stubborn man," said Shaky.

"He was a bright one too," I said. "Brighter than I am, at least, because I'm still not sure what he was doing nosing around an old church."

"Do you believe what that cop told you?"

"I've no reason not to. The job Jude's daughter spoke of could have fallen through. She might have changed her mind about it, or that old couple, if they existed at all, could have reconsidered their Good Samaritanism while she left to get her bags. Or she might just have been unlucky."

"Unlucky?"

"She was a vulnerable woman living on the streets. There are men out there who'd regard someone like her as easy prey."

Shaky nodded and took a long sip of his beer.

"I know," he said. "I've met enough of them in my time, and they don't all sleep on mats on floors."

"You may be right," I said. "In my experience, the worst of them wear suits and drive nice, well-maintained vehicles. But one thing is certain: as far as the services in Bangor are concerned, Annie dropped off the radar on the day she spoke about that job. I went by the women's shelter on my way back down here, and nobody has seen or heard from her since then."

"And this woman, this Candy, she's certain Annie said she was going to Prosperous?"

"Yes, but that doesn't mean Prosperous is where she ended up."

"So what are you going to do?"

"Go back there. Look for a blue car. See what happens."

"Wow, good plan. You have it all worked out. And people pay you for that?"

"Not a lot," I said, pointedly. "And sometimes not at all."

XXVI

In the living room of Hayley Conyer's house, Morland steepled his hands over his face, closed his eyes, and made a prayer of thanks to a god in whom he did not believe. It was force of habit, and no more than that. It looked good for him to go to church on Sundays. All of the most influential citizens in Prosperous were members of one congregation or another. Some even believed. Just like their ancestors back in England who had carved faces into the walls of their church, their faith could encompass more than one deity. Morland was not of their kind. He no longer even knew what he believed in, apart from Prosperous itself. All he could say for sure was that no Christian god impinged on his consciousness.

He was weary from arguing, but at least his view had prevailed, for now. As the guardian of the church, it was Warraner and not Morland who had Hayley's ear in times of crisis, but on this occasion Morland had managed to sway Hayley. He had been helped by the absence of two members of the board: Luke Joblin was attending a Realtors' convention in Philadelphia, and Thomas Souleby was currently under observation at a sleep clinic in Boston, having recently received a diagnosis of sleep apnea. In times of crisis Hayley could act without a vote from the board, but Morland had convinced her that the situation wasn't that desperate. The detective was simply asking questions.

There was nothing to link the death of the girl's father to the town, and the girl herself was no more. Unless the detective could commune with the deceased, he would find his avenues of inquiry quickly exhausted.

Hayley Conyer poured the last of her tea into her cup. It must have been cold and unbearably strong by now, but she wasn't one to let things go to waste. To her right sat Warraner, his face frozen. That was the other thing: Warraner had wanted them to take action, but he couldn't specify what kind of action. Killing the detective wasn't an option, and Warraner had no solution of his own to offer. He just didn't like seeing Morland get his way. Warraner would rather have been the king of nothing than the prince of something.

"I'm still not entirely happy," said Warraner. "This man is a threat to us."

"Not yet," said Morland, for what seemed the hundredth time. He removed his hands from his face. "Not unless we make him a threat."

"We'll discuss it again when Thomas and Luke have returned," snapped Hayley. She seemed as weary of Warraner as Morland was. "In the meantime, I want to be informed the moment he returns to Prosperous, *if* he returns here. I don't want to have to wait to hear it from the pastor."

Warraner's face thawed into a smile. Morland didn't react. He simply wanted to be gone from the house. He stood and took his coat from the chair.

"If he comes back, you'll know," said Morland.

He was hungry. Alina would have done what she could to save some dinner for him, but it would still be dried to hell and back by now. He'd eat it, though, and not just because he was hungry. He'd have eaten it even if Hayley Conyer had force-fed him caviar and foie gras during their meeting. He'd eat it because his wife had prepared it for him.

"Good night," said Morland.

"Just one more thing, Chief," said Hayley, and Morland stiffened as surely as if she'd inserted a blade into the small of his back.

He turned. Even Warraner seemed curious to hear what it was she had to say.

"I want the girl's body moved," said Hayley.

Morland looked at her as though she were mad.

"You've got to be kidding."

"I'm far from kidding. This detective's presence in Prosperous has made me uneasy, and if that body is discovered we'll all be fucked."

Warraner looked shocked. Even Morland was surprised. He hadn't heard Hayley Conyer swear in a coon's age.

"I want the girl's remains taken beyond the town limits," she continued. "*Far* beyond. How you dispose of her is your own concern, but get her gone, do you understand?"

In that moment, Morland hated Hayley Conyer more than he had ever hated anyone before. He hated her, and he hated Prosperous.

"I understand," he said.

This time, he didn't call her a bitch when he was alone again. He had a stronger word for her instead, and he used it all the way home. He'd dig up the body the next day, just as he had been told, but he wouldn't do it alone, because fucking Harry Dixon would be right there alongside him.

"Fuck!" shouted Morland, as he drove. "Fuck! Fuck! Fuck!"

He slammed the steering wheel hard in time with each use of the word, and the wind tugged at the branches of the trees as around him the woods laughed.

CHAPTER

XXVII

There were three towns within a two-mile radius of Prosperous's limits. Only one, Dearden, was of any significant size; the other two were towns in the same way that Pluto used to be a planet, or a handful of guys standing at a crossroads counted as a crowd.

Every town has someone who is a royal pain in the ass. This role divides pretty evenly between the sexes, but the age profile is usually consistent: over forty, at least, and preferably older; usually single, or with the kind of spouse or partner who is either lost in hero worship or one step away from murder. If a meeting is held, they're at it. If change is in the air, they're against it. If you say it's black, they'll say it's white. If you agree that it's white, they'll reconsider their position. They've rarely held an elected position, or, if they once did, no one was crazy enough to reelect them. Their self-appointed role in life is to ensure that they're nobody's fool, and they want as many people as possible to know it. Because of them, things get done more slowly. Sometimes things don't get done at all. Very occasionally, they inadvertently do some good by preventing from happening that which might ultimately have proved to be unbeneficial or actively destructive to their community, but they manage to do so only on the basis that even a stopped clock is right twice a day.

If a town is sufficiently large, there may be many such persons, but Dearden was big enough to contain only a single such entity. His name was Euclid Danes, and even a cursory Internet search in connection with Dearden threw up Euclid's name with a frequency that might lead one to suspect that he was the only living soul in town. In fact, so omnipresent was Euclid Danes that even Dearden wasn't big enough to contain him, and his sphere of influence had extended to encompass parts of Prosperous too. Euclid Danes owned a number of acres between Prosperous and Dearden, and it appeared that he had made it his lifelong business to singlehandedly resist the expansion of Prosperous to the south. His land acted as a buffer between the towns, and he had steadfastly and successfully fought every attempt by the citizens of Prosperous to buy him, or force him, out. He didn't seem interested in money or reason. He wanted to keep his land, and if by doing so he irritated the hell out of the wealthy folk up the road, then so much the better.

Euclid Danes's house was the original bad-neighbor nightmare: poorly kept, with a yard that was a kissing cousin to wilderness and littered with pieces of unidentifiable machinery that, with a little work and a lot of chutzpah, might even have qualified as some form of modern sculpture. An original Volkswagen Beetle was in the drive. In an open garage beyond stood the skeleton of a second Beetle, scavenged for parts.

I parked and rang the doorbell. From somewhere at the back of the house came the sound of excited barking.

The door was opened by a stick-thin woman in a blue housecoat. A cigarette smoldered in her right hand. In her left she held a small mongrel puppy by the scruff of the neck.

"Yes?" she said.

"I was looking for Euclid Danes."

She took a drag on the cigarette. The puppy yawned.

"Jesus, what's he done now?" she said.

"Nothing. I just wanted to ask him a few questions."

"Why?"

"I'm a private investigator."

I showed her my identification. Even the puppy looked more impressed by it than she did.

"You sure he's not in trouble?"

"Not with me. Are you Mrs. Danes?"

This provoked a burst of laughter that deteriorated into a fit of coughing.

"Jesus Christ, no!" she said, once she'd recovered. "I'm his sister. There's nobody desperate enough to marry that poor sonofabitch, or if there is, then I don't want to meet her."

I couldn't see a wedding ring on her finger either. Then again, she was so thin that it would have been hard to make one fit, or, if it did, the weight would have unbalanced her. She was so skinny as to be almost sexless, and her hair was cut shorter than mine. If it hadn't been for the housecoat, and the pale twig legs that poked out from under her skirt, she could have passed for an elderly man.

"So, is Mr. Danes around?"

"Oh, he's around somewhere, just not here. He's on his throne, holding court. You know where Benny's is?"

"No."

"Head into town and take the first left after the intersection. Follow the smell of stale beer. When you find him, tell him to get his ass home. I'm cooking meat loaf. If he's not sitting at the table when it comes out of the oven, I'll feed it to the dogs."

"I'll be sure to let him know."

"Much appreciated." She held the puppy up at eye level. "You want to buy a puppy?"

"No, thank you."

"You want one for free?"

The puppy, seeming to understand that it was the object of discussion, wagged its tail hopefully. It was brown, with sleepy eyes.

"Not really."

"Damn."

"What'll you do with it?"

She looked the puppy in the eyes.

"Feed it meat loaf, I guess."

"Right."

She closed the door without saying another word. I remained where I was for a few moments, the way you do when you've just had something that might have passed for a conversation if you weren't paying attention, then got back into my car and went to look for Benny's.

———

BENNY'S WASN'T HARD TO find. Dearden was no metropolis, and there was only one intersection of any size at the heart of town. It didn't even have a signal, just a quartet of stop signs, and Benny's was the sole business on its street. Actually, Benny's was the sole *anything* on its street. Beyond it lay only woods. Benny's was a squat redbrick building whose sign had been provided by the Coca-Cola Company at least thirty years earlier, and was now faded and yellowed. It also lacked a possessive apostrophe. Maybe Benny didn't like to boast. If so, it was a wise move.

A certain odor comes with a bar that isn't cleaned regularly. All bars smell of it a little—it's a product of spilled beer that has in-grained itself into the floors and storage spaces, along with whatever chooses to propagate in old yeast—but Benny's smelled so strongly of it, even from outside, that birds flying above were at risk of alcohol-induced disorientation. Benny's had added an extra component to the stink by combining it with rancid grease: the extractors at the back of the building were caked with it. By the time I got to the door, Benny's had put its mark on me, and I knew that I'd end up stinking of the place all the way home, assuming my arteries didn't harden and kill me first.

Curiously, it didn't smell as bad inside, although that would have been difficult under the circumstances. Benny's was more of a restaurant than a bar, assuming you were prepared to be generous with your definition of a restaurant. An open kitchen lay behind the counter to the left, alongside a couple of beer taps that suggested microbrews were regarded as a passing fad. A menu board on the wall above had adjustable plastic letters and numbers arranged into the kinds of prices that hadn't changed since Elvis died, and the kinds of food choices that had helped to kill him. The tables were Formica, and the chairs wood and vinyl. Christmas tree lights hung on all four walls just below the ceiling, providing most of the illumination, and the décor was old beer signs and mirrors.

And, you know, it was kind of cool, once my eyes had adjusted to the gloom.

Music was playing low: "Come Together," followed by "Something." *Abbey Road.* A big man in an apron stood at the grill, flipping burgers.

"How you doin'," he said. "Waitress will be with you in a minute. How is it out there?"

"It's cold. Clear skies, though."

"Weather Channel says it could go down to ten degrees tonight."

"At least you're warm in here."

He was sweating over the grill. Nobody was going to have to salt a hamburger.

"I always got insulation."

He patted his massive belly, and I instantly recalled Candy, back in the Tender House in Bangor, watching her weight and counting marshmallows. It reminded me of why I was here.

A compact middle-aged woman with huge hair materialized out of the darkness. I had already begun to make out half a dozen figures scattered around, but it would have taken a flashlight shined on their faces to discern their features.

"Table, hon?" said the woman.

"I was looking for Euclid Danes," I said. "His sister told me he might be here."

"He's in his office," she said. "Table at the back. She send you to bring him home?"

"Apparently she's cooking meat loaf."

"I can believe it. She can't cook nothing else. Get you a drink?"

"Coffee, please."

"I'll make it extra strong. You'll need it if you're going to stay awake listening to his ramblings."

Euclid Danes looked like his sister in male drag. They might even have been twins. He was wearing a shabby blue suit and a red tie, just in case he was suddenly required to interfere in someone else's business. The table before him was covered with newspapers, clippings, random documents, assorted pens and highlighters, and a half-eaten plate of french fries. He didn't look up as I stood over him, so lost was he in annotating a sheaf of reports.

"Mr. Danes?" I said.

He raised his right hand while the fountain pen in his left continued to scrawl across the page. His notes were longer than the report itself. I could almost hear the rise of frustrated sighs at some future meeting as Euclid Danes stood, cleared his throat, and began to speak.

A long time went by. My coffee came. I added milk. I took a sip. Oceans rose and fell, and mountains collapsed to dust. Finally, Euclid Danes finished his work, capped his pen, and aligned it with the paper on which he had been working. He clasped his hands and looked up at me with young, curious eyes. There was mischief in them. Euclid Danes might have been the bane of life in Dearden, but he was smart enough to know it, and bright enough to enjoy it.

"How can I help you?" he said.

"You mind if I take a seat?"

"Not at all." He waved at a chair.

"Your french fries?" I said, pointing at the plate.

"They were."

"Your sister is going to be annoyed that you've eaten."

"My sister is always annoyed, whether I eat or not. Is she now hiring detectives to monitor my habits?"

I tried not to show surprise.

"Did she call ahead?"

"To warn me? She wouldn't do that. She's probably at home praying that you make me disappear. No, I read the papers and watch the news, and I have a good memory for faces. You're Charlie Parker, out of Portland."

"You make me sound like a gunfighter."

"Yes, I do, don't I?" he said, and his eyes twinkled. "So how can I help you, Mr. Parker?"

The waitress appeared and freshened my coffee.

"I'd like to talk to you about Prosperous," I said.

———

CHIEF MORLAND PICKED UP Harry Dixon at his home. He didn't inform Harry as to why he needed him, just told him to get his coat and a pair of gloves. Morland already had a spade, his pickax, and flashlights in the car. He was tempted to ask Bryan Joblin to join them, but instead told him to wait with Harry's wife. Morland didn't want her to panic and do something stupid. He could see the way she was looking at him while Harry went to fetch his coat, as if he was ready to put her husband in the ground, but it hadn't come to that, not yet.

"It's all right," said Morland. "I'll bring him back in one piece. I just need his help."

Erin Dixon didn't reply. She sat at the kitchen counter, staring him down. She won, or he let her win. He wasn't sure which. In either event, he simply looked away.

Bryan Joblin was sitting by the fire, drinking a PBR and watching some dumb quiz show. Bryan was useful because he didn't think much, and he did as he was told. A purpose could always be found for men like that. Empires were built on their backs.

"How long is he going to stay here?" said Erin, pointing at Bryan with her chin. If Bryan heard her, he didn't respond. He took another sip of his beer and tried to figure out on which continent the Republic of Angola was situated.

"Just until the next girl is found," said Morland. "How's that coming along?"

"I've driven around some, as has Harry," said Erin. "It would be easier if we could move without that fool tagging along with us everywhere."

Bryan Joblin still didn't react. He was lost in his show. He'd guessed Asia, and was smacking the arm of his chair in frustration. Bryan would never serve on the board of selectmen, not unless every other living thing in Prosperous—cats and dogs included—predeceased him.

Morland knew that Bryan alternated his vigils between Harry and his wife. He was currently helping Harry out with an attic conversion on the outskirts of Bangor. Bryan might not have been smart, but he was good with his hands once he worked up the energy to act. In practical terms, there wasn't much Bryan could do if either Harry or Erin decided to try something dumb while he was with the other spouse, but his presence was a reminder of the town's power. It was psychological pressure, albeit with a physical threat implied.

"As soon as we have a girl, he'll be gone," said Morland. "You brought him on yourselves. You brought all of this on yourselves."

Harry had reappeared with his coat. He'd taken his time. Morland wondered what he'd been doing.

Harry patted his wife gently on the shoulder as he passed her. She reached out to grasp his hand, but it was too late. He had moved on.

"You have any idea how long we're going to be?" he asked Morland.

"Couple of hours. You got gloves?"

Harry removed a pair from his pocket. He always had gloves. They were part of his uniform.

"Then let's go," said Morland. "Sooner we get started, sooner we finish."

———

EUCLID DANES ASKED ME why I was interested in Prosperous.

"I'd prefer not to say," I told him. I didn't want the details to end up in one of Euclid's files, ready to be raised at the next meeting.

"You don't trust me?" said Euclid.

"I don't know you."

"So how did you find out about me?"

"Mr. Danes, you're all over the Internet like some kind of cyber rash. I'm surprised that the residents of Prosperous haven't paid to have you taken out."

"They don't much care for me up there," he admitted.

"I'm curious to know what your beef is with that town. You seem to be expending a lot of energy to insert splinters under the fingernails of its citizenry."

"Is that what they are—citizenry?" he said. "I'd say 'cultists' was a better word to use."

I waited. I was good at waiting. Euclid pulled a sheet of blank paper from a sheaf and drew a circle at the center of the page.

"This is Prosperous," he said. He then added a series of arrows pointing out toward a number of smaller circles. "Here are Dearden, Thomasville, and Lake Plasko. Beyond them, you have Bangor, Augusta, Portland. Prosperous sends its people out—to work, to learn, to worship—but it's careful about whom it admits. It needs fresh blood because it doesn't want to start breeding idiots in a shallow gene pool, so in the last half-century or so it's allowed its children to marry outsiders, but it keeps those new family units at arm's length until it's sure they're compatible with the town. Houses aren't sold to those who weren't born in Prosperous, or businesses either. The same goes for land, or what little the town has left to develop. Which is where I come in."

"Because Prosperous wants to expand," I said. "And you're in the way."

"Give that man a candy bar. The original founders of the town chose a location bounded by lakes and marshland and deep woods, apart from a channel of land to the southeast. Basically, they created their own little fortress, but now it's come back to bite them. If they want their children to continue to live in Prosperous, they need space on which to build, and the town has almost run out of land suitable for development. It's not yet critical, but it's getting there, and Prosperous always plans ahead."

"You make it sound like the town is a living thing."

"Isn't it?" said Euclid. "All towns are a collection of organisms forming a single entity, like a jellyfish. In the case of Prosperous, the controlling organisms are the original founding families, and their bloodlines have remained unpolluted. They control the board of selectmen, the police force, the school board, every institution of consequence. The same names recur throughout the history of Prosperous. They're the guardians of the town.

"And, just like a jellyfish, Prosperous has long tentacles that trail. Its people worship at mainstream churches, although all in towns outside Prosperous itself, because Prosperous only has room for one church. It places children of the founding families in the surrounding towns, including here in Dearden. It gives them money to run for local and state office, to support charities, to help out with donations to worthwhile causes when the state can't or won't. After a couple of generations, it gets so that people forget that these are creatures of Prosperous, and whatever they do aims to benefit Prosperous first and foremost. It's in their nature, from way back when they first came here as the remnants of the Family of Love. You know what the Family of Love is?"

"I've read up on it," I said.

"Yeah, Family of Love, my old ass. There was no love in those people. They weren't about to become no Quakers. I think that's why they left England. They were killing to protect themselves, and they had blood on their hands. Either they left or they were going to be buried by their enemies."

"Pastor Warraner claims that may just have been propaganda. The Familists were religious dissenters. The same lies were spread about Catholics and Jews."

"Warraner," said Euclid, and the name was like a fly that had somehow entered his mouth and needed to be spat from the tip of his tongue. "He's no more a pastor than I am. He can call himself what he wants, but there's no good in him. And, to correct you on another point, the Familists weren't just dissenters; they were infiltrators. They hid among established congregations and paid lip service to beliefs that weren't their own. I don't believe that's changed much down the years. They're still an infection. They're parasites, turning the body against itself."

This was a metaphor I had heard used before, under other circumstances. It evoked unpleasant associations with people who unwittingly sheltered old spirits inside them, ancient angels waiting for the moment when they could start to consume their hosts from within.

Unfortunately for Euclid Danes, his talk of jellyfish and parasites and bloodlines made him sound like a paranoid obsessive. Perhaps he was. Euclid guessed the direction of my thoughts.

"Sounds crazy, doesn't it?" he said. "Sounds like the ravings of a madman?"

"I wouldn't put it that strongly."

"You'd be in the minority, but it's easy enough to prove. Dearden is decaying, but compared to Thomasville it's like Las Vegas. Our kids are leaving because there's no work, and no hope of any. Businesses are closing, and those that stay open sell only stuff that old farts like me need. The towns in this whole region are slowly dying, all except Prosperous. It's suffering, because everywhere is suffering, but not like we are. It's insulated. It's protected. It sucks the life out of the surrounding towns to feed itself. Good fortune, luck, divine providence—call it what you will, but there's only so much of it to go around, and Prosperous has taken it all."

The waitress with the big hair came by to offer me yet more coffee. I was the only person in the bar who seemed to be drinking it, and she clearly didn't want to waste the pot. I had a long ride home. It would help me stay awake. I drank it quickly, though. I didn't think there was much more that Euclid Danes could tell me.

"Are there others like you?" I asked.

"Wackjobs? Paranoiacs? Fantasists?"

"How about 'dissenters'?"

He smiled at the co-opting of the word. "Some. Enough. They keep quieter about it than I do, though. It doesn't pay to cross the folk up in Prosperous. It starts with small things—a dog going missing, damage to your car, maybe a call to the IRS to say that you're taking in a little work on the side to cover your bar tab—but then it escalates. It's not only the economy that has led to businesses closing around here, and families leaving."

"But you've stayed."

He picked up his fountain pen and unscrewed the cap, ready to return to his papers. I glimpsed the name on the pen: Tibaldi. I looked it up later. They started at about four hundred dollars and went up to forty thousand. The one that Euclid Danes used had a lot of gold on it.

"I look like the crazy old coot who lives in a run-down house with more dogs than bugs and a sister who can only cook meat loaf," he said. "But my brother was a justice of the Massachusetts Supreme Judicial Court, my nephews and nieces are lawyers and bankers, and there's nothing anyone can teach me about playing the markets. I have money, and a degree of influence. I think that's why they hate me so much: because, except for an accident of birth, I could have been one of them. Even though I'm not, they still feel that I should side with wealth and privilege, because I'm wealthy and privileged myself.

"So Prosperous can't move against me, and it can't frighten me. All it can do is wait for me to die, and even then those bastards will find that I've tied so much legal ribbon around my land that humanity itself will be extinct before they find a way to build on it. It's been good talking with you, Mr. Parker. I wish you luck with whatever it is that you're investigating."

He lowered his head and began writing again. I was reminded of the end of *Willy Wonka & the Chocolate Factory*, when Gene Wilder dismisses Charlie and tries to lose himself in his papers until the boy returns the Everlasting Gobstopper as a token of recompense. I hadn't shared all that I knew with Euclid, because I was cautious. I had underestimated and misjudged him, although I thought Euclid might have done the same with me.

"A homeless man named Jude hanged himself down in Portland not long ago," I said. "He was looking for his daughter before he died. Her name was Annie Broyer. He was convinced that she'd gone to Prosperous. There's still no trace of her. I think she's dead, and I'm not alone in believing it. I also think that she may have met her end in Prosperous."

Euclid stopped writing. The cap went back on the pen. He straightened his tie and reached for his coat.

"Mr. Parker, why don't you and I take a ride?"

———

IT WAS ALREADY DARK. I had followed Euclid Danes to the northwestern limit of the town of Dearden. His fence marked the boundary. Beyond it lay woodland: part of the township of Prosperous.

THE WOLF IN WINTER

"Why haven't they built here?" I asked. "The land's suitable. It would just be a matter of knocking down some trees."

Euclid took a small flashlight from his pocket and shined it on the ground. There was a hole in the earth, perhaps eighteen inches in diameter, or a little more. It was partly obscured by undergrowth and tree roots.

"What is it?" I asked.

"I don't know. I've found three of them over the years, but there may be more. I know for sure that there are a couple around that old church of theirs. I haven't seen them myself for some time—as you can imagine, I'm persona non grata in Prosperous—but I have it on good authority from others who've been there."

"You think the ground is unstable?"

"Might be. I'm no expert."

I was no expert either, but this wasn't karst terrain, not as far as I was aware. I hadn't heard of any Florida-style sinkholes appearing in the area. The hole was curious, unsettling even, but that might have been a vague atavistic dread of small, enclosed places beneath the earth, and the fear of collapse they brought with them. I wasn't claustrophobic, but then I'd never been trapped in a hole below the ground.

"What made it?"

Euclid killed the flashlight.

"Ah, that's the interesting question, isn't it?" he said. "I'll leave that one with you. All I know is that I have meat loaf waiting, with a side of indigestion to follow. I'd ask you to join me, but I like you."

He began to walk back to his car. I stayed by the fence. I could still make out the hole, a deeper blackness against the encroaching dark. I felt an itching on my scalp, as though bugs were crawling through my hair.

Euclid called back a final piece of advice when he reached his car. He was driving a beautiful old '57 Chevy Bel Air in red. "I like them to know I'm coming," he had told me. Now he stood beside its open door, a chill breeze toying with his wispy hair and his wide tie.

"Good luck with those people up there," he said. "Just watch where you put your feet."

He turned on the ignition and kept the Chevy's lights trained on the ground in front of me until I was safely back at my own car. I followed him as far as his house, then continued south, and home.

———

ON THE OUTSKIRTS OF Prosperous, Lucas Morland and Harry Dixon were staring at another hole in the ground. At first Harry had been struck by the absurd yet terrible thought that the girl had actually dug herself out, just as he had dreamed, and what had crawled from that grave was something much worse than a wounded young woman who could name names. But then their flashlights had picked out the big paw prints on the scattered earth, and the broken bones, and the teeth marks on them. They found the head under an old oak, most of the face gnawed away.

"I told you," said Harry to Morland. "I told you I saw a wolf."

Morland said nothing, but began gathering up what he could retrieve of the remains. Harry joined him. They couldn't find all of the girl. The wolf, or some other scavenger, had carried parts of her away. There was an arm missing, and most of one leg.

Evidence, thought Morland. It's evidence. It would have to be found. For now, all he could do was put what they collected of the girl into more of the plastic sheeting, dump it in the car, and refill the grave. Nothing like this, nothing so terrible, so unlucky, had happened in Prosperous for generations. If the girl hadn't run . . . If Dixon and his bitch wife hadn't let her escape . . .

Morland wanted to punch Harry. He wanted to kill him. It was the Dixons' fault, all of it. Even if Harry and Erin located a suitable girl, Morland would find a way to make them pay. Hell, if Erin herself wasn't so fucking old and worn they could have used her. But no, the town didn't feed on its own. It never had. Those from within who transgressed had always been dealt with in a different way. There were rules.

They taped up the plastic, forming three packages of body parts. After that they drove north for an hour, far beyond Prosperous, and reburied what was left of the girl. The stench of her stayed with them both all the way to town. Later, back in their own homes, both men scrubbed and showered, but still they could smell her.

Erin Dixon knocked at the bathroom door fifteen minutes after the shower had stopped running, and her husband had still not emerged. Bryan Joblin had fallen asleep in the armchair by the fireplace. She had thought about killing him. She was thinking about killing a lot lately.

"Harry?" she called. "Are you okay?"

From inside the bathroom she heard the sound of weeping. She tried the door. It was unlocked.

Her husband was sitting on the edge of the tub, a towel wrapped around his waist and his face buried in his hands. She sat beside him and held him to her.

"Can you smell it?" he asked her.

She sniffed him, inhaling the scent of his hair and his skin. She detected only soap.

"You smell fine," she said. "You want to tell me what happened?"

"No."

She went to the bathroom doorway and listened. She could still hear the sound of Joblin snoring. She closed the door and returned to her husband, but she kept her voice to a whisper, just in case.

"Marie Nesbit called me earlier on my cell phone, while that asshole was snoring his head off," she said.

Marie was Erin's closest friend. She worked as a secretary at the Town Office, and was from one of the founding families, just like the

Dixons. Her husband, Art, was an alcoholic, but gentle and sad, for the most part, rather than violent. Erin had long provided her with a sympathetic ear.

"She told me that a detective came to town asking about the girl."

Harry had stopped weeping.

"Police?"

"No, a private investigator, like on TV."

"Did she say who had hired him?"

"No. She only overheard the start of what he had to say. She didn't want to be seen spying."

"What was his name?"

"Parker. Charlie Parker. I googled him on my phone, then erased the history. He's been in the newspapers."

So that's why Morland wanted the girl's body moved. The detective had come, and Morland had gotten scared. No, not just Morland. He might have been chief, but Morland did what he was told to do by the board. The order to dig up the corpse had probably come from Hayley Conyer herself, but a wolf had reached it first. First the girl, then the detective, now the wolf. The town was starting to unravel.

"Harry," said Erin. "I've decided: I'm not going to find them another girl."

He nodded. How could they, after setting the last one free? How could a couple who had wished for, but never been given, their own daughter collude in the killing of someone else's child?

"They'll be monitoring the detective," said Harry. "That's how they work. We can't contact him, not yet. Maybe not ever."

"So what will we do?"

"It's like I said. We'll leave, and soon. After that, we'll decide."

Erin gripped his hand. He squeezed hers in return.

"When?"

"A couple of days. No more than that."

"Promise?"

"Promise."

She kissed him. His mouth opened beneath hers, but before they could go any further they were disturbed by a knock on the door and Bryan Joblin said, "Hey, are you two in there?"

Erin went to the door and unlocked it. Joblin stood bleary-eyed before her, smelling of his cheap beer. He took in Erin, and Harry standing behind her, his towel around his waist, his body angled to hide his now diminishing hard-on.

"Havin' some fun?" said Joblin. "Shit, you got a bedroom. We all got to use this room, and I need to take a piss."

XXVIII

C hief Morland rarely dreamed. He was curious about this fact. He understood that everybody dreamed, even if they didn't always remember their dreams when they woke, but they could retain details of some of them at least. His wife dreamed a lot, and she had a recall of her dreams that bordered on the exhaustive. Morland could bring to mind only a handful of occasions on which he had awakened with some memory of his dreams. He couldn't associate them with any particularly difficult or traumatic periods in his life. It wasn't as though his father died, and that night he dreamed, or he was plagued by nightmares, following the time he nearly sent his car into a ditch at high speed after skidding on black ice, and was certain that his moment had come. He couldn't pinpoint that kind of cause and effect.

But he dreamed on the night that he and Harry Dixon found the girl's scattered remains. He'd gone to bed late because he'd been thinking about the wolf. He should have believed Dixon on that first night, when he claimed to have seen an animal on the road. He should have connected the sighting with the reports that had come to him of garbage bags torn apart, and Elspeth Ramsay's missing dog, but his mind was on other matters, like a girl with a hole in her chest, and the Dixons and their tales of bolts and wood splinters, and the slow decline in the fortunes of his town that had to be arrested.

And it had been decades since a wolf was last seen in the state. The St. Lawrence formed a natural barrier, keeping them in Canada, and that suited Morland just fine. He was aware that some in Maine were in favor of the reintroduction of wolves, arguing that they'd been an important part of the ecosystem until they were slaughtered out of existence. You could make the same argument for dinosaurs and saber-toothed cats, as far as Morland was concerned, but that wasn't a reason to bring them back. What might happen to a kid who got lost in the woods, maybe separated from parents who were hiking the trails? What about an adult stumbling and breaking a leg, and suddenly finding himself surrounded by a wolf pack—what would happen then? The same thing that happened to Elspeth Ramsay's pet, perhaps, or the same thing that happened to the girl, except that at least she was dead when the wolf started to gnaw on her. The world was full of do-gooders, but it was left to men like Morland to clean up their mess.

He poured himself a finger of bourbon. Just as he rarely dreamed, so too he only occasionally consumed hard liquor. He wondered if the two might not be connected. Didn't matter. Tonight was different. Tonight he'd gone to dig up a body and found that a wolf had done it for him, forcing him to scrabble in the dirt for bone, and rotting meat, and scraps of plastic and cloth. He'd seen dead bodies before—suicides, accidental shootings, traffic collisions, and the regular actions of mortality that called for the local cops to break a window or kick in a door because someone had been selfish enough to pass away without giving prior notice to his friends, relatives, and neighbors. Morland had never killed anyone himself, unlike his old man, but Daniel Morland had prepared his son well for the responsibility that would eventually pass to him when he became chief of police, and Morland had been surprised at how dispassionately he'd viewed the girl's body following the shooting. It reminded him of the sense of passing sadness he felt upon looking down at a deer felled during the course of a hunt.

He took a mouthful of bourbon—not a sip, a mouthful. This wasn't a night for sipping. He closed his eyes and briefly tried to pretend that he was chief of police in a normal town, but it didn't take. A "normal town"—his own words made him laugh aloud, and he covered his mouth like a child who feared being caught doing something naughty. The only thing normal about Prosperous was the way it proved that, over time, individuals could habituate themselves to the most appalling behavior. So many of the townsfolk, even the ones most closely involved in its secrets, regarded themselves as "good" people, and not without reason. They looked after their families, and they abided, for the most part, by the law. Politically, Prosperous was the most liberal town in this part of Maine: Proposition 1, to allow same-sex marriage in the state, had passed by as much of a majority in Prosperous as it had in Portland, and the town leaned slightly Democrat or liberal independent in elections. But the older citizens of Prosperous understood that the town was built on a lie, or a truth too terrible to be named. Some of them preferred to pretend not to know, and nobody begrudged them their show of ignorance. They weren't suited to leadership. In the end, it always came down to the original families, to the founders. They looked after the town for all.

Morland finished his drink. He should have called Hayley Conyer to tell her about the wolf and the turmoil at the grave site, but he didn't. He'd had his fill of Hayley. The call could wait until morning. Tomorrow he would see about putting together a hunting party, and they'd find the wolf and kill it quietly. Thomas Souleby had an old hound that might be useful in picking up the wolf's scent. Morland didn't know much about hunting wolves, apart from what he'd learned that evening from Google, but opinion seemed to be divided on the usefulness of packs of dogs in a hunt. Some said that a wolf would run from them, but in Wisconsin a couple of hundred dead hunting dogs said otherwise. Elspeth Ramsay's missing mongrel suggested that this wolf wasn't above taking down a domestic animal if it had the chance. No matter; Prosperous wasn't overflowing with the kinds of dogs that might be useful in a confrontation with a wolf anyway, not unless he had missed a news flash about the hidden strength of labradoodles. Trapping seemed the most effective way to deal with the animal, but they might be lucky enough to get it under their guns first, although right now luck was in short supply.

He went to bed. He kissed his wife. She mumbled something in her sleep.

He dreamed.

In his dream, Prosperous was burning.

———

THE HEADLINES IN THE newspapers in the days that followed were all very similar: "Triple Tragedy Strikes Small Town," "Maine Town Mourns Its Dead," "Trouble Comes in Threes for Close-Knit Community," . . .

In Afghanistan, a UH-60 Black Hawk helicopter carrying four U.S. "military advisers" and crew went down in Kandahar. Three of the men survived the crash, which was caused by a mechanical failure, but they didn't survive the firefight with the Taliban that followed. In the shadowy corners of the Internet, a photograph circulated of three severed heads placed in a line on the sand. Two of them were identified as Captain Mark Tabart and Staff Sergeant Jeremy Cutter, both natives of Prosperous, Maine.

On the same day that the two soldiers died, a woman named Valerie Gillson rounded a bend between Dearden and Prosperous and saw a wounded fawn lying in the middle of the road. The animal appeared to have been struck by a vehicle, for its back legs were twisted and broken. It scrabbled at the road with its front hooves and thrashed its head in agony. Valerie stepped from her car. She couldn't leave the animal in distress, and she couldn't run it over to put it out of its agony: she'd never be able to drive her car again. She took out her cell phone and called the police department in Prosperous. Chief Morland would know what to do. The number rang, and Marie Nesbit, who was on dispatch duty that day, picked up the call.

"Hi, Marie? This is Valerie Gillson. Yes, I'm fine, but I'm about a mile south of town and there's a wounded deer in the middle of the road. It's in a lot of pain, and I don't—"

She stopped talking. She had just noticed that there was something tangled around the back legs of the deer. It looked like wire. No, not wire: roots, or thick briars—she wasn't sure which. They extended into the undergrowth. It was almost as if the wounded deer had been placed there as bait. Instinctively, she raised her phone and took a photograph of the deer's legs.

She heard Marie's voice asking if she was okay.

"Sorry, Marie, I just noticed—"

Valerie Gillson never got to tell Marie what she had just seen, because at that moment a logging-company truck took the bend behind her just a fraction too fast. The driver swerved to avoid the car and struck Valerie instead, killing her instantly. Her cell phone was recovered in the aftermath. On it was the last photograph that Valerie had taken: the hindquarters of a fawn, its legs entwined with dark roots.

But of the animal itself there was no sign.

And in the gunsmithery at the back of his store Ben Pearson was carrying his favorite hunting rifle to the workbench. The gun was the same one that he had used to kill Annie Broyer. Chief Morland had advised him to get rid of it, and Ben knew that it made sense to do as Morland said. The bullet had gone straight through the girl, and Ben hadn't been able to find any trace of it, try as he might. The rifle linked him to murder, and it didn't matter how much time and effort he'd put into customizing it so that there wasn't a gun to rival it for miles; it had to be taken apart and destroyed.

He had been thinking a lot about the dead girl. He didn't regret what he'd done. If she'd escaped, that would have been the end for all of them, but he had a lingering sense of transgression. The girl hadn't been his to kill. She had been sourced for a particular reason. She was the town's girl. She belonged to Prosperous, and her life was the town's to take. By killing her, he had deprived the town of its due. That had never happened before, not in the long history of the community. Ben feared that if another girl wasn't found soon there could be repercussions. He would bury the rifle in the woods. It would represent his own small sacrifice, an act of recompense.

For the first, and last, time, Ben stumbled in his workshop, a place that he had known for decades. As he fell, his finger slipped inside the trigger guard. The rifle should not have been loaded. As far as Ben was concerned, the rifle *could* not have been loaded. He was obsessively careful about such matters, and never left a round chambered.

The bullet tore through his chest, nicking his heart.

And he held his beloved rifle in his arms as he died.

XXIX

I had been anticipating the call from Euclid Danes ever since the first reports began to link the deaths of the soldiers in Afghanistan to the town of Prosperous. A traffic fatality and an apparently accidental shooting in the same town in the space of twenty-four hours would have been unlikely to attract quite the same degree of media interest, but the addition of the military casualties, and the manner in which the soldiers had died, brought attention to Prosperous, and not just from the local and state outlets. The nationals turned their gaze on the town, and it was featured on the Web sites of the *New York Times* and *USA Today*. The task of dealing with the media fell to Hayley Conyer, as the head of the board of selectmen. (One unfortunate local TV reporter inadvertently referred to it as the board of "selectpersons" within earshot of Conyer, and was lucky to escape with his life.) She handled her role well. She was polite, dignified, and distant. She gave the reporters just enough to keep them from prying further, but in repeating the same sound bites over and over, along with ongoing pleas for privacy, she managed to dull their curiosity. Prosperous weathered the storm of attention for a few days, and then subsided into a traumatized calm.

Euclid Danes called me on the third day, when Prosperous was already starting to slide from prominence in the bulletins.

"Looks like Prosperous has emptied its barrel of good fortune," he said. He didn't sound triumphant, but concerned.

"It happens," I said.

"Not to Prosperous."

"I guess they'll just have to deal with it."

"That's what worries me. I received a call early this morning. There was no caller ID. The voice was male, but I didn't recognize it. He told me that my bullshit wasn't going to be tolerated any longer, and if I didn't keep my mouth shut I'd be put in a hole in the ground, and my bitch sister too. His words, not mine. I like my sister, apart from her cooking. I was also warned not to go shooting my mouth off to strangers in Benny's."

"Somebody ratted you out."

"Money's scarce in Dearden, so I wouldn't be surprised if someone was being paid a little on the side to keep an eye on me, but I thought you should know about the call. With all that's happened over the last day or two, Prosperous is going to be in pain, and wounded animals lash out."

"I'll bear that in mind. Thank you, Mr. Danes."

Euclid Danes said goodbye and hung up.

I waited until the remains of the soldiers were repatriated, and the bodies laid in the ground, before I returned to Prosperous.

————

IT WAS PASTOR WARRANER'S daughter who alerted him to the presence of a man in the cemetery.

Warraner had almost finished the final detailing on the last of the kitchen cabinets. It was an out-of-town order from a banker and his wife in Rockland, and they hadn't even blinked at his estimate, even though he'd added a premium of twenty percent to what was already an expensive quote. The recent tragedies, and their implications for the town, would not force him to miss his deadline. He was already a week ahead when the deaths occurred, for which he was grateful; he could not work well with fear in his heart, and his pace had slowed during Prosperous's recent troubles.

The board was scheduled to meet the following evening, now that the media circus had collapsed its tents and departed to seek out new miseries and misfortunes. Warraner had pressed for an earlier conclave, but Hayley Conyer had resisted. The presence of the newspapers and TV cameras, and the unwelcome attention they brought on Prosperous, had disturbed her, adding to her shock and grief at the four deaths. She and Ben Pearson had been close, even though their personalities had differed vastly. There was an element of the Brahmin to Hayley, while Ben had been an earthy Mainer through and through. Unlike so many others in Prosperous, Ben Pearson had no fear of Hayley Conyer, and she had admired his independence of thought. It made her respect his opinion more than those of the other board members, and she usually tended to listen when he disagreed with her, and adapt her views and actions accordingly.

Now there was a vacancy on the board. Under ordinary circumstances, the remaining members would have come up with the names of suitable candidates and presented them to the townsfolk for rubber-stamping, but Prosperous was in crisis and this was not the time for an election. The board would continue with only five members, and Morland and Warraner would remain as observers who could offer advice and arguments but were still not entitled to vote.

The soldiers, along with Valerie Gillson and Ben Pearson, were buried in the new cemetery to the south. Nobody had been interred in the grounds of the old church since the end of the last century, not even deceased members of the senior families, whose surnames already adorned so many stones in the churchyard. It was Warraner's father who had decreed that the cemetery was now closed to interments, and nobody had questioned his decision. The only reason he had given was this:

Why risk disturbing what is at rest?

In recent days his son had issued an even more restrictive edict. The cemetery and church were out of bounds to all. Nobody was to trespass there, and while the media was in town Morland and his deputies—aided by the most trustworthy of the younger citizens— had maintained a twenty-four-hour vigil to ensure that visitors and reporters were kept away. Had Warraner been asked for a reason, he would have given this one:

Why risk disturbing further what is no longer at rest?

Now here was his youngest daughter telling him that a man was walking among the stones, and taking photographs of the church with his phone. Warraner was so incensed that he didn't even go to the house to get a coat but ran in his shirtsleeves through the woods, ignoring the cold, ignoring, too, the branches that pulled at him even as he recalled the final photograph on Valerie Gillson's cell phone, the image of a deer with its legs bound by briars, a deer that had been crippled and laid out as bait. . . .

He burst from the woods and saw the intruder.

"Hey!" he cried. "That's private property, and sacred ground. You've no right to be in there."

The stranger turned, and at the sight of him Pastor Warraner im- mediately understood that the town's troubles had just increased considerably.

———

I WATCHED WARRANER AS he came to a halt at the iron railing that surrounded the cemetery. He was breathing heavily, and a scratch on his neck was bleeding into his shirt collar.

"What are you doing here?" he asked.

I walked toward him. He watched my progress carefully.

"Same as last time," I said. "Trying to find a missing girl."

"She's not in this place, and you're disturbing the peace of the dead."

I sidestepped a tilting stone cross. The names and dates on it were so old and faded as to be entirely illegible.

"Really? I've found that it takes a lot to wake the dead, unless some were never quite asleep to begin with."

"This is neither the time nor the place for mockery, Mr. Parker. Our town has been through a difficult period."

"I'm aware of that, Mr. Warraner," I said. "And I'm entirely serious."

I was facing him now. His hands gripped the railing so tightly that his knuckles showed white against his skin. I turned to the right and continued walking, forcing him to keep pace with me.

"The gate is to your left," he said.

"I know. That's how I got in."

"It's locked."

"It *was* locked. I found it open."

"You're lying."

"I suppose you could call Chief Morland and ask him to dust it for fingerprints. Or you could just buy a better lock."

"I fully intend to call Chief Morland," said Warraner. "I'll have you arrested for trespassing."

His hands searched his pockets for his cell phone but came up empty. I offered him mine.

"Feel free to call, but I was planning to pay him another visit anyway, just as soon as I've finished here."

I saw that Warraner was tempted to take my phone, but even he could appreciate the absurdity of doing so. The threat of police involvement was of limited effectiveness if the person being threatened was only a middleman away from calling the cops on himself.

"What do you want, Mr. Parker?" he said.

I paused beside a hole in the ground. It was similar to the one that Euclid Danes had pointed out to me close to the edge of his own land.

"I was wondering what this might be?"

I had stumbled across the hole by accident—literally; I had almost broken my ankle in it.

"It's a fox den," he said.

"Really?"

I knelt and examined it. An active den usually retained signs of the animal's comings and goings, but this had none. The ground around it was undisturbed.

"It's big for a fox hole," I said. "And I don't see any sign of foxes."

"It's an old den," said Warraner. Hostility flowed from him in waves.

"Do you have many old dens around here?"

"Possibly. I've never taken the time to count them. For the last time, I want you to leave this place. Now!"

If we'd both been nine years old and in a schoolyard I could have asked him to make me, or inquired about what he might do if I refused, but that didn't seem appropriate in a cemetery, and I'd annoyed him enough for now. He tracked me back to the gate and examined the lock once I was back on the right side of the fence. I hadn't been forced to break the lock; two decades of friendship with Angel had taught me the rudiments of picking. Warraner wrapped the chain from gate to fence and secured it.

"Do you want to follow me to the police department?" I said.

"No," said Warraner. "I know you'll go there. You have more questions to ask, don't you? Why can't you just leave us in peace?"

"Questions always remain, even when things work out. It comes with the territory."

"With being a self-righteous prick who can't allow a town to mourn its dead undisturbed?"

He savored the word "prick." I'd been called worse, but not by anyone with a degree in divinity.

"No, with being human. You should try it, Mr. Warraner, or Pastor Warraner, or whatever title you've chosen to give yourself. Your dead are past caring, and your mourning will do them no good. I'm searching for a missing girl. If she's alive, she's in trouble. If she's dead, someone else is. As an individual who professes to be a man of God, I'd suggest that your compassion is currently misdirected."

Warraner plunged his hands into the pockets of his jeans as though he feared the damage he might otherwise inflict on me. He was a big man, and strong as well. If he got his hands on me, he'd do some harm. Of course, I'd shatter one of his knees before he got that close, but it wouldn't look good on my résumé. Still, all of his weight was on his left leg, which was ramrod straight. If he moved, I'd take him.

Warraner breathed deeply to calm himself and recover his dignity. The moment passed.

"You know nothing of my god, Mr. Parker," he said solemnly.

I looked past him and took in the ancient stones of his church, and the leering faces visible in the fading afternoon light.

"You may be wrong about that, Pastor."

He stayed at the gate as I drove away, his hands deep in his pockets, his gaze fixed on me, standing in the shadow of his church.

In the shadow of his god.

Chief Morland was looking out the window of his office as I pulled up outside his department. If he was pleased to see me, he was trying manfully to hide it. His arms were folded, and he stared at me without expression as I walked up the path. Inside there was a strained silence among the staff, and I guessed that, not long before, Chief Morland had been shouting into a telephone receiver at Pastor Warraner. Nobody offered me coffee and a cookie. Nobody even wanted to catch my eye.

Morland's door was open. I stood on the threshold.

"Mind if I come in?"

He unfolded his arms. "Would it matter if I did?"

"I can talk to you from here, but it seems kind of childish."

Morland gestured me inside and told me to close the door. He waited for me to sit before doing the same himself.

"You've been keeping my phone busy," he said.

"Warraner?"

"The pastor was just the most recent caller. We've had reports of a man in a car like yours casing properties, and I already sent a deputy out to take a look. If you'd been driving your fancy Mustang I'd have known it was you, but you seem to have left your toy automobile back in Portland today."

"I was trying to be discreet."

"The pastor didn't think so. Maybe you failed to notice the sign that read PRIVATE PROPERTY out by the cemetery?"

"If I paid attention to every sign that read PRIVATE PROPERTY or NO ENTRY, I'd never get anything done. Besides, I figured that after the last tour I was practically a member of the congregation."

"It doesn't have a congregation."

"Yeah, I've been meaning to ask about that. I still find it strange that a religious sect would go to the trouble of hauling a church across the Atlantic, rebuild it brick by brick, and then just shrug and walk off."

"They died out."

"You're speaking metaphorically, right? Because the descendants of the original settlers are still here. This town has more old names than the Bible."

"I'm no historian, but there are plenty of folk in this town who consider themselves one," said Morland. "The Familists faded away. I've heard it said that the worst thing to happen to the Family of Love was leaving England. They survived because they were hunted and oppressed, and there's nothing more guaranteed to harden a man's convictions than to be told that he can't follow his own beliefs. With freedom to worship also came the freedom not to worship."

"And where do you worship, Chief?"

"I'm a Catholic. I go to Mary Immaculate down in Dearden."

"Are you familiar with a man there called Euclid Danes?"

"Euclid's a Methodist, although they'd disown him if they weren't so short on bodies to fill their seats. How do you know him?"

He didn't blink, didn't look away, didn't rub his left ear with his right hand or scratch his nose or whatever it is that men and women are supposed to do when they're lying or trying to hide knowledge, but he might just as well have. Morland was well aware that I'd been speaking with Euclid Danes. He wouldn't have been much of a chief of police if he weren't, not in a town like Prosperous. So he pretended, and I let him pretend, and each of us watched the other act.

"I found him on the Internet," I said.

"Looking for a date?"

"He's a little old for me, although I bet he cleans up nicely."

"Euclid's not very popular in this town."

"He wears it as a badge of pride. In his place, I might do the same. Are you aware that he's been threatened?"

"He's always being threatened. Doesn't do much good, though."

"You sound almost as though you approve."

"He's one stubborn man standing in the way of the expansion of a town and the money that would bring into the local economy."

"As you yourself said, there's nothing more likely to make a certain kind of man resolute than finding himself threatened for his beliefs."

"I don't think the First Amendment guarantees your right to be an asshole."

"I think that's precisely what it does."

Morland threw his hands into the air in despair. "Jesus, if I closed my eyes I could almost be talking to Danes himself, and you don't know how unhappy that makes me. So you talked to Danes? Go, you. I'll bet he told you all about how rich old Prosperous is bad, and its people are jerks just because they look after their own. I could give a fuck what Danes says. We're weathering the recession, and we're doing okay. You know why? Because we support one another, because we're close-knit, and that's helped us get through the bad times.

"In case you haven't noticed, Mr. Parker, this town has taken a kicking recently. Instead of busting into old cemeteries, you should go to the new one and pay your respects to the two boys we just buried there. Their crosses won't be hard to find. They have flags beside them. Close by you'll find fresh earth over Valerie Gillson's grave, and the messages her kids left on it for her. Look to your right and a pile of flowers marks where Ben Pearson is resting. Four dead in twenty-four hours, a town in mourning, and I have to deal with your bullshit."

He had a point. I just chose to ignore it.

"I'm looking for an older couple," I said, as though he had never spoken. "Sixties at least, at a guess, although you know how young people are; when you're in your twenties, everyone over forty looks old. This couple own a blue car. I saw a few blue cars during my ride through your very clean town, but I resisted the impulse to start knocking on doors until we'd spoken. You could save me time by giving me the names and addresses of anyone who might fit the criteria."

I took a small hardback notebook from my pocket, slipped the minipen from the spine, and waited. I felt like a secretary poised to take dictation.

"What are you talking about?" said Morland.

"I have a witness who says that the people who took Annie Broyer to this town were an older couple in a blue car. I thought I might try talking to older couples with blue cars. Sometimes the simplest options are the best. You're welcome to come along, unless you're preparing some more stump speeches."

There was a knock at the door behind me.

"Not now," said Morland.

The door opened a fraction. I turned to see one of the secretaries poke her head in.

"Chief, I—"

"I said, 'Not now!'"

The door quickly closed again. Morland hadn't taken his eyes from me throughout the brief exchange.

"I told you when you came through last time that there's no evidence the woman you're looking for ended up in Prosperous."

"I think she did."

"Has she been reported missing?"

"No," I admitted.

"So you're looking for a street person, a former junkie, who has probably fallen back into her old ways, and you want me to help you accuse seniors of kidnapping her?"

"Seniors, and younger," I corrected. "And only ones with access to a blue car."

"Get out!"

I closed my notebook and restored the minipen to the spine.

"I guess I'll just have to go through the DMV."

"You do that. Nobody here fits your bill. That girl is not in Prosperous. If I see you within the town limits again, you'll be charged with trespass and harassment."

I stood. I'd filled my aggravation quota for the day.

"Thank you for your time, Chief," I said, as I left the office. "You've been a big help."

He took it as sarcasm—I could see it on his face—but I was speaking the truth.

I had never told Morland that Annie Broyer was an ex-junkie.

———

THE WOLF CONTINUED TO circle the town. He had returned to the place in which he found the meat and bone belowground, but only the scent of it remained now. For a time, the streets had been filled with even more light and noise and men than before, and the activity had caused the wolf to flee into the woods, but his hunger had driven him back. He tore apart a garbage bag and fed on the chicken carcasses he smelled inside before slipping back into the woods. He remained thin, and even through the double layer of his fur, his ribs shone sharply carved. The temperature had started to drop again; that night it would plummet to minus seven. The wolf's thick subcutaneous fat had become depleted over the winter months as his body fed upon itself. The food from the town was sustaining him, but the damage had already been done. Instinct warned him to seek shelter from the cold, to find a dark, hidden place with warmth. In his youth, members of the pack had sometimes colonized abandoned fox dens, and the wolf now sought a hole in the ground in which to hide. The pain was spreading through his body, and he could put no weight on his damaged limb.

South of the town, he picked up the smell of a deer. The spoor was old, but the wolf identified the pain and panic that had marked the deer's final moments. He paused, wary now. The deer had died in terror, and beneath the sweet stink of prey the wolf could detect another smell, one that was unfamiliar and yet set his senses jangling. The wolf had no predators, aside from man. He would even take on a grizzly in a fight for food, and his pack had once come upon, and consumed, a hibernating black bear. The fear that the wolf now felt reminded him of his fear of man. Yet this was no man.

The scent of the deer drew the wolf on. He flattened his ears against his head and arched his back as a car passed. The light vanished, the sound faded, and he continued to pick his way through the trees until at last he came to a clearing.

In the clearing was a hole. Beside it, almost hidden by roots and branches, lay the deer. The wolf narrowed his eyes and pulled back his ears. His tail pointed straight out, parallel to the ground. The threat came from the hole. Now the wolf snarled, and his fur bristled. He crouched in anticipation of an attack. His senses were flooded by the smell of the deer. He would fight to eat.

And then the wolf's tail moved, withdrawing fully between his legs. He thrust out his tongue and lowered his hindquarters, his eyes still fixed on the hole but his muzzle pointing up. His back arched again, just as it had when the car passed, but this time it was a gesture not of fear but of active submission, the respect that one animal pays to the dominant other. Finally, the wolf approached the deer while maintaining a careful distance from the hole. Briars entangled around the deer's hind legs came away easily as the wolf pulled at the remains.

Despite his weariness and his hunger, he did not start to feed until he had managed to drag the deer as far from the hole in the ground as he could. The smell of danger grew fainter. The threat from the dominant animal was receding, moving farther away.

Moving deeper into the earth.

———

THE DOORBELL RANG IN Chief Morland's house. Morland's wife went to answer, but he told her that he would take care of it. He had barely spoken to her since coming home, and hadn't eaten dinner with the family. His wife said nothing, and did not object. Her husband rarely behaved in this way, but when he did he usually had good cause, and she knew better than to press him. He would tell her of his troubles in his own time.

Thomas Souleby stood on the doorstep. Beside him was a man whom Morland did not know. He wore heavy tan boots, and his body was hidden beneath layers of clothing. His red beard was thick, flecked here and there with gray. In his right hand he held a wolf trap on a length of chain.

The two visitors entered the house, and the door closed softly behind them.

3

KILLING

We humans fear the beast within the wolf because
we do not understand the beast within ourselves.

Gerald Hausman, *Meditations with the Navajo*

XXXI

They convened at the home of Hayley Conyer, as they always did when issues of great import had to be discussed in private. The board of selectmen conducted public meetings on a regular basis, but the agenda for such gatherings was decided well in advance, and sensitive subjects were resolutely avoided. They were also open only to residents of Prosperous, following an abortive attempt by Euclid Danes to hijack one session. The late Ben Pearson had advocated killing Danes following that particular incident, and he had not been joking. If it had gone to a vote of the board, the motion would almost certainly have been passed unanimously.

Luke Joblin arrived first at Hayley's house, accompanied by Kinley Nowell. Kinley had checked himself out of the hospital following Ben Pearson's death. He was still weak, and his breathing was shallow and labored, but he walked into the house under his own steam, aided only by the walker that he had been using for the past decade or more. Joblin carried his ventilator for him. After them came Thomas Souleby, and then Calder Ayton. Hayley was most solicitous of Calder, whose grief at the loss of Ben was etched on his face. She whispered to him as he sat silently at the table, the chair to his right—the chair that had always been occupied by Ben—now empty.

Pastor Warraner arrived at the same time as Chief Morland. Had

Hayley not known of the animosity that existed between them she might almost have suspected them of collusion, but the two men stood awkwardly apart on the porch when she opened the door to them, their body language speaking volumes about their distaste for each other. She knew that Morland had been out in the woods that day, setting traps for the wolf with Abbot, the hunter brought by Souleby to the town. Morland looked exhausted. Good, thought Hayley: it would make him more pliable. She took him by the arm as he passed, indicating to Warraner that he should go on ahead into the dining room. Warraner did as he was told. He had no concerns about what Hayley Conyer might have to say to Morland in his absence. Even after their last meeting, when Hayley had sided with Morland against him, Warraner remained secure in his position as Hayley's spiritual adviser.

"Did you find the animal?" asked Hayley.

"No, not yet, but it's still around. We discovered a deer carcass. It was all chewed up. Abbot reckoned it had been dead for a while, but the damage to it was recent—not more than twenty-four hours. We've laid bait and set traps. We'll get it soon. Abbot says that it's wounded. He could tell by the tracks."

But Hayley was now more interested in the deer. Like the others, she had seen the photograph on Valerie Gillson's phone.

"The deer, was it—?"

"Maybe. There wasn't much of it left to identify. And there was a hole not far from where we found it."

She nodded. "Go inside. The others are waiting."

Morland joined them. The four surviving members of the board sat on either side of the dining table, with a chair left empty at the head for Hayley. Warraner sat at the other end of the table, leaving two chairs between himself and Kinley Nowell. Morland seated himself across from Warraner, leaving three chairs between himself and Calder Ayton. If he squinted, he could almost see the ghost of Ben

Pearson occupying one of them, tearing open a pack of exotic cookies or passing around some British candy, because it was Ben who had always taken it upon himself to provide a small treat for the board and the observers. But the chair remained empty, and the table bare. There were no reports to be considered, and no notebooks lay open. No true record of this meeting would ever be kept.

Hayley turned off the lights in the hall and took her seat at the head of the table.

"All right," she said. "Let's begin."

———

HARRY DIXON KNELT INSIDE his bedroom closet and removed a section of baseboard. The house was quiet. Erin was at her quilting circle, where work had commenced on a quilt in memory of the town's recent dead. According to Erin, so many women wanted to participate that they had to bring in more chairs. Bryan Joblin had gone with her, although he would be drinking in a bar while Erin sewed. Harry wondered how long the board planned to keep up this farce of imposing Joblin on them: until he and Erin found another girl; until they proved themselves.

To that end, Harry had earlier gone out with Joblin, and together they had cruised the streets of Lewiston and Augusta, looking at women. It wasn't exactly difficult work. Harry figured that Joblin would have been doing something similar in his spare time anyway, even if it weren't a matter of some urgency. Hell, Harry had been known to cast a wistful eye at young beauties when his wife wasn't around, but he was nothing like Bryan Joblin. The Joblin boy had a reputation for being a pussy hound of the first order, to the extent that Hayley Conyer herself had taken Bryan and his father to one side following a chance encounter on Main Street and warned them that if Bryan didn't keep his pecker to himself, or at least limit its use to the vast swath of the United States beyond Prosperous, she would personally slice it off and hang it from the town's welcome sign as a warning to others who might be similarly tempted to screw around with the feelings and, indeed, bodies of Properous's generative future. Since then, Bryan Joblin had indulged himself largely in the relative flesh-pots of Bangor, and still tended to cross the street in order to avoid any further confrontations with Hayley Conyer, as though fearing that the old woman might whip out a blade at any moment and make good on her threat.

That afternoon, Harry and Joblin watched schoolgirls, and young housewives. One of them would be ideal, Joblin said. He was in favor of snatching a girl right there and then—a young, athletic-looking brunette out by the mall in Augusta—but Harry dissuaded him. These things needed to be planned properly, Harry told him. Taking a woman in broad daylight was too risky. They looked at some of the homeless women, but they were all too old or worn. Fresher meat was needed.

"What about a child?" said Joblin. "It's gotta be easy to take a child."

Harry didn't reply. He just pictured Bryan Joblin dying in painful ways.

Joblin had bitched all the way back to Prosperous, but Harry knew he would inform his father that the Dixons looked as if they were at least trying to fulfill their obligations to the town, and Luke Joblin would, in turn, tell the board. To add to the deception, Harry set Joblin to trawling prostitution Web sites: twenty-five or younger, Harry had stipulated, and they should be from out of state. No tattoos, and no ID requirements from prospective johns. Independents too, not agency girls. Bryan had dived into the work wholeheartedly. He even printed off a list of possible candidates for Harry.

"You know they can trace all those searches back to our computer?" Erin told Harry, when she learned of what Bryan was doing. Her quilting bag was on the bed behind her, ready for use. They were whispering. They spent most of their days in near silence now because of their unwanted houseguest. It was like living in some kind of religious retreat.

"It doesn't matter," said Harry. "It's all just smoke anyway."

"Well, I still don't like it. It makes the computer seem dirty. I won't feel the same about using it."

Give me strength, thought Harry.

"The computer won't be coming with us," he said. "I'll buy you a new one when we get—"

"Get where?" she asked.

"Get to wherever we're going," he finished.

"When?"

"I don't know. "

"When?" she repeated. There were tears in her eyes. "I can't do this much longer. I can't stand having Bryan Joblin around. I hate the smell of him, the sound of him. I hate the way he looks at me."

"Looks at you? What do you mean?"

"Jesus, you see nothing. Nothing! It's like you can't imagine that another man might find me attractive."

And with that she stormed out to start work on the great quilt. Harry had watched Erin as she walked to her car, Bryan Joblin trailing behind her. Of course, she was still a good-looking woman. He knew that better than anyone. It shouldn't have surprised him that Bryan Joblin might appreciate her too.

Now he placed the section of baseboard on the carpet and reached into the space revealed. His hands came out holding a red fireproof box, a smaller version of the one in which he and Erin kept their passports and valuable documents. The key was in the lock. He had no fear of anyone finding the box, and he didn't want Erin coming across the key by accident and asking what it was. They didn't have many secrets from each other, but this was one of them.

Harry opened the box. Inside were five thousand dollars in tens and twenties: it was Harry's emergency fund. He had resisted dipping into the cash until that week, even when his business was at its lowest. Harry didn't know how long five thousand dollars would last once he and Erin started running, but their main priority would be to put distance between themselves and Prosperous. After that, he'd make some calls. He still had friends beyond Prosperous.

The box also contained a letter written and ready to mail. The letter was addressed to Hayley Conyer, and its contents could be summarized as a promise to keep quiet about Prosperous if he and Erin were left in peace. Even after all that had occurred, Harry remained loyal to the town. He didn't want to betray its secrets.

The final item in the box was a handgun, a five-shot Smith & Wesson 638 with a concealed hammer, a barrel length of less than two inches, and a weight of just fourteen ounces when empty. It had been acquired for him by one of his subcontractors, a plumber with a string of convictions who owed Harry, because Harry gave him work when nobody else would. Harry had been afraid to purchase a legal firearm. He was worried that word would get back to Chief Morland, and then questions would be asked, and with questions came suspicions. The gun fit easily into the pocket of his favorite jacket, and was powerful, accurate, and easy to fire, even for a neophyte like him. Erin didn't approve of guns and wouldn't tolerate them in the house. If she'd discovered that he had the S&W, he'd have found a quick use for the box of self-defense round-nose loads that sat alongside the pistol.

Now he transferred the entire contents of the box to a small black canvas sack and hid it on the top shelf of the closet behind a stack of old T-shirts. He hadn't told Erin, but preparations for their departure were almost complete. He had spoken to a used-car dealer in Medway and arranged a trade-in, with some cash on the side, for his truck. One morning, while Bryan Joblin was watching Erin, Harry had driven to the T.J.Maxx in Bangor with a list of his wife's measurements and bought various items of underwear and casual clothing and sneakers, along with a pair of cheap suitcases. He didn't need to buy much for himself; he'd hidden a plastic garbage bag filled with jeans, shirts, and a new pair of boots in the spare toolbox in his truck, and these he added to one of the suitcases. He then went to the Walgreens on Broadway and replicated as many as possible of the toiletries and cosmetics he had seen in their bathroom and on his wife's dressing table. When he was done, he paid a quick visit to Erin's sister and asked her to take care of the cases for him. To his surprise, she didn't ask any questions. That made him wonder how much she already knew, or suspected, about Prosperous.

Harry restored the empty box to its space behind the closet and replaced the baseboard. It seemed to him that by removing the cash and the gun he had made his decision. There was only one final step to take. After that, there could be no going back.

Harry drove to the post office and, with only a slight hesitation, mailed the letter to Hayley Conyer.

XXXII

Hayley was playing with him, Morland knew, trying to put him off guard and make him ill at ease. He had seen her do this more than once with those who displeased her, and his father had warned him about it when it came time for him to take over as chief of police.

"She's a clever one, you mark my words," his father said. "You watch yourself around her, and never turn your back on her. She's crossed swords over the years with a lot of men and women who thought they were smarter than she was, and she's left them all lying dead in the ground."

Even then, Morland had wondered if his father was speaking literally or metaphorically.

Now Morland made himself as comfortable as possible in the creaky old dining chairs, and did his best to keep his temper in check as Hayley baited him. Almost an hour had gone by, and she hadn't yet even alluded to the detective. She was building up to it, allowing the tension in the room to coalesce around Morland, constraining him so that when at last they came to the issue at hand he would be both wound tight internally and compressed by her implied disapproval of his actions, although he didn't know how else he might have reacted to the detective's interest in the missing girl. What did Haley expect—

that he should kill anyone who so much as glanced curiously in the town's direction? Perhaps so; she had always been paranoid, although she tried to justify it by claiming that the fate of the town, and the responsibility for its citizens, lay in her hands. What was that line about power corrupting? Whatever it was, it was true, but also incomplete: power didn't just corrupt. After a time, it could also drive a person mad.

So it was that, over the past hour, Hayley had ignored Morland's interjections, even when it was clear that she had left space in the discussions for him to offer an opinion. If he remained quiet, she asked him to contribute and then ceased to listen almost as soon as he began speaking, until finally, while he was still in mid-flow, she would begin to talk over him, or turn to one of the others for an alternative view, or simply change the subject altogether, leaving Morland to wind down slowly into silence. It was humiliating, and Morland was certain that Hayley's ultimate intention was to drive him from the meeting entirely, but he refused to be forced into giving her what she wanted. It was crucial that he remain present. He guessed what she was planning to do, and he had to stop her. She hadn't met the detective, and didn't fully understand the danger that he represented. Even Warraner, who had twice encountered Parker, was guilty of underestimating him, but that was a function of Warraner's own misplaced sense of superiority. Morland had watched him with the detective in the chapel, behaving like some glorified tour guide, almost inviting Parker to draw conclusions about hidden knowledge that might or might not be true. But the detective was subtler and more cunning than Warraner had first assumed, and by the time Warraner came to that realization—with the detective's questions about the Familists and Vitel—it was too late.

And then the detective returned, with his talk of blue cars, baiting Morland and Warraner just as Morland himself was now being baited. He'd spoken to Danes too, and Danes was much more than a simple nuisance. He had the ear of people in the state legislature, although he didn't have much influence over the current governor, mainly because, as far as Morland could tell, the current governor didn't listen to anyone. But Morland and the board knew that Danes had managed to scatter seeds of suspicion about Prosperous down in Augusta. True, most people still dismissed him as a flake, but he was a flake with money, and money bought influence.

Morland recalled again the late Ben Pearson's rage at Danes's intrusion on the public meeting. The old bastard had been practically frothing at the mouth, and Souleby and the others weren't far behind him, howling for blood like the high priests before Pilate. On that occasion, it was Hayley who proved to be the voice of reason. They couldn't kill Danes, because who knew what trouble his death might bring on them if there was even a hint of foul play about it? They'd just have to wait for him to die naturally, but so far Danes had proved to be as stubbornly healthy as Hayley herself. Sometimes Morland even suspected that Hayley liked having Danes around. She seemed almost indulgent of his efforts to hamper the town's expansion, as though their intensity were a reflection of Prosperous's importance, and a vindication of her own stewardship.

Prosperous had influence in Augusta as well. It was natural in a town as wealthy as this one, and even though its citizens differed politically, they still recognized that contributions to politicians of all stripes served the common cause. But that influence had to be used subtly and carefully. Morland sensed that a time was coming when the town's investment in state politics might finally be required to yield profit. He would be happier if it could be saved for another moment, but he was growing increasingly ill at ease at this meeting. It was like watching a snake preparing to strike, unaware of the shadow of the blade behind it.

The board had almost concluded its discussion of the recent fatalities. Hayley asked about the families, and how they were coping, and Warraner gave her chapter and verse about his pastoral role, and each vied with the other to appear the more sympathetic, the more understanding, the more pained by the sufferings of others. It was quickly decided that a fund should be established to aid the families in their time of need. The selectmen immediately offered generous contributions, and Hayley matched their combined total. Once they had tapped the rest of the town for sums both big and small, it would represent a significant source of financial consolation for the families.

Call it what it is, thought Morland. Call it a bribe, a way of buying time and loyalty. There were already whispers among the townsfolk (for Morland was listening and, where possible, stoking the fires of discontent with the board). Why had this happened? Where had their protection gone? What was the board going to do about it? If the board could do nothing, or not enough, then it might be that it was time for others to step up and take the responsibility of running the town from these old men and this old woman who had served Prosperous so well for so long, but whose hour was now past.

And if any of them objected—and by "any" they could be referring only to one, Hayley Conyer—then, Morland thought, the town would understand if some bad luck were to befall her, for old women had accidents, and Prosperous would accept her passing as a different kind of sacrifice. So this was an important meeting, perhaps the most important in nearly a century. The town's survival might not have been at stake, not yet, but the survival of the current board certainly was.

"Well, so that's decided," said Hayley at last. She would write it all down the next day, creating inconsequential minutes for a meeting of great consequence. Let the town, and those whose eyes were upon it, see how it handled itself in times of strife. Meanwhile, the truth would be communicated in quiet words at gas stations, and on street corners, and in kitchens when the children were asleep. The whispers of doubt would be smothered. The board had acted. All would be well.

"That brings us to the main business of the evening."

There was shuffling around her. Heads turned toward Morland. He felt the wires tighten around him, and instinctively he breathed in, swelling his upper body, tensing his arms and hands against unseen bonds, making himself larger, gaining himself room to move.

Hayley sat back in her chair. It was a Carver, the only chair at the table that had arms. She rested her right elbow on one arm, her thumb beneath her chin, her index finger to her right temple, and stared thoughtfully at Morland, like a queen waiting for the courtier who had disappointed her to explain his way out of an appointment with the executioner.

"So, Chief Morland," she said. "Tell us about this detective. . . ."

XXXIII

Ronald Straydeer came by my house while I was once again reading through the material about the Familists culled from the archives of the Maine Historical Society. Ronald was a Penobscot Indian out of Old Town, north of Bangor. He had served with the K-9 Corps in Vietnam and, like so many men who fought in that war, he came back with a fracture running through his soul. In Ronald's case, that fracture was caused by the decision of the U.S. military to classify its war dogs as "equipment" and then leave them behind as "surplus to requirements" when the United States fled South Vietnam. Thousands of war dogs were either transferred to the South Vietnamese Army or euthanized, and many of the handlers, like Ronald, never quite forgave their country for its treatment of the animals.

The Vietcong hated the K-9 teams because they made surprise attacks almost impossible to carry out, and both the dogs and their handlers were hunted by the enemy with extreme prejudice. The bond between the K-9 soldiers and their dogs was immensely strong, and the emotional and psychological damage caused by the attitude of the U.S. Army toward the teams was impossible to quantify. A wiser military, one more attuned to the effects of combat on the psyche, would have allowed the men to adopt their dogs, but such legislation would not come into effect until 2000. Instead, the K-9 soldiers watched South Vietnam fall to the North Vietnamese, and they knew that their dogs would be slaughtered in revenge.

Now Ronald worked with veterans, but he did so almost entirely without the assistance of the U.S. government or its military. He wanted little to do with either. I think that was one of the reasons he sold pot. It wasn't so much that he cared one way or another about drugs; it was just a means of quietly socking it to Uncle Sam for sacrificing Elsa, Ronald's German shepherd, back in Vietnam. He was largely a recreational dealer, though; he probably gave away more than he sold, and smoked the rest himself.

I hadn't seen him in a while. Someone told me that he'd left town. His brother up in Old Town was ill, or so the story went, and Ronald was helping his family out. But, as far as I knew, Ronald didn't have a brother.

Tonight his eyes were brighter than usual, and he was wearing a blue sports jacket over jeans, a matching shirt, and off-white sneakers.

"You know," I said, "the denim shirt-and-jeans look only works if you're a country singer, or you own a farm."

Ronald gave me a hard look.

"Should I tell you of how, long before the white man came, my people roamed these lands?"

"In matching denim?"

"We move with the times."

"Not fast enough."

He followed me into my office. I offered him coffee, or a beer if he was in the mood, but he declined both. He took a seat in one of the armchairs. He was a big man, and he made the chair look too small for him. Actually, the way he had to squeeze himself into it made me start worrying about how we were going to get him out again when he tried to stand. I had visions of injecting Crisco down the sides from a pastry-icing bag.

"So, how have you been?" I asked.

"I stopped drinking," he said.

"Really?"

Ronald had never been a big drinker, from what I could recall, but he had been a steady one, although he stuck to beer, for the most part.

"Yeah. I quit smoking weed too."

This *was* news.

"You stop dealing as well?"

"I got enough money in the bank. I don't need to do that no more."

"You didn't fall off a horse on the road to Damascus, did you?"

"No, man. I don't like horses. You thinking of the Plains Indians. You ought to read a book, educate yourself."

Ronald said all of this with an entirely straight face. It was generally hard to tell if he was serious or joking, at least not until he started punching you in the gut.

"I heard you'd been out of town for a while," I said. "I guess now I know what you were doing. You were self-improving."

"And thinking."

"Mind if I ask what about?"

"Life. Philosophical shit. You wouldn't understand, being a white man."

"You look good for it, even to a white man."

"I decided it wasn't positive for me to be drinking and smoking and dealing when I was working with men for whom all of those activities might prove a temptation. If I was going to help them get straight and clean, I had to be straight and clean myself, you understand?"

"Absolutely."

"I kept up with the newspapers, though. You weren't in them. Looks like you haven't shot anyone in months. You retired?"

"I could be tempted to break my spell of gun celibacy, under the current circumstances. Are you just here to yank my chain, or is there something I can help you with?"

"I hear you been around the homeless shelters asking questions," said Ronald.

In his dealings with veterans, Ronald was often to be found working in the shelters, trying to form bonds with men and women who felt abandoned by their country once their period in uniform was over. Some of them even ended up staying with him on occasion. Despite his somewhat stony demeanor, Ronald Straydeer had a seemingly infinite capacity for empathy.

"That's right."

"Veterans?"

Ronald had helped me out in the past with cases involving soldiers or the military. It was his turf, and he was conscious of protecting it.

"Not really, or only by association. You knew Jude, right?"

"Yeah. He was a good man. Dressed funny, but he was helpful. I hear he died. Suicide."

"I don't think he killed himself. I believe he was helped into the next world."

"Any idea why?"

"Can I ask why you're interested?"

"Someone's got to look out for these people. I try. If the city's homeless are being targeted for any reason, I'd like to know."

That was as good a reason as any.

"It's early," I said, "but I think he might have been killed because he went looking for his daughter. Her name was Annie, and she was following in her father's footsteps, in both senses of the term. She'd lost her way, and ended up on the streets. I believe she was trying to draw him to her, while at the same time keeping him at a distance. She was staying at a women's shelter in Bangor, but she's not there any longer. There's nobody around to report her missing, but I have a feeling that she might have been snatched. Jude was concerned about her before he died."

"And what's this to you?"

"A friend of Jude's, a man named Shaky, told me that Jude had saved up to buy a few hours of my time. Call it an obligation on my part."

"I know Shaky. Any idea who might have taken the girl?"

"You ever been to the town of Prosperous?"

"No. Heard of it. Don't think they have much time for the natives, or anyone who isn't white and wealthy."

"Annie told someone up in Bangor that she'd been offered a job by an older couple from Prosperous. She collected her things from the shelter before taking a ride with them, and that was the last anyone saw of her."

"The couple might have been lying," said Ronald. "It's easy to say you're from one place when you're actually from another."

"I had considered that."

"It's why you're a detective."

"That's right. I like to think of myself as wise for a white man."

"That bar is set low," said Ronald.

"Not for all of us, and perhaps not for Annie Broyer. I get the sense, from the people I've spoken with about her, that she wasn't dumb. Otherwise she wouldn't have survived on the streets for as long as she did. I think she would have asked for some proof that these people were on the level. If she said she was going to Prosperous, then I believe that's where she ended up. Unfortunately, according to the local police there's no sign of her, and never has been."

I hadn't told Ronald anything that Shaky or the cops in Portland didn't already know, for the most part. Any other thoughts or suspicions, including the peculiar history of the Familists, I kept to myself.

Ronald remained seated silently in his chair. He appeared to be contemplating something, even if it was only how he was going to get out of the chair now that he'd found out what he wanted to know.

"How did the people who killed Jude find him?" said Ronald at last.

People: Ronald knew that it took more than a single person to stage a hanging, even one involving a man seemingly as weak as Jude.

"They watched the shelters," I replied. "He was, as you remarked, a distinctive figure."

"Someone might have noticed them. The homeless, the sharp ones, they're always watching. They keep an eye out for the cops, for friends, for men and women with grudges against them. It's hard and merciless at the bottom of the pond. You have to be careful if you don't want to get eaten."

Ronald was right. I hadn't asked enough questions on the streets. I had allowed myself to become sidetracked by Prosperous and what it might represent, but perhaps there was another way.

"Any suggestions as to whom I might talk with?"

"You go around using words like 'whom' and nobody will talk to you at all. Leave it to me."

"You're sure?"

"I'll get more out of them than you will."

I had to admit the truth of it.

"One thing," I said.

"Yes?"

"I'd be discreet about it. If I'm right, and Jude was murdered, the people who did it won't be reluctant to act if they have to cover their tracks. We don't need any more bodies."

"I understand."

Ronald rose to leave. As anticipated, he had some trouble extricating himself from his seat, but by pressing down hard with his arms he somehow managed it. Once he was free, he regarded the chair in a vaguely hostile manner.

"Next time, I will not sit," he said.

"That might be for the best."

He looked out the window at the moonlight shining on the marshes.

"I've been thinking about getting another dog," he said.

Ronald hadn't owned a dog since Vietnam.

"Good," I said.

"Yes," said Ronald, and for the first time since he arrived at my door he smiled. "Yes, I believe it is."

———

WHEN HE WAS GONE, I called Angel and Louis in New York. Angel answered. Angel always answered. Louis regarded telephones as instruments of the Devil. He used them only reluctantly, and his conversation was even more minimal over the phone than it was in person, which was saying something—or, in Louis's case, nothing at all.

Angel told me that he was working on finding more of the Collector's nests, but so far he'd come up empty. Maybe we'd taken care of all of them, and the Collector was now living in a hole in the ground like a character in a book I'd read as a boy. The man had tried to assassinate someone who might have been Hitler, and failed. Hunted in turn, he had literally gone underground, digging a cave for himself in the earth and waiting for his pursuers to show their face. *Rogue Male*—that was the title of the book. They'd made a movie of it, with Peter O'Toole. Thinking of the book and the movie reminded me of those holes in the ground around Prosperous. Something had made them, but what?

"You still there?" said Angel.

"Yes, sorry. My mind was somewhere else for a moment."

"Well, it's your dime."

"You're showing your age, remembering a time when you could make a call for a dime. Tell me, what did you and Mr. Edison talk about back then?"

"Fuck you, *and* Thomas Edison."

"The Collector's still out there. He can rough it, but the lawyer can't. Somewhere there's a record of a house purchase that we haven't found yet."

"I'll keep looking. What about you? Whose cage are you rattling these days?"

I told him about Jude, and Annie, and Prosperous, and even Ronald Straydeer.

"Last time I talked to you, you were process-serving," said Angel. "I knew it wouldn't last."

"How's Louis?"

"Bored. I'm hoping he'll commit a crime, just to get him out of the apartment."

"Tell him to watch a movie. You ever hear of *Rogue Male*?"

"Is it porn?"

"No."

"It sounds like gay porn."

"Why would I be watching gay porn?"

"I don't know. Maybe you're thinking of switching teams."

"I'm not even sure how *you* got on that team. You certainly weren't picked first."

"Fuck you again, and your team."

"Tell Louis to go find *Rogue Male*. I think he'll like it."

"Okay." His voice grew slightly fainter as he turned away from the phone. "Hey, Louis, Parker says you need to go find some rogue male."

I caught a muffled reply.

"He says he's too old."

"*Rogue Male*, starring Peter O'Toole."

"Tool?" said Angel. "That's the guy's name? Man, that's gotta be porn. . . ."

I hung up. Even "hung" sounded mildly dirty after the conversation I'd just had. I made some coffee and went outside to drink it while I watched the moon shine on the marshes. Clouds crossed its face, changing the light, chasing shadows. I listened. Sometimes I wished for them to come, the lost daughter and the woman who walked with her, but I had no sense of them that night. Perhaps it was for the best. Blood flowed when they came.

But they would return, in the end. They always did.

XXXIV

Morland told the board what he knew of the detective. He spoke of his history, and the deaths of his wife and child many years earlier. He told them of some of the cases in which the detective had been involved, the ones that had come to public notice, but he also informed them of the rumors that circulated about other investigations, secret investigations. It was a delicate line that Morland was walking; he wanted them to understand the threat that the detective posed, but he did not want them to feel concerned enough to act rashly. Morland was certain that Hayley already knew most of what he had to say. His performance was for the benefit of the rest of the board, and Warraner too.

"You say that he has crossed paths with the Believers?" said Souleby.

There was a rustle of disapproval from the others. The board of selectmen had been in existence in Maine longer than the sect known as the Believers, and it regarded them with a mixture of unease and distaste. The Believers' search for their brethren, for lost angels like themselves, was of no concern to the citizens of Prosperous. On the other hand, neither did the town wish to attract the attentions of others like the Believers, or those in whose shadows the Believers toiled. The Believers were only one element of a larger conspiracy, one that was slowly encroaching upon the state of Maine. The board wanted no part of it, although unofficial channels of communication with certain interested parties were kept open through Thomas Souleby, who retained membership in various clubs in Boston, and moved easily in such circles.

"He has," said Morland. "All I've heard are whispers, but it's safe to say that they regretted the encounters more than he did."

Old Kinley Nowell spoke up. He had to remove the oxygen mask from his face to do so, and each word sounded like a desperate effort for him. Morland thought that he already looked like a corpse. His skin was pale and waxen, and he stank of mortality and the medicines that were being used to stave it off.

"Why has the detective not been killed before now?"

"Some have tried," said Morland. "And failed."

"I'm not talking of thugs and criminals," said Nowell. He put his mask to his face and drew two deep breaths before resuming. "I'm not even speaking of the Believers. There are others in the background, and they do not fail. They've been killing for as long as there were men to kill. Cain's blood runs in their veins."

The Backers—that was how Morland had heard them described. Men and women with great wealth and power, like the board of selectmen writ large. Souleby's people.

"If he's alive," said Souleby, as if on cue, "then it's because they want him alive."

"But why?" said Nowell. "He's clearly a threat to them—if not now, then in the future. It makes no sense for them to let him live."

Hayley Conyer looked to Warraner for the solution, not to Souleby. It was, in her view, a theological issue.

"Pastor, would you care to offer a possible answer to this conundrum?"

Warraner might have been arrogant and conniving, thought Morland, but he wasn't a fool. He gave himself almost a full minute before he replied.

"They're afraid to kill what they don't understand," he said, finally. "What do they want? They wish to find their buried god and release him, and they feel themselves to be closer to that end than they have ever been before. The detective may be an obstacle, or it may be that he has a part to play in that search. For now, they do not understand his nature, and they're afraid to move against him for fear that, by doing so, they may ultimately harm their cause. I have listened to what Chief Morland has to say, and I confess that I may have underestimated the detective."

This surprised Morland. Warraner rarely admitted weakness, especially in front of Hayley and the board. It caught Morland off guard, so that he was unprepared when the blade was thrust into his back.

"That said," Warraner continued, "Chief Morland underestimated him as well, and should not have brought him to the church. The detective should have been kept far away from it, and from me. I was forced into a situation where I had to answer questions, and I dealt with them as best I could, under the circumstances."

Liar, Morland wanted to say. I saw you preening. You wretched man; I will remember this.

"Chief?" said Conyer. "Is this true?"

She was amused. Morland could see it. She enjoyed watching her pets snap at each other. He felt her willing him to grow angry. The small humiliations that she had aimed at him earlier hadn't been enough to make him lose his temper. It might be that she already had someone else in mind to succeed him, but Morland didn't believe she had thought so far ahead. She knew only that he was beginning to doubt her, and she wished to retain her position. If she had to sacrifice him in order to survive, she would.

But Morland said only "I did what I thought was best," and watched with some small satisfaction as disappointment clouded the old woman's face.

Souleby, ever the diplomat, chose that moment to intervene.

"Throwing blame around isn't going to help us," he said. "Chief Morland, the question is this: will the detective give up?"

"No, but—"

Morland thought hard about how he was going to phrase his next words.

"Go on," said Souleby.

"He has no evidence, no clues. He has only his suspicions, and they aren't enough."

"Then why did he return to the town a second time?"

"Because he's taunting us. In the absence of evidence, he wants us to act. He wants us to move against him. By acting, we'll confirm his suspicions, and then he'll respond with violence. He isn't just the bait but the hook as well."

"Only if he lives," said Nowell, filled with malice as the end neared, as though he were intent on expending all his viciousness before he passed on.

"He has friends," said Morland. "They would not allow any action against him to go unpunished."

"They can die too."

"I don't think you understand—"

"Don't!" cawed Nowell. He raised a withered finger, like an ancient crow clawing against the darkness. "I understand better than you think. You're afraid. You're a coward. You—"

The rest of his accusations were lost in a fit of gasps and coughs. It was left to Luke Joblin to secure the mask to Nowell's face and leave it in place. For now, the old man's contributions to the meeting, however worthless they might be, were over. Why don't you just die, Morland wished—die and free up a place for someone with an ounce of sense and reason left to him. Nowell eyed him over the mask, reading his thoughts.

"You were saying?" said Souleby.

Morland looked away from Nowell.

"The detective has killed," he said. "He has victims who are known, and I guarantee you there are just as many who are unknown. A man who has acted in this way and is not behind bars, or has not been deprived of his livelihood and his weapons, is protected. Yes, some on the side of law would be glad to see him removed from the equation, but even they would be forced to act if he was harmed."

There was quiet among the members of the board, broken only by the tortured breathing of Kinley Nowell.

"Could we not approach the Backers and seek their advice?" said Luke Joblin. "They might even work with us."

"We don't ask the permission of others to act," said Hayley Conyer. "Their interests and ours are not the same, not even in this case. If they're unwilling to move against him on their own behalf, they won't do so on ours."

"And there's the matter of another girl," said Calder Ayton. They were his first words since the meeting began. Morland had almost forgotten that he was present.

"What do you mean, Calder?" asked Conyer. She too seemed surprised to hear him speak at all.

"I mean that we have received a warning, or four warnings, depending on one's view of the current dilemma," said Ayton. "Our people are worried. Whatever threat this detective poses, another girl has to be found and delivered—and quickly. Can we take the chance of having this man nosing around at such a delicate moment in the town's history?"

"What news from the Dixons?" Souleby asked Morland. "Has there been progress?"

"Bryan is watching them," said Luke Joblin, answering for Morland. "He thinks they're getting close to finding someone."

But Morland had his own view of the situation.

"Bryan tells me that he's been out scouting with Harry, but—and please don't take this the wrong way, Luke—your son isn't the sharpest tool in the box. My view is that the Dixons aren't to be trusted. I think they're leading Bryan on. We should have given the job of finding a girl to someone else."

"But, Chief Morland, it was your suspicions that led us to test them with the hunt," said Conyer.

"There might have been better ways to satisfy ourselves as to their loyalty," said Morland.

"It's done now," said Conyer. "Your regrets are a little late."

Again, it was Thomas Souleby who intervened.

"But if they are leading Bryan on—and, by extension, the rest of us—they're doing so to what end?" he asked.

"I think they're planning to run," said Morland.

His opinion went down badly. People did leave Prosperous. After all, it wasn't a fortress, or a prison, and a larger world existed beyond its boundaries. But those who left were secure in their loyalty to the town, and many of them eventually returned. Running was another matter, for it brought with it the possibility of disclosure.

"There is a precedent for it on Erin's side," said Ayton.

"We don't blame the children for the sins of the adults," said Conyer. "And her mother more than made up for the failings of the father."

She returned her attention to Morland.

"Have you taken steps?" she said.

"I have."

"Could you be more precise?"

"I could, but I would prefer not to," said Morland. "After all, I may be wrong about them. I hope that I am."

"But the detective," Ayton insisted. "What of the detective?"

"We'll vote on it," said Conyer. "Reverend, do you have anything to add before we start?"

"Only that I believe the detective is dangerous," said Warraner.

A nicely ambiguous reply, thought Morland. *Whatever they decide, and whatever the consequences, no blame will fall on your head.*

"And you, Chief?

"You know my views," said Morland. "If you attack him and succeed in killing him, you will bring more trouble down on this town. If you attack him and fail to kill him, the consequences may be even worse. We should not move against him. Eventually he'll grow weary, or another case will distract him."

But Morland wondered if he was indulging in wishful thinking. Yes, the detective might leave them in peace for a while, but he would not forget. It was not in him to do so. He would return, and keep returning. The best they could hope for was that his visits might bring no reward and, in time, someone else might do them the favor of killing him.

Around him, the board meditated on what it had heard. He couldn't tell if his words had made any impact.

"Thank you both for your contributions," said Conyer. "Would you mind waiting outside while we make our decision?"

The two observers rose and left. Warraner wrapped his coat tightly around himself, thrust his hands into his pockets, and took a seat on the porch. It was strange, but Morland had the sense that something of his own words of warning had penetrated Warraner's carapace of blind faith and deluded self-belief. He could see it in the pastor's face. Warraner lived to protect his church. For him, the town's continued safety and good fortune were merely a by-product of his own mission. It was one thing for him to assent to the killing of a homeless man, one whom Warraner believed would not be mourned or missed; it was another entirely to involve himself in an attack on a dangerous individual which could well have negative consequences whether they succeeded in killing him or not.

"Bait," said Warraner.

"What?" said Morland.

"You said that the detective was prepared to use himself as bait. Why would a man put himself in that kind of danger, especially for someone he didn't even know?"

"A sense of justice, maybe. The world beyond the limits of our town isn't as entirely corrupt as we might like to believe. After all, look at how corrupt we ourselves have become."

"We do what is necessary."

"Not for much longer."

"Why do you say that?"

"Our ways can't continue in the modern world. In the end, we'll be found out."

"So you believe that we should stop?"

"We can stop, or we can be stopped. The former might be less painful than the latter."

"And the old god?"

"What is a god without believers? It is just a myth waiting to be forgotten."

Warraner gaped. To him, this was blasphemy.

"But what will become of the town?"

"The town will survive. It'll just be a town like any other."

Bile rose up and caught in Morland's throat, the acidity bringing tears to his eyes. How could Prosperous ever be such a town? The blood had permeated it too thoroughly. It was mired in redness and sin.

"No," said Warraner. "It can never be that."

And Morland was sure that Warraner had missed the point.

"You haven't answered my question," said Warraner. "Some vague concept of justice isn't sufficient to explain this man's actions."

"Justice is never vague," said Morland. "The law only makes it seem that way. And as for this man . . ."

Morland had been thinking about the detective a lot. In reading up on him, he believed that, on some level, he almost understood him. When Morland spoke again, he was talking as much to himself as to Warraner.

"I don't think he's afraid of dying," said Morland. "He doesn't seek out death, and he'll fight it until the end, but he's not frightened of it. I think he's in pain. He's been damaged by loss, and it's left him in agony. When death does come for him, it'll end his pain. Until then, nothing that anyone can visit on him will be worse than what he's already experienced. That makes him a formidable enemy, because he can endure more than his opponents. And the things he's done, the risks he's taken for others, they've won him allies, and some of them may be even more dangerous than he is, because they don't share his morals. If he has a weakness, it's that he's a moral being. Where possible, he'll do the right thing, the just thing, and if he does wrong he'll bear the guilt of it."

"You respect him."

"You'd have to be a fool not to."

"But you sound almost as though you like him."

"Yes," said Morland. "It may be that I like him even better than I like myself."

He stepped down into Hayley Conyer's garden and lit a cigarette. She wouldn't approve, but he didn't care. His position had been made clear—the inconsequentiality of his role in the town's affairs, the hollowness of his authority. After all this was over, he would have to resign. If he was fortunate, the board would accept his resignation and allow him to take his family and leave. Otherwise, it could force him to stay on, a pitiful figure good only for issuing parking violations and speeding tickets.

Although it could do worse.

He felt the end of things approaching, had felt it ever since the shooting of the girl. The arrival of the detective had merely compounded what he already knew. Even with the coming of spring there would be no rebirth, not for Prosperous. That might even be for the best.

He took a long drag on his cigarette, and thought of wolves.

———

THE WOLF SMELLED THE meat. The wind carried it to him. He had been resting in the shelter of a fallen tree, sleeping fitfully and feverishly through his pain when the scent of blood came. The wolf had only nibbled at the dead deer he had been permitted to take. The meat had tasted wrong, infected by the manner of the fawn's dying.

The wolf rose slowly. He was always stiff when he first stood, even if he had been lying down for only a short time, but the promise of fresh meat was enough to spur him on.

With the moon full in the sky, and blood in the air, he limped south.

It was Thomas Souleby who summoned Morland and Warraner back inside. By then, Morland had finished one cigarette and started another. The curtains at the living room window moved, and he glimpsed a face peering out at him. It might have been Hayley Conyer, but he couldn't be sure. He stamped out the remains of the second cigarette on the gravel, and considered leaving it there for the old bitch to find in the morning, but thought better of it. There was no percentage in pettiness, even if it did offer a passing sense of satisfaction.

Souleby sniffed at him as he reentered the house.

"She'll smell it on you," said Souleby. "It's one thing smoking on the sly, another bringing the evidence into her home."

Morland didn't look at him. He didn't want Souleby to see his desperation, his grim sense that it was important, above all, to let the detective be. The more he had paced and smoked, the more he dreaded what was to come.

"She'll smell worse on me once all this is over," said Morland. "This whole town is going to stink of blood."

And Souleby didn't try to deny it.

———

MORLAND KNEW WHAT THEY had decided as soon as he entered the dining room. He supposed he had known even before he left them to their deliberations, but the vindictively triumphant expression on the portion of Kinley Nowell's face not obscured by his mask removed any lingering doubt.

Now that her victory was assured, Hayley Conyer was content to soften her attitude toward her chief of police—because that, of course, was how she thought of him: "her" chief of police, "her" board, "her" town. She waited for him to take his seat, and smiled in the manner of a prospective employer preparing to break bad news to an unsuccessful job candidate.

"We've decided to deal with the detective," she said.

"There will be repercussions," said Morland.

"We have taken that possibility into account. The finger of blame will point . . . elsewhere."

Morland noticed that Conyer now had a sheet of paper in front of her. While he watched, she took a pen from the pocket of her cardigan and drew a symbol on the page. Wordlessly, she passed it to him.

Morland didn't touch the sheet. He didn't have to, for he could see what she had drawn clearly enough, but neither did he *want* to touch it. Conyer had drawn a trident. It was the symbol of the Believers. An already difficult and dangerous situation was about to become potentially disastrous.

"They'll know that it was us," said Morland.

"He's right," said Souleby. He looked genuinely frightened. Clearly this element of Conyer's plan hadn't been discussed. "It goes beyond the bounds of common sense."

"They won't know if we're careful," said Conyer. "And we are always careful."

That was a lie, but Morland didn't call her on it. If they had been truly careful, the detective would never have set foot in their town.

Nowell pulled off his mask.

"And what matter if it becomes known that it was us?" he rasped. "The Believers weren't many to begin with, and the detective has taken care of the rest."

"We don't know that for sure," said Morland. "There may be others. They hide. It's in their nature. And then there's the matter of the Backers. They have always maintained links with the Believers. There may even be Believers among them. They could have acted against the detective, but they chose not to. Making the decision to remove him for them may not be appreciated."

"No blame will accrue to us," Conyer insisted.

"You can't be certain," said Morland.

He felt a migraine coming on. He rubbed at his temples, as though that might somehow ward off the pain and the nausea. He was weary. He should have just kept his mouth shut, because this was a pointless discussion. The battle was lost, and soon the war would be as well.

"You're right; I can't be certain," said Conyer.

Morland glanced up in surprise.

"But they can," she concluded.

Morland heard movement behind him, and two shadows fell across the table.

It had all been a farce—the meeting, the arguments, the final private discussion. The decision had been made long before. These two would not have been present otherwise. They didn't travel unless killing was imminent.

"You don't have to worry about the detective any longer, Chief Morland," said Conyer. "Our friends will take care of him for us. For now, though, the Dixons remain your responsibility. I want them watched. If they try to run, I want them stopped.

"And if they get beyond the town limits," she added, "I want them killed."

———

THEY DRIFTED FROM THE meeting. Nobody spoke. Morland went outside to smoke another cigarette, and watched them go. He didn't care
what Hayley Conyer thought of his nicotine addiction now. It was the
least of his worries. Anyway, his days as chief of police were now definitely numbered. She had emasculated him back in the living room,
just as surely as if she had used on him the blade with which she had
threatened to remove Bryan Joblin's manhood. It was then appropriate, somehow, that it was only Luke Joblin who lingered after most of
the others had departed, Souleby leaving alone, Ayton taking responsibility for the fading vileness of Kinley Nowell.

Morland offered Joblin a smoke, and he accepted.

"I knew you hadn't really given up," said Morland.

Joblin had spent the last couple of months trumpeting the fact that
he'd kicked cigarettes, although he boasted loudest when his wife was
near.

"Barbara thinks that I have," he said. "I don't know which is costing
me more, the cigarettes or the breath mints."

Together they watched the rear lights of the last car disappear as the
vehicle turned onto the road and headed toward town.

"Something on your mind, Luke?" said Morland.

"I'm worried," said Joblin.

"About Bryan?"

"Jesus, no. You're right; he's not bright, but he can take care of
himself. If you need help with the Dixons, you can rely on him. He's a
stand-up young man."

Bryan Joblin wasn't a stand-up anything. He was borderline psy-
chotic, with a deep wellspring of viciousness and sexual deviance
from which to draw, but Morland kept that opinion to himself. He had
few friends on the board, and he didn't need to alienate Luke Joblin
too.

Joblin took a long drag on the cigarette. "No, it's the Backers. I don't
understand why we didn't approach them. We don't want to cross

them. They could crush us. We should have spoken to them before we acted, but Hayley shot down that idea as soon as it was raised. Why?"

"Because we worship different gods," said Hayley Conyer from behind them.

Morland hadn't even heard her approach. One second they were alone, and the next she had materialized at their backs.

"I'm sorry," said Joblin, although it wasn't clear whether he was referring to his criticism of the decision or the fact that he'd been caught smoking in Conyer's yard, or both. He looked for somewhere to put out the cigarette. He didn't want to drop it. Finally, he settled for lifting the sole of his left shoe and stubbing the butt out on the leather. It left a scorch mark. He would have to hide the shoe until he found time to get new soles made. His wife would wonder what a reformed smoker was doing stubbing out cigarettes on three-hundred-dollar shoes. Morland took the butt from him and put it in his now empty pack.

"Don't be," said Conyer. "It is at the root of all that we do here, all that we're trying to protect. We aren't like the Backers, and their god isn't like our god. Theirs is a wicked god, an angry god."

"And ours?" said Morland.

He saw Warraner standing on the porch steps, watching them. Behind him, two figures waited in the hallway.

Hayley Conyer laid a gentle hand on Morland's forearm. It was a peculiarly intimate gesture, equal parts consolation, reassurance, and, he recognized, regretful dismissal.

"Ours," she said, "is merely hungry."

———

THE WOLF HAD FOUND the meat: a slab of bloody venison haunch. He circled it, still wary despite his need, but at last he could no longer resist.

He took two steps forward, and the trap snapped shut upon his paw.

XXXVI

F ounded in 1794, and located on the shores of Casco Bay where the Androscoggin River flowed into the sea, Bowdoin College was routinely ranked among the top colleges in America. Its list of alumni included Henry Wadsworth Longfellow, Nathaniel Hawthorne, the explorer Robert Peary, and the sexologist Alfred Kinsey. Unfortunately, it did not appear to include Prosperous's own Pastor Warraner. An early morning call to the Office of Alumni Relations produced no record of a Michael Warraner among its former students, and a similar inquiry left at Bangor Theological Seminary also drew a blank.

While I was still sucking on a pencil and trying to figure out why Warraner would bother to lie about something that could so easily be checked, I received a follow-up call from a secretary at Bowdoin. Apparently, one of their associate professors was interested in meeting with me. He was free that afternoon, in fact, if I could find the time to "pop up" to the college.

"Did he really say that?" I asked.

"Say what?" said the secretary.

"'Pop up'?"

"That's how he speaks. He's from England."

"Ah."

"Yes. Ah."

"Please tell him that I'd be delighted to pop up."

Somewhere among Bowdoin's faculty of religion, the name Warraner had set a small alarm bell ringing.

———

PROFESSOR IAN WILLIAMSON LOOKED exactly as I'd always believed most academics should look but rarely did: slightly disheveled—but not so much as to raise too many concerns about his mental well-being—and fond of waistcoats and varieties of tweed, although in his case the potential fustiness of the cloth was offset by his choice of Converse sneakers as footwear. He was youthful, bearded, and cheerfully distracted, as though at any moment he might catch sight of an interesting cloud and run after it in order to lasso it with a piece of string.

As it turned out, Williamson was a decade older than I was, so clearly the academic life agreed with him. He'd been at Bowdoin for more than twenty years, although he still spoke like a weekend visitor to Downton Abbey. Frankly, if Professor Williamson's accent couldn't get him laid in Maine, then nothing could. He specialized in Religious Tolerance and Comparative Mystical Traditions, and his office in the lovely old faculty building was filled equally with books and assorted religious bric-a-brac, so that it was somewhere between a library and a market stall.

He offered me coffee from his own personal Nespresso machine, put his feet up on a pile of books, and asked me why I was interested in Michael Warraner.

"I could ask you the same thing," I said, "given that he doesn't appear to be one of your alumni."

"Ah, fencing," said Williamson. "Right. I see. Excellent."

"What?" I said, not seeing.

"Fencing." He made a parrying gesture with an imaginary foil and accompanied it with a swishing noise, just to make certain that I got the picture. Which I didn't.

"Sorry, are you challenging me to a duel?"

"What? No. I meant verbal fencing—the old thrust and parry. Philip Marlowe and all that. I say, you say. You know, that kind of thing."

He stared animatedly at me. I stared less animatedly back.

"Or perhaps not," said Williamson, and a little of his enthusiasm seemed to leach away. I felt as though I'd kicked a puppy.

"Let's say that I'm curious about Prosperous," I said. "And I'm curious about Pastor Warraner. He seems like a strange man in an odd town."

Williamson sipped his Nespresso. Behind him, on his otherwise empty desk, I noticed a trio of books with their spines facing toward me. All related to the Green Man. It couldn't have been a coincidence that they were displayed so prominently.

"Michael Warraner entered Bowdoin as a liberal arts student when he was in his midtwenties," said Williamson. "From the start, it was clear that his focus was on religious studies. It's a demanding regimen, and tends only to attract students with a real passion for the subject. A major consists of nine courses, a minor five, with two courses required: Introduction to the Study of Religion, or Religion 101, and Theories About Religion. The rest are composed of various options from Asian Religions, Islam and Post-Biblical Judaism, Christianity and Gender, and Bible and Comparative Studies. Clear enough?"

"Absolutely."

Williamson shifted in his chair.

"Warraner was not the most able of students," he said. "In fact, his admission hung in the balance for some time, but he had influential supporters."

"From Prosperous?"

"And elsewhere. It was clear that efforts were being made on his behalf. On the other hand, we were aware that space existed in courses for dedicated students, and . . ."

"Yes?"

"There was a certain amount of curiosity among faculty members, myself included, about Prosperous. As you're no doubt aware, it is a town founded by a secretive religious sect, the history and ultimate fate of which remain nebulous to this day. By admitting Warraner, it seemed that we might be in a position to learn more about the town and its history."

"And how did that work out?"

"We got what you might refer to as 'the party line.' Warraner gave us a certain amount of information, and we were also permitted to study the church and its environs, but we really found out very little about Prosperous and the Family of Love that we didn't already know. Furthermore, Warraner's academic limitations were exposed at a very early stage. He struggled to scrape together credits and D grades. Eventually, we were forced to let him go.

"Pastor Warraner, as he subsequently began to style himself, was later readmitted to this college as a 'special student.' Special students are people from the local community who, for whatever reason, desire to resume their education on a part-time basis. While they're assessed on their academic record, non-academic achievements are also considered. They pay course fees, and no financial aid is available to them. Their work is graded, and they receive a college transcript, but they are non-degree candidates, and therefore cannot graduate. Pastor Warraner took ten such courses over a period of about five years, some more successfully and enthusiastically than others. He was surprisingly open to issues of Christianity and gender, less so to Asian religions, Islam, and Judaism. Overall, my impression was that Warraner desired the imprimatur of a college education. He wanted to say that he had been to college, and that was all."

"I believe he also told me that he'd majored in religion at Bowdoin, and studied as a Master of Divinity at Bangor Theological Seminary."

"I suppose, if one were being generous-spirited enough, those statements might offer a certain latitude of interpretation, the latter more than the former. If you asked around, I bet you'd find that he approached Bangor at some point and was rebuffed, or tried to sit in unofficially on seminars. It would fit with that desire for affirmation and recognition."

"Any other impression he may have left on you?"

"He was a fanatic."

"Doesn't that come with the territory?"

"Sometimes. Warraner, though, could rarely string together more than a couple of sentences without referring to 'his' god."

"And what kind of god does he worship? I've met him, and I've seen his church, and I'm still not sure just what kind of pastor he is."

"Superficially, Warraner is a variety of austere Protestant. There's a bit of the Baptist in him, a sprinkling of Methodism, a dash of Quaker, but also a healthy dose of pantheism. None of it is particularly deep, though. His religion, for want of a better explanation, is his church—the bricks and mortar of it. He worships a building, or what that building represents for him. You say that you've seen it?"

"I got the grand tour."

"And what did you think?"

"It's a little light on crosses for my tastes."

"Catholic?"

"Occasional."

"I was raised in the Church of England—Low, I should add—and even I found Warraner's chapel positively spartan."

"The carvings apart."

"Yes, they are interesting, aren't they? Unusual here in the United States. Less so, perhaps, among the older churches of England and certain parts of Europe, although Warraner's are quite distinctive. It's a

Familist church, of that there can be little doubt, but a Familist church of a particular type. This is not the element of the sect that fed into the Quakers or the Unitarians, infused with a spirit of peace and gentleness. It's something harsher."

"And Warraner—is he still a Familist?"

Williamson finished his coffee. He seemed to be considering making more, then thought better of it. He put his cup down.

"Yes, Mr. Parker," he said. "I believe that not only is Warraner a Familist but that Prosperous remains a Familist community. To what end, I couldn't say."

"And their god?"

"Look again at those carvings inside the church, if you get the chance. My suspicion is that, somewhere along the line, the link between God—the Christian deity—and the rule of nature has become lost to Warraner and those who share his religious convictions. All that's left is the carvings. For the people of Prosperous, those are the faces of their god."

I stood to leave. As I did so, Williamson handed me the books from his desk.

"I thought these might interest you," he said. "Just pop them in the post when you're done with them."

There he was again, "pop"-ing, and putting things in the "post." He caught me smiling.

"Did I say something funny?"

"I was just wondering how many dates you'd gotten in the United States because of that accent of yours."

He grinned. "It did seem to make me very popular for a while. I suspect I may even have married out of my league because of it."

"It's the residual colonial admiration for the oppressor."

"Spoken like a history major."

"No, not me, but Warraner said something similar when I met him. He drew an analogy between detection and historical research."

"But aren't all investigations historical?" said Williamson. "The crime is committed in the past, and the investigation conducted in the present. It's a form of excavation."

"Do you feel a paper coming on?"

"You know, I might do, at that."

I flicked through the first of the books. It was heavily illustrated with images and drawings.

"Pictures too," I said.

"If you color any of them in, we may be forced to have a long talk."

"One last question?" I said.

"Go right ahead."

"Why are so many of these faces threatening, or hostile?"

"Fear," said Williamson. "Fear of the power of nature, fear of old gods. And perhaps, too, the early Church found in such depictions a literal representation of a metaphorical concept—the *radix malorum*, the 'root of all evil.' Hell, if you choose to believe in it, is beneath our feet, not above our heads. You'd have to dig deep to find it, but it wasn't difficult for Christians with ancient links to the land to conceive of the influence of the maleficent in terms of twisted roots and clinging ivy, of faces formed by something buried far beneath the earth trying to create a physical representation of itself from whatever materials were at hand. But the god depicted on the walls of the Prosperous chapel has no connection with Christianity. It's older, and beyond conceptions of good and evil. It simply *is*."

"You sound almost as though you believe in it yourself."

"Perhaps I just sometimes find it easier to understand how someone could conceive and worship a god of tree and leaf, a god that formed as the land around it formed, than a bearded figure living on a cloud in the sky."

"Does that count as a crisis of faith?"

He grinned again. "No, only a natural consequence of the study of every shade of religious belief, and of trying to teach the importance of being tolerant in a world in which tolerance is associated with weakness or heresy."

"Let me guess—you and Michael Warraner didn't exactly see eye to eye on that subject."

"No. He wasn't hostile toward other forms of religious belief, merely uninterested."

"When I see him again, should I pass on your good wishes?" I said.

"I'd prefer if you didn't," said Williamson.

"Frightened?"

"Wary. You should be too." He was no longer distracted, no longer smiling. "One of the challenges I like to set my students for their first class is a word association game. I ask them to list all the words, positive or negative, that come to mind when they think of 'god.' Sometimes I get pages of words, at other times a handful, but Warraner was the only student who ever wrote just one solitary word. That word was "hunger." He and those like him worship a hungry god, Mr. Parker, and no good can ever come of worshipping a deity that hungers. No good at all."

XXXVII

I drove back toward Scarborough, but stopped off at Bull Moose Music's massive warehouse store on Payne Road and browsed the racks for an hour. It was part pleasure, part displacement activity. I felt that I'd reached a dead end as far as Prosperous was concerned, and my talk with Williamson had served only to confirm my own suspicions about the town without opening any new avenues of inquiry.

I was no closer to finding Annie Broyer than I had been when I started out, and I was beginning to wonder if I might not have been mistaken in assuming that everything I had learned in the past week was useful or even true: an elderly couple, a blue car, a passing reference to a job in Prosperous made to a woman with the mental capacity of a child, and a homeless man's obsession with the carvings on an ancient church. Every piece of information I had gathered was open to question, and it was entirely possible that Annie Broyer would turn up in Boston, or Chicago, or Seattle in the days and weeks to come. Even Lucas Morland's passing reference to Annie as an "ex-junkie" could be explained away if he had made a simple phone call to Portland or Bangor after my first visit to the town. In the eyes of some, I had already violated the primary commandment of an investigation: don't assume. Don't create patterns where there are none. Don't conceive of a narrative and then force the evidence to fit it. On the other hand, all investigations involve a degree of speculation—the capacity to bear witness to a crime and imagine a chain of events that might have caused that crime to be committed. An investigation was not simply a matter of historical research, as Warraner had suggested. It was an act of faith both in one's own capacities and in the possibility of justice in a world that had made justice subservient to the rule of law.

But I had no crime to investigate. I had only a homeless man with a history of depression who might well have hanged himself in a fit of desperation, and a missing girl with a history of narcotic and alcohol abuse who had drifted for most of her life. Was I fixating on Prosperous because its citizens were wealthy and privileged, while Jude and his daughter were poor and suffering? Was I marking Warraner and Morland for simply doing what a pastor and a policeman should do, which was to protect their people?

And yet . . .

Michael Warraner wasn't quite a fraud, but something potentially much more dangerous: a frustrated man with a set of religious or spiritual principles that reinforced his inflated opinion of himself and his place in the world. It was also clear from the way Morland reacted to my unauthorized visit to the church that Warraner had a position of authority in the town, which meant that there were influential individuals who either shared his beliefs or didn't entirely discount them.

What—if anything—all that had to do with the disappearance of Annie and the death of her father, I did not know. Prosperous just felt wrong to me, and I'd grown to trust my feelings. Then again, Angel and Louis might have asked if I ever felt *right* about anything, and if I'd learned to trust those feelings too. I could have countered by replying that nobody ever asked for my help when there wasn't a problem, but I then found myself growing annoyed that I was having arguments—and, more to the point, losing them—with Angel and Louis even when they weren't actually present.

I headed into Portland, where I caught a movie at the Nickelodeon and then ate a burger at the Little Tap House on High Street. The building had once housed Katahdin before that restaurant's move to Forest Avenue. A tapas place had briefly occupied the location in the aftermath of the move, and now the Little Tap House had carved out a niche for itself as a neighborhood bar with good food. I drank a soda and tried to read a little of the books with which Williamson had entrusted me. They traced the development of foliate sculpture from at least the first century AD, through its adoption by the early Church, and on to its proliferation throughout Western Europe. Some of the illustrations were more graphic than others. My server seemed particularly dismayed by a capital in the cathedral at Autun that depicted a man disappearing into the jaws of a leafed face. Many of the carvings, such as a thirteenth-century mask from Bamberg Cathedral, in Germany, had a kind of beauty to them, which rendered them even more sinister.

I did find a source for Williamson's Latin reference: the apocryphal gospel of Nicodemus, in which Satan was described as *radix omnium malorum*, "the root of all evil," alongside a picture of a tricephalos, a three-faced demon from the façade of San Pietro, in Tuscany. Coiling tendrils pushed through the mouths of the demons, extrusions from the original root, and the text described them as "blood-suckers" in the context of another fifteenth-century head from Melrose Abbey. Here too there was a reference to the relationship between the human and plant elements in the masks as essentially hostile or parasitic, although the general consensus seemed to be that they represented a type of symbiosis, a long-term interaction and mutually beneficial relationship between two species. Man received the blessings of nature's fruits, or the rebirth wrought by the changing of the seasons, and in return—

Well, that last part wasn't so clear, although the cathedral at Autun, with its images of consumption, offered one possible realm of speculation.

I closed the books, paid my tab, and left the bar. The weather had warmed up a little since the previous night—not by much, but the weathermen were already predicting that the worst of winter was now behind us for another year; prematurely, I suspected. The sky was clear as I drove home, and the saltwater marshes smelled fresh and clean as I parked outside my house. I walked around to the back door to enter by the kitchen. It had become a habit with me ever since Rachel and Sam moved out. Entering by the front door and seeing the empty hallway was somehow more depressing than going in through the kitchen, which was where I spent most of my time anyway. I opened the door and had reached out to key in the alarm code when my dead daughter spoke to me from behind. She said just one word

daddy

and it contained within it the prospect of living and the hope of dying, of endings and beginnings, of love and loss and peace and rage, all wrapped up in two whispered syllables.

I was already diving to the floor when the first of the shotgun blasts hit me, the pellets tearing the skin from my back, the hair from my skull, the flesh from my bones. I burned. I fell to the kitchen floor, and found the strength to kick at the door, knocking it closed, but the second blast blew away the lock and most of the glass, showering me with slivers and splinters. The floor was slick with my blood as I tried to rise, my feet sliding in the redness. I somehow stumbled into the hallway, and now pistol shots were sounding from behind me. I felt the force of their impact in my back, and my shoulder, and my side. I went down again, but as the pain took hold I found it in myself to twist my body to the left. I screamed as I landed on the floor, but I was now halfway across the doorway of my office. My right hand found the corner of the wall, and I dragged myself inside. Again I kicked a door closed, and managed to seat myself upright against my desk. I drew my gun. I raised it and fired a round. I didn't know what it hit. I didn't care. It was enough that it was in my hand.

"Come on," I cried, and blood and spittle sprayed from my lips. "*Come on!*" I said, louder now, and I did not know if I was speaking to myself or to whatever or whomever lay beyond the door.

"Come on," I said a third time, to the approaching darkness, to the figures that beckoned from within it, to the peace that comes at last to every dead thing. Above it all sounded the wailing of the alarm.

I fired again, and two bullets tore through the door in response. One missed. The other did not.

"Come—"

———

THE WOLF LOOKED UP at the men who surrounded him. He had tried to gnaw his trapped paw off, but had not succeeded. Now he was weary. The time had come. He snarled at the hunters, the fur around his mouth wet with his own blood. A sharp, bitter scent troubled his senses, the smell of noise and dying.

He howled, the final sound that he would ever make. In it was both defiance and a kind of resignation. He was calling on death to come for him.

The gun fired, and the wolf was gone.

———

"HOLD HIM! HOLD HIM!"

Light. No light.

"Jesus, I can't even get a grip on him, there's so much blood. Okay, on three. One, two—"

"Ah, for Christ's sake."

"His back is just meat. What the fuck happened here?"

Light. No light. Light.

"Can you hear me?"

Yes. No. I saw the paramedic. I saw Sharon Macy behind him. I tried to speak, but no words would come.

"Mr. Parker, can you hear me?"

Light. Stronger now. "You stay with me, you hear? You stay!"

Up. Movement. Ceiling. Lights.

Stars.

Darkness.

Gone.

CHAPTER

XXXVIII

The house, larger than most of its neighbors, lay on a nondescript road midway between Rehoboth Beach and Dewey Beach on the Delaware coast. Most of the surrounding homes were vacation rentals or summer places used by Washingtonians with a little money to spend. Transience was the norm here. True, a handful of year-round residents lived on the road, but they tended to mind their own business and left others to mind theirs.

A significant number of the homes in the area were owned by gay couples, for Rehoboth had long been one of the East Coast's most gay-friendly resorts. This was perhaps surprising, given that Rehoboth was founded in 1873 by the Reverend Robert W. Todd as a Methodist meeting camp. Reverend Todd's vision of a religious community was short-lived, though, and by the 1940s the gay Hollywood crowd was carousing at the DuPont property along the ocean. Then came the Pink Pony Bar in the 1950s, and the Pleasant Inn and the Nomad Village in the 1960s, all known to be welcoming to DC's more closeted citizens. In the 1990s, some of the town's less tolerant residents made a vain attempt to restore what were loosely termed "family values," in some cases by beating the shit out of anyone who even looked gay. But negotiations among representatives of the gay community, homeowners, and the police largely put an end to the unrest, and Rehoboth settled gently into its role as not only the "Nation's Summer Capital" but the "Nation's *Gay* Summer Capital."

The big house was rarely occupied, even by the standards of vacation homes. Neither was its care entrusted to any of the local Realtors, many of whom boosted their income by acting as agents for summer rentals, and taking care of houses during the winter months. Nevertheless, it was well kept, and local rumor suggested that it had been bought either as part of some complicated tax write-off (in which case the fewer questions asked about it the better, especially in an area swarming with Washingtonians who might or might not have connections to the IRS) or as a corporate investment, for its ownership apparently lay with a shelf company, itself a part of another shelf company, on and on like a series of seemingly infinite matryoshka dolls.

And now, with the hold of winter still upon the land, and the beaches largely empty and devoid of life, the house at last was occupied. Two men, one young and one old, had been noticed entering and leaving, although they did not socialize in any of the local bars and restaurants, and the older gentleman appeared somewhat frail.

But two men, of whatever vintages, living together was not so unusual in Rehoboth Beach, and so their presence went largely unremarked.

———

INSIDE THE HOUSE, THE Collector brooded by a window. There was no view of the sea here, only a line of trees that protected the house and its occupants from the curiosity of others. The furnishings were largely antiques, some acquired through clever investment but most through bequests, and occasionally by means of outright theft. The Collector viewed such acquisitions as little more than his due. After all, the previous owners had no more use for them, the previous owners being, without exception, dead.

The Collector heard the sound of the lawyer Eldritch coughing and moving about in the next room. Eldritch slept more since the explosion that had almost cost him his life, and had destroyed the records of crimes, both public and private, painstakingly assembled over many decades of investigation. Even had the old man not been so frail, the loss of the files would have seriously curtailed the Collector's activities. He had not realized just how much he relied upon Eldritch's knowledge and complicity in order to hunt and prey. Without Eldritch, the Collector was reduced to the status of an onlooker, left to speculate on the sins of others without the evidence needed to damn them.

But in recent days some of Eldritch's old energy had returned, and he had begun the process of rebuilding his archive. His memory was astonishing in its recall, but his recent sufferings and losses had spurred him still harder to force it to relinquish its store of secrets, fueled by hatred and the desire for revenge. He had lost almost everything that mattered to him: a woman who had been both his consort and his accomplice, and a lifetime's work of cataloging the mortal failings of men. All he had left now was the Collector, and he would be the weapon with which Eldritch avenged himself.

And so, where once the lawyer had been a check on the Collector's urges, he now fed them. Each day brought the two men ever closer. It reminded the Collector that, on one level, they were still father and son, although the thing that lived inside the Collector was very old, and very far from human, and the Collector had largely forgotten his previous identity as the son of the ancient lawyer in the next room.

The house was one of the newest of the Collector's property investments, but also one of the best concealed. Curiously, he owed its existence to the detective Parker. The Collector had arrived in Rehoboth as part of his exploration of the detective's past, his attempt to understand Parker. It was an element of Parker's history—a minor one, admittedly, but the Collector was nothing if not meticulous—and therefore worthy of examination. The house, modest yet handsome, drew the Collector. He was weary of sparsely furnished hideouts, of uncarpeted rooms filled only with mementos of the dead. He needed a place in which to rest, to contemplate, to plan, and so it was that, through Eldritch, he acquired the house. It remained one of the few in which he still felt secure, particularly since the detective and his friends had begun tracking him, seeking to punish him for the death of one of their own. It was off to Rehoboth that the Collector had spirited the lawyer once his wounds had healed sufficiently to enable him to travel, and now the Collector too was sequestered here. He had never known what it was to be hunted before, for he had always been the hunter. They had come close to trapping him in Newark: the recurrent pain from the torn ligaments in his leg was a reminder of that. This situation could not continue. There was harvesting to be done.

Worse, when night came the Hollow Men gathered at his window. He had deprived them of life and returned their souls to their maker. What was left of them lingered, drawn to him not only because they erroneously believed that it was he alone who had caused their suffering—the dead being as capable of self-delusion as the living—but because he could add to their number. That was their only comfort: that others might suffer as they did. But now they sensed his weakness, his vulnerability, and with it came a terrible, warped hope that the Collector would be wiped from the earth, and with his passing might come the oblivion they desired. At night they gathered among the trees, their skin wrinkled and mottled like old, diseased fruit, waiting, willing the detective and his allies to descend upon the Collector.

I could kill them, thought the Collector. I could tear Parker apart, and the ones called Angel and Louis. There was enough evidence against them to justify it, enough sin to tip the scales.

Probably.

Possibly.

But what if he was wrong? What might the consequences be? He had killed their friend in a fit of rage, and as a result he was now little better than a marked animal, running from hole to hole, the ring of hunters tightening around him. If the Collector were to kill the detective, his friends would not rest until the Collector was himself buried. If the Collector were to kill Parker's friends yet leave him alive, the detective would track him to the ends of the earth. And if, by some miracle, he were to kill all three of them? Then a line would have been crossed, and those who protected the detective from the shadows would finish what he had started and hunt the Collector to death. Whatever choice the Collector made would end the same way: the pursuit would continue until he was cornered and his punishment meted out.

The Collector wanted a cigarette. The lawyer did not like him to smoke in the house. He said that it affected his breathing. The Collector could go outside, of course, but he realized that he had grown fearful of showing himself, as if the slightest moment of carelessness might undo him. He had never before been so frightened. The experience was proving unpleasantly enlightening.

The Collector concluded that he could not kill the detective. Even if he were to do so and somehow escape the consequences of his actions, he would ultimately be acting against the Divine. The detective was important. He had a role to play in what was to come. He was human, of that the Collector was now certain, but there was an aspect of him that was beyond understanding. Somehow, in some way, he had touched, or been touched by, the Divine. He had survived so much. Evil had been drawn to him, and he had destroyed it in every instance. There were entities that feared the Collector, and yet they feared the detective even more.

There was no solution. There was no escape.

He closed his eyes, and felt the gloating triumph of the Hollow Men.

———

THE LAWYER ELDRITCH TURNED on his computer and returned to the task in hand: the reconstruction of his records. He was progressing alphabetically, for the most part, but if a later name or detail came to him unexpectedly he would open a separate file and input the new information. The physical records had been little more than aides-mémoire; everything that mattered was contained in his brain.

His ears ached. His hearing had been damaged in the explosion that killed the woman and destroyed his files, and now he had to endure a continuous high-pitched tinnitus. Some of the nerves in his hands and feet had been damaged as well, causing his legs to spasm as he tried to sleep, and his fingers to freeze into claws if he wrote or typed for too long. His condition was slowly improving, but he was forced to make do without proper physiotherapy or medical advice, for the Collector feared that if Eldritch showed himself it might draw the detective down upon them.

Let him come, thought Eldritch in his worst moments, as he lay awake in his bed, his legs jerking so violently that he could almost feel the muscles starting to tear, his fingers curling so agonizingly that he was certain the bones must break through the skin. Let him come, and let us be done with all this. But somehow he would steal enough sleep to continue, and each day he tried to convince himself that he could discern a diminution in his sufferings: more time between the spasms in his legs, like a child counting the seconds between cracks of thunder to reassure himself that the storm was passing; a little more control over his fingers and toes, like a transplant patient learning to use a new limb; and a slight reduction in the intensity of the noise in his ears, in the hope that madness might be held at bay.

The Collector had set up a series of highly secure email drop boxes for Eldritch, with five-step verification and a prohibition on any outside access. Telephone contact was forbidden—it was too easy to trace—but the lawyer still had his informants, and it was important that he remain in touch with them. Now Eldritch opened the first of the drop boxes. There was only one message inside. Its subject line was "IN CASE YOU DID NOT SEE THIS," and it was only an hour old. The message contained a link to a news report.

Eldritch cut and pasted the link before opening it. It took him to that evening's News Center on NBC's Channel 6, out of Portland, Maine. He watched the report in silence, letting it play in its entirety before he called to the man in the next room.

"Come here," said Eldritch. "You need to look at this."

Moments later, the Collector appeared at his shoulder.

"What is it?" he said.

Eldritch let the news report play a second time.

"The answer to our problems."

XXXIX

Garrison Pryor was on his way to the chef's table at L'Espalier, on Boylston, when the call came through to his personal cell phone, the one that was changed weekly, and for which only a handful of people had the number at any time. He was particularly surprised to see the identity of the caller. Pryor hit the green answer button immediately.

"Yes?" he said.

There would be no pleasantries. The Principal Backer didn't like to linger on unsecured lines.

"Have you seen the news?"

"No, I've been in meetings all day, and I'm about to join some clients for a late dinner."

"Your phone has Internet access?"

"Of course."

"Go to Channel Six in Portland. Call me when you're done."

Pryor didn't argue or object. He was running late for dinner, but it didn't matter now. The Principal Backer didn't make such calls lightly.

Pryor hung up and found a spot against the wall by the entrance to the Copley T station. It didn't take him long to find the news report to which the Principal Backer had been referring. He went to the

Portland Press Herald's Web site, just in case it had further details, but there were none.

He waited a moment, gathered his thoughts, then called the Principal Backer.

"Are you at home?" asked Pryor.

"Yes."

"But you can talk?"

"For now. Was it one of ours?"

"No."

"You're certain?"

"Absolutely. Nobody would have made a move like this without consulting me first, and I would have given no such authorization. It was decided: we should wait."

"Make sure that we weren't involved."

"I will, but there's no doubt in my mind. The man was not short of enemies."

"Neither are we. There will be consequences for all of us if we're found to be anywhere near this."

"I'll send out word. There will be no further activity until you say otherwise."

"And get somebody to Scarborough. I want to know exactly what happened at that house."

"I'll make the call now."

There was silence on the other end of the line, then:

"I hear L'Espalier is very good."

"Yes." It took Pryor a second or two to realize that he had not told the Principal Backer where he was eating that night. "Yes, it is."

"Perhaps you should inform your clients that you won't be able to make it to dinner after all."

The connection was cut off. Pryor looked at the phone. He'd only had it for two days. He removed the battery, wiped it with his gloves, and tossed it in the trash. As he walked on, he broke the SIM card and dropped the pieces down a drain. He crossed Boylston, heading for Newbury. He stepped into the shadows of Public Alley 440, put the phone on the ground, and began grinding it beneath his heel, harder and harder, until finally he was stamping furiously on fragments of plastic and circuitry, swearing as he did so. Two pedestrians glanced at him as they passed down Exeter, but they didn't stop.

Pryor pressed his forehead against the wall of the nearest building and closed his eyes.

Consequences: that was an understatement. If someone had made an unauthorized hit on the detective, there was no limit to how bad things might get.

————

IN AN APARTMENT IN Brooklyn, the rabbi named Epstein sat before his computer screen, watching and listening.

It had been a long day of discussions, arguments, and something resembling slow progress, assuming one took a tectonic view of such matters. Epstein, along with two of his fellow moderate rabbis, was trying to hammer out compromises between the borough of Brooklyn and the local Hasidim on a lengthy series of issues, including the Hasidim's desire for the separation of the sexes on city buses and their religious objections to the use of bicycles, mostly with little success. Today, for his sins, Epstein had been forced to explain the concept of *metzizah b'peh*—the practice of oral suction from a baby's circumcision wound—to a disbelieving councilman.

"But why would anyone want to do that?" the councilman kept asking. "Why?"

And, to be honest, Epstein didn't really have an answer or, at least, not one that would satisfy the councilman.

Meanwhile, some of the young Hasidim apparently regarded Epstein with little more affection than they did the goyim. He even heard one of them refer to him behind his back as an *alter kocker*—an "old

fart"—but he didn't react. Their elders knew better, and at least acknowledged that Epstein was trying to help by acting as a go-between,
attempting to find a compromise with which both the Hasidim and
the city could live. Still, if they had their way the Hasidim would wall
off Williamsburg from the rest of Brooklyn, although they'd probably
have to fight the hipsters for it. The situation wasn't helped by certain
city officials publicly comparing the Hasidim to the Mafia. At times,
it was enough to make a reasonable man consider abandoning both
his faith and his city. But there was a saying in Hebrew, "We survived
Pharoah, we'll survive this too." In the words of the old joke, it was the
theme of every Jewish holiday: they tried to kill us, they failed, so let's
eat!

With that in mind, Epstein was hungry when he arrived home,
but all thoughts of food were gone now. Beside him stood a young
woman dressed in black. Her name was Liat. She was deaf and mute,
so she could not hear the news report, but she could read the anchor-
man's lips when he appeared onscreen. She took in the images of the
police cars, and the house, and the picture of the detective that was
being used on all the news reports. It was not a recent photograph.
He looked older now. She recalled his face as they had made love, and
the feel of his damaged body against hers.

So many scars, so many wounds, both visible and hidden.

Epstein touched her arm. She looked down at his face so that she
could watch his lips move.

"Go up there," he said. "Find out what you can. I will start making
inquiries here."

She nodded and left.

Strange, thought Epstein: he had never seen her cry before.

XL

It was Bryan Joblin who told them the news, just as he was running out the door. His departure at that moment, leaving them alone, seemed a godsend. Harry and Erin had been growing increasingly fractious with Joblin as his perpetual presence in their lives began to tell on them, while he had settled happily into his role as their watcher, houseguest, and sometime accomplice in a crime yet to be committed. He still pressed Harry to find a girl, as if Harry needed to be reminded. Hayley Conyer herself had stopped by the house that morning while they were clearing up after breakfast, and she had made it very clear to the Dixons that they were running out of time.

"Things are going to start moving fast around here pretty soon," Conyer said, as she stood at the front door, as though reluctant even to set foot once again in their crumbling home. "A lot of our problems are about to disappear, and we can start concentrating again on the tasks that matter."

She leaned in close to the Dixons, and Harry could smell on her breath the sour stink that he always associated with his mother's dying—the stench of the body's internal workings beginning to atrophy.

"You should know that there are folk in Prosperous who blame you for what happened to our young men in Afghanistan, and to Valerie Gillson and Ben Pearson, too," she said. "They believe that if you hadn't let the girl go"—Conyer allowed the different possible interpretations of that conditional clause to hang in the air for a moment—"then four of our people might still be alive. You have a lot of work to do to make up for your failings. I'm giving you three days. By then, you'd better produce a substitute girl for me."

But Harry knew that they wouldn't be around in three days, or, if they were, it would probably be the end of them. They were ready to run. Had Bryan Joblin not told them of what had occurred, then left them for a time to their own devices, they might have waited another day, just to be sure that everything was in place for their escape. Now they took his news as a sign: it was time. They watched him drive away, his words still ringing in their ears.

"We hit the detective," Joblin told them. "It's all over the news. That fucker is gone. *Gone!*"

And, within twenty minutes of Joblin's departure, the Dixons had left Prosperous.

———

HARRY MADE THE CALL on the way to Medway. The auto dealership closed most evenings at six, but Harry had the dealer's cell phone number and knew that he lived only a couple of blocks from the lot. He'd told the guy that, if it came down to the wire, he might have to leave the state at short notice. He had spun the man a line about a sick mother, knowing that the dealer couldn't have given a rat's ass if Harry's mother was Typhoid Mary, as long as he paid cash alongside the trade-in. So it was that, thirty minutes after leaving Prosperous, the Dixons drove out of the lot in a GMC Savana Passenger Van with 100,000 miles on the clock, stopping only at the outskirts of Medway to call Magnus and Dianne and let them know that they were on their way. The van was ugly as a mudslide, but they could sleep in it if they had to, and who knew how long they might be on the road, or how far they might have to travel? They couldn't stay with Harry's in-laws for long. Even one night would be risky. In fact, the closer Harry got to the house in Medway, the more he started to feel that perhaps he and Erin shouldn't stay with them at all. It might be wiser just to pick up their stuff, arrange some way of remaining in contact, and then find a motel for the night. The more distance they put between themselves and Prosperous, the better. He expressed his concerns to Erin, and he was surprised when she concurred without argument. Her only regret, as far as he could tell, was that they hadn't managed to kill Bryan Joblin before they left Prosperous. She might have been joking, but somehow Harry doubted it.

They pulled up in the driveway of the house. The lights were on inside, and Harry could see Magnus watching TV in the living room, the drapes open. He saw his brother-in-law stand as he heard the sound of the engine. He waved at them from the window. They were still getting out of the van when Magnus opened the front door.

"Come in," he said. "We've been worrying ever since we got your call."

"Where's Dianne?" said Erin.

"She's in the bathroom. She'll be right down."

Magnus stood aside to let Harry and Erin enter.

"Let me take your coats," said Magnus.

"We're not staying," said Harry.

"That's not what you told us."

"I know what I told you, but I think it's better if we just keep driving. They're going to come looking for us once they find that we've gone, and it won't take them long to make the connection to you and Dianne. We need to put ground between Prosperous and us. I can't tell you why. We just have to leave the town far behind."

Magnus closed the front door. Harry could still feel a draft on his face, though. It was coming from the kitchen. A gust of wind passed through the house. It blew open the dining room door to their left. Inside, they saw Dianne seated in the dark by the table.

"I thought you were—" said Erin, but she got no further.

Bryan Joblin sat across from Dianne. He held a gun in his right hand, pointing loosely at her chest. Behind him was Calder Ayton. He too held a gun, but his was aimed at the head of Dianne's daughter, Kayley.

Harry's hand slid slowly toward the gun in his jacket pocket, just as Chief Morland appeared from the living room. He laid a hand on Harry's arm.

"Don't," said Morland, and his voice was almost kindly.

Harry's hand faltered, then fell to his side. Morland reached into Harry's pocket and removed the Smith & Wesson.

"You have a license for this?" said Morland.

Harry didn't reply.

"I didn't think so," said Morland.

He raised the gun and touched it to the back of Erin's head. He pulled the trigger, and the cream walls of the hallway blushed crimson. While Harry was still trying to take in the sight of his wife's body collapsing to the floor, Morland shot Magnus in the chest, then advanced three steps and killed Dianne with a single bullet that entered her face just below the bridge of her nose.

It was Kayley's screams that brought Harry back, but by then it was all too late. Morland swept Harry's feet from under him, sending him sprawling to the floor beside his dead wife. He stared at her. Her eyes were closed, her face contorted in a final grimace of shock. Harry wondered if she'd felt a lot of pain. He hoped not. He'd loved her. He'd loved her so very much.

Morland's weight was on his back now. Harry smelled the muzzle of the gun as it brushed his face.

"Do it," said Harry. "Just do it."

But instead the gun disappeared, and Harry's hands were cuffed loosely behind his back. Kayley had stopped screaming and was now sobbing. It sounded as if there might have been a hand across her mouth, though, for the sobs were muffled.

"Why?" said Harry.

"Because we can't have a multiple killing without a killer," said Morland.

He lifted Harry to his feet. Harry stared at him, his eyes glazed. Morland's features formed a mask of pure desolation.

Calder Ayton and Bryan Joblin emerged from the second entrance to the living room, carrying Kayley between them. They walked through the kitchen to the back door. Shortly after that, Harry heard the trunk of a car closing, and then the vehicle drove away.

"What's going to happen to her?" he asked.

"I think you already know," said Morland. "You were told to find us a girl. It looks like you did your duty after all."

Bryan Joblin reappeared in the kitchen. He smiled at Harry as he approached him.

"What now?" said Harry.

"You and Bryan are going to take a ride. I'll join you both as soon as I can."

Morland turned to leave, then paused.

"Tell me, Harry. Did the girl really escape, or did you let her go?"

What did it matter, thought Harry. The girl had still died, and soon he would join her.

"We let her go."

The use of the word "we" made him look down at Erin, and in doing so he missed the look that passed across Morland's face. It contained a hint of admiration.

Harry felt as though he should cry, but no tears would come. It was too late for tears, anyway, and they would serve no purpose.

"I'm sorry it's come down to this," said Morland.

"Go to hell, Lucas," said Harry.

"Yes," said Morland. "I think that I probably will."

XLI

A day passed. Night fell. All was changed, yet unchanged. The dead remained dead, and waited for the dying to join their number.

On the outskirts of Prosperous, a massive 4WD pulled up by the side of the road, disgorging one of its occupants before quickly turning back east. Ronald Straydeer hoisted a pack onto his back and headed for the woods, making his way toward the ruins of the church.

XLII

The two-story redbrick premises advertised itself as BLACKTHORN, APOTHECARY, although it had been many years since the store sold anything, and old Blackthorn himself was now long dead. It had, for much of its history, been the only business on Hunts Lane, a Brooklyn mews originally designed to stable the horses of the wealthy on nearby Remsen and Joralemon Streets.

The exterior wood surround was black, the lettering on and above the window gold, and its front door was permanently closed. The upstairs windows were shuttered, while the main window on the first floor was protected by a dense wire grille. The jumbled display behind it was a historical artifact, a collection of boxes and bottles bearing the names, where legible at all, of companies that no longer existed, and products with more than a hint of snake oil about them: Dalley's Magical Pain Extractor, Dr. Ham's Aromatic Invigorator, Dr. Miles's Nervine.

Perhaps, at some point in the past, an ancestor of the last Blackthorn had seen fit to offer such elixirs to his customers, along with remedies stranger still. A glass case inside the door contained packets of Potter's Asthma Smoking Mixture ("may be smoked in a pipe either with or without ordinary tobacco") and Potter's Asthma Care Cigarettes from the nineteenth century, along with Espic and Legras powders, the latter beloved of the French writer Marcel Proust, who used it to tackle his asthma and his hay fever. In addition to stramonium, a derivative of the common thorn apple, *Datura stramonium*, which was regarded as an effective remedy for respiratory problems, such products contained, variously, potash and arsenic. Now, long fallen from favor, they were memorialized in the gloom of Blackthorn, Apothecary, alongside malt beverages for nursing mothers, empty bottles of cocaine-based coca wine and heroin hydrochloride, and assorted preparations of morphine and opium for coughs, colds, and children's teething difficulties.

By the time the final Blackthorn was entering his twilight years—in a store that, most aptly, eschewed sunlight through the judicious use of heavy drapes and a sparing attitude toward electricity—the business that bore his family name sold only herbal medicines, and the musty interior still contained the evidence of Blackthorn's faith in the efficacy of natural solutions. The mahogany shelves were lined with glass jars containing moldering and desiccated herbs, although the various oils appeared to have survived the years with little change. A series of ornate lettered boards between the shelves detailed a litany of ailments and the herbs available to counteract their symptoms, from bad breath (parsley) and gas (fennel and dill) to cankers (goldenseal), cancer (bilberry, maitake mushroom, pomegranate, raspberry) and congestive heart failure (hawthorn). All was dust and dead insects, except on the floor, where regular footfalls had cleared a narrow path through the detritus of decades. This led from a side entrance beside the main door, through a hallway adorned with photographs of the dead, and amateur landscapes that bespoke a morbid fascination with the work of the more depressive German Romantics, and into the store itself by way of a door with panels decorated by graphically rendered scenes from the Passion of Christ. The path's final destination was obscured by a pair of black velvet drapes that closed off what had once been old Blackthorn's back room, in which the apothecary had created his tinctures and powders.

Now, as a chill rain fell on the streets, specks of light showed through the moth holes in the drapes, and they glittered like stars as unseen figures moved in the room behind. Evening had descended, and Hunts Lane was empty, apart from the two men who stood beneath the awning of an old stable, watching the storefront on the other side of the alley, and the vague signs of life from within.

Two days had passed since the shooting.

"He gives me the creeps," said Angel.

"Man gives everyone the creeps," said Louis. "There's dead folk would move out if they found themselves buried next to him."

"Why here?"

"Why not?"

"I guess. How long has he been holed up in that place?"

"Couple of weeks, if what I hear is true."

The location had cost Louis a considerable amount of money, along with one favor that he could never call in again. He didn't mind. This was personal.

"It's homely," said Angel. "In a Dickensian way—it's kind of appropriate. Any idea where he's been all these years?"

"No. He did have a habit of moving around."

"Not much choice. Probably doesn't make many friends in his line of work."

"Probably not."

"After all, you didn't."

"No."

"Except me."

"Yeah. About that . . ."

"Go fuck yourself."

"That would be the other option."

Angel stared at the building, and the building seemed to stare back.

"Strange that he should turn up now."

"Yes."

"You know what he was doing while he was gone?"

"What he's always been doing—causing pain."

"Maybe he thinks it'll take away some of his own."

Louis glanced at his partner.

"You know, you get real philosophical at unexpected moments."

"I was born philosophical. I just don't always care to share my thoughts with others, that's all. I think I might be a Stoic, if I understood what that meant. Either way, I like the sound of it."

"On your earlier point, he enjoyed inflicting pain, and watching others inflict it, even when he wasn't suffering himself."

"If you believed in a god, you might say it was divine retribution."

"Karma."

"Yeah, that too."

The rain continued to fall.

"You know," said Angel, "there's a hole in this awning."

"Yes."

"It's, like, a metaphor or something."

"Or just a hole."

"You got no poetry in your heart."

"No."

"You think he knows we're out here?"

"He knows."

"So?"

"You want to knock, be my guest."

"What'll happen?"

"You'll be dead."

"I figured it would be something like that. So we wait."

"Yes."

"Until?"

"Until he opens the door."

"And?"

"If he tries to kill us, we know he's involved."

"And if he doesn't try to kill us, then he's not involved?"

"No, then maybe he's just smarter than I thought."

"You said he was as smart as any man you'd ever known."

"That's right."

"Doesn't bode well for us."

"No."

There was a noise from across the alley: the sound of a key turning in a lock, and a bolt being pulled. Angel moved to the right, his gun already in his hand. Louis went left, and was absorbed by the darkness. A light bloomed slowly in the hallway, visible through the hemisphere of cracked glass above the smaller of the two doors. The door opened slowly, revealing a huge man. He remained very still, his hands slightly held out from his sides. Had Angel and Louis wanted to kill him, this would have been the perfect opportunity. But the message seemed clear: the one they had come to see wanted to talk. There would be no killing.

Not yet.

There was no further movement for a time. Angel's gaze alternated between the shuttered windows on the second floor of the apothecary and the entrance to Hunts Lane from Henry Street. Hunts Lane was a dead end. If this was a trap, there would be no escape. He had questioned Louis about their approach, wondering aloud if it might not be better for one of them to remain on the street while the other entered the alley, but Louis had demurred.

"He knows that we're coming. He's the last one."

"Which means?"

"That if it's a trap he'd spring it long before the alley. We'd be dead as soon as we set foot in Brooklyn. We just wouldn't know it until the blade fell."

None of this did Angel find reassuring. He had met this man only once before, when he sought to recruit Louis—and, by extension, Angel—for his own ends. The memory of that meeting had never faded. Angel had felt poisoned by it afterward, as though by breathing the same air as the man he had forever tainted his system.

Louis appeared again. He had his gun raised, aimed directly at the figure in the doorway. The giant stepped forward, and a motion-activated light went on above his head. He was truly enormous, his head like a grave monument on his shoulders, his chest and arms impossibly massive. Angel didn't recognize the face, and he would surely have remembered if he had seen such a monster before. His skull was bald, his scalp crisscrossed with scars, and his eyes were very clear and round, like boiled eggs pressed into his face. He was extraordinarily unhandsome, as though God had created the ugliest human being possible and then punched him in the face.

Most striking of all was the yellow suit that he wore. It gave him a strange air of feigned jollity, the product, perhaps, of an erroneous belief that he might somehow appear less threatening if he just wore brighter colors. He watched Louis approach, and it struck Angel that he hadn't yet seen the sentinel in the doorway blink once. His eyes were so huge that any blinks would have been obvious, like the flapping of wings.

Louis lowered his gun, and simultaneously the man at the door raised his right hand. He showed Louis the small plastic bottle that he held and then, without waiting for Louis to respond, tilted his head back and added drops to his eyes. When he was done, he stepped into the rain and silently indicated that Angel and Louis should enter the apothecary's store, his right hand now extended like that of the greeter at the world's worst nightclub.

Reluctantly, Angel came forward. He followed Louis into the darkness of the hallway, but he entered backward, keeping his eyes, and his gun, on the unblinking giant at the door. But the giant didn't follow them inside. Instead, he remained standing in the rain, his face raised to the heavens, and the water flowed down his cheeks like tears.

CHAPTER
XLIII

Angel and Louis followed the trail through the dust, the interior lit only by a single lamp that flickered in a corner. The room smelled of long-withered herbs, the scent of them infused in the grain of the wood and the peeling paint on the walls, but underpinning it was a medicinal odor that grew stronger as they approached the drapes concealing the back room.

And there was another smell again beneath them all: it was the unmistakable reek of rotting flesh.

Louis had replaced his gun in its holster, and now Angel did the same. Slowly Louis reached out and pulled aside the drapes, revealing the room beyond, and a man seated at a desk lit only by a banker's lamp. The angle of the lamp meant that the man was hidden in shadow, but even in the darkness Angel could see that he was yet more misshapen than when they'd last met. As they entered he raised his head with difficulty, and his words were slurred as he spoke.

"Welcome," he said. "You'll forgive me for not shaking hands."

His twisted right hand reached for the lamp, its fingers so deformed that they appeared to have been lost entirely, the digits reduced to twin stumps at the end of the arm. Angel and Louis didn't react, except for the merest flicker of compassion that briefly caused Angel's eyes to close. It was beyond Angel's capacity not to feel some sympathy, even for one such as this. His response didn't go unnoticed.

"Spare me," said the man. "If it were possible to rid myself of this disease by visiting it instead on you, I would do so in an instant."

He gurgled, and it took Angel a moment to realize that he was laughing.

"In fact," he added, "I would visit it upon you anyway, were it possible, if only for the pleasure of sharing."

"Mr. Cambion," said Louis. "You have not changed."

With a flick of his wrist, Cambion moved the lamp so that its light now fell upon his ravaged face.

"Oh," he said, "but I have."

———

ITS OFFICIAL NAME WAS Hansen's disease, after the Norwegian physician Gerhard Armauer Hansen, who, in 1873, identified the bacterium that was its causative agent, but for more than four thousand years humankind had known it simply as leprosy. Multidrug therapies had now rendered curable what had once been regarded as beyond treatment, with rifampicin as the base drug used to tackle both types of leprosy, multibacillary and paucibacillary, but Cambion was one of the exceptional cases, the small unfortunate few who showed no clinical or bacteriological improvement with MDT. The reasons for this were unclear, but those who whispered of him said that, during the earliest manifestations of the disease, he had been treated unethically with rifampicin as a monotherapy, instead of in conjunction with dapsone and clofazimine, and this had created in him a resistance to the base drug. The unfortunate physician responsible had subsequently disappeared, although he was not forgotten by his immediate family, helped by the fact that pieces of the doctor continued to be delivered to them at regular intervals. In fact, it wasn't even clear if the doctor was dead, since the body parts that arrived appeared remarkably fresh, even allowing for the preservative compounds in which they were packed.

But truth, when it came to Cambion, was in short supply. Even his name was an invention. In medieval times, a cambion was the mutated offspring of a human and a demon. Caliban, Prospero's antagonist in *The Tempest*, was a cambion—"not honour'd with a human shape." All that could be known of Cambion for sure, confirmed by his presence in the old apothecary, was that his condition was deteriorating rapidly. One might even have said that it was degenerating, but then Cambion had always been degenerate by nature, and his physical ailment could have been taken as an outward manifestation of his inner corruption. Cambion was wealthy, and without morals. Cambion had killed—men, women, children—but as the disease had rotted his flesh, limiting his power of movement and depriving him of sensation at his extremities, he had moved from the act of killing to the facilitation of it. It had always been a lucrative sideline for him, for his reputation drew men and women who were at least as debased as he, but now it was his principal activity. Cambion was the main point of contact for those who liked to combine murder with rape and torture, and those who devoutly wished that their enemies might suffer before they died. It was said that, when possible, Cambion liked to watch. Cambion's people—if people they even were, as their capacity for evil called into question their very humanity—took on jobs that others refused to countenance, whether for reasons of morality or personal safety. Their sadism was their weakness, though. This was why Cambion's services remained so specialized, and why he and his beasts hid themselves in the shadows. Their acts had been met with promises of retribution that were at least their equal.

When Angel had last seen Cambion, more than a decade earlier, his features were already displaying signs of ulceration and lesions, and certain nerves had begun to enlarge, including the great auricular nerve beneath the ears and the supraorbital on the skull. Now the rav-

ages of the disease had rendered him almost unrecognizable. His left
eye was barely visible as a slit in the flesh of his face, while the right
eye was wide but cloudy. His lower lip had swollen immensely, causing his mouth to droop open. His nasal cartilage had dissolved, leaving two holes separated by a strip of bone. Any remaining visible skin
was covered with bumps that looked as hard as stone.

"What do you think?" said Cambion, and spittle sprayed from his
lips. Angel was glad that he hadn't chosen to stand closer to the desk.
After that first, and last, encounter with Cambion, he had taken the
time to read up on leprosy. Most of what he knew, or thought he knew
of the disease, turned out to be myths, including that it was transmitted by touch. Routes of transmission were still being researched, but
it appeared to be spread primarily through nasal secretions. Angel
watched the droplets of spittle on Cambion's desk and realized that he
was holding his breath.

"Don't look like you're getting no better," said Louis.

"I think that's a safe conjecture," said Cambion.

"Maybe you ought to try—" Louis clicked his fingers and turned to
Angel for help. "What's that shit you use? You know, for your scabies."

"Hydrocortisone. And it's not scabies. It's heat rash."

"Yeah, that's it," said Louis. He returned his attention to Cambion.
"Hydrocortisone. Clear that shit right up."

"Thank you for the advice. I'll bear it in mind."

"My pleasure," said Louis. "You give what ails you to SpongeBob
SquarePants outside too?"

Cambion managed to smile.

"I'll let Edmund know what you called him. I'm sure he'll find it
amusing."

"I don't much care either way," said Louis.

"No, I don't imagine you would. As for what troubles him, he has
a condition known as lagophthalmos—a form of facial paralysis that
affects the seventh cranial nerve, which controls the orbicularis oculi,

the closing muscle of the eyelid. It leaves him unable to properly lubri-
cate his eyes."

"Man," said Louis, "you quite the pair."

"I like to think that Edmund's exposure to me enables him to put
his own problems into some kind of perspective."

"It would, if you hired a bodyguard who can see right."

"Edmund's not just my bodyguard. He's my nurse, and my confi-
dant. In fact"—Cambion waved his right arm, displaying the stumps—
"you could say that he's my right-hand man. My left, though, continues
to have its uses."

He displayed his left hand for the first time. It still had three fingers
and a thumb. They were currently wrapped around a modified pistol
with an oversized trigger. The muzzle of the gun pointed loosely at
Louis.

"We was going to kill you, we'd have done it already," said Louis.

"Likewise."

"You were hard to find."

"Yet here you are. I knew you'd get to me eventually, once you'd exhausted all other avenues of inquiry. You've been tearing quite a swath
through the city, you and your boyfriend. There can't be a stone left
unturned."

It was true. Within hours of the shooting, Angel and Louis had
begun asking questions, sometimes gently, sometimes less so. There
had been quiet conversations over cups of coffee in upscale restaurants, and over beers in the back rooms of dive bars. There were phone
calls and denials, threats and warnings. Every middleman, every fixer,
every facilitator who had knowledge of those who killed for money
was contacted directly or received word: Louis wanted names. He desired to know who had pulled the trigger, and who had made the call.

The difficulty was that Louis suspected the shooter—or shooters, for
Louis believed that the combination of shotgun and pistol used pointed
to a team—hadn't been sourced through the usual channels. He had

no doubt that they were pros, or, at least, he had started off with that assumption. It didn't smell like amateur hour to him, not where Parker was concerned, and the likelihood of two gunmen reinforced that belief. If he was wrong, and it turned out that some enraged loner was responsible, then it would be a matter for the cops and their investigation. Louis might get to the shooter first if the information leaked, but that wasn't his world. In Louis's world, people were paid to kill.

But the detective's connections to Louis were well known, and nobody of Louis's acquaintance would have accepted the contract, either as the agent or as the trigger man. Nevertheless, it had been necessary to check, just to be sure.

There was also the distinct possibility that the hit was related to Parker's movements through darker realms, and with that in mind Louis had already made contact with Epstein, the old rabbi in New York. Louis had made it clear to him that, if Epstein discovered something relating to the hit and chose not to share it, Louis would be seriously displeased. In the meantime, Epstein had sent his own pet bodyguard, Liat, up to Maine. She was, thought Louis, a little late to the party. They all were.

A third line of investigation pointed to the Collector, but Louis had dismissed that possibility almost immediately. A shotgun wasn't the Collector's style, and he'd probably have come after Angel and Louis first. Louis suspected that the Collector wanted Parker alive unless there was no other option, although he still didn't understand why, despite Parker's efforts to explain the situation to him. If he ever did manage to corner the Collector, Louis planned to ask him to clarify it, just before he shot him in the head.

Finally, there was the case on which Parker had been working before the hit: a missing girl, a dead man in a basement, and a town called Prosperous, but that was all Louis knew. If someone in Prosperous had hired a killer, then it brought the hunt back to Louis. He would find the shooters and make them talk.

Which was why he and Angel were now standing before Cambion, because Cambion didn't care about Louis, or Parker, or anyone or anything else, and he dealt, in turn, with those who were too vicious and depraved to care either. Even if Cambion hadn't been involved—and that had yet to be established—his contacts extended into corners of which even Louis was not aware. The creatures that hid there had claws and fangs, and were filled with poison.

"Quite the place you have here," said Louis. His eyes were growing used to the dimness. He could see the modern medicines on the shelves behind Cambion, and a doorway beyond that, presumably, led to where Cambion lived and slept. He could not visualize this man making it up a flight of stairs. A wheelchair stood folded in one corner. Beside it was a plastic bowl, a spoon, and a napkin. A china bowl and a silver soup spoon sat on the desk beside Cambion, and Louis spotted a similar bowl and spoon on a side table to his right.

Curious, thought Louis: two people, but three bowls.

"I was growing fond of my new home," said Cambion. "But now, I think, I shall have to move again. A pity—such upheavals drain my strength, and it's difficult to find suitable premises with such a gracious atmosphere."

"Don't go running off on my account," said Louis. He didn't even bother to comment on the ambience. The apothecary's old premises felt to him only a step away from an embalmer's chambers.

"Why, are you telling me that I can rely on your discretion—that you won't breathe a word of where I am?" said Cambion. "There's a price on my head. The only reason you've got this close is because I know that you declined the contract on me. I still don't understand why."

"Because I thought a day like this might come," said Louis.

"When you needed me?"

"When I'd have to look in your eyes to see if you were lying."

"Ask it."

"Were you involved?"

"No."

Louis remained very still as he stared at the decaying man. Finally, he nodded.

"Who was?"

"No one in my circle."

"You're sure?"

"Yes."

Although it was only the slightest of movements, Angel saw Louis's shoulders slump. Cambion was the last of the middlemen. The hunt would now become much more difficult.

"I have heard a rumor, though. . . ."

Louis tensed. Here was the game. There was always a game where Cambion was concerned.

"Which is?"

"What can you offer me in return?"

"What do you want?"

"To die in peace."

"Looking at you, that don't seem like an option."

"I want the contract nullified."

"I can't do that."

Cambion placed the gun, which had remained in his hand throughout, on the desk and opened a drawer. From it he produced an envelope, which he slid toward Louis.

"Talking tires me," he said. "This should suffice."

"What is it?"

"A list of names—the worst of men and women."

"The ones you've used."

"Yes, along with the crimes for which they're responsible. I want to buy the contract back with their blood. I'm tired of being pursued. I need to rest."

Louis stared at the envelope, making the calculations. Finally, he took it and placed it in his jacket pocket.

"I'll do what I can."

"Those names will be enough."

"Yes, I think they will. Now, the rumor."

"A man and a woman. Married. Children. Perfect Middle Americans. They have only one employer. A handful of hits, but very good."

"Their motivation?"

"Not money. Ideology."

"Political?"

"Religious, if what I hear is true."

"Where?"

"North Carolina, but that may no longer be the case. It's all I have."

Behind them, the yellow-clad giant named Edmund appeared. He handed Louis a slip of paper. On it was written a cell phone number. The meeting was over.

"Soon I'll be gone from here," said Cambion. "Use that number to confirm that the contract has been rendered null and void."

Louis memorized the number before handing the paper back to Edmund. It vanished into the folds of the giant's hand.

"How long you got left?" he asked Cambion.

"Who knows?"

"Seems like it might be a mercy to let the contract run its course," said Louis, as Edmund stepped aside so that the two visitors could leave, and prepared to escort them out.

"You might think that," said Cambion, "but I'm not ready to die yet."

"Yeah," said Louis, as the drapes fell closed behind him. "That's a damn shame."

XLIV

Ronald Straydeer was not unfamiliar with sleeping outdoors. He'd bedded down in the jungles in Vietnam, the Great North Woods of Maine, and beside pot plantations in upstate New York during a period of misunderstanding with some rival growers, which came to an end when Ronald put one of them headfirst into a narrow hole and proceeded to fill it in.

Thus Ronald understood the necessity of good nutrition and proper clothing, particularly when it came to cold weather. He wore polypropylene, not cotton, next to his skin, because he knew that cotton trapped moisture, and the action of convection meant that cold air and damp drained the body's heat. A hat with earflaps covered his head, because when the head got cold the body began to shut off circulation to the extremities. He kept himself moving constantly, if only through the gentle shuffling of his feet and minute stretches of his arms, fingers, and toes, generating heat as a by-product. He had brought plenty of water, and an assortment of nuts, seeds, energy bars, jerky, and salami, as well as a couple of MREs—because sometimes a man needed a hot meal, even one that tasted as if it had been made for pets—and containers of self-heating soup and coffee. He didn't know how long he might be out in the wild, but he had packed enough food for four days, or more if he had to be abstemious. He was armed with a licensed hunting rifle, a Browning BAR Mark II Lightweight Stalker in .308. If it came down to it, he could claim to be hunting squirrels or hare, even coyotes, although the Browning wouldn't leave much of a varmint behind apart from bits of fur and memories.

He had been fortunate with this location. The woods around the ruined church were a mixture of deciduous and evergreen, but more of the latter. He bedded down in the thickest copse he could find and covered his sleeping bag with branches. He made a careful recce of his surroundings but did not enter the church grounds—not out of superstition but simply because, if Shaky was right, the church was important, and people tended to protect places that were important. He checked the gate and the fence, and saw nothing to indicate that the grounds were guarded electronically, but he still didn't want to risk setting off any kind of hidden motion sensor. Neither did he attempt an exploration of the town itself. Ronald was a striking, imposing man, and he attracted attention. Perhaps he would be seeing more of the town soon enough.

To pass the time, he read. He had brought with him a copy of *Bleak House*, by Charles Dickens, because he recalled the detective's recommending it to him once. He had bought it but never got around to reading it. Now seemed the appropriate time.

Shaky, like Jude before him, was convinced that Prosperous was rotten, and he had halfway managed to convince Ronald of the same thing, even before Ronald had ever come to the town. Shaky had accompanied Ronald around Portland and South Portland as he began quietly questioning the homeless about what they had seen in the days preceding Jude's death. Shaky had a way of calming folk. He was unthreatening, and generally well liked. It was, thought Ronald, a little like having a good dog with him—an old Labrador, maybe, something friendly and tolerant. He didn't share this with Shaky, though. He wasn't sure how it might be taken.

Despite their efforts, they learned nothing of worth until the end of a long day of searching and questioning. It came from an unlikely source: the woman known as Frannie, with whom Shaky had witnessed Brightboy arguing on the morning that Brightboy attacked him. Shaky usually did his best to avoid Frannie due to her intimidating nature, and the vision of a man having his nose gnawed off that she invariably conjured up, but Ronald Straydeer wasn't troubled by her in the least. He told Shaky that he knew Frannie from way back, when she still had most of her teeth.

"Is it true that she once bit a man's nose off and spit it out in front of him?" asked Shaky. After all, it seemed that Ronald Straydeer might be able to confirm the story, once and for all.

"No," said Ronald solemnly. "That's not true."

Shaky was relieved, but Ronald wasn't done.

"She didn't spit it out," he continued. "She swallowed it."

Shaky felt ill. During the subsequent conversation with Frannie, he found himself using Ronald's body as a bulwark between him and the woman. If she'd developed a taste for male flesh, she'd have to go through Ronald to get to him.

Frannie was pleased to see Ronald, although she was less pleased when she learned that he was no longer dealing. Using mainly four-letter words, she expressed the view that Ronald was a grave disappointment to her. Ronald accepted the judgment without complaint, and gave her the name of someone who might be able to help her find some pot, along with twenty bucks with which to treat herself.

In return, Frannie told them about the couple she'd seen near Jude's basement.

Frannie wasn't a mixer. She avoided the shelters. She was always angry, or briefly coming down from being angry prior to getting angry all over again. She liked no one, not even Jude. She'd never asked him for anything, and he'd never offered, knowing better than to do so. Shaky couldn't understand why she was opening up to Ronald Straydeer, even allowing for the money and the pot connection. It was only later that it dawned on him: Frannie had been flattered by Ronald's attention. Ronald spoke to her as he would to any woman. He was courteous. He smiled. He asked about a wound on her arm, and recommended something for it. None of this did he do in a false manner; Frannie would have seen through that in an instant. Instead, Ronald talked to her as the woman that she once was, and perhaps, deep down, still believed herself to be. How long had it been since anyone had done that for her, thought Shaky. Decades, probably. She hadn't always been this way and, like all of those who ended up on the streets, never wanted it for herself. As she and Ronald spoke, Shaky saw her change. Her eyes softened. She wasn't beautiful—she would never again be that, if she had ever been—but for the first time Shaky saw her as something other than an individual to be feared. She let her guard down while talking to Ronald, and it struck Shaky that Frannie lived her life in a state of perpetual fear, for, however bad it was to be a homeless man, it was infinitely worse to be a homeless woman. He had always understood that, but as an abstract concept, and generally applied it only to the younger girls, the teenagers, who were more obviously vulnerable. He had made the mistake of imagining that somehow, for Frannie, it might have become easier over the years, not harder. Now he knew himself to be wrong.

So Frannie told Ronald Straydeer of how she had walked past Jude's place the night before he died, and seen a car parked across the street. And because she was always desperate, and asking was free, she tapped on the glass in the hope that a dollar might be forthcoming.

"They gave me a five," she told Ronald. "Five bucks. Just like that."

"And did they ask for anything in return?" said Ronald.

Frannie shook her head.

"Nothing."

"They didn't ask after Jude?"

"No."

Because they already knew, thought Shaky, and they were smarter than to draw attention to themselves by bribing a homeless woman for information. Instead, they paid her—enough to be generous, but not too generous—and she went away, leaving them to wait for Jude to appear.

Ronald asked what Frannie remembered about them. She recalled a silver car, and Massachusetts plates, but she admitted that she might have been mistaken about the plates. The woman was good-looking, but in that way of women who try too hard to keep themselves in condition as they get older and end up with lines on their tanned faces that might have been avoided if they'd resigned themselves to a little flesh on their bones. The man was balding, and wore glasses. He had barely looked at Frannie. The woman gave her the money, and responded to Frannie's word of thanks with the briefest of smiles.

Frannie's information wasn't much, but it was a small reward for their efforts. Ronald prepared to take his leave of Shaky and return home. He would call on the detective along the way, and share what he had learned with him. Instead, he and Shaky saw the detective's face appear on the television screen of a bar on Congress as they passed. Ronald bought Shaky a beer while he sipped a soda, and together they watched the news. Shaky told him that it had to be connected to Jude and his daughter. If that was the case, it was also connected to Prosperous, and if Prosperous was involved it had something to do with the old church, which was how Ronald came to be lying in the woods eating MREs and reading Dickens. Even if Shaky was mistaken, at least Ronald was trying to do something, but he had to give it to the little homeless man: Prosperous felt wrong, and the old church felt multiples of wrong.

There had been little activity since he arrived. Twice a police cruiser had driven up the road to the church, but on each occasion the cop had simply checked the lock on the gate and made a cursory circuit of the cemetery. Ronald had used the telescopic sight to pick out the cop's name on a briefly visible shirt tag: Morland.

The only other visitor was a tall man in his forties with receding hair, dressed in jeans, work boots, and a brown suede jacket. He arrived at the cemetery from the northwest, so that his appearance in the churchyard caught Ronald by surprise. On the first occasion, Ronald watched as he opened the church and checked inside, although he didn't remain there for long. Ronald figured him for the pastor, Warraner. Shaky had learned about him from the detective, as well as something of the chief cop named Morland. Both Jude and the detective had endured run-ins with each of them, according to Shaky. Ronald didn't follow Warraner when he left, but later he found the path that led from the churchyard to the pastor's house. Better to know where he was coming from than not.

The pastor returned shortly before sunset on the first day, this time with a rake and a shovel, and began clearing undergrowth from an area about forty feet from the western wall of the church. Ronald watched him through the scope. When Warraner was done, a hole just a little over two feet in diameter was revealed in the earth. Then, apparently content with his work, the pastor left and hadn't yet returned.

Now darkness had descended again, and Ronald was preparing to spend another night in the woods when the car arrived. It approached slowly, because it was driving without lights, and it stopped well before it neared the cemetery's railings. Two men got out. Ronald turned his Armasight night-vision binoculars on them. One was Morland, although this time he was out of uniform. The second was an old scarecrow of a man wearing a long coat and a felt hat. They didn't speak as Morland unlocked the cemetery gate, and the two men entered.

A second car, a station wagon, came up the road. Morland and the scarecrow stopped to watch it approach. It pulled up alongside the first vehicle, and an elderly woman emerged from the driver's side. Two more men climbed out of the back, although one of them needed the assistance of his companion and the woman to do so. He wore a small oxygen tank strapped to his back, and a mask covered his mouth. Supported by the others, he made his way into the churchyard.

Finally, from the northwest, came the pastor, but he wasn't alone. There was a girl of eighteen or nineteen with him. She wore a padded jacket over what looked like a nightgown, and there were unlaced sneakers on her feet. Her hands were restrained behind her back, and tape covered her mouth. To her right walked another man, a decade or so older than the pastor. He held the girl's right arm above the elbow, guiding her so that she wouldn't trip over the old gravestones, whispering and smiling as he did so. The girl didn't struggle or try to run. Ronald wondered if she was drugged, for her eyes drooped slightly, and she dragged her feet as she came.

She was brought to the place by the western wall of the church from which Warraner had cleared the undergrowth earlier that day. Ronald tried to get closer to them, but he didn't want to risk making a noise and alerting the group below. He contented himself with shifting position slightly so that he might see more clearly what was happening. It was a still, quiet night, and the voices of the group carried to him if he listened carefully. He heard Warraner tell the girl to rest, that they were almost done. The man who held her arm assisted her as she sank to her knees, and the others formed a semicircle around her, almost obscuring her from sight. A blade appeared, and Ronald drew a breath. He put down the binoculars and switched to the night-vision scope on his rifle. It wasn't as powerful, and didn't give him such a wide view of proceedings, but if anyone tried to take the knife to the girl, then, cop or no cop, he planned to cut them down before the metal touched her skin. The Browning was self-loading, which gave him four shots before he'd have to pause.

But the knife was used only to cut the bonds holding the girl's hands. Ronald watched them fall loosely to her sides, and then the man who had been assisting her removed the padded jacket, leaving her with only the nightgown as protection against the cold. Through

Ronald's scope she looked like a pale ghost in the churchyard. He fixed his sights on the man with the knife and waited, his finger not quite touching the trigger of the rifle, but the blade disappeared, and none of the others was holding a weapon.

They backed away from the girl, partially obscuring Ronald's view of her. He could still see her nightgown, though, white against the dark. He moved his sights from one back to the next, watching for movement, waiting for someone to produce a gun or knife, to make a move on the girl, but nobody did. Instead, they appeared to be waiting.

Ronald moved back to what he could see of the girl, and a finger of shadow crept across the pallor of her nightgown, as though the moon had suddenly shone on an overhanging branch.

But there was no branch, and there was no moon.

A second shadow came, and a third, like cracks on ice. There was a flurry of movement, a blur of white, and a single dull snap, as of a bone breaking. The watching elders came together, and for an instant the girl's form was entirely hidden from Ronald.

When they separated again, she was gone.

Ronald removed his eye from the scope and blinked. It wasn't possible. He scanned the ground, but there was no sign of the girl in the white nightgown. Even had it somehow been stripped from her, her naked body would have been visible on the ground, but Ronald could see nothing.

Now the group was dispersing. Warraner was heading back to his house, while the man who had come with him joined the others as they returned to their cars. Within minutes, the gates were locked once again, and the vehicles were making their way back down the road to the highway, still driving without lights.

Ronald waited for fifteen minutes, then headed for the cemetery. He climbed the railing, heedless now of any hidden sensors, and approached the spot where he had last seen the girl. He knelt, and discerned signs of disturbance. Clumps of earth had been dislodged from the dry ground, and there were marks in the dirt where something had briefly been dragged through it. They ended where the hole once lay, but it had now collapsed, leaving only a slight depression in the ground.

Ronald put his rifle aside and started to scrabble at the dirt with his bare hands. He dug until one of his fingernails cracked, but there was no trace of the girl, only earth and thick roots, although Ronald couldn't tell their origin, for there were no trees in the cemetery. He sat back on the ground, breathing heavily. Above him, the old church loomed.

A fragment of something pale caught his eye. Lodged against a small stone in the dirt was a piece of pale cloth about half an inch square. Ronald held it between his finger and thumb.

I am not mad, he thought. I am not mad.

He picked up his rifle and, using his boots, tried to hide his efforts at digging. When he felt that he had done all he could, he returned to his hiding place, gathered his belongings, and prepared to leave. He checked to make sure that he had not left behind any trash or possessions, even though he knew himself to be more careful than that. Still, it paid to take the time to be sure. When he was done, he started walking. It was not yet 11 P.M., and by traveling carefully he made it to the town of Dearden shortly before midnight, where he huddled down at the outskirts and made himself as comfortable as possible against a tree. He called just one number along the way, but it was not 911. He used a cup of coffee to warm himself, but it didn't stop his shivering, and his whole body was aching by the time the truck arrived. The Fulci brothers helped him inside, and drove him back to Scarborough.

XLV

Angel and Louis were parked close to the intersection of Amity and Henry, about four blocks south of Hunts Lane. They spoke as they walked, heads down against the rain.

"So?" said Angel.

"He's not telling us all he knows," said Louis.

"But you believed what he did tell us?"

"Yes."

"Why?"

"Because there was a percentage in keeping information back from us, but none in lying, and he's a man who works the percentages. He wasn't the middleman on the hit, but he has more information about who was responsible than he's shared with us."

"You could tell that just by looking in his eyes?"

"I understand him. And I know that he's scared of me."

"It's not a very exclusive club."

"No, but not everyone in it has the resources to make a move against one of my friends. Cambion does, but he's smart enough to know that if he involved himself he'd have to take me out as well, and that didn't happen."

"Which means that the shooters either don't know about you or don't care."

"And you just know that it can't be the latter."

"God forbid. You'd have no reason left to live."

"Exactly."

"So what's Cambion holding back on the shooters?"

"Their names. Cambion doesn't trade in rumors. Maybe they crossed his path once. He might even have tried to recruit them."

"And, like you, they turned him down."

"But, unlike me, they sound like religious zealots."

"True. Nobody could ever accuse you of darkening church doors, not unless you were planning to shoot somebody from the shadows. So Cambion is waiting for you to get the contract voided, and then he'll give you more?"

"That would be my guess, theoretically."

"Can you do it? Can you burn the contract?"

"No. It's gone too far. There are too many people with an interest in seeing Cambion dead, either for what he's done or for what he knows."

"But if Cambion is as clever as you say, he must realize that."

"Probably."

"Then what's the game?"

"He's trying to buy time. Like I told you, he works the percentages. I think he knows exactly who we're looking for, so right now he's trying to figure if the people who were sent after Parker are more dangerous than I am. If they are, then he can sell me out to them in return for whatever it is he needs—money, a hiding place, or most likely the heads of some of those who are hunting him. If Cambion doesn't believe the shooters are good enough to take me out he'll feed them to us, but he'll wait until we have more to offer him. I don't think he was lying when he said he wanted to live out the rest of his days in peace. He wants a guarantee of protection, but he knows that's more than I alone can give him."

Angel considered this.

"Feds," he said, after a time. "He wants a government screen."

"Feds," confirmed Louis.

"But we only know one Fed."

"That's right."

"And he doesn't like you and me."

"No, but right now I'd say he's real interested in us."

"How can you be sure?"

"Because I reckon that's who's been following us for the last two blocks."

"The big blue Ford? I was wondering about that. Maybe he figures he's undercover."

"I don't think he cares."

Louis stepped out into the street in front of the creeping car, put his fingers to his lips, and gave a piercing whistle as it braked within feet of him.

"Yo, taxi!" he said.

Through the wipers and the rain, Special Agent Ross, of the Federal Bureau of Investigation, grimaced at him. His lips moved soundlessly as Angel joined Louis. Angel cupped a hand to his ear.

"Sorry, 'mother-what?'" said Angel.

The second time, Ross shouted the word, just to make sure.

———

THEY SAT TOGETHER IN Henry Public, at 329 Henry. Each ordered a Brooklyn Brown Ale. It seemed only right, given the neighborhood. They were almost alone in the bar, given the hour.

"I'll pay," said Ross, as the beers were brought to their table. "It's bad enough that I'm sitting with you. I don't want to be accused of corruption as well."

"Hey, wasn't this how that Fed in Boston got caught, the one who was tight with Whitey Bulger?" said Angel. "One minute you're just enjoying a drink with friends in Southie, the next you're doing forty years."

"To begin with, we're not friends," said Ross.

"I'm hurt," said Angel. "Now how am I going to get my parking violations fixed?"

"That's the fucking NYPD, knucklehead," said Ross.

"Ah, right," said Angel. He took a sip of his beer. "But suppose I get ticketed in DC?"

"Fuck you."

"You know, you swear more than the Feds on TV."

"I only swear under stress."

"You must be stressed a lot."

Ross turned to Louis.

"Is he always like this?" said Ross.

"Pretty much."

"I never thought I'd say it, but you must be a fucking saint."

"I believe so," said Louis. "He also has his uses."

"I don't even want to know," said Ross.

He took a long draft from his bottle.

"You been to see him?"

"Parker?" said Louis.

"No, the new pope. Who the fuck else would I be talking about?"

A look passed between Angel and Louis. Angel wanted to go up to Maine, but Louis had demurred. He believed they could be of more use to Parker in New York. He was right, of course, but it still sat uneasily with Angel. He was deeply fond of the detective. If Parker wasn't going to pull through, Angel wanted to be able to say his goodbye.

"No," said Louis. "They say he's dying."

"That's what I hear."

"Is it true?"

"He's like a cat: he has nine lives. I just don't know how many of them he's used up by now."

They let that one sink in while they drank.

"What do you want, Agent Ross?" said Louis.

"My understanding is that you're turning the town upside down trying to find out who shot him. I was wondering how far you'd got."

"Is this an attempt at an information exchange?" said Louis. "If so, you're about to be gravely disappointed."

"I know who you were seeing in Hunts Lane," said Ross.

Louis's left eye flickered. For him, it was an expression of extreme surprise, the equivalent of someone else fainting. Ross caught it.

"How fucking inefficient do you think we are?" he said.

"Is that a rhetorical question?"

"You want to see my file on you?"

Louis let that one pass.

"How long have you been watching him?" said Angel.

"Ever since he got back into town," said Ross. "How's he looking? We haven't been able to get a clear shot of him. The last pictures we had of him, he wasn't doing so good."

"He's probably still having a little trouble dating," said Angel.

"Was he involved?"

Ross watched them both, and waited. He was very patient. A full minute went by, but he didn't seem perturbed.

"No," said Louis, eventually. "Or not directly."

"Were you planning on bringing him in?" said Angel.

"We've got nothing but stories. We do hear there's money for whoever pushes the button on him, though." His gaze flicked back to Louis. "I thought you might be looking to cash in."

"You got the wrong guy," said Louis.

"Clearly."

"Were you listening?"

"I wish. He hasn't left that old store since he took up residence. There's no landline. If he's using cell phones, they're throwaways. He conducts all his business away from the windows, which means we can't pick up vibrations, especially with all those drapes."

"So?" said Louis.

"My understanding is that he's been making informal approaches, looking to have the contract lifted. Is it true?"

Again Louis waited awhile before answering. Angel remained silent. If this was to be an exchange, it was for Louis to decide how much to give and what he wanted in return.

"That's true," said Louis. "You considering offering him a deal?"

"Our understanding is that he holds a lot of secrets."

"He'll bleed you for every one he reveals, and you'll never get him to testify."

"Maybe we don't want testimony," said Ross. "Maybe we just want details. It's not just about putting people behind bars. It's about knowledge."

Angel thought of the list of names now in Louis's possession. It might be worth something. Then again, it might be worth nothing at all. The truth, in all likelihood, lay somewhere in between.

Ross finished his first beer and held up the bottle, signaling the waitress for another round, even though Louis had barely touched his first drink.

"I heard he tried to bring you into his fold," Ross said to Louis. "Way back in the day."

"Not so far back," said Louis.

"You didn't bite?"

"Like you, he seemed to be confused about what I did for a living."

"And you didn't like him."

"There wasn't a great deal to like. Even less now, seeing as so much of him has rotted away."

The second beers arrived, but no one reached for them. Angel sensed that they had reached a crucial point in whatever negotiation was unfolding, although, as far as he could tell, there didn't seem to have been much obvious progress of any kind. Angel wasn't built for negotiation. That U.N. job just got further out of reach every day.

"I'll ask you again," said Louis. "What is it you want from me, Agent Ross?"

He fixed Ross with his gaze, like a snake mesmerizing an animal before striking. Ross didn't blink. He'd taken the "three guys having a beer approach," and that hadn't worked. He must have known that it wouldn't, but it never hurt to try. As Angel watched, he transformed himself, sitting up straighter in his seat, his face tightening, the years seeming to fall away from him. In that moment, Angel understood why Parker had always been so careful around Ross. Like Cambion, he was a creature of concealment, a repository of secrets.

"I came to warn you that I won't tolerate a campaign of vengeance, even for your friend. I won't tolerate it because I'm concerned that it might interfere with my own work, with the bigger picture. For every man or woman you kill, a potential avenue of inquiry closes. That's not how this thing works."

"And what is the 'bigger picture,' Agent Ross?" asked Angel. "What is 'this thing'?"

"The hunt for something that's been hidden away since before the appearance of life on earth," said Ross. "An entity, long buried. Is that big enough for you?"

Angel picked up his beer.

"You know," he said, "maybe I will have this second one after all."

He drained half the bottle.

"And you believe in the existence of this 'entity'?" said Louis.

"It doesn't matter what I believe. What matters are the beliefs of those who are looking for it, and the havoc they've created, and will continue to create, until they're stopped."

"So you want us to step back and do nothing?" said Louis.

"I'm not a fool," said Ross. "Doing nothing isn't an option where you're concerned. I want cooperation. You share what you find."

"And then you tell us if we can act on it?" said Louis. "That sounds like the worst fucking deal since the Indians got screwed for Manhattan."

"It also sounds like a good way to end up in jail," said Angel. "We might as well just sign a confession in advance. We tell you what we'd like to do, you say, 'Hey, that sounds like a fucking great idea. Be my guest!' and next thing we're all staring awkwardly at one another in front of a judge."

"He has a point," said Louis. "No deal."

To his credit, Ross didn't appear particularly surprised or disappointed. Instead, he reached into his pocket and removed a manila envelope. From it he slid a single photograph and placed it on the table before them. It showed the symbol of a pitchfork, crudely carved into a piece of wood. Louis and Angel knew it immediately for what it was: the sign of the Believers. Parker had crossed paths with them in the past, Angel and Louis too. The Believers hadn't enjoyed the encounters.

"Where was it taken?" said Angel.

"At Parker's house, immediately after the attack. Now do you understand why I'm asking you to tread carefully?"

Louis used the edge of his bottle to turn the photograph so that he could see it more clearly.

"Yes," he said. "I understand."

It was Louis's turn to produce an envelope from his pocket. He handed it to Ross without comment. Ross opened it and glanced at a typewritten list of names, places, and dates. He didn't need Louis to tell him what it meant.

"From Cambion?" said Ross.

"Yes."

"Why did he give it to you?"

"He thought I could act as the go-between in his contract difficulties."

"What did you get in return?"

"It doesn't matter."

Ross folded the list and returned it to the envelope.

"Why are you giving this to me?"

"It's what you wanted, right?"

"Yes."

"Now you don't need to cut a deal with him, and you can call off your surveillance."

"Leaving him at your mercy."

"I don't have any mercy for him."

"Should that concern me?"

"I don't see why."

Ross balanced the envelope on the palm of his right hand, as though judging its weight against the cost to his soul.

"You went to Cambion because you thought he knew something about the hit on Parker," said Ross. "I'll bet a shiny new quarter that he gave you a taste of what he had, but you believe there may be more. Negotiating on his behalf was part of the deal. Don't bother telling me if I'm warm. I wouldn't want you to feel compromised."

"I'm a long way from feeling compromised, Agent Ross," said Louis.

"But now you've got nothing," said Ross.

"Except a clear run at Cambion, if I need it, right?"

The envelope stayed on Ross's palm for a few seconds longer, then vanished into his pocket.

"Right," he said. "And Parker?"

"If it leads us to the Believers, I'll let you know through the rabbi, Epstein. Otherwise, you stay out of our affairs."

"You're an arrogant sonofabitch, you know that?"

"At least you didn't call me uppity. That might have caused serious friction."

Ross stood and dropped a fifty on the table.

"It's been a pleasure doing business with you, gentlemen," he said.

"Likewise," said Louis.

"You're sure you can't help with parking violations?" said Angel.

"Fuck you," said Ross.

"I'll hold on to your number anyway," said Angel. "Just in case."

XLVI

A ngel and Louis didn't speak again until they were back in their apartment, as Louis was concerned that Ross might have decided to cover himself by bugging their car. A subsequent sweep of the vehicle revealed nothing, though. It didn't matter; Louis hadn't survived this long by being careless, and Angel really didn't have anything better to do than sweep the car for listening devices, or so Louis told him.

They were greeted on their return by Mrs. Bondarchuk, the old lady who lived in the apartment below theirs. Mrs. Bondarchuk, in addition to being their sole neighbor, was also their sole tenant, the building being owned by one of Louis's shelf companies. Mrs. Bondarchuk kept Pomeranians, on which she lavished most of her love and attention, Mr. Bondarchuk having long since departed for a better place. For many years Angel and Louis had labored under the misapprehension that Mr. Bondarchuk was dead, but it had recently emerged that he had simply bailed in 1979, and his better place was Boise, Idaho—"better" being a relative term in an unhappy marriage. Mrs. Bondarchuk didn't miss him. She explained that her husband had left rather than be killed by her. The Pomeranians were a more than satisfactory replacement, despite their yappy natures, although Mrs. Bondarchuk raised exclusively male dogs, and made sure to have them neutered at the earliest opportunity, which suggested to Angel and Louis that she retained some residual hostility toward Mr. Bondarchuk. Mrs. Bondarchuk defended the noisiness of her Pomeranians on the grounds that it made them good watchdogs, and hence they constituted a virtual alarm system of their own. Louis took this with good grace, even though the building had the kind of alarm system that governments might envy, and that usually only governments could afford.

Some years earlier there had been what Mrs. Bondarchuk continued to refer to as "the unpleasantness," during which an effort had been made to access the building through hostile means, an effort that ultimately concluded with the deaths of all those responsible. It was an incident that failed to trouble the police, once Angel had explained to Mrs. Bondarchuk, over milk and chocolate cake, the importance of sometimes avoiding the attentions of the forces of law and order, such forces perhaps not always understanding that there were times when violence could be met only with violence. Mrs. Bondarchuk, who was old enough to remember the arrival of the Nazis in her native Ukraine, and the death of her father during the encirclement of Kiev, actually proved very understanding of this point of view. She told a startled Angel that she and her mother had transported weapons for the Ukrainian partisans, and she had watched from a corner as her mother and a quartet of other widows castrated and then killed a private from the German police-battalion 'Ostland' who had been unfortunate enough to fall into their clutches. In her way, as a Jew whose people had been slaughtered at Minsk and Kostopil and Sosenki, she knew better than Angel the importance of keeping some things secret from the authorities, and the occasional necessity of harsh reprisals against degenerate men. Ever since then, she had become even more protective of her two neighbors than before, and they, in turn, ensured that her rent was nominal and her comforts were guaranteed.

Now, with Mrs. Bondarchuk greeted and the building secured, the talk turned once more to the events of that evening as Louis poured two glasses of Meerlust Rubicon from South Africa, a suitably wintry red. Flurries of snow obscured the view through the windows, but they were halfhearted and ultimately inconsequential, like the parting shots of a defeated army. Angel watched as Louis shed his jacket and rolled up his shirtsleeves. The shirt was immaculately white, and as smooth as it had been before it was worn. It never failed to amaze Angel how his partner's appearance could remain so pristine. If Angel even looked at a shirt, it started to wrinkle. The only way he could have worn a white shirt for an evening and returned home without evidence of grievous use was to add so much starch to it that it resembled the top half of a suit of armor.

"Why did you give Ross those names?" Angel asked. He spoke without a hint of accusation or blame. He was simply curious to know.

"Because I don't like Cambion, and I'll be happy when he's dead." Louis swirled the wine in his glass. "Did you notice anything odd about Cambion's little pied-à-terre?"

"If I knew what that was, I might be able to answer. I'll take a guess that you're talking about the apothecary."

"You have a lot of room for self-improvement."

"Then you have something to look forward to. And, in answer to your question, there was *only* odd when it came to Cambion's little whatever-you-said."

"I counted three soup bowls, one of them plastic. I didn't count but two people."

"One of the bowls could have been from earlier."

"Maybe."

"But you don't think so."

"The place was old, and weird, but it was tidy. Apart from those bowls."

"A plastic bowl," said Angel. "You think he has a child in there?"

"I don't know. I just don't think he and his boy Edmund are the only ones holed up in that old store."

"You planning on going back there to clarify the situation?"

"Not yet. We're prioritizing."

"On that subject: you gave Ross the list, but what did we get in return?"

"We know that the Believers had nothing to do with the hit."

Angel wondered if the wine and the two earlier beers had somehow interacted disastrously, destroying some of his already threatened brain cells. Ross had shown them a picture. Had Ross been lying?

"What about the photograph?"

"The photograph is meaningless. It's a false trail. These people, or whatever they are, they don't sign their names. That's for dime-store novels. You think I ever put a bullet in a man, then rolled up a business card and stuck it in the hole because it pays to advertise?"

Angel doubted it, but you never knew.

"You think Ross figures it's a false trail?"

"Ross don't care one way or the other. It's one more nail in their coffin, and it don't matter to him who hammered it in."

"Doesn't. It *doesn't* matter. You have inconsistent grammar, you know that?"

Louis's public and private personae were different, but sometimes he forgot which role he was supposed to be playing.

"Fuckin' Ross was right about you, you know *that*?" said Louis.

"Ross can't even get a parking ticket fixed. He said so himself. So we go back to Cambion and tell him what—that we sold out his future to the Feds? Or do we just lie and make out like you're still trying to burn the contract?"

"Neither. I know people in the Carolinas. If there's a team of husband-and-wife shooters operating out of there, someone's got to have heard."

"Not if they're selective. Not if they don't work for money but out of some misguided sense of purpose."

"What, you mean like us?"

"Exactly like us, except without the religion."

"Yeah, and look how hard we were to find. It wasn't so long ago we had delivery men with explosives trying to blow our door off, and tonight Ross could have run our asses over if he'd felt like it. But we'll nail them, however long it takes."

"And then?"

"We make them talk."

"And after that?"

Louis tried the wine. It was good.

"We kill them."

———

LOUIS WAS CORRECT IN more than one of his assumptions. Even the most cautious of men can be found, if his pursuer has the commitment and the resources. The man who stood at the rain-soaked corner on the Upper West Side, where the poor were in sight of the rich and, more worryingly for those who feared imminent societal collapse, the rich were in sight of the poor, had spent a long time, and a not inconsiderable amount of money, trying to establish where Angel and Louis lived. In the end, it was the attack on the building—"the unpleasantness" over which Angel and Mrs. Bondarchuk had bonded—that brought them to his attention. Louis had made every effort to ensure that word of what happened didn't leak to the police, but the man on the corner represented a different form of law and justice, and such matters were very difficult to keep from him and his father.

The Collector cupped his hands over the match and held it to the cigarette at his lips, then smoked it with the butt held between the thumb and index finger, the remaining fingers sheltering it from the rain. He had arrived just as Angel and Louis entered the building. He did not know where they had been, but he could guess: they would be tracking those responsible for the attack on the detective. The Collector admired their single-mindedness, their focus: no mercy dash north to be at the detective's bedside, none of the fruitless beating at the darkness that comes from those who have grief without power, and anger without an object. They would even have set aside their pursuit of the Collector himself in order to concentrate on the more immediate matter. The Collector knew that most of that impetus probably came from Louis, but his lover was not to be underestimated either. Emotionless killers rarely survived for long. The trick was not to stifle the emotions but to control them. Love, anger, grief—all were useful in their way, but they needed to be kept in check. The one called Angel enabled Louis to do this. Without him, Louis would have died long ago.

But Angel was dangerous too. Louis would calculate the odds and, if the situation wasn't to his liking, back off and wait for a better opportunity to strike. The logician in him was always at the fore. Angel was different. Once he made the decision to move, he would keep coming at his target until one of them went down. He knew how to channel emotion as a weapon. That kind of force and determination wasn't to be underestimated. What most people failed to realize was that fights were decided in the opening seconds, not the closing ones, and there was something about facing an attacker of apparently relentless belligerence that could psychologically undo even a bigger, stronger opponent.

But what was strangest of all for the Collector, as he assessed these two men, was the realization that he had come to admire them. Even as they hunted him from nest to nest, and destroyed the hiding places that he had so carefully constructed for himself, he was in awe of their ferocity, their guile. Neither could he deny that he and these men, through their allegiance to Parker, were engaged in variations on the same work. True, the Collector had been forced to kill one of their number, but in that he had erred. He had let emotion get the better of him, and he accepted that he must pay a price for his lapse. The loss of his nests had been the price, but now he was tiring of the chase. He would give these two men what they wanted in order to secure a truce. If they did not agree, well, there was work to be done, and their pursuit of him was getting in the way of it. The distraction and threat that they posed, and the time and effort they were causing him to expend, enabled men and women of profound viciousness to continue to prey on those weaker than themselves. Judgments were waiting to be handed out. His collection needed to be replenished.

He called Eldritch from a pay phone. Over the old man's objections, the Collector had secured the services of a nurse for the period of his enforced absence. The Collector trusted the nurse implicitly. She was a niece of the woman who had kept Epstein's office in order, and put warmth in his bed, until her recent passing. She was discreet, and selectively deaf, mute, and blind.

"How are you feeling?" said the Collector.

"I'm well."

"The woman is taking good care of you?"

"I can take care of myself. She just gets in the way."

"Consider it a favor to me. It puts my concerns at rest."

"I'm touched. Have you found them?"

"Yes."

"Have you approached them?"

"No, but soon I'll have a message delivered to them. Tomorrow we will meet."

"They may not agree."

"One is a pragmatist, the other driven by principle. What I offer will appeal to both."

"And if it doesn't?"

"Then this goes on and, inevitably, more blood will be spilled. They will not want that, I guarantee it. I believe that they are as weary of it as I am. The detective is their priority—the detective, and those who pulled the trigger on him. And, who knows, I may manage to negotiate a little extra for us—a prize that you've been seeking for many years."

"And what would that be?"

"The location of a corrupted man," said the Collector. "The lair of a leper."

XLVII

G arrison Pryor's tame cop had experienced difficulty gaining access to the scene of the shooting. Not only was the Scarborough PD all over it; so were the Maine State Police's Major Crimes Unit and the FBI, which had immediately sent agents not just from its field office in Boston but from New York too. The house and its environs had been locked down from the instant the first patrol car arrived, and the flow of information was being tightly controlled amid threats of suspension and possible imprisonment for any breaches by police or emergency personnel.

But, despite all those precautions, Pryor's guy was able to talk to one of the ambulance crew, and—cops being cops—managed to piece together small details just by keeping his mouth shut and listening. Nevertheless, days went by before Pryor learned of the symbol that had been carved into the wood of the detective's kitchen door. The knowledge placed him in a difficult position: should he alert the Principal Backer immediately, or wait until he had clarified the situation? He decided to take the former course of action. He did not want to give the Principal Backer any cause to doubt him, and better to plead ignorance initially, and work to correct it, than be accused of withholding information, leaving himself open to suspicion.

As the morning sun tried to pierce the gray clouds over Boston, the

Principal Backer listened in silence while Pryor communicated what he had learned. The Principal Backer was not the kind of man who interrupted, or who tolerated being interrupted in turn.

"Well, was this the work of Believers?" he said when Pryor had finished.

"It's possible," said Pryor. "But, if so, it's not any of whom we have knowledge. There's no connection to us."

He didn't need to mention that most of the Believers were dead. Only a handful had ever existed to begin with, and the detective and his allies had wiped most of those out. Although it had never been formally discussed, many of the Backers regarded the elimination of the Believers as something of a blessing. Each group had its own obsessions, its own motives, and while its ultimate aims sometimes intersected or followed a similar path, neither party entirely trusted the other. But generations of Backers had been content to use the Believers when it suited them. Some had even allied themselves to the Believers' cause. Connections existed.

"If someone is scratching the Believers' symbol into the woodwork of scenes of attempted murder, then there is potentially a connection to all of us," said the Principal Backer. "Any investigation could damage us."

"It may be the action of renegades," said Pryor. "If so, they could be difficult to find. We know the identities of the ones who have crossed Parker. Any others have kept themselves hidden, even from us. Ultimately, my instinct says that the symbol is a false trail. Whoever carried out the attack, or ordered it to be carried out, wants to divert attention from themselves."

"There are those who would willingly use even a suspicion of involvement to act against us. What of the detective?"

"His condition remains critical. Privately, the doctors are suggesting that he won't survive. Even if he does, he will not be the same man. Perhaps he has no part to play in what is to come after all."

"Perhaps not, or it could be that his role has simply changed."

Laurie, Pryor's personal assistant, knocked at his office door. He waved her away in irritation. How urgent could it be? If there was a fire, he'd hear the alarm bells.

But she persisted, and her face contorted into a rictus of anxiety.

"Sir, I may have to get back to you," said Pryor.

"Is there a problem?"

"I think so."

He hung up the phone, and Laurie immediately entered.

"I had asked—" he began, but she cut him off.

"Mr. Pryor, there are agents from the Economic Crimes Unit downstairs. Security is trying to delay them, but they have warrants."

The Economic Crimes Unit was the branch of the FBI's Financial Crimes Division tasked with investigating securities and commodities fraud, among other areas. The Principal Backer's fears were being realized. The attack on the detective had given their enemies an opening. This might just be a fishing expedition, but through it a message was being sent to them.

We know of you.

We *know*.

———

WHILE GARRISON PRYOR PREPARED to confront the federal investigators, Angel called Rachel Wolfe. She had just returned to her home in Vermont, having spent a couple of nights in Portland to be close to the father of her child. Her daughter had not stayed with her. Rachel felt that it was important for Sam to continue her routines, and not be engaged in some ongoing deathwatch, but she had been permitted to see him briefly in the ICU. Rachel was worried about exposing Sam to the sight of her father lying broken and dying in a hospital bed, but the child had insisted. Jeff, Rachel's partner, drove Sam over to Portland, then took her home again. He might not have been particularly enamored of Rachel's former lover, but he had behaved sensitively since the attack, and she was grateful to him for it. Now Rachel spoke to Angel of tubes and needles, of wounds and dressings. One kidney gone. Shotgun pellets painstakingly removed from his skull and back, including a number perilously close to his spine. Potential nerve damage to one arm. Murmurs of possible brain injury. He remained in a coma. His body appeared to have shut down all but the most essential of systems in order to fight for survival.

"How did Sam do?" asked Angel.

"She didn't shed a tear," said Rachel. "Even Jeff looked broken up, and he doesn't even like Charlie. But Sam, she just whispered something to him, and wouldn't tell me what it was. Apparently she was quiet on the ride home. She didn't want to speak. Then, when Jeff looked back at her somewhere around Lebanon, she was fast asleep."

"You try talking to her about it since the visit?"

"I'm a psychologist—all I ever do is talk about things. She seems . . . fine. You know what she told me? She said she thought her daddy was deciding."

"Deciding what?"

"If he wanted to live or die."

And Rachel's voice broke on the last word.

"And how are you doing?"

He could hear her trying to control herself, trying not to cry.

"Okay, I guess. It's complicated. I feel disloyal to him, somehow, like I abandoned him. Does that make any sense?"

"It's guilt."

"Yes."

"For fucking an asshole like Jeff."

She couldn't help but splutter with laughter.

"You're the asshole, you know that?"

"I get that a lot."

"Jeff's been good, you dick. And, hey, you know what the weirdest thing about being at that hospital was?"

"I get the feeling you're going to tell me."

"You bet I am. It was the number of women who kept coming into the place asking about him. It's like waiting by the bedside of King Solomon. There was a little dark-haired cop, and a woman from that town, Dark Hollow. You remember it? You ought to. There was shooting."

Angel winced, not so much at the memory of the town itself but at the mention of the woman. Her name was Lorna Jennings, and she was the wife of the chief of police up in Dark Hollow. There was history there, the kind you didn't want to discuss with the mother of a man's child, even if they were now separated and he was dying in a hospital bed.

"Yeah, it rings a bell."

"Do you remember her?"

"Not so much."

"Liar. Did he sleep with her?"

"I don't know."

"Come on."

"Jesus, I don't know! I don't follow him around with a towel and a glass of water."

"What about the cop?"

That had to be Sharon Macy. Parker had told Angel about her.

"No, he didn't sleep with her. I'm pretty certain of that."

Angel tried to remember a more awkward conversation that he'd had, but failed.

"And there's another woman. She doesn't stray far from the ICU, and I get the impression she has police permission to be there, but she's no cop. She's a deaf mute, and she carries a gun. I've seen how she looks at him."

"Liat," said Angel. Epstein must have sent her to watch over Parker. She was a curious choice of guardian angel. Effective, but curious.

"He slept with her, didn't he? If he didn't, he should have."

What the hell, thought Angel.

"Yeah, he slept with her."

"Trust him to sleep with a woman who couldn't answer back."

"It was just once," said Angel.

"What are you, his personal apologist?"

"You've *made* me his apologist! I only called to see how you were. Now I'm sorry I asked."

Rachel laughed. It was genuine, and he was happy that he had given her that, at least.

"Will you come up to see him?" she asked.

"Soon," he said.

"You're looking for them, aren't you, the ones who did this to him?"

"Yes."

"Nobody ever got this close to him before. Nobody ever hurt him so badly. If he dies . . ."

"Don't say that. Remember what your daughter told you; he's still deciding, and he has a reason to come back. He loves Sam, and he loves you, even if you are fucking an asshole like Jeff."

"Go away," said Rachel. "Do something useful."

"Yes, ma'am," said Angel.

He hung up. Louis stood beside him, waiting. He handed Angel a Beretta 21 fitted with a suppressor that was barely longer than the pistol itself. The Beretta could now be fired in a restaurant and would make a sound only slightly louder than a spoon striking against the side of a cup. Louis carried a similar weapon in the pocket of his Belstaff jacket.

They were off to do something useful.

They were going to meet and, if necessary, kill the Collector.

XLVIII

Ronald Straydeer sat in the living room of his home near the Scarborough Downs racetrack. He held in his hands a photograph of himself as a younger man in uniform, his left arm encircling the neck of a massive German shepherd. In the picture, Ronald was smiling, and he liked to think that Elsa was smiling too.

He wished that he still smoked pot. He wished that he still drank. It would have been easy to return to doing one or the other, or even both. Under the circumstances, it would not have been surprising or blameworthy. Instead, he spoke to the picture, and to the ghost of the dog within it.

He was often asked, by those who didn't know any better, why he hadn't found himself another dog in the intervening years. He knew there were some who said that those who kept dogs had to resign themselves to their eventual loss because of the animals' relatively short lives. The trick—if "trick" was the right word—was to learn to love the spirit of the animal, and to recognize that it transferred itself from dog to dog, with each one representing the same life force. Ronald believed that there might be some sense in this, but he felt, too, that men might equally say the same thing about women, and vice versa. He had known plenty of women, and had even loved one or two of them, so he had a degree of experience in the matter. But some men and women lost a partner early in life and never managed to give themselves again to another. Ronald thought there might have been something of that catastrophic sense of loss to his feelings for his abandoned dog. He wasn't a sentimental man—although, again, some mistook his grieving for a dead animal as sentimentality. Ronald Straydeer had simply loved the dog, and Elsa had saved his life and the lives of his brother soldiers on more than one occasion. In the end, he was forced to abandon and betray her, and the sight of her, caged and scratching at the wire as she was taken from him, had torn at him every day since then. His only hope was that he might eventually be reunited with his dog in a world beyond this one.

Now he told the ghost of the dog about the church, and the girl, and the shadows that had encircled her before she was dragged beneath the ground. He could have gone to the police, but there was a policeman involved. And what could he have told them—that he saw a girl kneel by a hole in the earth and then disappear? All he had was a fragment of pale material. Could they extract DNA from it? Ronald didn't know. It depended, he supposed, on whether it had touched the girl's skin for long enough, if it had touched her at all. He had placed the material in one of the resealable bags that he used for food and waste. It was before him now. He held it up to the light, but he could see no traces of blood on it, and it seemed to be stained only by dirt. He didn't know her name, and he wasn't sure if he could have identified her from the glimpse that he caught of her in the greenish light of his night-vision lens. He knew only that she was not Jude's daughter. He had seen photographs of Annie. Jude had shared them with him, and Ronald retained an uncanny recall for faces and names. The girl swallowed by the churchyard was younger than Jude's daughter. Ronald wondered if Annie too lay somewhere in that cemetery, if her fate had been the same as that poor girl's. If so, how many others slept beneath the church, embraced by roots? (For those were not shadows that had wrapped themselves around the girl before she was taken. Oh, no . . .)

But Ronald also understood instinctively that, even if people were to believe him and a search was eventually conducted, men could dig long and deep in that churchyard without finding any trace of the girl. As he worked at the collapsed earth with his bare hands, hoping to reveal some sign of her, he had felt the presence of a perfect and profound hostility, a malevolent hunger given form. It was this more than any inability to keep digging that had caused him to abandon his efforts to find a body. Even now, he was glad that he had used the water in the Fulcis' truck to clean his hands of the soil from that place, and one of their towels to dry them, and had then disposed of the towel in a Dumpster so that it wouldn't be used again. He was grateful not to have contaminated his home with even a fragment of that cursed earth, and he kept sealed the bag containing the piece of material lest some minute particle of grit should fall from it and pollute all.

The detective would have known what to do, but he was dying. He had friends, though: clever men, dangerous men. Right now, those men would be looking for the ones responsible for shooting him. Ronald didn't find it hard to make a connection between the detective's inquiries into the disappearance of Annie Broyer and the sight of an unknown girl being dragged beneath the ground while a group of men and one woman watched. It wasn't much of a stretch from there to imagine a set of circumstances in which those same people might have seen fit to try and take the detective's life.

And if he was wrong? Well, the men who stood by the detective were more like him than perhaps even they knew, and they had wrath to spare. Ronald would find a way to contact them, and together they would avenge those trapped in uneasy rest beneath the dirt of Prosperous.

———

AS RONALD STRAYDEER SAT in contemplation and mourning, the bodies of Magnus and Dianne Madsen, and Erin Dixon, were discov-

ered by the police after Magnus failed to appear as scheduled for his
hospital duties. The Maine State Police informed Lucas Morland of the
Prosperous Police Department once Erin's identity was established.
With both Kayley Madsen and Harry Dixon apparently missing, a
patrol car was immediately dispatched to the Dixon house, but there
was no sign of Harry or his niece. Their faces duly began showing up
on news channels, and an auto dealer in Medway came forward to say
that he'd taken a trade-in on a GMC Passenger Van from Harry Dixon
just a few days earlier. The van was soon found in a patch of woodland just outside Bangor, with Harry seated at the wheel and holes
in his head where the bullet from the gun in his hand had entered
and exited. On the seat beside him was a woman's shirt, stained with
blood at the collar. Its size matched clothing found in Kayley Madsen's
closet, and DNA tests would subsequently confirm that the blood was
Kayley's, although no other trace of her was ever found.

"Prosperous: Maine's Cursed Town," read one of the more lurid
newspaper headlines in the aftermath. Prosperous crawled with MSP
investigators, but Morland handled them all well. He was diligent,
cooperative, and unassuming. He knew his place. Only once did he
experience a shred of alarm, and that was when an FBI agent named
Ross visited from New York. Ross sat in Morland's office, nibbled on
a cookie, and asked about the detective Parker. Why had he come to
Prosperous? What did he want to know? And then he gave Morland
a possible out: had Parker spoken to Harry Dixon or his wife at any
point? Morland didn't know, but he conceded that it was possible, although why Parker might have wanted to meet with the Dixons Morland couldn't say. But anything that linked Parker to the Dixons was
good for Morland, and good for Prosperous. That was a dead end, and
the FBI and the state police could spend decades peering into it for
all Morland cared.

"Can I ask why the FBI is interested in the fact that a private detective was shot in Maine?" said Morland.

"Curiosity," said Ross. Then: "Your town seems to be having a bad time of it lately."

"Yeah," said Morland. "They say these things come in threes."

"Really?" said Ross. "I count, uh—" He worked it out on his fingers. "Six," he concluded. "Or nine, if you include the Madsens and their missing daughter. Or, wow, eleven allowing for that homeless guy in Portland and *his* missing daughter. That's a lot. More than three, anyway."

It wasn't the first time Morland had heard something of the kind. The MSP investigators had intimated as much, and now Morland replied to Ross just as he had responded to them.

"Sir, my reckoning is two killings by religious terrorists thousands of miles from here; one accidental self-inflicted gunshot wound on an elderly man; one automobile incident; and, to our shame and regret, an apparent murder-suicide involving two of our townsfolk. I can't speak to suicides in Portland, or missing girls. I just know what this town has endured. I can't say why Harry Dixon might have killed those people. I heard that he had money problems, but a lot of folk have money problems and don't take a gun to their family as a consequence. It could be that the town's troubles caused something in him to snap. I'm no psychiatrist. But if you can establish a connection between all those disparate events, then I'll never again question the amount of taxes our government plows into the bureau."

Ross finished his cookie.

"And the attempted murder of a private investigator," said Ross. "I almost forgot to add that."

Morland didn't respond. He was all done with the FBI for now.

"Can I help you with anything else today, Agent Ross?"

"No," said Ross. "I think that'll be all. I appreciate your time. And the cookie was very good. My compliments to the baker."

"My wife," said Morland.

"You're a fortunate man," said Ross.

He stood and buttoned his coat before heading out. There was still a chill in the air.

"And this is quite a town. Quite a town indeed."

———

THIRTY MINUTES LATER, MORLAND received a call from Pastor Warraner. Ross had been out at the church.

XLIX

At first, Angel and Louis believed the missive from the Collector to be little more than a taunt. It was delivered by a bike messenger, and consisted of a padded envelope containing a single final bear claw from the necklace that had once belonged to their friend, the late Jackie Garner, and a business card from the Lexington Candy Shop on Lexington, the old soda-candy store and luncheonette that had been in operation at that location since 1925. It was only when Louis turned over the card and saw a date (that same day) and a time (11 A.M.—written on the back) that they understood that this might be different, although whether it would prove to be an olive branch or a trap they were not certain.

Even the Collector's choice of location for the meeting wasn't without resonance: the Lexington Candy Shop was where Gabriel, Louis's late master, would hold his meetings with clients, and sometimes with the operatives for whom he acted as a middleman, Louis among them. Perhaps, thought Louis, the distance between Cambion and Gabriel wasn't as great as Louis might have liked to believe. Gabriel was merely Cambion with a more highly developed moral sense, but that wasn't saying a whole lot. There were things breeding in petri dishes with a more highly developed moral sense than Cambion's. By extension, the distance between Louis and Cambion might well have been significantly less than it was comfortable to imagine. The difference was that Louis had changed, while Cambion had not. Cambion didn't have a man like Angel by his side, but then a man like Angel would never have allied himself with one such as Cambion to begin with. It made Louis wonder if Angel had seen the possibility of redemption in him long before Louis himself had recognized it. Louis found this simultaneously flattering and slightly worrying.

The Collector's decision to nominate the Lexington Candy Shop as the venue for their meeting was his way of telling Louis that he knew all he needed to know about Louis and his past. It added another layer of peculiarity to the Collector's invitation. This was not the action of a man laying a trap but of a man willingly walking into one.

The only other customers at the diner when Angel and Louis entered were two male Japanese tourists excitedly taking photographs of the interior, with its gas-fired coffee urns and its ancient signage. The Collector sat at the back of the diner, near the door marked NO ADMITTANCE. STAFF ONLY. His hands lay flat on the table before him, resting on either side of a coffee cup. He was dressed as he nearly always was, in a long dark coat worn over dark pants, a dark jacket, and a tieless shirt that had once been white but now, like his nicotine-stained fingertips, had more than a hint of yellow about it. His hair was slicked back from his forehead and hung over the collar of his shirt, adding touches of grease to the yellow. He was, thought Angel, even more cadaverous than when last they'd met. Being hunted will do that to a man.

Once Louis and Angel were inside, a middle-aged woman moved from behind the counter, locked the door, and turned the sign to CLOSED. She then unhurriedly poured two cups of coffee and left through the private staff door without looking at them or at the man who sat waiting for them, stinking of cigarette smoke.

The two Japanese tourists laid down their cameras and turned to face the Collector. The younger of the men signaled almost imperceptibly to a pair of his countrymen watching from the southeastern corner of Lexington and Eighty-Third. One of them now crossed the street to cover the front of the store, while the other watched the side.

"You think I didn't notice them?" said the Collector. "I spotted them before they were even aware of my presence."

Louis sat at the table facing, but to the right of, the Collector, and Angel took a similar position to the Collector's left, forming a kind of lethal triangle. By the time they were seated the guns were in their hands, visible to the Collector but not to anyone glancing in casually from the street.

"We've been looking for you," said Louis.

"I'm aware of that. You must be running out of houses to burn down."

"You could have saved us a lot of gas money by just showing up here months ago."

"And maybe I could have marked the spot on my forehead for the bullet to enter."

"You should have been more careful about your choice of victims."

Louis reached into his coat pocket with his left hand and withdrew Jackie Garner's bear claw necklace. The claws rattled like bones as he fed them through his fingers. In his right he held the final claw, broken from the necklace and included with the Collector's invitation.

"I might say the same about your late friend," said the Collector.

Slowly, precisely, so as not to cause the men before him to react, he picked up his cup and sipped his coffee.

"We can, if you choose, play the blame game until the sun starts to set, but none of us is that naïve," he said. "Mr. Garner miscalculated, and someone close to me paid the price. I reacted in anger, and Mr. Garner died. You'll forgive me if I refuse to allow someone like you, a man with the blood of both the innocent and the guilty on his hands, to admonish me about the appropriateness or otherwise of killing. Hypocrisy is a particularly galling vice."

Angel inclined slightly toward Louis.

"Are we being lectured by a serial killer?"

"You know, I do believe we are."

"It's a novel experience."

"Yes, it is. I still won't miss him after we kill him."

"No, me neither."

The Collector's hands were, once again, resting on the table. He showed no sign of unease. It might have been that he was not aware of how close he was to death, or he simply might not have cared.

"I hear that your friend, the detective, is dying," he said.

"Or still living," said Angel. "It's a matter of perspective."

"He is an unusual man. I don't claim to understand him, but I would prefer it if he survived. The world is more colorful for his presence. He draws evil to him like moths to light. It makes its practitioners easier to dispose of."

"You come here to deliver a get-well-soon wish?" said Louis. "We'll be sure to pass it on. And if he does die, well, you may just be in a position to express your regrets to him personally."

The Collector stared out the window at the two Japanese men, then took in the second pair in the diner.

"Where do you find these people?" he asked.

"We attract them," said Louis. "Like moths to light," he added, appropriating the Collector's metaphor for himself.

"Is that what you are now? The force of light?"

"In the absence of another."

"Yes, I suspect yours is only reflected light," said the Collector. "You're looking for the ones who shot him. I can help you."

"How?"

"I can give you their names. I can tell you where to find them."

"And why would you do that?"

"To cut a deal. Eldritch is ill. He needs rest, and time to recuperate. The strain of the hunt is telling on him. As for me, it's interfering with my work. While I try to stay one step ahead of you, vicious men and women go unpunished. So I will give you the names, and as part of the bargain you will abandon the hunt. You must be tiring of it as much as I, and you know that your Mr. Garner did wrong. If I hadn't killed him, he would be spending the rest of his days in a cell. In a way, I did him a favor. He wouldn't have lasted long in prison. He wasn't as strong as we are."

Angel's grip tightened on his gun. For this creature to suggest that Jackie's murder was some kind of blessing was almost too much for him to bear.

"At least he'd have received a trial," said Angel.

"I tried him. He confessed. You're speaking of the trappings of legality, and nothing more."

Louis spoke. He said only one word, but it was both a warning and an imprecation.

"Angel."

After a second or two, Angel relaxed.

"You mentioned us backing off as 'part' of the bargain," said Louis. "What's the rest?"

"I know that your search for the ones who did the shooting has brought you into contact with all kinds of interesting individuals. I'm assuming one of those was Cambion."

"Why?"

"Because when you'd exhausted all other avenues, he would have been the only one left. I doubt that he gave you the answers you needed."

"We met him," confirmed Louis.

"And?"

"He told us that a couple, a man and a woman, carried out the attack. He promised more."

"Of course he did. What did he ask in return for the information?"

"The same thing that you just did—for us to call off the dogs. But it's like this: he may be a freak, but he's a freak who didn't kill one of our friends. If it comes down to it, I might be more inclined to take my chances with him."

"You'd be disappointed. He's going to feed you to the shooters, you and your boyfriend. They're potentially more valuable to him than you are. You'll never do his bidding, but they'll owe him a favor, and they're very, very good at what they do."

And Louis understood that the Collector was right. It simply confirmed what Louis had suspected: there would be more benefits to Cambion in siding with the shooters.

"Go on."

"Here is what I'm offering," said the Collector. "I give you the names. In return, I want a truce between us, and I want to know where Cambion is. He is long overdue a blade."

"And if we don't agree?" said Louis. "What if we just decide to kill you here?"

The gun in his hand moved so that it was aiming at the Collector beneath the table. The first shots would take him in the gut, the last in the back of the head as he fell forward and Louis delivered the coup de grâce from above.

The Collector gestured with his right hand toward the chair beside him. On it, unnoticed by Angel and Louis, until now, was a green cardboard folder.

"Open it," he said, as he restored his hands to the table.

Louis stood, never taking his eyes from the Collector as he went to retrieve the folder. The two Asian men in the diner moved too, their guns now visible. The Collector remained very still, his gaze fixed on the tabletop before him. He remained like that as Louis flipped through the file. It contained typewritten sheets, photographs, even transcripts of telephone conversations.

"It's your history," said the Collector. "The story of your life—every killing we could trace, every piece of evidence we could accumulate against you. By good fortune, it was one of a handful of records for which Eldritch retained secure copies. There's enough in there to have damned you, should I have chosen to take the knife to you. If I don't walk safely out of here today, Eldritch will ensure that a copy of it goes to the U.S. Attorney for the Southern District of New York, the New York County District Attorney, twelve different police departments throughout the nation, and the Criminal Investigative Division of the FBI. It should fill in any annoying gaps in their own research."

For the first time, the Collector relaxed. He sat back in his chair and closed his eyes.

"I told you, I'm tired of the hunt," he said. "It ends now. I could have used this material alone to force you to relent, but I feel that I have to make recompense for what happened to Mr. Garner. I want your promise that the chase is over. I want Cambion. In return, you get vengeance for what happened to the detective."

Louis and Angel looked at each other. Louis could see that Angel didn't want to make a deal with this man, but the file had tipped the scales, and Angel, Louis knew, would agree to whatever protected him. Bringing them closer to those who had carried out the attack on Parker would just have to be considered a bonus.

"Agreed," said Louis.

"If the detective survives, I'll take it that your word is a guarantee of his good behavior too," said the Collector. "Otherwise, our truce is void."

"Understood."

"The couple for whom you're looking are named William and Zilla Daund. They live in Asheville, North Carolina. They have two sons, Adrian and Kerr. The sons have no idea of their parents' sideline in killing."

"Who hired them?"

"You'll have to ask them."

"But you know."

"I believe the name Daund comes from the northeast of England—Durham, or possibly Northumberland. I'll let them fill in any other details themselves. Now, I'd like you to fulfill the second part of our arrangement."

"Cambion is in Hunts Lane, over in Brooklyn," said Louis. "Assuming he hasn't already moved on. He's holed up in an old apothecary."

"Does he have anyone with him?"

"A big man named Edmund."

The Collector stood.

"Then we're done here," he said. "I wish you luck in your investigation."

He buttoned his coat and stepped around the table.

"And you can keep the file," he told Louis as he passed him. "We have more than one copy now."

They let him go, and he lost himself in the crowds on Lexington Avenue.

"I notice that you didn't mention the possibility of a third person at Hunts Lane with Cambion and his buddy," said Angel.

"No," said Louis. "I guess it must have slipped my mind."

CHAPTER

L

I sat at the edge of a lake, on a wooden bench painted white. I was cold, even with a jacket on, and I kept my hands in my pockets to hold the worst of the chill at bay. To my left, at the top of a small hill, was the rehabilitation center, an old nineteenth-century sea captain's house surrounded by a series of more recently built single-story redbrick buildings. Evergreen trees bounded the lake, and most of the snow had been cleared from the grass. The grounds were quiet.

All was quiet.

A small black stone lay by my feet. It looked incredibly smooth. I wanted to hold it in my hand. I reached down to pick it up, and found that it was flawed beneath. A shard of it had fallen away, leaving the underside jagged and uneven. I stared out at the still expanse of the lake and threw the stone. It hit the water and the surface cracked like ice, even though it wasn't frozen. The cracks extended away from me and across the lake, then fractured the woods and mountains beyond, until finally the sky itself was shattered by black lightning.

I heard footsteps behind me, and a hand lit upon my shoulder. I saw the wedding ring that it wore. I remembered the ring. I recalled putting it on that finger before a priest. Now one of the nails was broken.

Susan.

"I knew that it wasn't real," I said.

"How?" said my dead wife.

I did not turn to look at her. I was afraid.

"Because I could not remember how I got here. Because there was no pain."

And I was speaking of the wounds left by the bullets, and the wounds left by loss.

"There doesn't have to be any more pain," she said.

"It's cold."

"It will be, for a time."

I turned now. I wanted to see her. She was as she had been before the Traveling Man took his knife to her. And yet she was not. She was both more and less than she once was.

She wore a summer dress, for she always wore a summer dress in this place. In every glimpse of her that I had caught since losing her, she had been wearing the same dress, although at those times I never saw her face. When I did, it was under other circumstances. The dress would be stained with blood, and her features a ruin of red. I had never been able to reconcile the two versions of her.

Now she was beautiful once again, but her eyes were distant, focused elsewhere, as though my presence here had called her from more pleas-ant business and she wished to return to it as quickly as possible.

"I'm sorry," I said.

"For what?"

"For leaving you. For not being there when he came for you."

"You would have died with us."

"I might have stopped him."

"No. You weren't as strong then, and he had so much rage. So much rage . . ."

Her nails dug into my shoulder, and I was transported with her, back to our home, and together we watched as the Traveling Man had his way with her and our daughter. As he worked, another version of my wife stood behind him, her face a scarlet blur as her head and body shook. This was the one whom I had seen before. This was the wife who walked through my world.

"Who is she?" I asked. "What is she?"

"She is what remains. She is my anger. She is all my hatred and my sorrow, my hurt and my pain. She is the thing that haunts you."

Her hand stroked my cheek. Her touch burned.

"I had a lot of anger," she said.

"So I see. And when I die?"

"Then she dies too."

The remains of our daughter were stretched across her mother's lap. Jennifer was already dead when he began cutting. It was, I supposed, a mercy.

"And Jennifer?"

I felt her hesitate.

"She is different."

"How?"

"She moves between worlds. She holds the other in check. She would not desert you, even in death."

"She whispers to me."

"Yes."

"She writes upon the dust of windowpanes."

"Yes."

"Where is she now?"

"Close."

I looked, but I could not find her.

"I saw her here, in this house, once before."

I had been stalked through these rooms years after their lives were ended, hunted through my former home by a pair of lovers. But my daughter had been waiting for them—my daughter, and the creature of rage she tried to control, but which on that occasion she was content to unleash.

"I'd like to see her."

"She'll come, when she's ready."

I watched the Traveling Man continue his cutting. There was no pain.

Not for me.

———

WE WERE BACK AT the lake. The cracks and fissures were repaired. The fragile world was undisturbed. I stood by the shore. The water did not lap. There were no waves.

"What should I do?" I asked.

"What do you want to do?" she asked.

"I think I want to die."

"Then die."

I could not see my reflection, but I could see Susan's. In this world, it was she who had substance and I who had none.

"What will happen?"

"The world will go on. Did you think that it revolved around you?"

"I didn't realize the afterlife had so much sarcasm in it."

"I haven't had cause to use it in a while. You haven't been around."

"I loved you, you know."

"I know. I loved you too."

She stumbled over the words, unfamiliar in her mouth, but I sensed that speaking them aloud caused something deep inside her to thaw. It was as though my proximity reminded her of what it had once been like to be human.

"If you stay here," she said, "events will play out without you. The world will be different. You will not be there for those whom you might have protected. Others may take your place, but who can say?"

"And if I go back?"

"Pain. Loss. Life. Another death."

"To what end?"

"Are you asking me your purpose?"

"Perhaps."

"You know what they seek. The One Who Waits Behind the Glass. The God of Wasps. The Buried God."

"Am I supposed to stop them?"

"I doubt that you can."

"So why should I go back?"

"There is no 'should.' If you go back, you do so because you choose it, and you will protect those who might not otherwise be protected."

She moved closer to me. I felt the warmth of her breath against my face. It bore a trace of incense.

"You wonder why they come to you, why they're drawn to you, these fallen ones." She whispered the words, as though fearful of being overheard. "When you spend time close to a fire, you smell of smoke. These things seek not only their Buried God. They are looking for a fire that they wish to extinguish, but they cannot find it. You have been near it. You have been in its presence. You carry its smoke upon you, and so they come for you."

She stepped away from me. Her reflection receded, then disappeared. I was alone. I closed my eyes. When I opened them again, my daughter was beside me. She put her hand in mine.

"You're cold," said Jennifer.

"Yes." My voice broke on the word.

"Would you like to go for a walk, Daddy?" she asked.

"Yes," I said. "I'd like that very much."

LI

The Battery Park Book Exchange stood in the center of Asheville, North Carolina. It sold rare and used books, to which Louis had no objection, and wine and champagne, to which, if possible, he had even fewer objections.

The woman named Zilla Daund was taking part in a book club in the store. She and four other women were discussing Stacy Schiff's biography of Cleopatra over sparkling wine and the kind of single-mouthful treats that passed for food where thin, attractive women were concerned. Louis sat with a glass of Pinot Noir by his right hand and a copy of *Max Perkins: Editor of Genius*, by A. Scott Berg, on his lap. He had picked up the Berg book because Perkins had edited Thomas Wolfe, probably Asheville's most famous son, and Louis, who couldn't stand Wolfe's writings, was trying to understand why Perkins had bothered. As far as he could tell from reading the relevant sections in Berg's biography, the only reason that Wolfe's début, *Look Homeward, Angel,* was even marginally tolerable was that Perkins had forced Wolfe to remove more than sixty thousand words from it. At Louis's rough estimate, that still left *Look Homeward, Angel*—which, in the store's Scribner edition, ran to about 500 pages—at least 499 pages too long.

Zilla Daund looked like the kind of woman who took reading

books very seriously without actually understanding how the act could be enjoyable as well. Her copy of *Cleopatra* was marked with narrow Post-it notes of different colors, and Louis felt certain that the interior was dotted with words such as "Interesting!" "Agree strongly!" and "VIP!" like a high schooler in freshman year working her way through *The Catcher in the Rye* for the first time. She was slim and blond, with the build of a long-distance runner. She might even have been considered good-looking had she not prematurely aged herself through a probable combination of excessive exposure to the elements and a steely determination that had left her brow permanently furrowed and her jaw set in a thin rictus, like a serpent about to strike.

Louis had been watching Daund for the past thirty-six hours, but this was as close as he had yet come to her. It was his way: begin at a distance, then slowly move in. So far, from his brief exposure to her routine, she seemed an ordinary suburban housewife living a moderately comfortable existence. She'd gone to her local gym that morning, training for an hour before returning home to shower and change, then leaving shortly after lunch to come to her book club. The day before, she'd eaten a late breakfast with some friends, shopped at the Asheville Mall, browsed the aisles at Mr. K's Used Books at River Ridge, and had dinner at home with her husband and their younger son—their older son, a sophomore at George Washington University, being currently absent. The younger son was just sixteen, but he wouldn't be coming home for dinner anytime soon. At that precise moment, he was in the back of a van being driven deep into the Pisgah National Forest by two men whose faces he had not even glimpsed before he was snatched. He was probably terrified, but the boy's terror didn't concern Louis. He wanted something to use against the Daunds if they proved unwilling to talk.

Meanwhile, Angel was staying close to William Daund, who was on the faculty of the Department of Literature and Language at the University of North Carolina at Asheville. Louis would have bet a dollar that William Daund had read *Look Homeward, Angel* so often he could recite passages of it by heart. He probably even liked the book. Louis was looking forward to killing him.

Zilla Daund finished giving her opinion on Cleopatra's ruthlessness, which apparently extended to slaughtering her own relatives when the situation required it. "She lived in an age of murder and betrayal," Daund told her friends. "I don't believe that she killed because she liked it. She killed because it was the most effective solution to the problems that she faced."

The other women laughed—that was their funny old Zilla, always following the shortest route between two points, no matter who or what happened to be in the way—and Louis watched as Daund laughed along with them. The group broke up. Louis returned his attention to Maxwell Perkins. In a letter dated November 17, 1936, Perkins was trying to come to terms with the fact that Wolfe was severing ties with him. "I know you would not ever do an insincere thing, or anything you did not think was right," wrote Perkins to Wolfe.

Louis had to admire Perkins's faith, even if he adjudged it ultimately to have been misplaced.

"He ruined Thomas Wolfe, you know."

Louis looked up. Zilla Daund was standing before him, her copy of *Cleopatra* cradled beneath her left arm, her right hidden in a pocket of her coat.

"He did good by Hemingway and Fitzgerald," said Louis. "Can't win 'em all."

He didn't allow his eyes to drift to her right hand. He held her gaze.

"No," she said. "Maybe you can't. Enjoy your wine—and your book."

She walked away, and Louis thought: She's made me, or thinks she has. It didn't matter. If she and her husband were as smart as Cambion and the Collector seemed to think, they must have learned quickly that the private detective they'd tried to kill was different, and that the perpetrators of the attack on him were being hunted not only by the police but by men who weren't unlike themselves. Perhaps they had simply not expected to be found so quickly, if they were found at all. Louis wondered if Cambion had already warned them.

He called Angel as he watched her walk across the street to the parking garage.

"Where is he?"

"In his office," said Angel. "He's been in tutorials since this morning, and he's about to give a class until four."

"If he cancels, call me."

"Why?"

"I think the woman is spooked. If I'm right, she'll contact him. You know where he's parked?"

"Yes."

"Watch the car."

"What about you?"

"I'll take the house. Stay with the husband. And, hey?"

"What?"

"You ever read *Look Homeward, Angel*?"

"Fuck, no. It must be a thousand pages long. Why would I want to do that?"

"I knew there was a reason why I liked you," said Louis.

"Yeah?" said Angel. "Well, if I think of one in return I'll let you know."

———

LOUIS WAS AHEAD OF the woman all the way. He had parked at a meter just outside the store, so as soon as she was out of sight he left cash for his wine and returned to his car. Angel had already taken care of the house alarm earlier in the day, once he was certain that William Daund was committed to his tutorials. It meant that when Zilla

Daund entered the house Louis was waiting for her. She said only one word, Louis's suppressed .22 just inches from her head.

"Fuck."

"I prefer 'fucked,'" said Louis. "And, just for the record, you're wrong about Maxwell Perkins."

He closed the front door with his foot and took a step back from her.

"You know what this is about?" he asked.

"The hit in Maine."

"Someone told you to expect trouble?"

"We knew from the aftershock, but we got a call."

"Cambion?"

She didn't respond.

"Not that it's any consolation, but he told us about you as well," said Louis. "Not everything, but a start."

"Like you say, we got fucked."

"Yes, you did. Drop the bag."

A big purse hung from her left shoulder. He'd watched her as she drank her wine earlier, so he knew that she was right-handed, even before she'd spoken to him with that hand concealed, probably holding a weapon aimed at him. He figured she had at least one gun on her person, and maybe another in the purse.

"If you're armed, you better tell me now."

"In my purse."

"But not your right coat pocket?"

"Oops."

Louis stepped back and told her to let the coat fall from her body. It landed on the wood floor with a heavy thud.

"You got anything else?"

"You're welcome to frisk me."

"We're below the Mason-Dixon Line. Us colored folks got to be careful with the white women down here. I'd prefer it if you just told me."

"Left side, on the belt."

"You expecting war to break out?"

"We live in a dangerous world."

She was wearing a loose-fitting cardigan under a light suit jacket, the kind that would easily cover a gun.

"Use your left hand," Louis said. "Thumb and index finger only. Slowly."

Zilla Daund lowered her left hand, pushed aside her jacket with her forearm, and used the palm of her hand to raise the cardigan, exposing the gun. It looked like a little hammerless S&W 642 in a .38 Special.

"This is awkward," she said. "The holster's tight."

He saw her tense, and was a second ahead of her. She was fast, twisting her body at the same time that she raised her right hand to lash out at him, but by then Louis was already bringing the butt of his gun down on her right temple. He followed her to the floor, wrenching the .38 from its holster and tossing it aside. She was stunned but conscious. He kept the gun at the base of her neck while he pulled her jacket and cardigan to her elbows, trapping her arms, then patted her down. Her jeans were skintight, but he still checked them for a blade. He released her when he was done, and watched as she rearranged her clothing. He found her phone and handed it to her.

"Call your husband," he said.

"Why?"

She looked dazed, but he thought that she might have been exaggerating for his benefit. He allowed her to sit up with her back against the wall, although he insisted that she keep her legs outstretched and her hands away from her body. This would make it harder for her to raise herself up if she tried to attack him again. Louis was under no illusions about how dangerous this woman was.

"Because I know that you called your husband after you spoke to me at the bookstore. My guess is that he's expecting the all clear."

Angel had called Louis when he was within sight of the house to tell him that William Daund was on the move. "Let him come" had been Louis's instruction.

Louis waited while she went to her recent calls and found "Bill." He let the gun touch her left temple as her finger hovered above the call button.

"If I was aware that your husband was coming, then you understand I'm not working alone. Your husband is being followed. If you say anything to alert him, we'll know. This doesn't have to end badly for you."

She stared at him. Any aftereffects, real or feigned, of the blow to her head were now almost entirely gone.

"We both know that's not true," she said. "I've seen your face."

"Ma'am," said Louis, "right now you have no idea just how much worse this could get for you and your family."

It was the mention of her family that did it. This wasn't just about her and her husband.

"Fuck," she said again, softly.

"You were that concerned about the safety of your boys, maybe you should have picked another line of work," said Louis. "Make the call. Raise the volume, but don't put it on speaker."

She did as she was told. Louis listened.

"Zill?" said her husband.

"I'm home," she said. "But we still need to talk."

"I'm on my way. No more over the phone."

"Okay. Just be quick."

The call ended.

"Zill and Bill," said Louis. "Cute."

She didn't reply. He could see her calculating, trying to figure out what moves were open to her. Seconds later, Louis's phone buzzed.

"Angel."

"He's about five minutes from you."

"Stay as close as you can."

"Got it."

Louis continued to point the gun at Zilla Daund.

"Crawl into the kitchen on your belly," he said. "Do it."

"What?"

"If you try to get to your feet, I'll kill you."

"You're an animal."

"Now you're just being hurtful," said Louis. "Kitchen."

He stayed behind her as she crawled, keeping the gun on her all the way. The kitchen was mostly walnut, with a matching table and four chairs at the center. When Zilla Daund reached the table, Louis told her to get up slowly and take a seat facing the door. He removed a cup from a shelf and placed it in front of her. The kitchen extended the width of the house, with a connecting door leading to a big living room with a dining area at one end. Between the table and the connecting door was a refrigerator and a glass-fronted cabinet filled with canned goods. It was there that Louis took up position. He couldn't see the front door, but he could see the woman.

The sound of a car pulling up came from the front of the house. About a minute later, there was the rattle of a key in the door. This was the moment. This was when Zilla Daund would warn her husband.

The door opened. Three things happened almost simultaneously.

Zilla Daund screamed her husband's name and threw herself to the kitchen floor.

William Daund raised the gun that was already in his hand and prepared to fire.

And Angel appeared behind William Daund and killed him with a single suppressed shot to the back of the head. Angel then proceeded into the house and closed the door behind him. He didn't look at Daund's body as he stepped over it. It wasn't callousness. He just didn't want to see what he had done. He checked the street from the living room window, but there was no indication that anyone had witnessed what had occurred. Then again, they wouldn't know for sure unless the cops arrived on the doorstep. This had to be quick.

When he joined Louis in the kitchen, Zilla Daund was standing by the utility room. She was under Louis's gun, but she had a big kitchen knife in her hand. On whom she intended to try to use it wasn't clear, but turning it on anyone in that room, including herself, wouldn't have a good result.

"You were only ever going to let one of us live," she said.

"No," said Louis. "Neither of you was ever going to live. The first one into the house was just going to live longer."

Zilla Daund turned the knife in her hand and placed the tip of it against her throat.

"You'll leave with nothing," she said.

"Before you do that," said Louis, "you ought to call your son."

He placed a cell phone on the kitchen table and slid it carefully to the end nearest Zilla. He lowered his gun. Angel did the same. Zilla Daund approached the table. She picked up the phone. There was one name on the display: Kerr, her younger boy.

She called his number. He answered.

"Kerr?" she said.

"Mom? *Mom?*"

"Kerr, are you okay?"

"I don't know where I am, Mom. I got jumped by some men, and they've been driving me around for hours. Mom, I'm scared. What's happening?"

"You're going to be fine, honey. It's a big mistake. Those men are about to let you go. I love you."

"Mom? What—"

Zilla Daund killed the connection. She placed the knife back in its block. She bit her lower lip and shook her head. Her eyes were elsewhere. A tear trickled down one cheek, but whether it was for her son, her husband, or herself could not be known.

"Your word?" she said.

"He'll be released unharmed," said Angel.

He didn't like this. He didn't like it at all. Threatening kids wasn't in his nature. It was necessary, but that didn't make it right.

"How can I trust you?" said Zilla Daund.

"Without overstating the obvious," said Louis, "you don't have much choice. But I figure Cambion told you enough about us, and you've maybe learned a little more in the meantime."

"We made some calls," she admitted.

"And?"

"If we'd known about you, we'd have killed you before we went after the detective."

"Ambitious."

"And careful."

"No. If you were careful, you'd have done your homework first."

Zilla Daund conceded the point.

"Who told you to kill the detective?" said Louis.

"Hayley Conyer."

"Who's Hayley Conyer?"

"The chief selectman of the town of Prosperous, Maine."

"Why?"

"I didn't ask, but everything Hayley does is for the good of the town."

"You kill for anyone else?"

"No, just her."

"For money?"

"She pays, but we'd have helped her for nothing if we had to. We're of the town from generations past."

"Who else knew?"

"Morland, the chief of police. Pastor Warraner. The rest of the board of selectmen."

"Did you kill a homeless man named Jude in Portland and make it look like suicide?"

"Yes."

"And his daughter?"

"No."

"What's so special about Prosperous?" asked Angel.

Zilla Daund's mouth settled into the odd grimace of determination that Louis had identified back at the bookstore, her teeth gritted, her lips slightly parted.

"That's all you get," she said.

"You sold out your town pretty easily," said Louis.

"I didn't sell it out at all," said Zilla Daund. "Prosperous will eat you alive."

Louis shot her twice. She shuddered on the kitchen floor for a time before she died. Louis walked to the front window of the house and looked out. It was already getting dark. The houses in this modern dormitory community all sat on large lots divided by hedges and trees. Lights burned in some of the homes, but there was nobody on the streets. Louis wondered how anyone could live in a development like this, with its near-identical dwellings on clearly delineated lots, the tiny differences in detail or aspect designed to give a false impression of individuality. Maybe killing people was the only way the Daunds could keep from going crazy.

Given more time, they would have searched the house, but Angel was uneasy and eager to be on the move. From his jacket pocket he produced two flasks of carbolic acid, or liquefied phenol. He and Louis retraced their steps through the house, spraying the carbolic acid as they went. Phenol was a useful contaminant of DNA samples. Once they were done, they left the house and returned to their cars. Each had a false adhesive number plate attached to the original. They took only seconds to remove, and melted in open flame. Louis made the call to Kerr Daund's captors, but they were instructed not to release him until the following morning, by which time Angel and Louis would be far from Asheville, North Carolina—but considerably closer to Prosperous, Maine.

CHAPTER

LII

They did not immediately descend on Prosperous. Instead, Angel and Louis waited, and they planned.

An apartment on Eastern Promenade, in Portland, was rented in the name of one of Louis's shelf companies. At the Great Lost Bear, Dave Evans turned a blind eye as a succession of meetings took place in his office, until eventually he resigned himself to doing his paperwork in a booth by the bar. Prosperous was visited by a pair of Japanese businessmen and their wives, who endeared themselves to everyone they met with their courtesy and their enthusiasm. They took a lot of photographs, but then that was to be expected of tourists from the Far East. They even accepted it in good spirits when they were prevented from entering the cemetery that surrounded the old church. The ground was unsafe, they were told, but plans were being put in place to mark a route through the gravestones to the church itself. Perhaps next time, if they returned.

And one evening, shortly after Angel and Louis's arrival in Portland, Ronald Straydeer came to the Great Lost Bear. Ronald had rarely frequented the city's bars when he did drink, and now that he had given up he had no cause to visit them at all, but Angel and Louis preferred to conduct their business away from their apartment, for the fewer people who knew about it the better. The meeting with Ronald had been arranged through Rachel Wolfe, as Ronald did not know of any other way to contact the two men whom he sought. He had left a message for her at the hospital where the detective still lay in a coma. Ronald's short note requested simply that Rachel call him. Rachel had met Ronald on a couple of occasions while she was living in Scarborough, so she knew who he was, and was aware of the mutual respect that existed between him and her former lover. She asked no questions when he told her that he wanted to be put in touch with Angel and Louis, but simply passed the message on to them. When Angel eventually called, Ronald had said only this: "I saw something happen in Prosperous, something bad."

And Angel knew that they were about to be handed another piece of the puzzle.

Over coffee in the back office, Ronald told Angel and Louis what he had witnessed: a girl swallowed by the earth in the shadow of an old church, while a group of older men and a woman, accompanied by a pastor and a policeman, stood by and watched. If the two men were surprised by his tale, they didn't show it. If they were skeptical, Ronald could detect no trace.

"What do you think happened to her?" asked Louis.

"I think something pulled her underground," said Ronald.

"*Something?*" said Louis.

It seemed to Ronald to be the first expression of any doubt, but he was mistaken. It came to him that these men had seen and heard things stranger even than this.

"It's not enough," Louis continued. "We need more. We can't go in blind."

Ronald had thought on this too. He had ransacked his memories of tribal lore—the Cherokee worship of the cedar tree, based on the belief that the Creator had imbued it with the spirits of those who had perished during the times of eternal night; the Canotila, or tree dwellers, of the Lakota; the Abenakis' tale of the creation of man from the bark of ash trees; and the forest-dwelling Mikum-wasus of his own Penobscot people—but he could find no explanation for what he had seen. He had a vision of a great tree growing upside down, its leafless crown far below the ground, its trunk extending upward to roots that twitched and groped, breaking through the earth to the air above; and at its heart, surrounded by the husks of dead girls, was an entity that had come from far away, a spirit that had infused the stones of an old church, traveling with it as it crossed land and sea before retreating into the new ground in which the foundations of that church were laid, creating a form for itself from wood and sap. But the question that consumed him most was its nature, for he believed that men created gods as much, if not more, than gods created men. If this old god existed, it did so because there were men and women who permitted it to continue to exist through their beliefs. They fed it, and it, in turn, fed them.

Ronald took from his jacket a sheaf of photocopied pages and laid them before Angel and Louis. The images on them were undated, but they depicted the carved heads that could be seen both inside and outside the Blessed Chapel of the Congregation of Adam Before Eve & Eve Before Adam. He had found the pictures buried in the archives of the Center for Maine History, and then, unbeknownst to him, had followed a research path similar to the one pursued by the detective, staring at images of the foliate heads to be found on the churches and cathedrals of Western Europe. The English had called it the Green Man, but it predated that name by more than a millennium, and its spirit was older still. When the first men came, it was waiting for them among the trees, and in their minds it formed itself in their image: a human face rendered in wood and leaf.

"It may be that it looks like this," said Ronald.

Angel picked up one of the pictures. It was the face of winter, the bleakest and most hostile of the visages from the Prosperous church. He thought of what Agent Ross had said to them back in Brooklyn. It didn't matter whether a thing existed or not. What mattered was the trouble caused by those who believed in its existence.

"You talked of roots," he said.

"Yes," said Ronald. "I think roots drew the girl down."

"Roots and branches," said Angel. "Wood."

"And what does wood do?" asked Louis.

Angel smiled as he replied.

"It burns."

———

THE KILLINGS IN ASHEVILLE hadn't gone unremarked in Boston, for Garrison Pryor's people had been following trails similar to those walked by Angel and Louis, albeit a little more discreetly. The deaths of William and Zilla Daund simply confirmed what Pryor had begun to suspect: that the attack on the detective had been ordered from the town of Prosperous. This indicated that the decision to leave the Believers' mark at the scene had also been taken there, which meant, finally, that all of Pryor's current troubles could be laid at the town's door.

Prosperous had rarely troubled Pryor until now. It was a community unto itself, and he saw no reason to interfere with it as long as it was discreet in its activities. Now the town's very insularity—its refusal to recognize its relationship to the larger world and the possible impact of its decisions upon those beyond its boundaries—and the commitment of its protectors to its preservation, at any cost, had disturbed this state of equilibrium.

Prosperous, by its actions, had made retribution inevitable.

———

THE CALL CAME THROUGH to Angel's cell phone, its ID hidden. Louis felt that he should have been more surprised when Angel handed him the phone and he heard the Collector's voice.

"Very impressive," said the Collector. "To be honest, I had wondered if Cambion might not have been right to bet everything on them, but clearly they weren't quite as accomplished as he believed them to be."

"I think killing homeless men had blunted their edge," said Louis.

"Oh, they've killed more than homeless men, but I won't disagree. They swam in a small pool."

"How did you know about them?"

"A process of elimination. I asked questions, and found out that Parker had been nosing around in Prosperous's business. It was possible that the town might not have been involved, but Cambion sealed it for me. He's long been interested in Prosperous's pet husband-and-wife killers."

"You could just have told us. You could just have given us the name of the town."

"But where would be the sport in that? And I know you, Louis, perhaps better than you know yourself. You're meticulous. You want to fill in the blanks. What did the Daunds give you? Prosperous, or more? Wait, names; they gave you names. You wouldn't have left without them. Am I correct?"

Louis put down his glass of orange juice. He'd just been settling into the business pages of the *New York Times*, but now he recognized that any interest he might have had in the newspaper or, indeed, the orange juice had largely dissipated.

"*A* name," he conceded. "The woman gave me a name."

"Hayley Conyer."

"Shit."

"Oh, she wouldn't like to hear you swear like that. She's a god-fearing woman. That's 'god' with a small 'g,' incidentally."

"You interested in her? Looking for a date?"

"She's very old."

"Begging your pardon, but I don't believe you can afford to be particular."

"Don't be facetious. She's an interesting woman, and Prosperous is a fascinating town. You'll like it."

"Is she on your list?"

"Oh, yes."

"So why haven't you taken her?"

"Because it's not just her but the whole town. And *generations* of it. To do the sins of Prosperous justice, I'd have to dig up centuries of bones and burn them on a pyre. The whole town would have to be put to the torch, and that's beyond my capabilities."

Louis understood.

"But not beyond ours."

"No."

"Why should we destroy an entire town?"

"Because it colluded in what happened to the detective, and if you don't wipe it from the earth it will continue its traditions into future generations, and those traditions are very, very nasty. Prosperous is a *hungry* town."

"So you want us to do your dirty work for you? Fuck you."

"Don't be like that," said the Collector. "You'll enjoy it, I guarantee it. Oh, and pay special attention to that church of theirs. Flames won't be enough. You'll have to dig much deeper, and tear it apart with something far stronger."

Louis sensed that the conversation was coming to a close.

"Hey, since we're being all civil and all, you find your friend Cambion?"

The Collector was standing in the premises of Blackthorn, Apothecary. He held a blade in his hands. Upon it was just a hint of blood.

"I'm afraid he seems to have made his excuses and left before we could become better acquainted."

"That's unfortunate," said Louis. And he meant it.

"Yes, it is," said the Collector, and he meant it too.

Seconds passed.

"You told me that he lived here with someone else," said the Collector.

"Yeah, big man. Dressed in yellow. Hard to miss."

"And no other?"

"Not that I was aware of."

"Hmmm."

The Collector stared at the tattered, partial wreckage of a human being that lay on a gurney before him. The man had no eyes, no ears, and no tongue. Most of his fingers and toes were also missing. Stitches marked the site of his emasculation. The Collector had killed him as an act of mercy.

"You know," he said, "I believe I may have discovered Mr. Cambion's missing physician. Be sure to send me a postcard from Prosperous."

The Collector hung up. Angel looked up at Louis from over the *Portland Press Herald*.

"Are you two, like, all buddies now?"

Louis sighed.

"You know," he said, "sometimes I wish I'd never heard the name Charlie Parker. . . ."

———

GARRISON PRYOR WAS SITTING in a quiet corner of the Isabella Stewart Gardner Museum in Boston. He could see into the next public room, so he knew that he was not being overheard or observed. Since the FBI's visit to his offices, Pryor had grown concerned about surveillance to the point of paranoia. He no longer made or received delicate calls outside or on the office phones, especially when he was dealing with the Principal Backer. The most important of the Backers now exchanged numbers for clean cell phones each day, but otherwise they had fallen back on a primitive but virtually untraceable means of communicating sensitive information like cell phone numbers, a simple code based on the print edition of the *Wall Street Journal:* page, column, paragraph, line. Many of the older Backers found the routine almost reassuring, and Pryor thought that some might advocate retaining it once the FBI had exhausted itself chasing after imagined breaches of financial regulations.

The bureau's attention was irritating and an inconvenience, but little more than that. His business, Pryor Investments, had learned from past mistakes, and was now entirely scrupulous in its dealings. Of course, the business was merely a front: a fully functioning and lucrative one, but a front nonetheless. The Backers' real machinery had been hidden so deeply, and for so long, in established companies—in banks and trusts, charities and religious organizations—as to be untraceable. Let the FBI and its allies expend their energy on Pryor Investments. Admittedly, it was unfortunate that the private detective in Maine had become interested in Pryor Investments to begin with. It was a piece of bad luck, and nothing more. But he had clearly spoken to others of his suspicions, which was why the FBI had ended up on Pryor's doorstep. But they would find nothing, and eventually their attention would turn elsewhere.

Now, in the quiet of the museum, he spoke on the phone with the Principal Backer.

"Who killed this couple in Asheville?"

"We don't know for sure," said Pryor, "but we believe it was Parker's pet assassins."

"They did well to find what we couldn't."

"We were close," said Pryor. "The Daunds' blood was still pooling on the floor of their house when I got their names."

"So they saved us the trouble of killing the Daunds ourselves."

"I suppose they did. What now?"

"Now? Nothing."

Pryor was surprised. "What about Prosperous?"

"We let Parker's friends finish what they started. Why should we involve ourselves when they'll do the job for us?" The Principal Backer laughed. "We won't even have to pay them."

"And then?"

"Business as usual. You have mines to acquire."

Yes, thought Pryor. Yes, I have.

LIII

Lucas Morland felt as though he had aged years within a matter of days, but for the first time he was starting to believe that Prosperous might be free and clear, at least as far as the law was concerned. The MSP hadn't been in touch with him in forty-eight hours, and its investigators were no longer troubling the town. A certain narrative was gaining traction: Harry Dixon, who had been depressed and suffering from financial problems, killed his wife, her half sister and her husband, and, it was presumed, their daughter, before turning his gun on himself. Extensive searches of the town and its environs had failed to uncover any trace of Kayley Madsen. The state police had even done some halfhearted exploring in the cemetery under Pastor Warraner's watchful eye. The only tense moment occurred when some disturbance to the earth near the church walls was discovered, but further digging exposed only the remains of what was believed to be an animal burrow of some kind—too narrow, it seemed, to allow for the burial of a young woman's body.

Then there was the matter of the detective. The hit on him had been botched, and, just as Morland had warned, the attack had brought with it a series of convulsive aftershocks, culminating in the killing of the Daunds. Morland didn't know how the couple had been tracked down. Neither did he know if they had kept silent as they died, or confessed all to their killers in an effort to save themselves or, more likely, their son, who had been held captive while his parents were shot dead in their own home. At best, those who were seeking to avenge the shooting of the detective were now only one step away from Prosperous. He had tried to get Hayley Conyer and the others to understand the danger they were in, but they refused to do so. They believed that they had acted to protect the town, and that the town, in turn, would protect them. Why wouldn't it? After all, they had given a girl to it.

Now he was back in Conyer's house, sitting at that same table in that same room, sipping tea from the same mugs. Sunlight flooded through the trees. It was the first truly warm day in months. The air was bright with the sound of snow and ice melting, like the dimly heard ticking of clocks.

"You've done well, Lucas," Conyer told him, as she sipped her tea. Morland had barely touched his. He had begun to resent every minute he was forced to spend in Conyer's presence. "Don't think the board doesn't appreciate all your efforts."

He was there only because that old bastard Kinley Nowell had finally given up the ghost. He had died that morning in his daughter's arms. It was a more peaceful passing than he deserved. As far as Morland was concerned, Kinley Nowell had been severely lacking in the milk of human kindness, even by the standards of a town that fed young women to a hole in the ground.

But Nowell's death had also provided him with what might be his final chance to talk some sense into Hayley Conyer. The board would need a replacement, but Conyer had vetoed the suggestion that the young lawyer Stacey Walker should be the one, despite the majority of her fellow board members being in favor. Instead, Conyer was holding firm on Daniel Cooper, who wasn't much younger than Nowell and was among the most stubborn and blinkered of the town's elders, as well as an admirer of Conyer's to the point of witlessness. Even after all that had occurred, Conyer was still attempting to consolidate her position.

"We just need to stand together for a little while longer," Conyer continued. "And then all this will pass."

She knew why he was here, but she wasn't about to be dissuaded from her course. She'd already informed Morland that she felt that Stacey Walker was too young, too inexperienced, to be brought onto the board. Hard times called for old heads, she told him. Morland couldn't tell whether she'd just made that up or it was an actual saying, but he rejected it totally in either case. It was old heads that had gotten them into all this trouble to begin with. The town needed a fresh start. He thought of Annie Broyer, and a question that had come to mind after he and Harry Dixon had spent a cold night burying her.

What would happen if we stopped feeding it?

Bad things, Hayley Conyer would have told him had she been there. She would have pointed to the misfortunes that had blighted Prosperous so recently—the deaths of those boys in Afghanistan, of Valerie Gillson, of Ben Pearson—and said, "There! See what happens when you fail in your duty to the town?"

But what if this was all a myth in which they had mistakenly chosen to believe? What if their old god was more dependent on them than they were on it? Their credence gave it power. If they deprived it of belief, what then?

Could a god die?

Let the town have its share of misfortunes. Let it take its chances with the rest of humanity, for good or ill. He was surprised by how much Kayley Madsen's fate had shaken him. He'd heard stories, of course. His own father had prepared him for it, so he thought he knew what to expect. He hadn't been ready for the reality, though. It was the speed of it that haunted him most—how quickly the girl had been swallowed by the earth, like a conjurer's vanishing trick.

If Morland had his way, they would feed this old god no longer.

But Hayley Conyer stood in his way: she and those like her.

"We have to put old disagreements behind us and look to the future," said Hayley. "Let all our difficulties be in the past."

"But they're not," he said. "What happened to the Daunds proves that."

"You're making assumptions that their deaths are linked to their recent efforts on our behalf."

"You told me yourself that they worked only for the town. There can be no other reason why they were targeted."

She dismissed what he said with a wave of her hand.

"They could have been tempted to take on other tasks without our knowledge. Even if they didn't, and they were somehow tracked down because of the detective, they wouldn't betray us."

"They might, to save their child."

But Hayley Conyer had no children, had apparently never shown any desire to be a mother, and to possess such feelings for a child was beyond her imaginative and emotional reach.

"Hayley," said Morland, with some force, "they will come here next. I'm certain of it."

And it's your fault, he wanted to tell her. I warned you. I told you not to take this course of action. I love this town as much as you. I've even killed for it. But you believe that whatever decision you take, whatever is right for you, is also right for Prosperous, and in that you are mistaken. You're like that French king who declared that he was the state, before the people ultimately proved him wrong by cutting off his descendant's head.

Morland wasn't the only one who felt this way. There were others too. The time of the current board of selectmen was drawing to a close.

"If they do come, we'll deal with them," said Conyer. "We'll . . ."

But Morland was no longer even listening. He drifted. He wasn't sleeping well, and when he did manage to doze off his dreams—he had begun to dream in earnest—were haunted by visions of wolves. He removed a handkerchief from his pocket. Hayley Conyer was still talking, lecturing him on the town's history, his obligations to it, the wisdom of the board. It sounded to him like the cawings of an old crow. She mentioned something about his position, about how nobody was irreplaceable. She talked of the possibility of Morland's taking a period of extended leave.

Morland stood. It took a huge effort. His body felt impossibly heavy. He looked at the handkerchief. Why had he taken it from his pocket? Ah, he remembered now. He walked behind Hayley Conyer, clasped the handkerchief over her nose and mouth, and squeezed. He wrapped his left arm around her as he did so, holding her down in the chair, her sticklike arms pressed to her sides. She struggled against him, but he was a big man, and she was an elderly woman at the end of her days. Morland didn't look into her eyes as he killed her. Instead, he stared out the window at the trees in the yard. He could see the dark winter buds on the nearest maple. Soon they would give way to the red and yellow flowers of early spring.

Hayley Conyer jerked hard in her chair. He felt her spirit depart, and smelled the dying of her. He released his grip on her face and examined her nose and mouth. There were no obvious signs of injury: a little redness where he had held her nostrils closed, but no more than that. He let her fall forward on the table and made a call to Frank Robinson, who operated the town's only medical practice and who, like Morland, felt that the time for a change was fast approaching. Robinson would make a fine selectman.

"Frank," he said, once the receptionist put him through. "I've got some bad news. I came over to talk to Hayley Conyer and found her collapsed on her dining table. Yeah, she's gone. I guess her old heart gave out on her at last. Must have been the stress of all that's happened."

It was unlikely that the state's chief medical examiner would insist on an autopsy, and even if one was ordered, Doc Robinson had the designated authority to perform it. Meanwhile, Morland would take photographs of the scene to include in his report.

He listened as Robinson spoke.

"Yeah," said Morland. "It's the town's loss. But we go on."

Two down, thought Morland. Three, and he could take over the board. The one to watch would be Thomas Souleby, who had always wanted to be chief selectman. Warraner too might be a problem, but it was traditional that the pastor did not serve on the board, just as Morland himself, as chief of police, was prevented from serving by the rules of the town. But Warraner didn't have many friends in the town, while Morland did. And perhaps, if Morland were finally to put an end to this madness, he would have to take care of Warraner as well. Without a shepherd, there was no flock. Without a pastor, there was no church.

He stared down at his hands. He had never even fired his gun in anger until the evening he killed Erin Dixon and her relatives, and now he had more deaths on his conscience than he could count on one hand. He had even fired the bullet that killed Harry Dixon. Bryan Joblin had offered to do it, but Morland wasn't sure that Joblin could do something that was at once so simple, yet so dangerous, without botching it. He'd let Bryan watch, though. It was the least he could do.

He should have been more troubled than he was, but, Kayley Madsen's final moments apart, he felt comparatively free of any psychological burden, for he could justify each killing to himself. By fleeing, Harry Dixon had given Morland no choice but to move against him. Eventually, he would have told someone about Annie Broyer and how she had come to die in the town of Prosperous. The town's hold on its citizens grew looser the farther from it they moved. This was true of any belief system. It was sustained by the proximity of other believers.

A car pulled up outside, and he watched Frank Robinson emerge from it. Morland wished that he could get into his own car and drive

away, but he had come too far now. A line from a play came to him, or
the vaguest memory of it. It had to be from high school, because Morland hadn't been to a play in twenty years. Shakespeare, he guessed,
something about how, if it were to be done, then it was best to do it
quickly.

If Morland could get rid of Souleby, the board would be his.

The board, and the town.

———

THE NEWS OF HAYLEY Conyer's passing made the papers, as anything
involving Prosperous now tended to do. The general consensus was
that the old woman's heart had been broken by the troubles visited on
her town, although this view was not shared by everyone.

"Jesus!" said Angel to Louis. "If it goes on like this there'll be
nobody left for us to kill."

He remained surprised by Louis's patience. They were still in Portland, and no move had yet been made on Prosperous.

"You think it was natural causes, like they're saying?" said Angel.

"Death is always by natural causes, if you look hard enough."

"That's not what I meant."

"I'd be surprised if she didn't die kicking at something," said Louis.
"Zilla Daund told us that the order to hit Parker came from the board
of selectmen, and this Conyer woman in particular. Now she's dead.
If I was on that board, I'd start locking my door at night. It's like that
Sherlock Holmes thing. You know, once you eliminate the impossible,
whatever is left, no matter how improbable it seems, is the truth."

"I don't get it," said Angel.

"Once everyone else in the room is dead, the person left standing,
no matter how respectable, is the killer."

"Right. You have anyone in mind?"

Louis walked over to the dining room table. An array of photographs lay on it, including images of the town, its buildings, and a

number of its citizens. Some of the pictures had been provided by the Japanese "tourists." Others had been copied from Web sites. Louis separated pictures of five men from the rest.

"Souleby, Joblin, Ayton, Warraner, and Morland," he said.

He pushed the photographs of Joblin and Ayton to one side.

"Not these," he said.

"Why?" said Angel.

"Just a feeling. Souleby might have it in him, I admit, but not the other two. One's too old; the second's not the type."

Louis then separated Warraner.

"Again, why?"

"Makes no sense. If this is all connected to something in their old church, then Conyer and the board acted to protect it. The church is Warraner's baby. He has no reason to hurt anyone who took measures for its benefit."

Louis touched his fingers to Souleby's picture. A file had been compiled on each of the selectmen, as well as on Warraner and Morland. Souleby was an interesting man—ruthless in business, with connections in Boston. But . . .

"Lot of killing for an old man," said Louis. "Too much." And he put Souleby's photograph with the rest.

"Which leaves Morland," said Angel.

Louis stared at Morland's photograph. It had been taken from the town's Web site. Morland was smiling.

"Yes," said Louis. "Which leaves Morland."

CHAPTER
LIV

Thomas Souleby tried to pack a bag as his wife looked on. Constance was growing increasingly disturbed at the casual way in which her husband was tossing his clothing into the big leather duffel. He never could pack for shit, she thought. She didn't say this aloud, though. Even after forty years of marriage, her husband still professed to be shocked by what he termed her "salty tongue."

"Here, let me do that," said Constance. She gently elbowed Thomas aside, removed the shirts and pants, and began folding them again before restoring them to the bag. "You go and get your shaving kit."

Thomas did as he was told. He didn't opine that there might not be time for the proper folding and placement of his clothing. She was working faster and yet more efficiently than he could have done anyway—he was all haste without speed—and there was little point in arguing with his wife, not when it came to the organizational details of his life. Without her involvement, they would never have achieved the degree of financial security and comfort they now enjoyed. Thomas had never been a details man. He worked in concepts. His wife was the meticulous one.

When he returned to the bed, she had half filled the bag with shirts, a sweater, two pairs of pants, and a second pair of shoes with his socks and underwear neatly fitted inside. To these he added his shaving kit and a Colt 1911 pistol that had belonged to his father. The Colt was unlicensed. Long ago, his father had advised him of the importance of keeping certain things secret, especially in a place like Prosperous. As Souleby had watched the slow, steady ascent of Lucas Morland, he came to be grateful for the bequest. Thomas Souleby considered himself a good judge of character—he couldn't have succeeded in business if he weren't—and had never liked or trusted Lucas Morland. The man thought he knew better than his elders, and that wasn't the way Prosperous worked. Souleby had also noticed a change in Morland in recent weeks. He could almost smell it on him, an alteration in his secretions. Conyer had sensed it too. That was why, before her death, she had been planning to remove Morland from his post and replace him with one of his more malleable deputies. Souleby could still feel the old woman's hand on his arm, the strength of her grip, as she had spoken to him for the last time the day before.

"You listen, Thomas Souleby, and you listen good," she said. "I'm as healthy as any woman in this town. My mother lived to be ninety-eight, and I plan on exceeding that age with room to spare. But if anything happens to me you'll know. It'll be Morland's doing, and he won't stop with me. You're no friend to him, and he sure as hell doesn't care much for you. He doesn't understand the town the way we do. He doesn't care for it the way we care. He has no *faith*."

And then the call came from Calder Ayton: Calder, who was everyone's friend, but hadn't been the same since the death of Ben Pearson. Souleby figured that Calder had loved Ben, and had Ben not been resolutely heterosexual, and Calder not a product of a less enlightened, more cloistered time, the two of them could have lived together in domestic bliss, protected by the amused tolerance of the town. Instead, Calder had settled for a sexless relationship of a sort, aided by Ben's status as a widower and Calder's share in the store, the two of them clucking and fussing over each other, snipping and sniping and making up like the old married couple that they secretly were. Calder wouldn't last long now, thought Souleby. Morland wouldn't have to kill him, even if Calder had the backbone to stand up to him, which Souleby doubted. Calder had been widowed, and without Ben to keep him company he would fade away and die quickly enough.

It was Calder who got in touch to tell Souleby of Hayley Conyer's passing. That didn't surprise Souleby. They were two of the last three selectmen, and he had always been closer to Calder than to Luke Joblin, who was too flash for Souleby's liking. What did surprise Souleby was Calder's tone. He knew. He *knew*.

"Who found her?" Souleby asked.

"Chief Morland," Calder told him, and it was there, in the way that he said "Chief." "He thinks she might have had a heart attack."

"And I'll bet Frank Robinson is signing off on it as we speak."

"That's what I hear." A pause. "Morland will be coming for you, Thomas."

The phone felt slick in Souleby's hand. His palms were sweating.

"I know," he said. "What about you?"

"He's not afraid of me."

"Maybe he's underestimated you."

Souleby heard Calder chuckle sadly.

"No, he knows me inside and out. This is my little act of defiance, my last one. I'll be resigning from the board."

"Nobody resigns from the board."

Only death brought an end to a selectman's tenure. The elections were just for show. Everyone knew that.

Calder was sitting in the back of Ben Pearson's store. In reality it was as much his as it had been Ben's, but Calder didn't regard it as anything other than Ben's store, even with Ben no longer around. He looked at the bottles of pills that he had been accumulating since Ben's death.

Soon, he thought. Soon.

"There are ways, Thomas," he said. "You step lively."

Now, with his bag packed, Thomas kissed his wife and prepared to leave.

"Where will you go?" asked Constance.

"I don't know. Not far, but far enough to be safe from him."

Calls had to be made. Souleby still had plenty of allies in the town, although he couldn't see many of them standing up to Morland. They weren't killers, but Morland was.

"What will I tell him when he comes?" asked Constance.

"Nothing, because you know nothing."

He kissed her on the mouth.

"I love you."

"I love you too."

She watched him drive away.

He had been gone less than an hour before Lucas Morland arrived at her door.

———

SOULEBY DROVE AS FAR as Portland and parked in the long-term garage at the Portland Jetport. He then took a bus to Boston, paying cash for the ticket. He didn't know how far Morland would go to track him, and he was no spy, but he hoped that, if Morland did somehow discover the whereabouts of the car, it would throw him a little. He asked his son-in-law to book a room for him under the name Ryan at a club off Massachusetts Avenue that advertised through Expedia. Souleby knew that the club didn't ask for ID, but simply held a key for the name listed on the reservation. He then walked over to Back Bay, sat in a coffee shop across from Pryor Investments, and waited. When Garrison Pryor eventually appeared, cell phone to his ear, Souleby left the coffee shop and followed him. Souleby caught up with Pryor when he stopped at a pedestrian signal.

"Hello, Garrison," he said.

Pryor turned.

"I'll call you back," he said, and hung up the phone. "What are you doing here, Thomas?"

"I need help."

The light changed. Pryor started walking, but Souleby easily kept up with him. He was considerably taller than Pryor, and fitter too, despite his age.

"I'm not in the helping business," said Pryor. "Not for you or your board."

"We've exchanged information in the past."

"That was before tridents began appearing in the woodwork of houses in Scarborough, Maine. Have you any idea of the trouble you've caused me?"

"I counseled against that."

"Not hard enough."

"We're having difficulties in Prosperous. Serious difficulties."

"I noticed."

"Our chief of police is out of control. He has to be . . . *retired* before we can restore stability. Recompense can be made to you and your colleagues."

"It's gone too far."

"Garrison." Souleby put a hand out to stop Pryor, forcing the shorter man to look up at him. "Morland is going to kill me."

"I'm sorry to hear that, Thomas," said Pryor. "Truly, I am. But we're not going to intervene. If it's any consolation to you, whatever happens, Prosperous's days are drawing to a close. In the end, it doesn't matter who's left standing—you, Morland, the board. There are men coming to wipe you from the map."

Souleby's hand dropped. "And you'll let this happen?"

Pryor took out his cell phone and redialed a number. He watched it connect, raised the phone to his ear, and patted Souleby on the shoulder in farewell.

"Thomas," said Pryor, as he walked away, "we're going to watch you all burn."

———

MORLAND SAT IN HIS office. He was frustrated, but no more than that. Souleby would have to return. His life was here. In Souleby's absence, Luke Joblin and Calder Ayton had agreed that elections to the board should be held just as soon as Hayley Conyer was safely interred. Neither had objected to Morland's list of nominees for the three vacant positions.

Morland had a fourth name ready too. He had a feeling that another vacancy would soon arise.

LV

Chief Morland next faced Thomas Souleby as they stood over Hayley Conyer's open grave. In recognition of her long and generous service to the town of Prosperous, she was buried in the old cemetery, in the shadow of the church whose legacy she had done so much to protect, and in which her body had reposed on the night before its burial. Only a handful of the most important citizens were permitted to enter the church for the funeral service, although a temporary sound system relayed the proceedings to the townsfolk who stood outside. God played a part, but so too did nature, and the metaphor that ran through Warraner's oratory was of the changing of the seasons, a life's journey from spring to winter, and thence to a new form of rebirth.

Once the coffin was lowered into the ground, it was left to the selectmen, assisted by Morland and Warraner, to fill in the grave. It was a sign of respect, but Morland was inevitably reminded of the last time he had wielded a spade in service of a body. The townsfolk started to leave. Tea and coffee were being served at the Town Office, where memories of Hayley Conyer would be exchanged, and talk would turn to the election of the new selectmen. In addition, nobody wanted to miss the chance to gossip a little under the flag of mourning: Thomas Souleby's absence until the morning of the funeral had not gone unremarked, and the tension between him and Chief Morland was common knowledge in the town, even if the catalyst for this particular bout of hostilities—Hayley Conyer's forced departure from this world—was not.

Morland caught up with Souleby halfway across the churchyard. He grabbed the older man's arm, steering him away from the gate.

"Walk with me awhile, Thomas," he said.

Souleby's wife was waiting for him outside the railings. Morland thought that she might spring over them to protect her husband when she saw the chief approach him, but Souleby raised a hand to let her know that he was okay. If Morland intended him harm, he would do so another day, and under other circumstances.

"We missed you," said Morland. "Your absence was unfortunate. The town was in mourning. It looked to the board for leadership, and the board, in its turn, looked to you as the senior selectman, but you weren't there."

Souleby wasn't about to accuse Lucas Morland of murder—not here, not anywhere. There remained a possibility that he could still survive this, and even turn the situation to his advantage. The three nominees to the board were comparatively young, and open to manipulation. They were not his creatures, but neither were they Morland's. He could not give Morland an excuse to act against him, although the flaw in this line of reasoning was easily apparent, for Morland might not even need a reason to act.

"I had business to conclude," said Souleby.

"You mind my asking what kind of business?"

"Private. Personal."

"You sure about that? Because if it had to do with the town I really ought to know about it. This is a delicate time. We all need to pull together."

Souleby stopped walking and faced Morland.

"What do you want, Chief Morland?"

"I want you to give up your place on the board."

"You know that's not possible. Under the rules—"

"The rules have changed. The board met while you were away."

"There *was* no board," said Souleby. "Two members isn't a quorum."

"Like I said, this is a delicate time. We didn't know what had happened to you, and your wife was of little help. Decisions had to be made. Calder Ayton and Luke Joblin consented to temporary measures pending the election of a new board and the permanent retention of those rules. Selectmen will no longer serve for life, and no selectman will be able to serve more than two terms in succession. I'd have informed you of the changes before now if I'd been able to find you."

Souleby understood what was happening. If he resigned from the board, any power that he had would disappear. He would have no protection.

And, eventually, Morland would come for him. He would do so because, alive, Souleby would always be a threat. Calder Ayton would soon be dead, while Luke Joblin was on Morland's side, and perhaps always had been. Only Souleby knew the details of what had been done in the board's name, and what Morland himself had done.

"And if I refuse to resign?"

Souleby noted movement among the trees, and saw that many members of the senior families hadn't left the environs of the cemetery. They were watching from the woods, and as he stared they began to turn their backs on him, one by one, until he could see their faces no longer. Then, and only then, did they begin to disperse.

"The will of the people will prevail, Thomas," said Morland, and Souleby knew that he was alone.

Morland smiled sadly and walked away. Only when Souleby had seen Morland's Crown Vic drive off, and was certain the chief was gone, did he join his wife outside the railings.

"What did he say to you?" said Constance.

"I want you to go and stay with Becky and Josh," he told her.

Becky was their eldest daughter. She lived down in Portsmouth. Her husband, Josh, was Calder Ayton's nephew. Souleby trusted him.

"No, I won't."

"You will," he said. "All this will pass, but for a time things will be difficult. I can't be worrying about you while I try to make this good."

"No," she said. "No, no . . ."

She started to cry. He held her.

"It'll be all right," he lied. "Everything will be all right."

———

CONSTANCE LEFT LATE THAT afternoon. Becky drove up to collect her. Becky tried to question her father, but he wouldn't answer her, and she knew the ways of Prosperous well enough to pursue the matter no further for now.

Souleby poured himself a glass of brandy. He watched the sun set. He felt drowsy, but he didn't sleep.

It was Luke Joblin who came for him, shortly after eight. His son Bryan waited in the backseat. Souleby saw him when the interior light came on as Luke opened the driver's door. He could have fought them, of course, but what would have been the point? Instead, the old Colt now lay under his wife's pillow. She would find it there, and she would know.

"Come along, Thomas," said Luke. He spoke gently but firmly, the way one might speak to an elderly relative who refused to do what was best for him. "It's time to go. . . ."

LVI

The call came through the following evening as Morland was preparing for bed. He was fresh out of the shower, and had changed into pajama pants and an old Red Sox T-shirt. He was quietly eating a late-night sandwich in the dark prior to hitting the sack and maybe spending some quality time with his wife. They hadn't made love in more than a week. Understandably, Morland hadn't been in the mood. His wife didn't like him eating late at night, but Morland took the view that what she didn't know, or couldn't prove, wouldn't hurt her. It was, he thought, true of so many things.

He had just returned from a visit to Souleby's bitch wife, Constance, at her daughter's house, accompanied by Luke Joblin and three representatives of the most senior families. They'd commented on Constance Souleby's lovely grandchildren, and the fine house in which her daughter and son-in-law lived, for the best kind of threat was the one that didn't sound like a threat at all, the kind that planted bad pictures in the imagination. Becky, Constance's daughter, offered coffee, but nobody accepted.

"What have you done with Thomas?" Constance asked Morland, once the pleasantries were done with.

"Nothing," he said. "We just want him to stay out of the way until after the election. We don't need him interfering, and you know he'll interfere. He's safe."

The election was scheduled for Saturday. Elections to the board were always held on Saturdays, just to be sure that the maximum number of people could vote.

"Why hasn't he called me?"

"If you want him to call, we'll have him do that," said Luke Joblin, all reasonableness and reassurance. "We had to take away his cell phone. You understand why."

If Constance Souleby did understand, she wasn't giving any sign of it.

"You had no right," she said. "No right."

"The town is changing, Mrs. Souleby," said Morland. "We just barely survived the mess of the last couple of weeks. That can't happen again. There can be no more blood spilled in Prosperous. The old board, and all that it did, has to be consigned to history. We have to find a way to survive in the twenty-first century."

A shiver of unease ran through the three representatives of the senior families—two men, one woman, all as old as any in the town. Morland had convinced them of the necessity for change, but this didn't mean that they weren't frightened by it.

"Thomas can adapt," said Constance. She was trying not to plead, but it bled into her voice nonetheless.

"That's not the issue," said Morland. "The decision has been made."

There was nothing more to be said. Morland, Joblin, and the three other visitors got to their feet. Someone mumbled an awkward good-bye, to no reply.

Morland was almost at his car when he heard Constance Souleby begin to wail. Luke Joblin heard it too. Morland could see him tense, even as he tried to ignore the old woman's cries.

"Why did you tell her that her husband would call her?" said Morland. Thomas Souleby wouldn't be calling anyone ever again. There would probably be no body. Once the elections were concluded, he would be reported missing.

"I was trying to keep her calm."

"You figure it worked?" said Morland, as the cries rose in intensity and then were smothered. Morland could almost see Constance Souleby's daughter holding her mother's head, kissing her, shushing her.

"No, not really," said Joblin. "You think she knows?"

"Oh, she knows."

"What will she do?"

"Nothing."

"You sound very certain of that."

"She won't turn on the town. It's not in her blood."

———

NOW, AS MORLAND LISTENED to the ringing of his cell phone, he wondered if he had been right to sound so confident. Great change was always traumatic, and with trauma came actions that were unanticipated, and out of character.

His wife appeared on the stairs, come to see where he was. She was wearing a sheer nightgown. Through it he could see the curves of her body. He tossed the remains of the sandwich into the sink before she noticed. He'd get rid of them in the morning. He was usually awake before her.

"Can't you ignore it?" she asked.

"Just let me see who it is."

He went to the hall and looked at the display.

Warraner.

He had yet to tackle the pastor. Rumors of what Morland was proposing had certainly already reached him. Warraner would have to be convinced of the necessity of acceding to the will of the town, but it wouldn't be easy. Still, he could continue to tend his church, and pray to his god behind the silence of its walls. Perhaps the pastor also hoped that, when bad times came, the town would turn once again to the church, and the old ways could resume. If that was the case, Morland thought that Warraner's prayers to his god would have to be powerful as all hell, because Morland would send Warraner the way of Hayley Conyer and Thomas Souleby before he let another girl end up kneeling by a hole in the cemetery.

Morland considered ignoring the call, but he remained the chief of police. If Warraner wanted to argue, Morland would put him off until morning, but if it was something more urgent . . .

He hit the green button.

"Pastor," he said. "I'm just about to go to bed."

"There's a homeless man on the church grounds," said Warraner. "He's shouting about a murder."

Shit.

"I'm on my way," said Morland.

He looked to his wife.

"I'm sorry," he said.

But she was already gone.

———

WARRANER HUNG UP THE phone. In a corner of the living room lay the body of Bryan Joblin. It was Joblin's misfortune to have been present at Warraner's house when the men arrived, and to have reached for his gun at the sight of them. Joblin had died instantly. He had recently fixed his eye on Warraner's eldest daughter, Ruth, a development about which Warraner had been deeply unhappy. That problem, at least, now appeared to have been solved.

Nearby, Warraner's wife and children were under a gun. One not dissimilar to it was only inches from the pastor's face. If he focused on the muzzle—and he *was* focusing, because it was very, very close to him—the masked face of the man holding the weapon became a blur. Warraner could only see one or the other properly, but not both: the instrument of killing, or the man who might let him live.

"You did good."

Warraner couldn't reply. It was all he had been able to do just to keep his voice steady as he spoke to Morland. He managed to generate some spittle in his mouth, and found his voice.

"What's going to happen to my family?"

"Nothing," replied the gunman. "Although I can't promise the same for you."

———

THE PROSPEROUS POLICE DEPARTMENT kept one officer on duty at night. In the event of an emergency, that officer could call the chief, or even the Maine State Police, but so far no nighttime incident had ever been sufficiently serious to require the assistance of the MSP. The officer on duty that night was Connie Dackson, and she was trying to rewire the plug on the coffee machine when two men entered the Town Office. One carried a shotgun, the other a pistol. Both wore black ski masks.

"Not a move," said the one holding the shotgun, which was now pointing at Dackson.

Nobody had ever pointed a gun at her before. She was so scared that she couldn't have moved even if she wanted to. She was forced facedown onto the floor, and her hands were secured with her own cuffs. A gag was placed over her mouth, and she was shown into the town's single holding cell. It was more than a hundred years old, just like the building that housed it. The bars were green, and Dackson had a clear view through them as the two men began disabling the department's entire communications system.

———

MORLAND COULDN'T RAISE Connie Dackson on her cell phone as he drove. He wasn't worried, though, not yet. She might have left it in her vehicle if she was patrolling, or simply be in the john. She might already even be with Warraner, trying to coax some bum out of the churchyard, a bum who was muttering about murder. That was when Morland knew that he was tired: Warraner wouldn't be dumb enough to call Dackson if there was a chance that she might hear something she shouldn't. This was up to him, and him alone.

The first thing that struck him as he reached the churchyard was the fact that the door of the church was open. The gate to the church-yard was unlocked, the chain lying on the ground. The chain had been cut, just like the one farther down the road.

The second was that he could find no trace of any bum.

He didn't call out Warraner's name. He didn't have to. He could now see the pastor kneeling in the doorway of the church. Beside him stood a tall man in a ski mask. He held a gun to the pastor's head.

"Chief Morland," said the man. "Glad you could make it."

Morland thought that he sounded like a black man. Prosperous didn't have any black residents. This wasn't unusual in such a white state. Maine was one of the few places where nobody could try to blame blacks for crime. The white folk had that one all sewn up.

Morland raised his own gun.

"Lower your weapon," he said.

"Look around you, Chief," said the man.

Morland risked a glance. Three other figures, also masked, ma-terialized from the gloom of the cemetery. Two were armed, their weapons pointing in his direction. The third held a coil of wire, and the sight of it caused Morland to notice for the first time the cables that crossed the cemetery and hung over some of the gravestones. He moved slightly to the right, and saw one of the holes that had so interested the state police investigators when they'd come looking for Kayley Madsen. A length of wire led into its depths.

"What are you doing?" said Morland.

"Putting the finishing touches to thermite and Semtex devices," said the man. "We're about to destroy your town, starting here. Now put down your gun. I want to talk. The pastor has been telling me a lot about you."

But Morland wasn't about to talk to anyone.

Instead, he simply started shooting.

———

NOBODY LIVED ON PROSPEROUS'S Main Street. It was strictly businesses only. As midnight approached, the street and its surround stood empty.

Slowly, men began to emerge from the shadows, eight in all. Ronald Straydeer led them, his features, like those of the others with him, concealed.

"You sure you're okay to do this?" asked Ronald.

"I'm sure," said Shaky.

He held an incendiary device in his good hand. A cold wind was blowing from the east. That was good. It would fan the flames.

There came the sound of breaking glass.

Minutes later, Prosperous started to burn.

———

MORLAND WAS RUNNING FOR his life. Shots struck the old gravestones, or whistled past his ear to vanish into the forest beyond. He stayed low, using the monuments for cover—weaving, dodging, firing blindly, but never stopping. He was outnumbered, and these men could easily surround and kill him, but he knew the woods and they did not. Anyway, staying in the cemetery was not an option, for it was now one massive explosion waiting to occur.

He didn't head for the gate. That would be too obvious. Instead, he sprinted for the railings and scrambled over them. He took a shot to the upper arm but didn't pause. The woods were ahead of him, and he lost himself in their darkness. He risked only one look back, and saw that the church door was now closed. The shooting had stopped, and in the silence Morland heard Warraner's voice raised in song from behind the old stone walls. Somehow, in the confusion, he had managed to lock himself inside.

"*When men begin to weed,*" sang Warraner, "*the thistle from the seed . . .*"

The figures in the churchyard started to run. Morland reloaded his gun and drew a bead on the nearest man. Perhaps he could yet stop this. His finger tightened on the trigger.

But he didn't fire. Was this not what he wanted, what he sought? Let this be an end to it. He lowered his gun, and retreated deeper into the trees, faster now, putting as much distance between him and the church as he could. If he could get to his car and return to town, he and Dackson could hole up in the Town Office while they called for backup.

He reached the road and saw an orange glow rising from Prosperous. The town was already burning, but he barely had time to register that fact before a massive blast rent the night. The ground shook, and Morland was knocked off his feet by the force of it. Debris was hurled high into the air, and earth, stone, and wood rained down on him where he lay. He could feel the heat of the detonation, even from the road.

He covered his head with his hands, and prayed to every god and none.

CHAPTER

LVII

Main Street was gone, reduced to brick shells and vacant, charred lots. At least one of the ruined buildings had dated back to the eighteenth century, and others were only marginally younger. Historians and architecture experts described it as a tragedy.

The Chapel of the Congregation of Adam Before Eve & Eve Before Adam was scattered over woods, roads, and what was left of the cemetery, which wasn't much at all. Charred human remains, most of them long interred, would be discovered for years after. Incredibly, the total number of fatalities amounted to just three: Pastor Michael Warraner, who had been inside his church when it was blown sky high; Bryan Joblin, killed in cold blood at Warraner's house; and Thomas Souleby, the senior selectman of the town, who was said to have accompanied Chief Morland to the cemetery when the original call was received about a homeless trespasser, and who had not been able to get clear of the cemetery before the explosion occurred. Frank Robinson conducted the autopsy on Souleby, just so that there could be no confusion about the matter. Unlike Pastor Warraner, Souleby's body remained undamaged enough to allow for a proper burial. Morland had suffocated Souleby, just as he had done with Hayley Conyer. If nothing else, the chaos at the church had given him a way of avoiding another cold night of burying a body.

It was not much, but it was enough.

The newspapers and TV cameras were back. It would be a long time before they left. When asked about plans to rebuild, Morland told them that work would begin on Main Street almost immediately, but he was unsure about plans for the church. The damage caused by the high explosives used meant that rebuilding the original structure would be ruinously expensive if it was possible at all, which was doubtful. Perhaps a monument might be erected in its place, he suggested. Discussions on the issue would begin, said Morland, once the new board of selectmen was elected.

It remained unclear who might have been responsible for what was described, almost immediately and inevitably, as an "act of terrorism." Attention was focused variously on Muslims, fascists, secessionists, opponents of the federal government, radical socialists, and extreme religious organizations, but Morland knew that none of those avenues of inquiry would ever yield any results.

The truth was that they should never have gone after the detective.

The Town Office had suffered significant damage, mostly in a successful effort to destroy the engines in the fire department. Officer Connie Dackson had watched it burn. Her captors had removed her from her cell and left her tied up at a safe distance from the conflagration. She thought that they might have been Asian, judging by their accents and their unusual politeness, but she couldn't be certain. The Prosperous Police Department had immediately moved to temporary lodgings at the local Veterans of Foreign Wars meeting hall.

On the third day after the attack on his town—for that was what it now was, "his" town—Lucas Morland watched the thawing snow from his window in the local hall. Meltwater ran down what remained of Main Street, starting clear at the top and ending up black as oil by the time it reached the bottom. More snow might come, but it wouldn't last long. They were done with winter, and winter was done with them. They had survived—*he* had survived—and the town would be better and stronger for this purging. He felt a deep and abiding sense of admiration for its people. No sooner were the fires extinguished than the cleanup operation had begun. Buildings were being assessed for demolition or restoration, according to the damage they had sustained. Pledges of aid numbering into six figures had already been received. Calls had been made to the heads of the insurance companies involved, warning them that any weaseling out of their commitments would not be tolerated, those calls having significant impact, since they came from members of their own boards who had ties to Prosperous.

Morland was under no illusions that the town's troubles—or, more particularly, his troubles—were at an end. Those responsible for the partial destruction of his town might well decide to return. He recalled the words of the man at the cemetery: "The pastor has been telling me a lot about you." Even in his final moments, Warraner had found a way to screw him over. At least Bryan Joblin was dead too. He was one loose end about whom Morland no longer needed to worry.

Let them come, Morland thought. Let them come, and I will face them down. Next time I'll be ready, and I will kill them where they stand.

Morland didn't hear the woman approach. He no longer had his own office. His desk was just one part of the jumble of town services in the old hall. People were constantly arriving and departing, and there was a steady hum of noise.

"Lucas."

He turned from the window. Constance Souleby was standing before him. She held a gun in her hand: an old Colt. It did not shake, for the woman holding it was a picture of calm.

"You could have spared him," she said.

He was aware of movement behind her, of someone approaching fast. He heard cries of shock. The gun had been noticed.

"I am—" Morland said.

The gun spoke in denial, and he ceased to be.

4

RETURNING

The forenoon is burn-faced and wandering
And I am the death of the moon.

Below my countenance the bell of the night has broken
And I am the new divine wolf.

Adonis (Ali Ahmad Said Esber), "The Divine Wolf"

LVIII

R onald Straydeer was standing in his yard when the car arrived. Winter was departing, and he was piling the snow behind the woodshed, where it could melt away and be damned without him having to see it.

He rested his hands on his shovel as the car drew to a halt, and felt a small ache of fear when the two men emerged from it. He hadn't seen or spoken to them since that night in Prosperous, but they weren't men who liked to leave loose ends. They had no cause for concern on his part, nor on the part of those whom he had brought with him to put Prosperous to the torch. Some had already left the state. Those who remained would keep silent.

The two men leaned on their car doors and regarded him.

"Beautiful day," said Angel.

"Yes, it is."

"Looks like winter may be ending."

"Yes."

Angel looked at Louis. Louis shrugged.

"We came to thank you," said Angel. "We're going to see Parker, then we're heading home. It's time for us to get back to civilization."

"I've called the hospital," said Ronald. "They tell me there's no change."

"There's always hope," said Angel.

"Yes," said Ronald. "I believe that's true."

"Anyway," said Angel, "we have a gift for you, I guess, if you want it."

He opened the rear door of the car and reached inside. When he emerged again, he held a female German shepherd puppy in his arms. He walked up to Ronald, placed the dog at his feet, and held out the leash. Ronald didn't take it. He looked at the dog. The dog sat for a moment, scratched itself, then stood and placed its front paws against Ronald's right leg.

"Parker talked about you," said Angel. "He used to tell us it was time you got another dog. He thought you might be starting to feel the same way too."

Ronald put the shovel aside. He leaned down and scratched the puppy's head. It wriggled with joy and continued trying to climb his leg.

Ronald took the leash from Angel and unclipped it from the dog's collar.

"You want to come with me?" he said to the dog.

He began walking toward his home. Without looking back at Angel, the dog followed, leaping to keep up with the long strides of its master.

"Thank you," said Ronald Straydeer.

Louis got back into the car. Angel joined him.

"Told you he'd keep the dog," said Louis.

"Yeah. I think you're getting soft in your old age."

"That may be."

He reversed out of Ronald's drive.

"How come we never got a dog?" said Angel.

"I don't need a dog," said Louis. "I got you."

"Right," said Angel.

He thought about it for a moment.

"Hey . . ."

LIX

I sat on the bench by the lake, my daughter by my side. We did not speak.

On an outcrop of land to the east stood a wolf. He watched us as we watched him.

A shadow fell across the bench, and I saw my dead wife reflected in the water. She touched my shoulder, and I felt the warmth of her.

"It's time," she said. "You must decide."

I heard the sound of a car approaching. I glanced over my shoulder. Parked on the road was a white 1960 Ford Falcon. I had seen pictures of it. It was the first car that my father and mother ever owned outright. A man sat in the driver's seat, a woman beside him. I could not see their faces, but I knew who they were. I wanted to talk to them. I wanted to tell them that I was sorry. I wanted to say what every child wishes to say to his parents when they're gone and it's too late to say anything at all: that I loved them, and had always loved them.

"Can I talk to them?" I asked.

"Only if you go with them," said my dead wife. "Only if you choose to take the Long Ride."

I saw the heads of the people in the car turn toward me. I still could not see their faces.

No more pain, I thought. No more pain.

From the hills beyond the lake arose a great howling. I saw the wolf raise his muzzle to the clear blue sky in response to the summoning, and the clamor from the hills grew louder and more joyous, but still the wolf did not move. His eyes were fixed on me.

No more pain. Let it end.

My daughter reached out and took my hand. She pressed something cold into it. I opened my fingers and saw a dark stone on my palm, smooth on one side, damaged on the other.

My daughter.

But I had another.

"If you take the Long Ride, I'll go with you," she said. "But if you stay, then I'll stay with you too."

I stared at the car, trying to see the faces behind the glass. I slowly shook my head. The heads turned from me, and the car pulled away. I watched it until it was gone. When I looked back at the lake, the wolf was still there. He gazed at me for a moment longer, then slipped into the trees, yipping and howling as he went, and the pack called out its welcome.

The stone felt heavy in my hand. It wanted to be thrown. When it was, this world would shatter, and another would take its place. Already I could feel a series of burnings as my wounds began to sing. My dead wife's hand remained on my shoulder, but its touch was growing colder. She whispered something in my ear—a name, a warning—but I was already struggling to remember it once the final word was spoken. Her reflection in the water began to dim as mine started to come into focus beside it. I tried to hold on tighter to my daughter's hand.

"Just a little while longer," I said. "Just—"

ACKNOWLEDGMENTS

First of all, the Family of Love did exist, and much of their history as recounted in this book is true. Whether they ever made it to the New World, I cannot say, but I am grateful to Joseph W. Martin's *Religious Radicals in Tudor England* (Hambledon Continuum, 1989) for increasing my small store of knowledge of them. The history of the foliate heads on churches is also true, and the following books proved highly illuminating, and slightly disturbing: *The Green Man in Britain*, by Fran and Geoff Doel (The History Press, 2010); *The Green Man*, by Kathleen Basford (D. S. Brewer, 1998); and *A Little Book of the Green Man*, by Mike Harding (Aurum Press, 1998).

The Oxford Street Shelter, the Portland Help Center, Skip Murphy's Sober House, and Amistad are all real agencies that provide critically important services to the homeless and the mentally ill in the Portland area. Thanks very much to Karen Murphy and Peter Driscoll of Amistad, Sonia Garcia of Spurwick, and Joe Riley of Skip Murphy's for permission to mention these organizations by name. If you would like to donate to any of these organizations, or get more information about their services, you may do so here:

Amistad Inc.
www.amistadinc.com
PO Box 992
Portland, ME 04101
207-773-1956

Oxford Street Shelter
203 Oxford Street
Portland, ME 04101
207-761-2072

The Portland Help Center (Spurwink Services)
www.spurwink.org
899 Riverside Avenue
Portland, ME 04013
888-889-3903

Skip Murphy's Structured Sober Living
www.skipmurphys.com
449 Forest Avenue, Suite #14
Portland, ME 04101
207-245-1867

My thanks, as always, go to Sue Fletcher, Swati Gamble, Kerry Hood, Lucy Hale, Auriol Bishop, and all at Hodder & Stoughton; Breda Purdue, Jim Binchy, Ruth Shern, Siobhan Tierney, Frank Cronin, and all at Hachette Ireland; Emily Bestler, Judith Curr, Megan Reid, David Brown, Louise Burke, and the staff at Atria/Emily Bestler Books and Pocket Books; and my agent Darley Anderson and his wonderful team. Clair Lamb and Madeira James do sterling work, looking after Web sites and much, much more. Jennie Ridyard has now become my fellow author as well as my other half in life, but continues to show remarkable forbearance with me, as do our sons, Cameron and Alistair. To you, the reader, thank you for continuing to read these odd little books. Without you, there really wouldn't be much point to all this.

And hello to Jason Isaacs.

Read on for the newest chilling installment in the
Charlie Parker series by bestselling author John Connolly

A TIME OF TORMENT

Available online and wherever books are sold in Summer 2016

I

They're circling now, then falling, descending in a slow gyre, dropping so gently that their approach can barely be discerned. They are hawks in the form of men, and the one who leads them is a being doubly transformed: lost and found, human and bird; youngest of them, yet strangely old. He has endured, and in this endurance he has been forged anew. He has seen a world beyond this one. He has glimpsed the face of a new god.

He is at peace with himself, and so he will wage war.

Faster they come, the spiral narrowing, the three almost as one, their coats mantling in the chill fall air; and not a whisper of their approach, not a passing shadow nor a sparrow startled, only the stillness of a world waiting to be shattered, and the perfect balance of a life, perhaps, to be saved and a life, perhaps, to be ended.

The clouds part, pierced by a shaft of light that catches them in flight, as though they have attracted, however briefly, the attention of a deity long slumbering but now awake, roused by martial clamor and the raising of armies in the name of the Captain, the One Who Waits Behind the Glass, the God of Wasps.

And the old deity will set His child against them, and the hawks will follow.

———

IT WAS A LONG time since the Gray Man had considered the possibility of being caught, for the Gray Man did not truly exist. He had no physical form. He dwelt alongside another, sharing the same skin, and only at the final breath might there have been a glimpse of the essence of his true nature, although even then he preferred to remain unseen, concealed by darkness. He was not above causing pain, although this was as much a matter of whim as any particular tastes that he might have possessed. A death was only the beginning, which was why he had survived undetected for so long. He could make a kill last for years. Physical pain was finite, for ultimately the body would surrender the soul, but emotional agony was capable of infinite variations, and the subtlest of modifications might release from the wound a new torrent of distress.

In the persona that he presented to the world, the Gray Man was a reverse chameleon. His name was Roger Ormsby, and he was small, colorful, and greatly liked. He was in his early sixties, with an impish humor. His hair and beard were white, but neatly trimmed. He proudly carried before him his little potbelly, like a happily expectant mother demonstrating the pleasure she takes in her burden. He favored red suspenders and vests of unusual design. He wore tweed in winter and linen in summer, preferring creams and tans but offsetting them with tastefully bright ties and handkerchiefs. He could play the piano, and waltz and two-step with ease, but inside Ormsby was a foul thing animating him as a puppeteer works a marionette, and only an expert might have detected the sterility of his renditions of beloved classics as his fingers moved across the keys, or the joyless precision of every move he made on a dance floor.

Ormsby did not discuss politics or religion. He took only frivolous subjects seriously, and as a consequence was much valued as a dinner guest. He was a happy widower, faithful to the memory of his departed wife to the extent that he would do no more than flirt with the less lonely widows of Champaign, Illinois, but not so in love with the ghost of his departed spouse as to allow the loss of her to cloud his spirit or the spirits of others. He was always in demand as a companion for theater, movies, and the occasional light opera, and the absence of a sexual component to his relationships meant that he moved in and out of social situations with ease. He was a Friend of the Library, a member of the Audubon Society, a regular fixture at lectures on local history, and a generous—but not overgenerous—donor to good causes. True, there were some who disliked him, for no man can be loved by all, but in general such naysayers were regarded by the majority as willfully ornery, unable to accept that someone might simply be a force for contentment in the world.

And so Roger Ormsby bobbed through life in his vibrant plumage, advertising his presence, hiding nothing, but when he closed his front door behind him the artificial light in his eyes was suffocated, and the face of the Gray Man was pendent like a dead moon in the blackness of his pupils.

This is what Roger Ormsby did—or, if you wish, what the Gray Man did, for they were two aspects of the same entity, like a coat and its lining. He typically targeted his victims carefully, spending months in preparation. He had been known to engage in crimes of opportunity, but they were riskier now than they once were, because cameras were everywhere. In addition, it was difficult to gauge just what one might be appropriating in such a situation, for Ormsby required a very particular set of social circumstances from his victims. They couldn't be loners, isolated from their families and friends. He did not desire discards. The more beloved they were, the better. He wanted offspring who were cherished. He wanted teenagers from happy homes. He wanted good mothers of children beyond the age of infancy. He wanted emotional engagement.

He wanted many lives that he could slowly and painstakingly destroy over a period of years, even decades.

Ormsby made people disappear, then watched as those who loved them were left to wonder at their fate. He understood the half-life of hope: it is not despair that destroys us, but its opposite. Hope is the winding, despair the unwinding. Despair brings with it the possibility of an ending. Taken to the extreme, its logical conclusion is death. But hope sustains. It can be exploited.

Ormsby's actions had caused some to take their own lives, but he considered this a failure, both on his own part and theirs. The ones he killed were merely the first victims, and also the least interesting to him. He liked to watch those who remained as they tried to cope with what had been visited upon them. He knew that they would wake each morning and briefly forget what they had lost: a mother, a son, a daughter. (Ormsby avoided taking adult men. He was stronger than he looked, but not so much that he believed he could tackle a grown man, especially not as he grew older.)

Then, seconds after waking, they would remember again, and this was where the pleasure lay for Ormsby.

He was not above goading, reminding, but that was a dangerous business. He had sent items to relatives in the mail—a necklace, a watch, a child's shoe—to enjoy the commotion that followed. He had forced children that he had taken to write letters to their mothers and fathers, informing them that they were in good health and being looked after. (Adults, too, might be persuaded to write similar missives, but only under threat of physical harm.) He might wait years before sending such notes, depending on the age of the child and the reaction of the parents. He dropped the letters in mailboxes far from home, often when he was on vacation, and always ensured that he was not overlooked by cameras.

The Internet made it easier for him to monitor the progress of his real victims, but Ormsby was wary of leaving an electronic trail. He concealed his searches amid random examinations of newspapers and magazines, often in public libraries or the kind of cybercafes frequented by immigrants. He did not attend public gatherings for the disappeared, or church services at which the congregation prayed for their safe return, because he believed the authorities monitored such events. It was usually enough for Ormsby to know that the suffering he had inflicted continued unabated. If nothing else, the Gray Man had a vivid imagination. This was how Ormsby could survive for so long without killing: as the years went by, so too his store of victims increased. He could dip in and out of destroyed lives. He was an emotional vampire.

Now, as he drove home, he thought that this metaphor had a pleasing precision under the circumstances. He recalled a scene from Bram Stoker's *Dracula*, in which the Count returns to his castle and throws to his three vampire brides an infant contained in a sack. At that moment, the trunk of Ormsby's car also contained a child in a sack. Her name was Charlotte Littleton. She was nine years old, and represented one of his rare crimes of opportunity: a child playing with a ball as the afternoon sunlight died, an open gate, the ball drifting into an empty street of big houses set back from the road . . .

Good fortune: God—if He existed—finding His attention briefly distracted.

And inside, the Gray Man danced.

CHAPTER

II

O rmsby's wife had died suddenly when she was in her early forties
and her husband was in his midthirties. It was a blessing, of a kind.
By then, Ormsby, the Gray Man, had already begun playing his
long game, and was concerned that his wife, who was not a stupid woman,
and even actively curious, might begin to take an interest in his activities.
Sometimes he wondered if, had her heart not simply failed unexpectedly
while she was testing the firmness of avocados at a sidewalk market—such
a curious detail, and one that had led him to avoid avocados ever since—he
might have been forced to get rid of her. He wasn't even certain why he
had married her to begin with. He suspected he had craved some form of
stability, given his own family background of divorce and acrimony, and
a mother whose maternal instincts extended no further than occasionally
taking it upon herself to heat some mac and cheese instead of delegating
the task to her only son. Ormsby's relationship with his late wife had been
affectionate, if almost entirely passionless, a situation that had not troubled
either of them unduly.

But perhaps also, even then, he was already creating a framework for his
life, and an identity for himself, that would arouse the least amount of suspicion: Roger Ormsby, contentedly if unexceptionally married, with a job
selling painting and decorating supplies that required him to spend time
on the road, staying in dull motels, mostly eating alone, but always watching, always listening.

He heard a thumping from the trunk of his car and turned up the
volume on the radio: a news program on NPR, which was just the kind

of show to which a man like Roger Ormsby might have been expected to listen. He used to smoke a pipe too, puffing contentedly on it as he drove, but then he'd learned about throat and tongue cancer, and decided that Roger Ormsby would be sensible enough to let this particular pleasure go. He missed the pipe, though. It had given him something to do with his hands.

He'd have to kill the girl quickly, of course. The unplanned ones were always difficult. He might not have taken her had winter not recently crept into the air, giving him an excuse to light the furnace in his big, old house. He'd spend the night questioning her, find out as much as he could about her family, then put an end to her: a single blow to the head, knocking her out cold, then strangulation. He didn't want her to suffer.

After that, the game could begin.

He fantasized about the months and years to come.

And the shadows that were following him, the arc of the hunters, went entirely unnoticed.

———

IN A CURIOUS WAY, Ormsby had been inspired to pursue his particular appetites by base conflicts in lands that he had never visited, and in which he had little interest on a political or social level. He had found himself fascinated by the actions of the military dictatorships in Argentina and Chile, which routinely "disappeared" those with whom they differed, leaving the families to mourn phantoms, nearly certain that their loved ones were dead but unable to let go of them until they could identify their remains and lay them in the ground, although the chances of this were remote when the military's favorite methods of dispatch included dropping the bound bodies of living captives into the sea from aircraft, or, in the case of the Chileans, using railway ties to ensure that the corpses didn't float to the surface.

And then there were the Irish terrorists who dragged widowed mothers from their homes and tortured them in secret before shooting them in the head and burying their bodies on some desolate stretch of beach. When the deed was done, they returned with clear consciences to their own families and communities, there to pass the desolate, orphaned children on the street, continuing to do so for decades after in a strange dance of murderers and victims, each party knowing the identity of the other but never confronting the truth of what had been done, and so the dance went on. Ormsby, who was depraved beyond comprehension, thought that he might have enjoyed fighting for freedom if he could have passed some of his time so pleasantly: the misery for those left behind lay in not knowing, in uncertainty. It was sadism refined to its purest essence.

Ormsby's house appeared before him. He turned into the driveway and activated the garage door. The garage connected directly to the house through the utility room, which in turn had another door leading to the basement. It meant that he was able to move his victims easily, and without being noticed. He pulled into the garage, killed the engine, and hit the button on his key fob a second time, causing the door to begin its descent. He was already out of his car, and poised to open the trunk, when he saw that the door had frozen.

Ormsby stared at it. He tried the button again. Nothing happened. The door didn't even jerk slightly, as might have been expected if the mechanism had somehow become fouled. He took a flashlight from the shelf and checked the door's workings, but could see nothing wrong. The street beyond appeared empty, but the door was not even a quarter of the way down, and while the light was fading, it was not yet dark enough to guarantee he wouldn't be seen by one of his neighbors if he tried to move the child.

Regardless of this, he couldn't just leave the door unsecured. The garage was connected to his house alarm, and the button on the fob automatically deactivated it. His home was now vulnerable, and it wasn't as if he could call someone to take a look at the door, not with a child tied in a sack in the trunk of his car. The girl was kicking again: he could hear her, and the lid of the trunk shook with the impact.

He tried the button one more time and, miraculously, the door began to descend. He held his breath until it stopped again an inch or two from the floor. It wasn't perfect, but from outside it would appear closed. He'd worry about it again in the morning, once the girl was dead.

Ormsby turned on the garage's interior light. Only now did he open the trunk of the car. The child in the sack was wriggling, and screaming against the material. He'd managed to get cable ties around her hands by working fast, but not her legs. They remained free, and the best he'd been able to do was cinch the drawstring of the sack around her shins and tie it off. He'd been forced to hit her once to stun her, but he hadn't enjoyed it, and had no desire to do it again.

Ormsby spoke.

"If you continue making noise, you'll force me to hurt you," he said, "and I don't want to hurt you. Keep quiet and listen to me."

The child stopped moving. He could see the sacking inflating and deflating where it was closest to her mouth. She was sobbing.

"I'm going to help you out of the car. If you struggle, you risk falling, and the floor here is hard. Also, if you try to lash out at me, you'll make me strike you, and I hate striking children. Nod if you understand."

There was a pause, and then he saw the girl nod.

"Good. Now I'm going to help you out of the trunk."

He leaned in carefully, still wary of her, and he was right to be. As soon as she sensed him drawing close, she tried to swing at him with her legs, hoping to catch him on the head with her knees or her feet. Objectively, he had to admire her spirit, but he couldn't risk incurring a broken nose, or even a bruise to his face. Any injury might be enough to raise suspicions, even in the case of harmless Roger Ormsby.

He stepped back.

"I warned you," he said. "Now you're going to make me do something I didn't want to do."

The girl began wailing and writhing. Ormsby was just drawing back his hand to give her a sharp slap on the head when the doorbell rang.

Ormsby listened. He wasn't expecting anyone. He could try to ignore the bell, and hope that whoever it was went away. On the other hand, if one of his neighbors had seen him pull into the garage they'd know he was home, and if he didn't answer they might begin to worry. The last thing he needed was for the police to be called.

And what if it was the police? Suppose he had been seen? The street had appeared to be empty and unwatched, but one could never be sure . . .

The bell rang a second time. Ormsby struck the girl once to subdue her before he closed the trunk again. He moved through the house, turning on a lamp as he entered the hallway. He saw a shape through the glass fan of the door: a tall figure.

Ormsby paused when he was still five feet away.

"Who is it?" he called, but received no reply.

Ormsby shuffled his feet and tried again.

"Who's there? What do you want?"

Finally, the voice spoke. It sounded to Ormsby like that of a black man.

"Delivery for Mr. Cole."

Ormsby relaxed.

"You have the wrong house," he said. "Cole lives in fourteen thirty-seven, across the street. This is fourteen thirty-six."

"You sure? Says fourteen thirty-six on the slip."

"Well, your slip's wrong."

"Shit," said the man, and Ormsby saw his shape ripple as he took in the street. "Don't look like anybody's home over there. Maybe you could sign for it, save me a wasted trip."

Ormsby experienced a creeping sense of unease.

"I don't think so," he said. "I don't open my door to strangers after dark."

"It's not dark yet."

"Even so."

"Shit," said the man again. "Okay, you have a good evening."

He went away. Only when Ormsby heard his footsteps moving down the path did he slip into the living room and ensure that he had departed. The caller was wearing a jacket, and didn't look like any delivery man Ormsby had ever seen, but as he paused at the sidewalk, Ormsby saw that he was holding a box. The man hung a right, and was lost behind the tall hedge. Ormsby waited, but he did not reappear.

Ormsby returned to the garage and opened the trunk of his car.

The sack lay limp and flat on the rubber matting.

The girl was gone.

III

L et us leave Roger Ormsby for now, staring into the empty trunk of his clean, well-maintained car, in his big, anonymous house with its many unused rooms, the whole surrounded by a pretty garden with beds that flower throughout the year, for Ormsby prided himself on his plants, and they flourished thanks to his care and attention, the addition of copious amounts of old coffee grounds . . .

And human ash.

———

IT WAS ONE MONTH earlier, and the town of Rehoboth Beach, Delaware, had witnessed the final exodus of its summer tourists. The boardwalk concessions had closed, along with those bars, restaurants, and stores that relied exclusively on the season for their income. Here and there rainbow flags still flew, for Rehoboth was as gay-friendly as such towns came, and anyway, the pink dollar was only pink in a certain light. Once it arrived at the bank, it was as green as any other.

In the bathroom of a house at the edge of the town limits, the lawyer Eldritch was shaving, working at his sparse whiskers with an old straight razor. His was the only room with a mirror, and even then it was barely large enough to enable him to see his own face. Beyond the bathroom was his bedroom, and downstairs was his home office, where he continued the work of reassembling the records he had lost in the explosive fire that had destroyed his original business premises in Lynn, Massachusetts, some years earlier. Eldritch had almost entirely recovered from the physical injuries he received in the blast, but he remained frailer than before. His right hand shook slightly as he cut swaths through the shaving foam.

Beside him was a window that gave a partial view of the sea through some trees. A man stood smoking on the lawn, his back to the house. This was Eldritch's son, although the old lawyer had long conceded that he was his son in name only. At the moment of his birth, something had colonized his being: a wandering spirit, an angel, a demon. Call it what you would, but it was not human.

The doctors were surprised that the child had lived: his umbilical cord had become wrapped around his neck during delivery, asphyxiating him. The boy had, in fact, been born dead, and only the swift actions of the attending staff had resuscitated him. Eldritch and his late wife—who lived barely long enough to see her boy begin to walk—had feared brain damage or some other disability, but their son appeared to be entirely healthy, if unusually quiet. Eldritch could only remember him crying, really bawling, a handful of times, and he had slept for seven hours a night throughout his infancy. Other fathers told him he was blessed. Mothers, too.

But he was not blessed: his son *had* died, and just as his soul left his body another force had taken its place, one that had only gradually revealed itself to Eldritch as the years passed. Even now, after many decades, it remained something of an enigma to him. As it grew and matured, so too did it alter Eldritch's own nature, so that a once ordinary attorney with the usual slate of minor civil and criminal work became an examiner of the consciences of men, an assembler of evidence of base acts, and he presented his records to this being, who decided if action should be taken. The man now smoking on the lawn was an instrument of justice, although of whose justice Eldritch was uncertain.

Eldritch had been raised Lutheran, but his faith quickly became a half-remembered matter irregularly indulged, like the expensive coat that he only wore to church for his biannual attendances at Easter and Christmas. Then, as the creature that hid itself in the guise of his dead son became manifest, the reality of a world beyond this one concretized for Eldritch, but it was not a realm that bore any resemblance to the paradise of which the preachers spoke. From the little that Eldritch could glean, the being responsible for the creation of the universe had been silent for millennia. For all anyone knew, He might even be dead. (Perhaps, Eldritch's son had suggested, spurred into an astonishing blasphemy by a rare indulgence in hard liquor, He had killed Himself in despair at what He had created.) God, to give the entity a name, might have been unheard and unseen, but other creatures were waiting, and listening, and it was best not to draw their attention through loose talk.

Kushiel: when Eldritch had asked his son for his true name, that was the one he gave, but he did so with a crooked smile, as though this, too, were part of some great cosmic joke to which Eldritch was not privy.

Kushiel: Hell's jailer.

But to those he hunted, he was the Collector.

Eldritch finished shaving and washed away the remains of the foam. Just as his son stank of nicotine from the cigarettes that had stained his fingers a deep ocher, so, too, could Eldritch smell his own mortality. His body odor had changed, and no matter how clean he kept himself, or how much cedarwood aftershave he used, he could still detect it. It was the stink of his physical form in decline. It was the reek of the mud in the bottom of the pond of existence, and flies buzzed around it. He wondered how much time he had left. Not long. He felt it in his bones.

He carefully turned the mirror so that its reflective surface faced the wall. The Collector—let Eldritch think of his son as others did—was strict about this. He had a distrust of mirrors. He had once described them as "reflecting eyes." Eldritch had thought it a superstition, until an incident involving a dead child killer named John Grady. The Collector had retrieved a mirror from Grady's former home, and, just before he removed it from Eldritch's presence, he had turned it toward the lawyer. Eldritch had seen his own features and, behind them, those of another: the terrified face of John Grady, who, in death, had somehow sequestered himself in a reflected version of his house, wandering through it with the ghosts of dead children, believing himself to be immune from justice, until the Collector proved him wrong.

But Eldritch knew that the Collector had seen other faces looking back at him from polished surfaces, and one face in particular, for behind the surface of mirrors moved the Buried God, the God of Wasps, the one whom even the Collector feared. If God slept, the Buried God did not. The Buried God watched, and waited to be found.

Eldritch entered his bedroom and put on a clean shirt. He was going to see a movie, and later he would have a quiet dinner in one of the local bars that remained open. He was rereading Montaigne's *Essays*. He found a kind of consolation in them.

He went downstairs and called from the open back door to say that he was leaving. He received only a slight wave of the hand in reply, but the Collector did not turn around. Even six months before, it would not have been possible for Eldritch to leave the house in this way, because the Collector would not have permitted it. They were being hunted by the detective named Charlie Parker and the men who stood with him, all of them seeking revenge for the death of one of their friends at the Collector's hands. But a truce of kinds had been declared, and they were safer now, although Eldritch knew that the Collector remained wary of Parker.

Sometimes, Eldritch thought, *I think he fears Parker almost as much as he fears the Buried God.*

Eldritch got in his car and drove onto the road, turning right for Rehoboth. He didn't even know what movie he'd go see. They all started at the same time, more or less. And they were all the same, more or less. It would be enough just to sit in the darkness and forget, for a while.

———

THE COLLECTOR TOOK ANOTHER drag on his cigarette, and listened to the sound of his father's car fading away. There was a new moon in the sky. He tracked the progress of a dying insect, its flight erratic, until it finally fell by the feet of the man who was holding a gun on him.

"I knew you'd come," he said, as Charlie Parker emerged from the shadows.